# ONE LUMP OR TWO

## BOOK I
## THE TEA COZY MYSTERIES SERIES

by Miss J.S. Devivre

E. Gads Hill Press

ISBN-10: 1522961909
ISBN-13: 978-1522961901

Published by E. Gads Hill Press

"Tea! The panacea for everything from weariness to a cold to a murder. Love and scandal are the best sweeteners of tea."
Henry Fielding

# PREFACE

Heartfelt appreciation to you, gentle reader, for joining wallflower protagonist Penelope Price as she navigates the worlds of tea, antiques and mystery. This first in the Tea Cozy series is part of a greater body of whodunits, to be sandwiched between suffragette Dorothea Tate's Marvels & Mysteries and the Social Bluebook Murders.

I look forward to meeting many of you over a cuppa at Tea Travellers Societea events or while playing a *Cup of Mystery* tea parlour game at one of Southern California's delightful tearooms. Until then, may your cups overflow with contentment and wellbeing.

Warmly,

Joy

CALIFORNIA ~ 31 DECEMBER, 2015

# CONTENTS

# ONE LUMP OR TWO

# Chapter One

Penelope sat shaking in the heavy armchair, its wooden frame straining and creaking beneath her gyrations. The tidy office struck her as ominous and oppressive, and she struggled to produce enough saliva to enable her parched mouth to speak. After performing several involuntary facial twitches, none of which had the desired effect of producing an audible answer, she stammered, "May I have a glass of water, please?"

"It's a simple question, Miss Price," said the scowling, buttoned-up man facing her. "Are you or are you not the grandniece of the deceased?"

"Yuh-y-yes," Penelope whimpered, fidgeting with the clasp on her ponderous purse.

"Speak up!" he snapped.

"Yes, I'm a great niece."

"What?!"

"I mean she was my niece," Penelope answered, breathing in sharply and causing her corset to give a cobra-like squeeze to her ribs. She was certain she would faint.

"Miss Price!" the scowler bellowed, standing up abruptly, the veins in his neck pulsating against his starched collar.

"Rather, I'm her aunt ... great aunt ... grandaunt, that is," Penelope said, the right side of her facing twitching again.

"This is ridiculous," the man snarled, slamming closed his briefcase, his annoyance now bordering on rage, "and a complete waste of time."

"I'm sorry, Mr. Beekham. I get nervous when it comes to legal matters," Penelope offered in explanation.

Her comment was made in understatement. Penelope Price went through life in a state of perpetual guilt, always fearing she'd either just said or done something wrong, illegal, or uncouth, or that she was on the verge of doing so. Those who knew her only slightly tended to view this trait with suspicion. Those who knew and loved her well found the innocent quirk endearing, especially given that Penelope had never in her life broken the law—at least, not to her knowledge.

The impeccably groomed man looked hard at her, easing back into his chair. "You're not on trial here, Miss Price," he said evenly. "I am merely attempting to settle your grandaunt's estate, of which you are a principal beneficiary."

"Yes, I understand." A ray of sun pierced the cloudy sky and bathed the oak and leather-bound room in warm, encouraging light. Penelope sat up, closed her eyes and took a single slow breath. "Yes, Dorothea Tate was my grandaunt, my grandmother's sister. I am her grandniece, or is it great niece—one of two—the other being my sister, Pauline, who was named after her actually."

"But Miss Tate's Christian name was Dorothea. And you just said your sister is named Pauline."

"It's a funny family story really, you see—"

"I'm sure it's quite the knee-slapper," the man said brusquely, collecting his things as if in preparation of departure.

"Perhaps another time," Penelope muttered, recoiling

in her chair.

He merely glowered at her. "Here are the keys and all of the attendant paperwork including the deed. Remember, your grandaunt's will stipulates that you maintain an antique shop on the premises. To do otherwise would find you in breach of contract; and you wouldn't want that, now would you, Miss Price?" He handed her a well-worn key ring and overstuffed file folder held together with a frayed ribbon as he made his way to the door to open it. "Do you have any further questions?"

"Yes, several, thank you. I was wondering—"

"I thought not," he said, striding over to her chair and lifting her by the elbow to lead her to the door. "Goodbye, Miss Price."

"But how do I—" were the last words she got out before the lawyer's door closed behind her.

Once again, she breathed deeply and slowly so as not to antagonize her corset. "I need tea," she said, using both hands to hoist and transport her gargantuan carpetbag as she shuffled off to her car, her hobble skirt inhibiting her strides and causing her to take petite geisha-like steps. She arrived at her Model T panting, and for several minutes fumbled with the shop keys and papers as she sought her own keys in her massive all-purpose satchel.

After experiencing a variety of tactile sensations ranging from fluffy to sticky, her gloved hand emerged holding a coin. She made her way to the nearby telephone booth, trying desperately to flick the sticky stuff off of her glove. All she managed to accomplish was the flinging of her telephone-designated coin into the great beyond. In searching for another coin, she fortuitously found her car keys—but then lost both the phone number she was to call and her train of thought as to whom she was calling or why, and then proceeded to lose track of her keys again. When she finally sorted herself and placed the call, the voice on the other end put her immediately at ease.

"Z, is that you?" Penelope shouted into the telephone

"... Yes ma'am, it's really and truly mine. Now I just need to figure out what to do with it ... How did you know I was just about to ask you ... Ten minutes sounds grand. Wait, is that ten minutes my time or Zara time? Because ten minutes for you generally means about three hours for others...

"Why do you need to know the number of this telephone? ... Pardon me? Oh all right, Franklin one, eight-six-seven-four ... Hello ... Hello? Well can ya beat that! She hung up on—Ooh were those my keys?" she squealed, digging down through several strata of paraphernalia in her cavernous repository.

Just then, the public telephone rang. With her hands buried deep in her bag, she employed her chin and shoulder to answer. "Hello? ... Zara, why on earth? ... I don't understand ... What do you mean you're on the road? You're talking nonsense ... And how do you propose to see me in a 'minute or two' when you're still at the hotel which is a good twelve minutes away? ... Aha!" she exclaimed, espying the tip of her room key poking through the edge of her bag.

A moment later, she was seated behind the wheel, glancing left and right, and checking her rear view mirror for the third time as she inched back out of her parking space. Gripping the steering wheel for life in a stable ten and two configuration, she motored conservatively toward her new business, previously known as *Dorothea's Finds, Treasures of Rare Value from Exotic Lands*. A rather high-falootin' business name in Penelope's estimation, but then again, Aunt Dee had always been the romanticist in the family.

Penelope cruised at her usual speed—exactly two miles below the posted limit. A car careened around a corner behind her, narrowly missing her as the driver honked wildly and swerved to pass. "Why is everyone always in such a hurry these days?" she said aloud. Indeed, Penelope was seldom in a hurry. Her methodical and exacting nature demanded she take her time when accomplishing any task to ensure she'd done it correctly and not forgotten a step. Her mind and mouth operated on the other end of the velocity spectrum, often working so quickly that when excited, she tended to speak in fragments to the confounding of those with whom she conversed.

When she pulled up to the antiques store five minutes later, she found Zara waiting for her in the back of her Model A Duesenberg touring car, the fastest, most powerful machine on the road. Zara lowered her window and held a bubbling flute aloft for Penelope who grabbed a handful of skirt and speed-shuffled over to the auto. Penelope did her best to grasp the glass stem while opening the sedan door and taking a seat inside—a feat which resulted in her standing paralyzed and confused for a moment, then passing the glass to herself through the car window from one hand to the other and back again, eventually managing to sit next to her best friend and tap champagne glasses with her.

"How … where …" Penelope began.

"Just drink, darling," Zara cooed.

"But you were on the telephone—"

"Yes, I was. It's a portable telephonic device—invented by a brilliant Swede with whom I spent a week at his dairy farm. Three days later I was still finding pieces of straw in the strangest places."

Penelope responded by taking a gulp of the champagne to calm her nerves and wet her parched whistle. Immediately she spat it out. "Zara! This is real champagne!"

"Real expensive champagne, you mean, and not the kind you spit out! What were you expecting?"

"Ginger ale, I suppose, under the circumstances." Penelope used her sticky handkerchief to wipe the sparkling wine off her tongue, and accidentally got the gummy cloth stuck in her hair.

"And what circumstances would those be?" Zara asked,

running a finger around the rim of her flute.

Penelope looked out the car windows for observing passersby before responding. "Prohibition," she mouthed.

"Oh that! It's just a passing gimmick, mark my words. Fortunately, I have enough booze stored to wait it out. Besides, I have a medical prescription for the stuff."

"But you're breaking the law!" Penelope said, her heart racing and mouth going dry again.

\* \* \* \*

The two women could not have been more opposite. While Penelope was inordinately law-abiding and considered by friends and family to be a consummate 'goody two shoes,' Zara had always been a wild spirit, going anywhere the wind blew, or at least where the nearest dashing rogue whisked her away on his motorbike. Zara had no sense of peril or impropriety. Penelope was in constant fear of offending someone and always made a point to look for pitfalls and signs of jeopardy before taking a step, both figuratively and literally.

Whereas close friends often grow to resemble one another, whether through mannerisms or similar fashion and style, there was no mistaking Penelope for Zara. Penelope was a wisp of a woman—diminutive, though full of energy, and far more physically fit than her delicate frame suggested. Her hair was of the lightest chestnut and was wavy unless it determined to be unmanageably curly or unbudgingly straight. With a peaches and cream complexion, she always had a glow to her cheeks and charming color in her lips. Her green eyes were pale and inviting, and were it not for the look of worry that contorted her features on most occasions, by all accounts, she was lovely and, at times, even captivating.

Zara's appearance commanded attention, even at a young age. She was part Apache and had the sort of natural raven-black hair that was uncommonly shiny and tinged with midnight blue. She'd worn her hair in a bob as a schoolgirl, and now as an adult flapper, she'd bobbed it again, occasionally swinging its strands or mussing them up to punctuate her speech. The pupils of her dark chocolate eyes were surrounded by a starburst of gold, and her enviably long black lashes spoke a language all their own. When in a jam, she would activate her dimples in a sweet cherubic smile that melted hearts of both genders and all ages. As she matured, she grew taller than all the girls in her class, and her shape developed alluring buxom curves. She learned in her teens how to use her physical attributes as tools of persuasion, and she'd mastered a room-hushing gait.

Her friendship with Penelope had been forged in the sandbox in their hometown of San Pedro, California, and throughout their lives they had remained close at heart, despite changing circumstances and habitats. Penelope was Zara's touchstone. Zara was Penelope's adventurous alter-ego.

\* \* \* \*

Zara disregarded her friend's protestations about liquor laws and asked, "How did it go?" parting her red lips to tip the golden brut into her practiced mouth.

"It went," Penelope said, sighing and turning her gaze to the sign over the shop's door. "I haven't a notion as to how to run an antiques store."

"They won't let you turn it into a tea room then? Pity, that had always been your dream, to have a tea room," Zara said, leaning back into the bench seat like a femme fatale in the first stages of seduction.

"I suppose we should go in and face the music," Penelope said, letting out a defeatist sigh and slumping her shoulders. "Ready?"

"Always," Zara said, downing the remainder of the costly vintage in one easy quaff, then patting the headrest of the driver's seat. "Paolo, we're going into the shop. Feel free to wander around, but stay close by, if you don't mind—no telling how long we'll be."

The chisel-jawed Italian driver responded with a tilt of his head and look of confusion.

"Stay," Zara said, raising her palm in a *stop* gesture. "I'll ring you in the car when I need you … Then again, I suppose I *always* need you, Paolo," she said coquettishly, sharing a long, smoldering look with him by way of the car's rear view mirror.

Penelope glanced about the spacious back seat, at a loss for where to place her glass. Zara wrested it from her hand, slid the stem into a polished mahogany rack, scooted Penelope out of the car, and locked arms with her. "Your new world awaits."

Once at the front door, Penelope realized she was without her shop keys. Zara sauntered over to the display window and peered in as Penelope returned to the car and fumbled through her bag, grumbling under her breath and shaking her head as she began yet another key search—an activity in which she invested a substantial portion of each day. Eventually, Penelope unlocked the door, and the friends entered, both awed by the vast collection of curiosities, artifacts, antique furniture, and objets d'art.

The main room rose two stories and was jam-packed with items representing various eras, cultures, and countries. Having originally been the public library, the space still featured a sliding ladder used to fetch items from the higher shelves. Bookcases displayed the bulk of the stock, while new and seasonal items graced the two bay windows that flanked the entry door, each a magical nook surrounded by beveled diamond-shaped panes of glass. Overhead, the sun streamed in through a stained glass skylight decorated with an ornate pair of intertwined peacocks.

Visitors to the shop were known to spend hours contentedly losing themselves in the curios, and so the center of the room strategically boasted a red, crushed velvet, doughnut banquette sofa, where shoppers sat in the round with their backs against a shared column. Across from the entrance stood an old-fashioned, bank teller's cage where orders were rung up and the shop's high-end valuables were stored under glass, lock, and key. The cage also featured a door secured by a heavy bolt.

"Zara, this place is like a gold mine. I had no idea Aunt Dee collected things like this," Penelope said, inspecting a glass case packed with arrowheads and thumb-sized animal figurines.

"I get the feeling there's a whole lot we don't know about Aunt Dee. Really, this stuff is incredible. You sure you don't want to own an antiques shop? The stories these trinkets could tell."

"Looks like I don't have a choice. I'd had my heart set on owning a tearoom as long as I can remember," Penelope said with a wistful sigh. "Too bad I can't do both."

"Who says you can't?" Zara asked.

Penelope opened her mouth to reply, but realized she had no rebuttal. "No one, come to think of it," she said, her eyes widening and thoughts racing.

The concept of taking the bull by the horns was foreign to Penelope. In most situations, she was too timid to ask for permission in order to make a move, let alone make the move sans prior permission. If not given specific directions on what she could or should do, she did nothing. That way, she reasoned, she would avoid taking a misstep, upsetting someone, or getting into hot water.

"C'mon, let's see what's in the back," Zara said, grabbing Penelope by the hand and tramping toward a doorway concealed by a heavy brocade curtain.

Penelope gasped upon entering. Stacks of unlabeled crates and cartons in various stages of deterioration teetered precariously, and each step Penelope took caused the towers to jiggle just a little. The air in the room was thick, and Penelope felt she was breathing in the millennia as she ambled through the room, running her hand along a row of boxes. The only thing more fascinating to her than the unknown contents of the containers was the promise of what she could do were the space cleared out.

"Why, this room is even bigger than the shop itself!" she exclaimed, looking up to the inexplicably sooty ceiling.

"It's also overflowing with unpacked crates and a ton more stuff."

"This would make a perfect tearoom!"

"Did I mention it's floor to ceiling with stuff?" Zara said, turning sideways as she entered to avoid knocking into one of the unsteady containers and causing an avalanche.

"I could just move it all to the garage at the boarding house. Mrs. Prescott, the landlady, would likely drool at the thought of extra rent money," Penelope said.

Zara looked unconvinced.

"Or I could rent out a couple of additional garages …"

"Or ten," Zara added.

"My point is, *this* could be the tearoom!"

Just then, Penelope dashed outside to view the space from the street. Zara followed at a leisurely stroll.

"Look at these majestic windows!" Penelope chirped. "They're enormous! I didn't even notice them when we were in the tearoom."

"Oh, we're calling it the tearoom already, are we? And the reason you didn't notice the large windows is because not only are they blacked out with paint, but there are boxes blocking them, bottom to top. Do you have any idea how much work you're in for?"

"Small price to pay to make a lifelong dream come true," Penelope said, dashing back into the room in question and making mental calculations as Zara ambled back in as far as the doorway. "I wonder what other mysteries this place has in store."

"You and me both."

"Come on. Let's go find out," Penelope said, tiptoeing out of the room to prevent the containers from jostling.

\* \* \* \*

Across from the proposed tearoom's streetside windows was situated a closed door that opened onto a small hallway—a hallway that extended the length of the store down to the door of the teller's cage at the front end. On the other side of the hall stood three doors—one leading to yet another crammed storage room, one leading to a small office, and one leading to a fully functional bathroom, complete with a large clawfoot bathtub and working shower fixture.

Penelope beamed as she and Zara peeked their heads into the crowded, dirty, dank storage space. "This will be the kitchen."

"Appetizing," Zara said. "You realize you're gonna spend a fortune on garages!"

"Since when are you the pragmatist and I the dreamer?"

"Since Mercury went into retrograde … Don't worry—it won't last."

"Let's go see the office!"

Zara covered her mouth as she followed Penelope down the hall, the smell of musty disuse making her gag.

"Zara, look at this—a Murphy bed! Do you think Aunt Dee lived here onsite? Come to think of it, I don't recall seeing anything in the court documents regarding a residence for her, and all of her correspondence always came from this address."

The desk was covered with a thick coating of dust and little else. A faded blotter set, dried inkwell, a pen with a rusty nib, and an ordinary looking rock sat quietly enveloped in the layers of time and buildup. Penelope opened the top drawer to find a ball of rubberbands, an empty envelope postmarked from Istanbul, and a silver letter opener in the shape of a small sword engraved with the name Edward Teach, an appellation Penelope failed to recognize as the Christian name of the famed pirate known as Blackbeard.

"This is strange," Penelope said, opening the desk's filing drawer. "It's empty! For all her chattels, Aunt Dee's cache of bookkeeping and mail is surprisingly sparse." She opened the closet door and her breath caught. "Look! Aunt Dee's personal effects. So she *did* live here then."

"And why not—did you get a look at that enormous tub? Sheer heaven."

"You know, I have a marvelous feeling about this place. I think I'm going to be very comfortable here in Pacific Grove."

Just then, a loud rapping on the shop's front door startled the two friends, and they screamed in unison.

"You were saying?" Zara remarked, taking a deep breath and following Penelope to the shop entrance.

"May I help you?" Penelope said as she opened the front door to find a tall, rugged man wearing stylish dark tweed trousers, a bespoke grey button-down shirt, black leather braces, and a charcoal fedora, carrying an industrial tool belt that looked out of place with the rest of his dapper ensemble.

"Actually, I came here to see if I can help *you*," the man said, smiling.

"You most certainly can," Zara purred, sashaying toward the door and undressing the visitor with her gaze. In an instant, she'd taken in his tall, muscular workman's build, his ice blue eyes, easy smile, sun-streaked hair, and effortless debonair posture.

Caught off-guard by Zara's burrowing stare, he searched one of the pouches on his tool belt and produced a business card.

"*Handy Hank's Handyman service*," Penelope read as she accepted the card. "*Hank Edwards, licensed and bonded.* I'm afraid I don't understand."

"I just wanted to introduce myself and offer my condolences. Dee and I were good friends."

"I see. Well that was awfully thoughtful of you to come by, Mr. Edwards," Penelope said, eyeing the stranger with a mixture of suspicion and curiosity.

"Right neighborly, if you ask me," Zara said, posing provocatively.

Penelope glared at her, wise to the coquette's antics.

"Did Aunt Dee engage you often?" Zara asked, her every word delivered with innuendo.

"That's an understatement," he answered, glossing over her advances. "I've been doing the work on this shop nearly daily for oh, more than nine years now."

"Gracious! Is there really that much wrong with the place?" Penelope asked, her heartbeat accelerating with the fear of the cost required to keep the shop in operable shape.

"Not any more, there isn't!" he said with a casual smile. "When Dee first contracted me, the place was a powder keg, faulty electrical wiring, life-threatening asbestos insulation, decades worth of code infractions and neglect. It took us a few years to get it up to scratch. By then, we'd become chums, and she really just liked having company, so she'd trump up excuses to get me down here to fix something or other. She even got me taking afternoon breaks to drink tea with her—not exactly the usual modus operandi of a handyman! But boy, the stories she'd tell of her adventures and the lengths she went to obtain some of her rarer treasures. She was quite a gal!"

"And all this time I just thought she was a docile spinster from Northern California," Penelope said, reflecting on the annual visits her aunt would make to San Pedro, always bearing unusual gifts from places of which Penelope had never heard.

She'd viewed her aunt as a simple hobbyist, rather like a philatelist or numismatist, and the trinkets Dorothea proffered as inconsequential and uninteresting mementos that only a devotee could appreciate. She assumed Dorothea had mundanely purchased the items at a specialty shop or through a catalogue. Never did it occur to her that her aunt had embarked on harrowing adventures to distant lands in order to acquire the objects in person, and often at personal peril.

Hank's words snapped her out of her mental meanderings. "Where are you from, umm, Miss ..."

"Penelope Price," Penelope said, extending her hand to shake his. "And this is my lifelong friend, Zara."

Zara poised her hand in a manner that begged Hank to kiss it. He grasped a pair of her fingers and shook them quickly, avoiding eye contact.

"We're both from San Pedro in Southern California," Penelope said.

"Once upon a time," Zara amended. "When I came of age, I became a citizen of the world."

"That's true," Penelope said. "Zara's lived all over this great planet of ours."

"What about you, Hank? Where were you born and so heartily bred?" Zara asked, looking him over again to appreciate his statuesque posture, effortless elegance, and classic features.

"I've lived here and there around California, but Pacific Grove is where I call home. Do you two live in town?"

"I do. Zara's just visi—"

"We're *both* new in town—and looking forward to getting to know the locals," Zara said, trailing the back of her hand down her long slender throat.

"We are?" Penelope said, cocking her head and looking at her friend to divine what she was up to. *Is Zara's visit more than the brief stopover I had anticipated?* she wondered.

"Well," Hank said, clearing his throat. "It was a pleasure to meet you both. Give me a ring if anything goes haywire. Ladies," he finished as he pulled down the front brim of his fedora.

"Wonderful to meet you, Hank. And we look forward to working with you. Can you swing round in a couple of days and show us the lay ... of the land, so to speak?" Zara said, her tone unmistakably sultry.

"Come again?" he slurred, clearly flustered by Zara's boldness.

"How's noon, Wednesday?" she asked.

"Noon?" Hank mumbled, still somewhat dazed.

"Twelve it is. See you then, Hank," Zara concluded with a dimpled smile.

"It was delightful to meet you, Hank," Penelope said, attempting to put him back at ease.

"Miss Price," he said, nodding and backing into an amphora planter placed at the shop entrance, nearly knocking over the enormous, heavy stone pot.

Once Hank was out of sight, Penelope closed the door and locked it, then turned to Zara, looking for some sort of explanation.

"My, my, who knew they grew 'em like that in this teeny tiny township?" Zara said, peering out the window to ogle Hank's shapely backside as he strode to his truck.

"Just what are you playing at, Z?" Penelope asked, raising an eyebrow and crossing her arms in front of her.

"Nothing yet ... but I hope to be up to my neck in local color soon enough." Zara sat on the shop's banquette sofa and surveyed the room. "I think I'm going to like it here."

"That reminds me. I've been meaning to ask you—how long do you plan to stay in town?" Penelope said, dropping onto the couch next to her and causing a puff of dust to issue from the fabric.

"Sick of me so soon, P?" Zara asked, gently tucking a stray strand of Penelope's hair into her Gibson Girl pompadour.

"Just the opposite! I don't want you to go, actually. I don't know how I'll get through all of this without you once you go home … Where exactly is home these days, by the way?"

"Pacific Grove, Califor-ni-a!" Zara said, opening her arms wide.

"Yes, I know that, but I mean once you leave. Who are you going back to … and where? Was it Costas in Greece? I lose track." Penelope said, absentmindedly drawing abstract stars and flowers on the dusty sofa with her finger.

"You're not following me, chérie. I'm staying here."

"Here here? In the shop here? I'm confused," she said, looking up into Zara's face for answers.

"You know, one of these days that technical, analytical mind of yours is going to get you in trouble. I mean here in Pacific Grove … with you."

It took a moment for Penelope to process what Zara was saying as well as its import. "Really?! That's fantastic! Oh, thank you, Z! You have no idea what this means to me. I can't believe you'd—" she broke off, becoming choked up with emotion.

"Calm down, P. I'm not doing it just for you. I'm doing it for me too. I may be Costas' favorite, but I'm certainly not his *only*." She paused as a shadow crept across her typically vibrant visage. "The time's come for this courtesan to hang up her garter belt and settle down. Let's face it, at my age, I'm in the twilight of my career. Why not go out while I'm still on top, so to speak?" she said, adding a wink to camouflage her heartache and trepidation.

"But won't a sleepy little town like this be too dreary and simple for you? They roll up the sidewalks at about eight in the evening," Penelope replied, oblivious to her friend's despondency.

"The quiet life is an adventure I've never had. Besides, Pacific Grove just got a whole lot more exciting—it's the new home of an internationally famous courtesan!" she said with a cheeky flip of her shaggy bob.

"True," Penelope said, weighing the veracity of Zara's statement. "For my part, I'm looking forward to uneventfully running my new little business and enjoying my spinsterhood in peace. And this quaint community seems like the perfect spot—a place where I can be myself … without explanation or apology, I might add," she said, followed by a satisfied exhalation.

"You mean a place away from your sister's stranglehold and imperious rule."

"You read my mind."

"I always do," Zara said with a grin. "Now, what do you want to do first? I've no doubt you've a plan already."

"But of course," Penelope said with a wry smile. "At some point today, I want to ring up the realty office and ask them to look for something more permanent than the Mrs. S.A. Virgin House boarding facilities, given Pacific Grove's looks to be home for the long haul. I can ask them to start looking for something for you too, if you like."

"Would you? You know how I detest business transactions … well, other than carnal business, that is."

Penelope shook her head and looked to the heavens. Having gone through her adolescence with Zara, she was well versed in salacious banter, though discourse was as far as her prudery had taken her; and she felt that Zara made enough whoopee for the both of them.

"Tell them I require a palatial powder room and an outdoor Turkish bath," Zara said. "For the rest, anything goes … I don't even care if it has a kitchen."

"I'm fairly confident kitchens are standard issue. Where else would you store your caviar and Brie de Meaux?" she said, smiling, and getting up to look for paper and a writing implement.

"Good point—I'll need a wine cellar, of course. And a hookah lounge—"

"A what?" Penelope replied from the teller's cage,

blowing the dust from off a receipt book and picking up a fountain pen.

"I suppose I can be flexible on that if need be … See? I'm already adapting to suburban life!"

"You're a real trooper, Z … There," she said, ripping off one of the receipts and tucking it into her sleeve. "I've written myself a note to call the realtor later this afternoon."

"Ee gads, would you really forget to call this afternoon without a note?"

"I like to keep a record of all my important activities and conversations—helps eliminate muddles and comes in handy for later reference."

"I need to teach you to have some fun."

Penelope returned to the banquette and heaved her purse into her lap to initiate the ritual of searching for her keys. "I have plenty fun—just not courtesan fun."

"For now," Zara said with a devilish smirk. "So, where are we off to next?"

"Nowhere, unless I find my keys. I just had them!" Penelope said, her voice muffled as she burrowed with both hands in her gaping satchel.

"Some things never change."

Penelope peeked up over the brim of her carpetbag and smiled. "Comforting, isn't it?"

# Chapter Two

Several minutes and curses later, Penelope found her errant keys, and the friends sat safely ensconced in the back seat of Zara's Duesenberg—or rather, Zara sprawled, Penelope perched.

Paolo turned his comely face around to address the ladies and simply said, "*Dove?*"

"Yes?" Penelope said, staring at his olive skin and green eyes. She had no idea what he'd said, but was willing to agree with anything as she gazed at his beauty.

Zara smiled. She knew Penelope's goofy look all too well—a look most women, and at least a few men, adopted when face to face with Paolo. It bolstered her morale and confidence in her powers of allurement to know she could still capture the attention and affection of such a sought-after young man, and to the devil with Costas! "Do-vay' is how you say, 'where' in Italian. Paolo wants to know where we want to go now."

Before Penelope could speak, her growling stomach answered.

"Food ... restaurant," Zara said loudly.

"Ahh, *ristorante*!" Paolo said, turning back toward the steering wheel and putting the car in gear.

Penelope and Zara gloried in the view of the town that was to be their new home. Buildings and streets all appeared to have been freshly washed down and tended with great care. Surfaces gleamed, floral blooms burst forth in colorful joy, and the complexion of the sky changed to match the mood of the time of day.

The coastal four-square-mile city was considered by many to be the jewel of California's Monterey County. Dubbed *Butterfly Town USA*, Pacific Grove served as home to a yearly migration of monarch butterflies, and Penelope regarded the place as a fairy tale township where she could live in tranquil independence. Now that her parents had both passed away, she no longer felt obligated to remain in Southern California. No, her sister, Pauline, could find someone else's life to disparage and manage into the ground.

As the childhood friends motored down the picturesque streets toward the city center, each smiled and pondered her dreams and prospects for their new life together. Their school days were the last during which they'd lived in the same municipality, and both women were looking forward to continuing their friendship in person. While they'd remained in contact during the intervening years, they really didn't know much about the women into whom they'd grown or what to expect now that they'd reunited.

Zara's large luxury automobile drew more than a few stares from the local gentry, and when Paolo parked the long vehicle across two parking spaces, a small crowd assembled around it. He got out and greeted the onlookers, posing against the car like a haute couture model, commanding even more attention as a chattering of young women flocked around him, blushing and whispering to one another.

Zara regarded the scene, thinking back on the days when she and Penelope would have been among the group of tittering teen girls. More accurately, Zara would have walked right up to a handsome older man such as Paolo and asked him to light her cigarette. Penelope would most likely have been secreted behind a tree, looking on covertly.

"I suppose I'll have to hire a full-time local driver. Pity. Paolo has certain … skills," Zara purred, trying to cover her growing forlornness with bawdy suggestiveness.

"Can't he stay on?" Penelope asked, glossing over Zara's provocative patter.

"I fear this town would bore him to distraction. He's used to the pace of San Francisco. Come to think of it, it might be a nice change to have a bed all to myself," Zara lied, looking out the window to avoid eye contact with Penelope while waiting for Paolo to open her door.

Penelope held the auto's door closed. "You mean he's staying in your bed with you?!" she whispered, worried the town folk might hear and disapprove.

"Oh don't be such a wet blanket. Of course he shares my bed. Do the math, P."

Penelope pulled the brim of her large festooned hat down over her eyes as a means of hiding from the milling townies in case they overheard her conversation with Zara.

"I'll say one thing for you," Zara said. "The size of your carpetbag is matched only by the size of your hat!"

"Balance, it's all about balance, Z," Penelope sputtered, opening the Duesenberg's door and breaking a sweat as she toiled to pull her carpetbag from the backseat.

Once inside city hall, they found the real estate registry was closed for lunch. Penelope wrote a note and slid it under the registry office's door, explaining that she and Zara were interested in purchasing lodgings. Zara busied herself looking at a board listing homes for sale in the area.

The friends had been raised in a seaside bedroom community, in some ways similar to the new town, but that was where the similarity in their previous residential situations ended. Until coming to Pacific Grove, Penelope had never ventured more than twenty miles beyond San Pedro. Since leaving home, Zara had lived in nine countries and visited dozens more. Most recently, she too had lived in a coastal village—that of Mykonos, Greece. There, she was treated like local royalty. In Pacific Grove she despaired of being treated like everyone else, or far worse, like a harlot, should anyone learn of her career as a courtesan. Penelope was not nearly so reflective—she was too caught up in the sudden tempest of life changes and requisite activity to pay her status or place any heed.

A short time later, the ladies got back into the Duesenberg and instructed Paolo to look for the bustling El Carmelo Hotel Penelope had read about prior to coming to town. When they arrived at the site, they found the place had been dismantled due to lack of business. Instead, they toured the streets looking for restaurants, ultimately opting for The Butterfly Café, a small lunchroom with six cramped tables. They invited Paolo to join them for lunch, but he chose to sleep in the car. Penelope suspected he wanted a reprieve from female prattling.

Penelope generally had a hard time deciding what to eat, whether at a restaurant or standing in front of her open icebox, and that day was no exception. After several irresolute minutes, she took the bold step of proclaiming she'd narrowed down her selection to the hot sandwich column. Zara was impressed with her friend's relative decisiveness. But when a lethargic waitress arrived to find Penelope in a panic over whether to get the meatloaf or open-faced turkey with gravy, Zara intervened and ordered both.

"We can share," Zara said, gently lowering the menu into which Penelope was gabbling unintelligibly.

Penelope heaved a relieved sigh. "You really know how to live, Z."

Zara let out a hearty laugh. "Amen! Who needs caviar and champagne when you can have meatloaf and hot turkey?!"

"I'm sincere! You're always so cool and relaxed. Nothing flusters you. I don't know how to operate like that. I wish I did."

"Well, there are plenty of things that fluster me, but no, I generally don't let the flotsam and jetsam send me into a tailspin. It's a matter of abiding in the given moment, and it takes practice."

"I'm not sure what 'abiding in the given moment' means exactly, but if it means being calm and poised like you, I could go for some *given momentness* myself."

"We're going to have a marvelous time being together as adults," Zara said, reaching a hand across the table.

"We most certainly are," Penelope replied, squeezing Zara's hand and sighing again, this time in contentment.

Just then, the waitress approached with their beverages, her tedium having turned to admiration at the sight of the two women holding hands. "That's beautiful," she said, placing the drinks on the table and nodding her approval. "Love is where you find it. This conservative town needs people like you. Your drinks are on me, ladies!"

Penelope's mouth dropped open as she watched the

waitress bounce up to the kitchen's pass-through window and whisper to the cook. When the two employees looked over and caught Penelope's eye, the waitress placed her fist over her heart and nodded.

"I ... I don't ... What just happened?" Penelope said to Zara.

"Looks to me like she thinks we're partners ... in the Sapphic sense," Zara said, blowing a kiss to Penelope over the rim of her iced tea glass.

"We're what!?" Penelope screeched, knocking her knees hard on the underside of the table as she involuntarily began to rise.

"Don't tell me you're homophobic, P."

"I won't ... because I am not!" she rejoined, rubbing her knees.

"Not homophobic or not a lesbian?" Zara returned, leaning back in the booth and languidly stirring her drink with her straw.

"Not either ... neither! ... This is terrible ... right when we're about to settle in town."

"And now that I'll be staying with you ..."

"Oh no! We're doomed!"

"Relax, P. Our small town stock just skyrocketed. Trust me ... lover," she added, punctuating the term with an exaggerated wink.

"Stop that, Z. I'm serious."

"Seriously too tightly laced, you mean. Loosen up those corset strings."

"You don't understand. I'm a business owner now."

"Good grief, you mean to tell me—"

Just then the waitress brought their order.

"I pre-split both sandwiches for you already. I think it's so endearing how you both share," she said, smiling approvingly. "And here—I dished you up some apple crumble—my treat!"

\* \* \* \*

Penelope was reclined nearly horizontally in the car as Paolo commenced a leisurely motor circuit of the neighborhoods.

"Don't tell me you're hiding in embarrassment after our scenario in the diner," Zara said.

"I'm not hiding. I'm just painfully full … It was that apple crumble did me in … *groan.*"

"You didn't have to eat every morsel of everything served, P."

"Clearly, you don't remember childhood dinners at my house. 'You'll sit at that table 'til you've swallowed every crumb, young lady! There are urchins starving in the gutters of New York!'"

"Your mom did have a flair for the dramatic," Zara remembered with a smile. "… P …"

"Z," Penelope moaned as she slid further down the seat, her digestive discomfort building.

"How did they … you know."

"No, I don't know. How did who do what?" Penelope blurted, wriggling to sit upright.

"How exactly did they die … your parents, that is."

"Oh …"

"You don't have to tell me if you don't want to."

"Nice of you to pretend, but you and I both know you're not letting me out of this car until I tell you."

Zara blinked slowly in a beguiling sort of way—a habit she was used to employing on gentlemen whom she wished to bend to her will.

Penelope exhaled. "The truth is, they never got over Joe's death—especially Mother. She cried herself into a state daily, off in the pantry with the door closed, where she thought no one could hear her. I think she truly died of a broken heart. Nothing nefarious happened. She just passed in her sleep. Three months later, Father did the same—which was frankly just as well. He was a shell of himself after first losing his only son to the war and then his wife of forty years."

"Did their passing bring you and Pauline closer?"

"You'd think so, but unfortunately not. My little sister just got meaner and more judgmental. She became nothing short of an ogress."

"The war tore so many families apart. Sounds like Pauline hasn't handled the loss of Joe or your parents so well."

"I never thought of it that way, Z. Thank you. That makes me think a little more kindly of her."

"Really? Well how 'bout that," Zara said with a triumphant mien.

"I said 'a little,'" Penelope added.

The friends both laughed, a warm yet weary laugh of those who had seen better days, as well as some they'd sooner forget.

Zara reached for the telephone embedded in the backseat's console. "Paolo?"

"*Olá*," Paolo answered, speaking into the front seat's telephone.

"Oh, brother," Penelope said, sliding down in her seat once more. "He's sitting right in front of us. You can hear each other plenty well without resorting to those gadgets.

"We could … but this is much more fun. Isn't it, Paolo?" Zara said, speaking loudly into the phone.

"*Si, Signorina Zara*," Paolo replied, his ardent gaze once more catching hers by way of the rear view mirror.

Zara let out a slight squeak and bit her lower lip seductively as she and Paolo continued to hold their respective telephones in silence, relying on their eyes to convey their lusty desires.

"Weren't you going to tell him something, Z?"

"Oh, there's plenty I'd like to tell him."

"*Ugh,*" Penelope protested, still annoyingly full from lunch and feeling the apple crumble creeping up her throat as she labored to stomach Zara's libidinous banter.

"Yes," Zara said, snapping out of her steamy daydream and tapping the auto's canvas top. "Paolo, be a pet and lower the cabriolet."

"The what?" Penelope asked.

"It's French for the fabric top of the car that folds away like an open carriage," Zara said. "Down, *per favore,*" she reiterated to Paolo, pointing downward to get her point across.

Paolo pulled the car to the side of the road, unlatched the top's front hooks, then got out to push the covering back and secure it.

"What's going on? This can't be safe," Penelope said, gripping the back of the driver's seat in front of her tightly and rubbernecking to keep an eagle eye on Paolo's actions.

"Hold onto your hat, P," Zara said, pulling her cloche down tight as Paolo got in the car and stepped on the gas.

"Whatever for?" Penelope asked as a gust of wind sent her picture hat soaring. Miraculously, in less than a second, she managed to catch the hat mid-air, locate a hatpin in her junk-laden carpetbag, and secure her hat against all flurries.

"Why on earth do you insist on still wearing Gainsborough Chapeaux? They've been out of style for nearly a decade," Zara said, shaking her head in disapproval.

"I figure if I wear them long enough they'll come back in style," Penelope answered with a grin.

"You actually may be on to something there," Zara said, her brow creased in contemplation.

At the ladies' command, Paolo inched up and down the neighborhood streets. Penelope gasped in veneration at each of the many Victorians they passed. Zara groaned her displeasure.

"Ooh look at that one!" Penelope cried, jumping to her knees on the back seat in order to gawk out the rear of the open car at a corner house bearing a for-sale sign.

"That tired old thing? Victorian architecture is so passé, P. Let's get something bolder, more daring, minimalist. Frank Lloyd Wright is starting to do some compelling things with concrete blocks, I hear. Let's get him to design something for us."

"Us? You mean you're actually setting up house with Paolo?" Penelope asked, raising an eyebrow.

"No! I mean for you and me!"

"Oh no, unh unh. You're my best friend, and I want to keep it that way. So moving in together permanently is out of the question."

"But—" Zara interjected.

"I'm in earnest, Z. I'm putting my foot down on this."

"Good lord, not with those feet, you're not. Look at those court shoes and Louis heels! I really must take you to the City of Paris Dry Goods store in San Francisco for a day. That should be enough time to burn your existing wardrobe. How do you feel about arson, Paolo?" Zara called out loudly.

"You'll do no such thing. Besides, the new Holman's Department Store here in town is said to be quite posh, you'll be happy to know," Penelope said.

"Very happy to know, in fact," Zara said.

"Paolo, stop the car, please," Penelope said with authority. "I'd like to get out and look at that corner Victorian we passed."

"Well if you're going to be a fuddy-duddy ... Paolo, *arresto*. Be a love and turn the car around? Penelope wants us to retire to a dusty, styleless, antediluvian old folks home."

"Say what you will, I love Victorian architecture. It will make a comeback someday too. Mark my words."

"Whatever you say, P," Zara said, rolling her eyes.

Paolo pulled to the side of the street, and Penelope bounded out of the car.

"Ya know, for someone who prides herself on not attracting attention, this place is awfully gaudy," Zara said, following her up to the house.

"Isn't it grand?" Penelope asked in wide-eyed wonder. "It's a Queen Anne. That's my favorite style. Do you see how every surface is ornamented?"

"Oh yes, it's hard to miss."

Built in 1888, the multi-gabled seaside home was a standout among Pacific Grove's exquisitely maintained Victorian homes. British engineer and amateur architect William Lacy had originally built the residence as a vacation home for his family who lived in Los Angeles. Sadly, they never had the opportunity to occupy the place. Framed entirely of redwood, the house boasted solid maple floors along with a massive mantelpiece accenting the parlor's fireplace. The doors and window fixtures were constructed of copper and brass.

"Look at the multi-textured façade. And do you note all the gables? There are windows overlooking the ocean from every angle ... it even has stained glass flanking the chimney! It's perfect!"

"It's something, all right," Zara said.

"And an English garden! I adore English gardens."

"Of course you do," Zara lamented.

"I'm going to see if I can peek in the windows ... Oooooh ... don't you just love this archway with the creeping roses? Don't answer that!" Penelope said just as Zara's mouth opened to hurl a creatively scurrilous comment.

"I'm heading back to the car," Zara said with a languid wave of her hand.

"It already feels like home. Look at the imposingly high ceiling and that stately banister! The crown molding is exquisite and … will you look at that … it has a floor to ceiling built-in bar."

"Did you say bar?" Zara asked, turning around and double-timing her steps to meet Penelope at the window.

"Not just any bar—a proper bar with a carved bar-back. Do you see that gilt mirror and those tall bar chairs?

"Oh, P, you were right. This place is rather stunning. I don't know how I didn't see it before. Just think how we could do up that parlor!"

"You're not just saying that because of the prospect of evening cocktails on a daily basis?"

"Of course not … well, not entirely anyway. Let's go around the other side."

The boon companions locked arms and tittered their way around the house, dirtying their noses and gloves on the windows, verbally decorating and redecorating each room they came upon, and nearly getting into an altercation over the potential dining room's color scheme.

"Hello … is someone here?"

The ladies froze in their tracks, clutching each other for moral support.

"Is somebody back there?"

Sheepishly, the two spies extricated themselves from the flower bed they'd inadvertently trampled in their enthusiasm to view the kitchen.

"Is there something I can do for you ladies?" said a smartly dressed women carrying a sign resembling the one Penelope had first seen on the front lawn.

"How do you do?" Penelope said, clearing her throat and smoothing her skirt. "I'm Penelope Price and this is Zara …"

"Just Zara," the cohort in question interjected.

"I'm interested in possibly purchasing this place. Might we go inside?" Not waiting for the expected answer,

Penelope strode toward the front door.

"I'm afraid that's impossible, Miss Price. This house has just been sold. I'm Nell Stewart, the realty agent representing the seller," the woman said, handing Penelope a business card.

"A female realtor. Good for you!" Zara said, slapping the unwitting Nell on her back in triumph.

"Thank you, Miss … ehrm, Zara. I'd be happy to show you something else in the area … perhaps something more modern?"

Zara snickered. Penelope kicked her in the shin.

"That's very kind of you …" Penelope began, crestfallen and not the least bit interested in seeing or considering any other residence.

"Unfortunately, it is imperative Miss Price own *this* house," Zara said, rubbing her calf against her aching shin.

"That's out of the question. Escrow has already closed, and the new family will be moving in a week Saturday."

"Family, you say …" Zara said slowly, her eyes flitting as she hatched a plan.

"Yes, the husband, Mr. Jenkins, has procured employment just outside of town at the new Del Monte Lodge in Pebble Beach. He starts on Monday actually, and he's staying at the town inn here in Pacific Grove until his family arrives."

"So there's absolutely nothing we might say or do to persuade you or him to release the house to my friend, Penelope here."

"Not a thing. And now if you'll excuse me, I really must go. I moonlight as a switchboard operator. The real estate market in California just doesn't pay the bills. Never will, I dare say."

\* \* \* \*

Twenty minutes later, Zara called out from a bedroom on the upper floor of the Queen Anne Victorian. "This is my room, definitely. Did you get a load of this closet? I think it could hold a football field."

"I counted three fireplaces and six rooms. Can you beat that? And one of the bedrooms has a bathroom actually set in a gable! Plus, there's a carriage house," Penelope returned, ambling around the top level of the house in an incredulous daze.

"Lucky thing. You'll need an entire house to store all of the stuff from the antiques store!"

Zara crawled into the shared bathroom's empty tub and glanced out the window at the Pacific. "Every room in this place has an ocean view! And did you see my room's adorable window seat?"

"I still don't understand how you did it," Penelope called out from within the fireplace she was inspecting from the inside out.

"It wasn't me! All the credit goes to John Knox," Zara called back.

"I don't follow," Penelope said, entering the shared bathroom.

Zara snickered as she noted the soot on her friend's face, but decided not to mention it. "Hundred dollar bills?"

"Huh?"

"You know, John J. Knox … the financier whose face is on the hundred dollar bill?"

"Oh, sorry, yes. I don't see many of those. But I promise, I'll pay you back, Z. You really didn't have to do that."

"Oh, but I did if you were to get your dream house … Why don't you look ecstatic?"

"I am … I guess … It's just … that poor man and his family … They were all set to move in and—"

"And now they have enough money to move wherever

they want, with a tidy nest egg to boot. Relax, P. A few months from now they won't remember a week's worth of inconvenience when they're living in their new and bigger home. This place was too small for that enormous family of theirs anyway."

"I didn't think of it that way. That makes me feel better."

"Of course it does."

"But truly, I *will* pay you back … just as soon as—"

"I know, as soon as the tearoom is making a profit. There's no rush, P."

"No, you didn't let me finish. I was going to say, 'As soon as we can go to the bank.'"

"I don't follow. Where would you get that kind of money? We courtesans tend to have money coming out of our ears … at least for a time … but you respectable types…"

"It's from my parents' inheritance," Penelope said quietly, looking to the ground and exiting the room to sit at the top of the second floor landing.

Zara vaulted out of the tub and hurried after her. "I wasn't thinking. I apologize, P."

"Nothing to apologize for," Penelope said, her voice quavering in emotion. "They'd be proud and pleased to see me getting settled in a home of my own in such a lovely little town."

Unlike her mercurial sister, Pauline, who was at constant loggerheads with their mother, Penelope had always been close to both of her parents. In fact, she considered them her best friends. As a result, she'd never thought to move out of San Pedro, and had only left the nest to take a room at the local boarding house at her mother's prodding.

At the time, Mr. Price's own mother came to live with Penelope's family when she turned ninety-three and required a good deal of looking after. Penelope was happy to surrender her room to Gran and had planned to camp out on the living room couch throughout the rest of her grandmother's days.

Penelope's mother kindly suggested that, as a young working woman, Penelope might want to move into lodgings where she could live among her peers instead of spending her nights playing board games with her elders. Penelope had reluctantly agreed, though she wished daily to return to the loving comfort of home. The plus side of the move was that sister Pauline had stopped giving her grief about 'mooching' off of their parents.

Meanwhile, Pauline rarely contacted her mother or father unless to ask for money for her own family, comprised of herself, her henpecked husband, and spoiled six-year-old son. Based on how often Pauline wanted money, she spoke to her parents frequently.

Penelope stood up and looked around the top floor before descending the stairway. "Mother and Father would be even happier to see me take up residence in such a beautiful home … especially if they knew I was keeping an eye on you," she added with bittersweet humor.

"Brat!" Zara said, swatting Penelope's backside as they headed down the stairs and out the front door. Once on the porch, Penelope fumbled through her bag, feeling for her key fob.

"Now you have another key to lose," Zara jested.

"I really must make a list of all these keys."

"Paolo, start your engine!" Zara shouted. "Too bad he's oblivious to my lurid double meanings," she added as she bounded into the back seat of the luxurious auto and basked in the seaside sun while Penelope continued her key search.

At length, a jingle of metal resonated from the bowels of the carpetbag, and Penelope thrust her arm into the depths, seized the brass ring, attached the new key to it, and locked the door of the home, *her* home, the first home of her very own.

"Thanks, Mother. Thanks, Father," she whispered as she gently placed her palm on the front door.

"Shake a leg, P!" Zara called.

Penelope walked to the car, carrying her large bag in her arms as if it were a stack of wood. Reaching the sidewalk, she turned around to take in the view of the house and grounds. She let out a humble and grateful sigh, then crawled into the back seat of the automobile, still holding the bag, her eyes fixed on the domicile until the car turned the corner.

"Now where to? We should celebrate!" Zara exclaimed. "Paolo, we really must locate the speakeasies in this town," she said, imitating the gesture of drinking.

"Si, signorina," Paolo replied, paying little attention to what had been said.

"I'm choosing to disregard that last incendiary comment of yours, Z. Really, I'd like to go to the boarding house, if it's all the same to you. My head is swimming, and I just want to be somewhere quiet where I can think."

"And make lists?"

"That too."

"Home, Paolo! And don't spare the horsepower!" Zara cheered.

# Chapter Three

Back in Penelope's room at the boarding house, things were far from quiet. Penelope had taken to brainstorming her ideas for the new home while standing on top of the flimsy cot on which she slept, and Zara smuggled Paolo into the dwelling through a second-story window. The jazz-loving flapper blared Duke Ellington at decibels of which Mrs. Prescott would surely disapprove if she were home which, mercifully, she was not. Paolo prepared cocktails and struck Charles Atlas style poses as Zara used her long cigarette holder to direct him. In her reverie, Penelope failed to comment on the illegality of having either a male or alcoholic beverages in her bedchamber.

The room shook with a brief jolt, causing the three revelers to freeze. "P, kill the music," Zara said.

Penelope's mind raced to recall from her youth what to do in case of earthquake.

"Paolo, under the bed, *now!*" Zara said, pushing him down to the ground.

"Actually, I think you're supposed to stand under a doorway when there's an earthquake," Penelope said, opening the door and surprised to find Mrs. Prescott standing before it. "Mrs. Prescott, ehrm good afternoon."

"Miss Price, was that loud music I heard coming from your window as I walked up?"

"I'm afraid so, Mrs. Prescott. It was my fault," Zara said, penitently approaching Mrs. Prescott and standing with her hands folded like a virtuous schoolgirl. "When I turned the Victrola on, I didn't realize how loud it would be. I was unable to find a volume lever so I turned it off completely."

"And you are …?" Mrs. Prescott said, sizing up Zara with an experienced eye.

"Minnie Clark," Zara returned, adopting an air of innocence.

At hearing Zara's real name, Paolo emitted a brief chortle from his hiding place beneath the bed in front of which Penelope stood. Penelope let out a small cough to cover up his laugh.

"You're not coming down with a cold, are you, Miss Price? Come to my room and I'll dose you with some castor oil. Can't afford to infect the whole of the boarding house, now can we?"

"No, ma'am," Penelope said, scratching her cheek to disguise the wince she felt coming on at the thought of the castor oil.

"Really, I'm surprised at you, Miss Price. I believe I was quite clear about our policy on guests. All must be approved prior to ascending to the dormitory level."

"I ... ehr ..." Penelope stammered.

"No exceptions," Mrs. Prescott added, a look of sadistic satisfaction taking hold of her features as she watched Penelope squirm.

"Mrs. Prescott, Penelope—I mean Miss Price—and I are childhood friends, and after hearing her praise your hostel so highly, I begged to view it for myself. You see, I'm new in town and looking for lodgings," Zara said, winning over Mrs. Prescott with ease.

"Oh ... well ... that's different. I require two months payment up front," Mrs. Prescott said, eyeing Zara as a tiger does its prey.

"Two? Huh, I planned for three. All the better," Zara said, toying with the avaricious housekeeper. "Shall we, Penelope? Miss Price is going to show me the town. I should really freshen up first. Delightful to meet you at last, Mrs. Prescott. I see everything Penelope said about you is true. Now if you'll excuse me ... all those hours on the road ... the water closet calls. Which way is it, Penelope?"

"Oh, uh, down the hall on the left," Penelope answered, struggling to comprehend what had just happened while maintaining Zara's ruse.

Zara strode down the hall with Mrs. Prescott hard on her heels.

"Three months would be fine too," Mrs. Prescott called, running to catch up to Zara.

Zara stopped at the lavatory door and turned to face Mrs. Prescott. "Thank you, Mrs. Prescott. I think I can handle things on my own from here." She cocked her head, smiled broadly, and closed the door, humming as she ran the water in the sink.

Mrs. Prescott retreated slowly down the hall, her

fingers calculating what she could do with Zara's three month's rent. Fortunately, Penelope found the presence of mind to send Paolo out the window. He dropped silently to the ground with catlike agility, and after looking around to make sure no one had witnessed his escape, he returned to the Duesenberg. A moment later, Penelope caught sight of the half-full magnum of champagne that sat open next to the bed. Panicked, she prepared to pour it out the window, but just as she began to tilt the bottle over the ledge, she noticed two girls from the boarding house approaching.

"Lovely evening, Penelope," one of them called up to her.

She smiled and waved, unsure of what to do with the incriminating evidence. Just then, a knock came at the door.

"Oh, Miss Price," Mrs. Prescott called.

"Uh, umm, I'm just dressing. I'll be right there," Penelope called back.

She quickly looked around the room in search of a suitable hiding place to stash the sloshing, capless container—a hiding place beyond the detection of her ever-suspicious landlady. With nowhere to dispose of the drink, the intrepid teetotaler downed the lot of it, gulping it as quickly as she could and stowing the bottle in her stocking drawer. She hiccupped, causing her corset to constrict her breathing again, and was certain she was going to faint. She quickly grabbed a hat and gloves and opened the door.

"I thought you said you were dressing. Isn't that what you were already wearing?" Mrs. Prescott said.

"Uh ... yes ... I changed, but I didn't care for the ensemble, so I changed back again," Penelope fibbed.

Mrs. Prescott pursed her lips and looked Penelope up and down. "You girls, so fickle these days. In my day there was no choice. We had one dress and that was all. Why, I —"

"Was there something you wanted to tell me, Mrs.

Prescott?" Penelope said, doing her utmost not to belch. "I don't want to keep Zar … Miss Clark waiting."

"Yes, about Miss Clark, I think she would make a fine addition to the S.A. Virgin boarding house. Don't you?"

"Oh, yes, quite."

"And a single lady able to pay three months in advance, most impressive. What does Miss Clark do for income, may I ask?"

"Nothing. She's rich," Penelope said, quickly putting on her gloves. She dared not look the lady in the eye lest she be caught in her lie.

The corners of Penelope's mouth began to turn up involuntarily as she heard Mrs. Prescott gurgle the words, "She's rich."

Penelope put a hand on the doorknob. "And now I really must go. Good day, Mrs. Prescott."

"It is a good day indeed," Mrs. Prescott said to herself, rejoicing over her perceived good fortune. "And you'll encourage our Miss Clark, of course, won't you?" she asked Penelope.

"Of course. Ahh, here she comes now. Ready, Minnie?"

Zara lowered her eyes, detesting the sound of her given name. "I don't know, are we?" she asked, looking around the room for Paolo.

"We are indeed. Here are your hat and gloves. Shall we?"

Penelope shooed Zara and Mrs. Prescott out the door and locked it. After taking a few steps, Penelope announced, "Silly me. I forgot my bag. You two go on without me." She then returned to the room and closed the door, making sure to lock it. She opened her stocking drawer and retrieved the empty bottle of brut, placing it in her enormous bag and burying it deep within the gallimaufry. She then exited and locked the door once more.

When she caught up to Zara, she found Mrs. Prescott

extolling the merits of the boarding house and her strict policies, all designed to produce exemplary women with pristine morals. To her dismay, Penelope noticed Zara slowly inching her skirt up to reveal the hip flask concealed in the top of her stocking. Zara batted her eyes at Penelope. Penelope simply shook her head *no*. Mrs. Prescott was happy to walk the girls to their car, and Penelope did her best to prevent the champagne bottle from clanking with the noise-making contents of her carryall.

When they reached the Duesenberg, Mrs. Prescott let out a squeak of surprise upon finding a man behind the wheel. "Oh ... I didn't realize ..."

"Mrs. Prescott, may I present my driver, Paolo?"

Paolo alighted from the vehicle, reached for Mrs. Prescott's hand, and slowly kissed it. She stood speechless.

"I don't believe women should drive themselves, do you, Mrs. Prescott?" Zara said.

"Indeed, no," the woman responded, gawking at Paolo.

"Piacere, signora," Paolo said smoothly, never taking his eyes off of those of Mrs. Prescott."

"Wha ... What did he say?" Mrs. Prescott tittered, her face instantly flushing in cerise blotches.

"He said, 'pleasure,' Mrs. Prescott ... as in it is a pleasure to meet you," Zara replied to calculated effect.

"Pleasure, you say?" Mrs. Prescott said, unwittingly caressing the hand that had just been kissed.

"And now we *really* must be off. So many things to do for a fledgling shopkeeper like Penelope. I'm sure you'll have many tips for her, as a successful businesswoman yourself," Zara said, landing the final blow that would ingratiate both Penelope and herself to Mrs. Prescott. "Paolo?"

Paolo opened the grand automobile's door for Zara who slid into the seat with regal grace. Penelope followed her, albeit less gracefully, as she labored to load her bag into the car without drawing Mrs. Prescott's attention, even as she swayed under the effects of the guzzled champagne. Fortunately, Mrs. Prescott was aware of nothing other than Paolo.

Paolo donned a driver's cap, clicked his heels and said, "Ciao, Signora," to Mrs. Prescott.

"Ciao!" Zara called out, smiling and waving at Mrs. Prescott as the automobile pulled away.

"Ciao," Mrs. Prescott returned dreamily, having no idea what she was saying.

Once the car had rounded the corner, Penelope dared to speak. "I knew you were good, Z, but jeepers, that was some show you put on."

"Comes with the territory," Zara replied off-handedly. "Now, what the devil are you trying to hide in that abyss of chaos you call a handbag."

"This," Penelope said, squelching a burp and producing the contraband bottle.

"But where did you pour the contents? Shame to let such a banner vintage go to waste."

"It didn't ... I drank it," Penelope said, her eyelids beginning to lower of their own volition.

Zara sat for a moment staring in amazement at her friend, then burst into hearty laughter. "I believe there's hope for you yet, P."

Penelope opened her mouth to respond, but what came out was a long, low, robust combination hiccup and rumbling eructation. Zara gave in to more laughter causing Penelope to laugh in turn and in so doing, experience yet even more hiccups. This sent Zara into a fit of jocularity that saw her rolling on the floor of the car, holding her abdomen, and kicking her feet wildly in the air.

When the shenanigans had subsided, Paolo got a word in. "*Dove?*"

"Pardon, Paolo?" Penelope replied, happy to move on from the embarrassment.

"He wants to know where we want to go next," Zara said, blinking tears of laughter from her eyes and working to catch her breath.

Penelope breathed in the convertible's fresh air in an effort to sober up. "I didn't know you spoke Italian, Z."

"Just a little. Paolo's been teaching me. And I've taught him a thing or two as well," she said, running her hand through the back of Paolo's hair.

He growled seductively in response. Penelope grunted in mild disgust, then continued breathing deeply to regain sobriety.

"Signorina Penelope?" Paolo prompted.

"Yes? … Oh, yes, where to? Well, I suppose we need furnishings and basic housewares. The shop next door to mine is a general store, I believe. We're sure to find some staples there. And giving them our business would show goodwill as neighbors," Penelope said, reasoning her way through her words.

"Why, Penelope Price!" Zara exclaimed.

"Oh no, what did I do now?" Penelope asked in the preliminary stage of panic, assuming she'd committed some sort of faux pas.

"If I didn't know better, I'd say you're beginning to talk like a bona fide woman of business!"

Penelope smiled, her cheeks turning pink owing to the compliment, along with the champagne.

"Paolo, il negozio di Penelope!" Zara called out enthusiastically.

"Si, signorina!" Paolo cheered in response, releasing the parking break and driving toward the antiques store.

"What did you say?" Penelope asked.

"I think I said, 'Penelope's store'—at least I hope I did."

As the Duesenberg headed to the shop, the ladies began a rapid-fire verbal list of all the things they'd need for the house. Penelope's list tended to favor the practical, whereas Zara's favored illegal substances and practices.

* * * *

"There it is! Allen's General Store," Penelope said.

"*We've got it all in Allen's*," Zara added, reading the sign on the store's window.

Paolo turned off the motor and pulled his driver's cap over his eyes, settling in for a nap in anticipation of a long shopping spree.

"Paolo!" Zara admonished.

He groaned, pushed his cap back up, got out of the car, and sluggishly opened the car door. Zara emerged from the Duesenberg as if she were a motion picture star arriving at a premiere. Penelope backed out unceremoniously, her posterior leading the way as she battled to extricate her carpetbag from the car.

"Not this time, P. Just take your coin purse."

Penelope looked lost at the idea of being separated from the *pit of no return*, Zara's preferred term for Penelope's mammoth tote. Penelope stood clutching her coin purse, turning it this way and that and trying to work out what to do with the palm-sized pouch. Zara wrested it from her hands and tucked it in her own décolleté. Penelope gasped at the sight as Zara slid her arm through Penelope's and tramped through Allen's door.

"Good afteernoon, ladiz. How may I beh of asseestance?" Hubert Allen said, slithering out from behind the front counter and admiring Zara.

"How do you do? Mr. Allen, I presume?" Zara said coolly.

"Een thee fleesh," he replied, not bothering to regard Penelope.

"It's a real pleasure to meet you. I'm Miss Price, Penelope Price."

"Dellighteed," Hubert said in a perfunctory tone, lavishing all of his attention on Zara. "And you are?" he asked, taking Zara's hand in his.

"Zara," Zara replied, pulling him into her web.

"Zara ...?" he prodded.

"Just Zara," she replied, meeting his gaze with bewitching eyes.

"Eez theer something een parteekular you are looking for today, Mees Zara?" he asked, still grasping her hand.

"A good many things, I should think," Zara said, looking him up and down for his benefit. "My friend, Miss Price, and I are setting up house and need ... Well, I suppose we should defer to you to tell us what we need."

"Right thees way," he said, taking the liberty of putting his hand on Zara's back to lead her through the emporium.

Comprised of three rooms, the store was well stocked, and its items tastefully displayed. Hubert led them out of the foyer—a room with gleaming windows that featured a sales counter and assortment of novelty, impulse-buy gadgets—into a generous space lined with shelves brimming with housewares organized according to the rooms found in the average household.

"Wow," Penelope whispered in raptured awe as Hubert escorted them into a large warehouse filled with furniture arranged in attractive tableaux.

"I thinnk you weell find our seeleection to beh vast, and our pricees to beh far more rezzonable than that of Mr. Holman and heez so-called *Popular* Dry Good Store. Our seerveece eez behyond compare ... so I've behn told."

"I see you're very well equipped," Zara said, twirling a lock of hair between her gloved fingers and parting her lips.

"That I am ... ehr, *weh* are," he said, gobbling up Zara's verbal bait. "Now, leet's start in thee parlor arehya and work our way to ... thee boudoir."

"I like how you think," Zara replied.

"Do you plan to do much eenteertaining?" he asked, parading her around the perimeter of the room.

"Oh yes," Zara said. "No, not really," Penelope responded in unison.

"And who are you, aggehn?" Hubert said, turning to Penelope and taking note of her for the first time.

"Miss Price ... your new business neighbor," she added with a wasted smile.

"New ..." he said, his eyes glancing about as he tried to sort out her answer. "Do I take you to minn you are Mees Tate's niss?" he asked.

"I am indeed," she said, forcing another smile. "I'm looking forward to working alongside you, Mr. Allen. You have such an interesting accent, may I ask where you're from?"

"From? I'll have you know I'm a Paceefeec Grove nateev. Peerhaps our way of spikking is foreen to confeedeerates like you, Mees Price, who eez, I beelivv, from San Peddro."

Penelope stood agog, unsure how to respond, and quite sure she'd not heard anyone from Northern California—or anywhere else for that matter—speak in such an unusual dialect.

"Shall we continue?" Zara said, taking Hubert's arm.

Ninety minutes later, the ladies exited Allen's General Store. Paolo looked up to see Penelope massaging one of her temples with her knuckle, her countenance that of one who'd seen a ghost. Zara's demeanor was cool and confident, as was so often the case when she'd charmed a new male acquaintance.

"I'll have Dan Coopeer, our uteeleetteh man, start moving your thinns een tomorrow morninn," Hubert said. "And wheere shall I seend heem?"

"The corner of Oceanview Boulevard and Fifth Street," Penelope chirped.

"Ah, thee old Lacy house. Some steel call it Iveh

Teerrace Hall, the name geeveen to thee home by eets last reeseedeent. Judge Weelbur of Pasadenna. An eexceeleent choice, Mees Zara," he said, ignoring Penelope.

"I'll have my man, Paolo, assist your Mr. Cooper," Zara said, waving daintily at Paolo who sat up when he heard his name mentioned.

"You have a man, Mees Zara?" Hubert said, prying in his oily manner.

"What a leading question, Mr. Allen," she returned flirtatiously.

"Thank you, Mr. Allen. We'll be going now," Penelope said, taking Zara's arm to pull her away.

"Unteel tomorrow," Hubert said to Zara.

"Until tomorrow," she replied, turning on her heel and returning to the car, her hips drawing figure eights as she walked.

"Oh, brother, what was that?" Penelope asked once they were sequestered in the Duesenberg.

"Goodwill insurance, P. Goodwill. Oh, and Paolo, darling, will you be a love and assist with some lifting tomorrow morning?"

"*Come?*" Paolo said, his brow furrowed in confusion.

Zara pantomimed the act of moving furniture.

"Si," Paolo said with a smile.

"I think you just gave him the impression he will be lifting weights at the gymnasium," Penelope said.

"Close enough, he'll be exercising," Zara said, flipping up her skirt to reach her flask. "Alla Del Monte Hotel, Paolo … We're taking off, P. See ya tomorrow … P? …" Zara said, nodding toward the car door.

"Huh?! Oh!" Penelope said, exiting the Duesenberg and dragging the *pit of no return* behind her.

"Don't forget this!" Zara said, producing Penelope's coin purse.

Penelope dropped the petite bag into its cavernous

counterpart and waved goodbye as Zara and Paolo pulled away. She then got into her Model T and conducted her usual series of steps and safety procedures in preparation of driving. After checking the mirrors several times, she paused, turned off the motor, and dived with both hands into her monstrous portmanteau where she quickly found her shop keys to which she'd attached her car keys. She then opened the car door, got out, took an authoritative breath, straightened her posture, and marched with uncharacteristic deliberateness to the front door of her new shop.

Once inside, she locked the door behind her and collapsed onto the red velvet doughnut settee. She peered around for some minutes then fell into a brief crying jag, her way of dealing with the abrupt and unexpected changes in her life.

"Auntie Dee, what have you gotten me into?" she whispered aloud.

She then stood and wandered around the sales room, marveling at the diversity and intricacy of the various relics, most of which were foreign to her. She made a point to look for furnishings from the shop that she could take home to fill in the gaps where Hubert Allen's goods left off. A gold-fringed, brown velvet chaise—what her mother would have called a *fainting couch*—caught her eye, along with a few Tiffany lamps, and several ornate mirrors. She put the items aside as best she could in the crowded shop area, then absentmindedly walked into her grandaunt's quarters, pulled down the Murphy bed, and dropped onto it, asleep in seconds.

# Chapter Four

She awoke in the dark, having no idea where she was, how she got there, or what time it might be. Stumbling toward the light from the shop's front windows, she began to recall her surroundings. Still in a sleepy stupor, she made her way to the door. Fortunately, she noticed her shop key wedged into the interior lock, as she would have had no idea where to look for keys otherwise.

After gathering her thoughts and her things, she locked the door behind her. Consulting her wristwatch, she noted the time was 9:45, three quarters of an hour past Mrs. Prescott's weeknight curfew.

"That's an awfulleh beeg eenteerprise for such a leettle ladeh," a voice said from the shadows.

Penelope recognized the unusual speech of Hubert Allen and located him by the waft of smoke floating up from his cigarette.

"This leetle ladeh has beeg plans for the place," Penelope replied, unintentionally mimicking his irregular speech.

He dropped his cigarette to the sidewalk and extinguished it with a long, thin worn-out loafer. "Eef eet becomes too much for you, I'd beh happeh to take a good dell of thee meerchandise off your hands. I herr you are more inteereesteed een running a teh shop than seeling dusteh antiks."

"That's very kind of you, Mr. Allen."

"Eet's what good neighbors do," he said, coming out of the shadows and giving her a fixed stare.

"Well … I best get going. Mrs. Prescott runs a tight ship," she said, fumbling with her keys.

"Theen I'll say goodnight. And seh you and Mees Zara in the morneng," he said with a lecherous grin.

When Penelope got to the boarding house, she was immediately chastised by the sight of Mrs. Prescott sitting on the front steps and clutching a broom for defense, her hair in curling rags.

"Not the sort of behavior I expect from a Virgin girl, Miss Price. I'm very disappointed. I dare say your fine friend, Miss Clark, would be as well."

"I'm so sorry, Mrs. Prescott. I fell asleep at my new

shop and lost track of the time."

"That's what comes from being a female merchant, Miss Price," Mrs. Prescott said, hoisting up her dressing gown and walking to the front door, the broom handle waving beneath her arm and narrowly missing Penelope's chin.

"Yes, ma'am," Penelope said, wanting nothing more than to crawl into bed and forget all about curfews and boarding houses and shops and business—at least until morning.

* * * *

Her sleep was sound and dreamless, and she didn't wake until the noise of bedroom doors in the hallway alerted her to the fact it was time to get up and get going.

She looked at her watch and calculated she had just ten minutes to get down to breakfast before Mrs. Prescott stopped serving. She desperately needed to bathe, but chose rankness over hunger, and simply splashed her face with water from the room's basin, smoothed her hair, replaced a few bobby pins, dabbed her neck and wrists with a bit of Après L'Ondée, chewed a breath mint, jumped back into her clothes from the day before, slid into her shoes, and made a beeline for the dining room with only a few minutes to spare.

"Lost track of time again?" Mrs. Prescott said with a forced frown that belied the kind of smug smile one wears when they believe they've been vindicated in some way. She then handed Penelope a pitcher of just-squeezed orange juice. "Toast, Miss Price?"

"Yes, please, ma'am," she said, still in a state of frazzlement.

The dormitory matron carved two slices from a large loaf of fresh-baked soda bread and deposited them in the toaster on the sideboard. "When might we have the pleasure of seeing Miss Clark again?" Mrs. Prescott said, her tone abnormally sweet and lilting.

"Oh, uh, we'll be working at the shop today, so …" Penelope took a swig of orange juice to avoid fully answering the question.

"Let her know I send my regards?" Mrs. Prescott said, carrying a tray of breakfast things back to the kitchen. "She'd make a fine Virgin girl, to be sure."

Penelope partially spit out her orange juice. Fortunately, there was no one to witness the gaffe since she was the only one left at the table. "I certainly will, Mrs. Prescott," she gasped.

A moment later, Mrs. Prescott returned to the dining room just as the toaster popped. Penelope was nowhere to be seen.

**✳ ✳ ✳ ✳**

Penelope was thankful to be ahead of schedule once she arrived at her new house. It would be an hour or two before the moving men would pull up to begin unloading. She toured the abode several times, plotting what furnishings would go where, bickering with herself as she was wont to do when figuring out any sort of puzzle. She was keen to have refreshments awaiting the movers, but hadn't anything to serve them, let alone the means with which to do so. In a flash of inspiration, she drove down Oceanview Boulevard in search of take-away food.

After a short drive, she came upon the Butterfly Café, the lunchroom where she and Zara had dined less than twenty-four hours prior, though it seemed weeks ago to Penelope given all that had transpired. When she entered the restaurant, the same waitress who had served them previously recognized her.

"Back so soon? Where's that choice bit of calico you came in with yesterday? You two make a hotsy-totsy pair."

"Oh, uh, do you mean Zara? She's on her way to the new house right now actually."

"Zara, what a name. It suits her. And what's your name, Miss …"

"Price … Penelope."

"I'm Ruby. What can I get for ya today, 'Price … Penelope?'"

"Umm, we have some movers who will be working at the house—fatigued and sweaty, I'm guessing. Can you recommend something nice for them to snack on?"

"Absolutely. It's all the rage. Key lime pie!"

"I'm afraid I've never heard of it. Is it like lemon chiffon?"

"It's like nothing you've ever had—an old recipe from the sponge fisherman down Key West way in Florida. Ya don't even cook it!"

"Why ever not?"

"'Cause fishermen on boats don't have ovens to bake in! They just throw together pelican eggs and sweet canned milk and these key limes while they're out at sea, and the whole thing sort of cooks itself!"

"Is it any good?"

"Any good?! Criminy, it's the bee's knees!"

"And that's good?"

"That's tops! We make ours the 'Aunt Sally' way with a graham cracker crust and dollops of fresh whipped cream. Trust me, your gang will go mad for it."

"Well then, one key lime pie …"

"Make it two."

"Two key lime pies then, and a pair of large thermoses of coffee, please. Also, by any chance, may I borrow some plates and cups and utensils? Ours haven't arrived yet."

"Sure thing!" said Ruby as she bounced away to fetch the pie and eating-ware.

As Penelope stood waiting for her order, she sensed a pair of eyes burrowing into the back of her head. She turned around to see the rough and ready female line-cook staring at her with a knowing smirk. Penelope gasped and immediately set off to promenade around the room, whistling and feigning intense interest in the bottles of condiments sitting on each table. Just when Penelope felt she would have to run from the café screaming in discomfort, Ruby returned.

"Don't take any wooden nickels!" the girl said, handing Penelope a large basket. "And come back soon with that sheba of yours!"

Penelope stuttered in an attempt to answer that Zara was not her sweetheart, but decided the correction wasn't worth the effort, so pre-occupied was she with the events of the last twenty-four hours, let alone those to come.

As she drove back toward the house, she made a point to take in the panoramic picture of the Pacific Ocean. Thus far, she'd neglected to pay any attention to the beauty of her new surrounds. "Breathtaking," she said aloud. The jagged shoreline with its wildflowers and lapping waves filled her with a contentment she'd rarely felt. Something was shifting within her psyche—something she was aware of only in a peripheral way.

Back at the Victorian, she arranged the plates, napkins, silverware, and pie on one side of the sink, and the coffee cups and thermos on the other, along with a jug of milk and bowl of sugar provided by Ruby. She'd never done much in the way of entertaining and had never cooked for anyone, not that she'd baked the key lime pie or even made the coffee herself. But suddenly, she felt a yearning to engage in hospitality. *Perhaps it comes with being a homeowner*, she reasoned.

After making the rounds through the house a few more times, she heard the rumble of a large truck coming up the lane. She ran downstairs and out the front door to find her tufted Victorian sofa being carried toward the house, a smiling Zara lounging atop it, posed like Cleopatra being conveyed to Caesar.

Penelope whisked back to the kitchen to fetch a clipboard bearing lists and charts, a pencil tied to the board's metal clamp lest the pencil go missing.

"I have no idea where all of this will go," Zara said, alighting from the sofa.

"I know exactly," Penelope said, directing Paolo and Hubert Allen's utility man Dan Cooper with a confidence and decisiveness Zara had never witnessed in her friend.

Dan unloaded the truck with a smile and a song. Paolo just glared and cursed the ladies under his breath. He may have been a muscular bodybuilder, but he loathed manual labor. Then again, he loathed most labor.

In under an hour, the entire contents of the immense moving truck had been emptied, thanks in great part to Dan. When Penelope offered the workmen some refreshment, they, along with Zara, were delightfully surprised to find the key lime pie and coffee waiting in the kitchen.

"I believe Emily Post would give you top marks," Zara said, referring to the famed etiquette expert of the day.

Penelope smiled bashfully. "You'll have to eat it all, gentleman. I'm afraid the icebox doesn't work."

"That's because the electricity is off, Miss Price," Dan noted. "You'll need to get it turned back on down at City Hall. If you'd like, I can remove this old icebox and install your new Kelvinator tomorrow while you're downtown."

"That's awfully nice of you, Dan," Zara said, impressed with his magnanimity.

"Thank you, Dan. That would be … the bee's knees," Penelope said with a shy smile.

Zara giggled.

Dan Cooper was what most in town considered a tragic figure. He'd run a booming business at the Half-Way House Saloon just outside of Pacific Grove's 'dry city' limits until the Eighteenth Amendment put an end to his livelihood. Since then, he'd fallen on hard times. He had to sell his saloon furnishings for pennies on the dollar and was forced to dispense with all his costly alcohol without remuneration.

With four young children and a wife, he'd taken to accepting any odd job he could find in order to provide for the family. Whereas just a year ago he was looked to as a pillar of the community, now he was little more than a charity case. He'd become gaunt and haggard, often going without meals to ensure his offspring had sufficient nutrition. He did not wear his newfound poverty well, and was at turns desperate and withdrawn since his financial woes began.

He'd married his high school sweetheart, Lillian Michaels, before shipping off to the war, and he was devoted to her and their children in every way imaginable. Lily had a promising career as a concert harpist that was cut short when she proved to be uncommonly fertile, producing four heirs in just as many years.

During the glory days of the Half-Way House—a name chosen based on its New Monterey location mid-way between Pacific Grove and Monterey—Dan earned a reputation for liberality and compassion, never pestering patrons to pay off their tabs, often driving inebriates home if they were in no state to travel on their own. The Half-Way House was the most popular watering hole in the area with live music on weekends and a hearty Sunday Supper served weekly to those who had no family with whom to dine. Dan himself was an accomplished musician, skilled at trumpet, clarinet and piano. Nearly every night at the saloon someone cajoled Dan to come out from behind the bar and play with the given night's band.

Recently, Dan's only performances involved the performing of random jobs for Hubert Allen, and Dan was always grateful for the extra work. His only goal was the welfare and happiness of his family, but he feared if his financial situation didn't improve, he could very well lose guardianship of his children.

Penelope was tickled to see with what zeal he gobbled down his pie and coffee. When she offered him a second piece, he eagerly accepted—same when she offered him a third. It was then she sensed that he was a soul in need. When Paolo refused a second helping, patting his waste to indicate he was watching his physique, Penelope asked Dan if he'd mind taking the rest of the pie home since she didn't have a working icebox. He was delighted to help her out. She was overjoyed to provide him with food.

As Dan and Paolo boarded the truck to return to Allen's General Store, Penelope asked Dan if he'd be available for some extra work. "I can pay you a dollar fifty per hour, if that's all right," Penelope offered.

"If that's all right?!" Dan gushed, overwhelmed at the amount that was fifty percent more than he was accustomed to earning. "When do I start?" he cried.

"Tomorrow morning, if you're able. Nine o'clock sharp at Aunt Dee's antiques shop," Penelope said.

"Oh that's right. Dorothea was your great aunt. My condolences, Miss Price."

"Thank you, Mr. Cooper. Aunt Dee lived a full and thrilling life, as I'm beginning to learn. I look forward to finding out more about her from all of you who worked and lived here in town with her."

"Your great aunt and I spent many nights together at the saloon into the wee hours. The secrets we shared," he said with a chuckle.

Zara's eyes widened in fascination. Paolo huffed his disinterest in the conversation and closed his eyes to snooze.

"Well ... thank you again for taking the pie off my hands. We'll see you in the morning then," Penelope said, sensing Paolo's impatience.

"Good day, Miss Price, Miss Zara," Dan said, tipping his cap.

"Good day, Dan," Zara returned, smiling compassionately.

"Poor man," she said to Penelope once the truck was out of sight.

"You sensed it too?" Penelope asked, walking back into the house.

Zara nodded. "Something about him … he seems like a broken man … and yet, a very good man."

"I agree. It's hard to see a person with so much promise brought so low. You and I are both so fortunate that we're prospering as we are," Penelope said, taking a seat on her new sofa and spreading her arms out wide.

Just then Zara shivered involuntarily, a pall coming over her usually radiant face.

Penelope put her hands in her lap and sat up. "What is it, Z? Did I say something to upset you? Golly, that was the furthest thing—"

"No, it's not you, P … it's me …" Zara said as she took a seat in one of Penelope's new tufted armchairs. "Actually, it's Costas … was Costas."

"Your former … ehrm … paramour?"

"Patron would be the more apt term."

"Why exactly did you leave him, Z? I thought you really cared for him."

"I did. You know how I used to scorn those chump women who fell in love with their patrons and even believed that baloney about their lovers leaving their wives for them?"

"Yes?"

"Well I became one of those chumps," Zara said, her eyes welling. "I made the ultimate mistake and fell in love with my lover. When I told Costas—when I bared my heart to him—he tenderly kissed me and told me he could bear to live without me as his wife no longer. He proposed on the spot. We even chose a date for the ceremony! That night we made love as never before."

"So romantic," Penelope whispered, resting her chin

and hands on the arm of the sofa as she hung on Zara's every word.

"Is it?" Zara said, forcing a smile and looking at Penelope with doleful, probing eyes. Her facial expression hardened as she continued, "The next morning I received a formal letter from his lawyer warning me to refrain from ever making contact with Costas again. The letter was delivered by a page and came with a large check."

Penelope sat silent for a moment, concentrating to grasp the import of what Zara had shared. "What did you do?" she quietly asked.

"I ripped it up of course!"

"The check or the letter?"

"Both!"

Penelope felt a lump filling her throat. She'd never known Zara to have a care in the world. Penelope realized Zara may have had many cares, but just never let on about them. "Good for you, Z," she cheered as enthusiastically as she could. "That showed him you didn't need him *or* his filthy money."

"That showed him all right," Zara said, putting her head in her hands and breaking down in a torrent of tears.

"Oh no! Is it something I said again? I always say the wrong thing. I'm sorry, Z," Penelope said, hastening over to the armchair to embrace and comfort her dearest friend, a friend Penelope viewed as her own family.

"I'm so ashamed," Zara sobbed.

"Of what, Z? Being a courtesan? You're not the first to—"

"No, it's not that … the check … I tried to put it back together!" she wailed.

Penelope sat on the floor next to Zara's chair, unsure as to what to say next. "Oh … well … bully for you! You earned that money! I'm glad you kept it."

"But, P, I couldn't put it back together and had to beg

the lawyer for a new one," she said, her reddened eyes pleading. "When I did, he just sneered at me and instructed the doorman to escort me out. You must think me a pathetic wretch," she said, sobbing anew.

"I think no such thing!" Penelope declared, shaking Zara's knee to emphasize her point. "I think you are the most beautiful, cultivated lady I've ever met and the best friend a girl could ask for. I've never been anything but proud of you."

Zara glanced into Penelope's eyes and her anxiety-ridden features once again softened. "Thanks, P. It means the world to me … truly."

Penelope put her head on Zara's knee and the two sat in silence for several minutes.

"Do you mind if I stay here tonight?" Zara asked. "I'm nearly out of money and need to vacate the hotel."

"Mind? I insist! Besides, you told me you were moving in with me, remember?" Penelope said with a hopeful smile.

Zara returned the smile. "That's true. In that case, I think I'll go to my room and lie down for a while. Wake me up for dinner?"

Penelope nodded. "While you nap, I'm going to take a long hot bath. These clothes are on the verge of becoming permanently attached to my skin!"

Much to her relief, Penelope found the hot water heater was working, thanks to Dan lighting its pilot light. The cares of the day seemed to evaporate with the steam rising from the tub as she stepped into the soothing soak. When the water began to cool, she wrapped herself in a pair of new over-sized bath towels, and tiptoed to Zara's room, trying hard to prevent the wooden floor from creaking.

She thought Zara looked like an innocent angel when sleeping, nothing like the formidable vamp Zara played when awake. Penelope crept to her own room and decided to try out her new canopy bed. She didn't intend to doze, just get off her feet for a few minutes.

# Chapter Five

The crow of the cock informed Penelope that she'd slept the night away. "Oh no! How will I face Mrs. Prescott?!" she exclaimed as she bolted upright in bed, still wrapped in bath sheets. Without a change of clothes at the new house, she was forced to wear the same outfit for the third day in a row. At least she'd had a chance to bathe.

Not wanting to take the time to wake Zara or even explain, she picked up her shoes and bag, and crept out to drive to the boarding house. As she hurriedly checked her side view mirror for the fifth time, she noticed Zara's car parked on the other side of the street. *Paolo must be here. I'll cross that bridge later.*

Driving quickly but conservatively to the Virgin House, she weighed several options as to what to say to Mrs. Prescott. She considered an account of kidnapping, one involving gypsies, even amnesia.

Upon arrival, Penelope burst through the front door and espied Mrs. Prescott bustling about the dining room, laying out the breakfast dishes.

Before Mrs. Prescott could emit a word from her crimson, ire-flushed face, Penelope blurted out the truth. "I'm terribly sorry for being out all night without telephoning you to let you know, Mrs. Prescott. You must have been worried sick."

Mrs. Prescott snarled and opened her mouth to speak.

"The thing is, I've just purchased the old Lacy home on Oceanview and fell asleep there from exhaustion after a busy day of furniture moving."

Mrs. Prescott's jaw dropped, as did the basket of muffins she was about to put on the dining table.

"Miss Clark, who actually goes by the name Zara by the way, will be moving in with me."

Mrs. Prescott fell into a chair, her eyes glazed and lower lip twitching.

Penelope opened her carpetbag and began to rummage through it, her words hardly audible as she spoke into the abyss. "I know there is nothing I can say to make up for being such a disappointment as a Virgin girl, but I hope this token of gratitude will help assuage a little of your disappointment over my many shortcomings." She then scribbled on a blank check and handed the slip of paper to Mrs. Prescott.

All the color drained from the boarding house matron's face, and for the first time since Penelope had known her, the woman was rendered speechless.

*The truth really is the best policy,* Penelope thought as she grabbed a muffin from the basket on the floor and walked up the stairs to her room. *At least when it's accompanied by an obscene amount of money.*

She made short work of packing up her belongings, full of adrenaline and exhilaration was she. A fresh change of clothing and a thorough brushing of teeth were all she really desired at that point. Once those tasks were completed, she put her things in the car, then strode back inside for a last breakfast at the boarding house. When she entered the dining room, she found Mrs. Prescott still sitting in the same chair, the same dumbfounded look on her face as she reviewed the information on the check over and over.

"Delicious spinach pie, Mrs. Prescott," Penelope said, exhibiting a carefree confidence she'd never experienced until arriving in town. "I do hope you'll stop by the tea shop for a cup with me when we open."

Mrs. Prescott gave her a look both perplexed and somewhat terrified.

"Oh yes, I'm adding a tearoom to the antiques store. In fact, I'm calling it AntiquiTeas—rather clever, if I do say so myself," Penelope added as she dabbed the corners of her mouth with a napkin.

Mrs. Prescott steadied herself by holding on to the edge of the dining table.

"Thank you again for your understanding and hospitality. We businesswomen must stick together, mustn't we?" Penelope said, surprised at the words coming out of her mouth. "Good day, Mrs. Prescott."

\* \* \* \*

Penelope hummed cheerfully as she motored back to the Victorian. Suddenly, the world seemed so much less daunting and oppressive to her, and she was sure she was dreaming or perhaps living someone else's life. She arrived home to hear tousling and giggling coming from Zara's room upstairs, and she surmised Paolo was with her. Visiting the servant's room downstairs that had been designated for Paolo, she saw his clothes strewn across the still-made bed. Clearly, he had not slept there. This level of co-habitation was not the sort of activity Penelope felt she could condone. She was a single woman in a new town. What's more, she was now a homeowner and a proprietress. Certainly, she could not afford to be saddled with scandal.

She made her way to the kitchen with plans to make a pot of restorative coffee, but several disheartening and frustrating minutes later, she gave up as the coffee maker refused to percolate. It was then she remembered the electricity was turned off and would require a visit to City Hall to see it turned back on. The civic building would not open for another forty-five minutes, but she decided waiting outside in the car would be preferable to enduring the illicit sound effects provided by Zara and Paolo upstairs, so she threw herself together and dashed out the door.

Once in the car, Penelope realized she had no idea where City Hall was located, so she decided to take advantage of the opportunity to get to know the area by letting herself roam the streets. After taking in the sights of the main thoroughfares of Lighthouse Avenue and Sunset Drive, she turned down Forest Avenue and happened upon the civic center. Her breath caught for a moment when she noticed that, like her new home, the City Hall building boasted a view of the Pacific. *This town truly is heaven on earth,* she thought as she gazed out at the ocean's horizon.

A few moments later, the building's clock tower chimed eight urging Penelope to gather her things and head to the entrance. When she arrived, she found a smiling man just unlocking the doors.

"Looks like you'll be the one catching the worm today," the man said in a jolly tone.

"Worm?" Penelope replied, befuddled. "Ohhhhhh, I get it … you mean because I'm the early bird," she said, smiling in response.

The man chuckled and the corners of his warm eyes crinkled. "What can I do ya for, Miss …" he asked, opening the door wide to accommodate her imposing satchel.

"Price, thank you."

The man's smile faded instantly. "Miss Penelope Price, niece of Miss Dorothea Tate?" he asked, his jowls drooping and face stern.

"Yuh, yes," she said, suddenly as nervous as she was just two days earlier when in Bernard Beekham's law office picking up the keys to the antiques shop. "How do you do, officer?" she said, extending a trembling hand.

"It's Chief, Chief Harrison. I run this town, Miss Price," he said, giving her hand a begrudging single shake.

"Nice to meet you, Chief Harrison," she said weakly, unsure of what she'd done to make the police chief's tone change so dramatically.

He addressed her sharply as he strode down the hall, not bothering to wait for her. "Is there something I can do for you, Miss Price?"

"Yes, sir, thank you. I was told to come here to arrange for the electricity to be turned on at my home," she said, jogging to keep up with him.

He stopped and turned toward her. "The electricity's off at the Virgin House? That's odd. Mrs. Prescott hasn't reported any problems."

"No, umm, I meant at *my* house … say, how did you know I was staying at the Virgin House?"

"This is a small town, Miss Price, and I'm its guardian." He resumed walking as he spoke. "Now, why don't you tell me what exactly is going on?" he said, opening the door to his small, cramped office and taking a seat behind his overloaded desk.

"Oh, well, no, you see, actually … I just bought a place … the old Lacy house, I'm told it's called." She lowered herself into the room's only other chair.

"Miss Price, do you expect me to believe that a spinster bookkeeper such as yourself has the means to buy a seaside home?"

Penelope felt attacked and defensive, though she didn't know precisely why. Her throat tightened and her eyes began to fill with tears. At that moment, she wanted nothing more than to bolt from the room, from the building, and possibly even from Pacific Grove. She thought of the women she admired—her mother, Aunt Dee, Zara—and sought to handle the situation the way any one of them might; thus, she summoned her courage and opened her trembling mouth to speak.

"Chief Harrison, I do not see how my financial affairs are your business, or anyone else's for that matter," she said, her confident tone waning with each word.

He glowered at her and commenced giving her a thorough tongue-lashing. "Madam, I am the chief of police in this town. Everything that happens here is my business, because everything affects the residents I've sworn to look after and protect. A single woman suspiciously buys a home the minute she sets foot in town—that gets me asking questions. Only people who have that kind of money these days are rumrunners. Are you a rumrunner, Miss Price?" the chief demanded, placing both hands on his desk and standing up as he leaned toward her.

Penelope wrung her hands, determined to answer and not to cry. "I used the money from my parents' inheritance to buy the house. Not only my Aunt Dee, but both of my parents recently passed. My sister got the family home and I got some money, if you insist on knowing," she said, breaking down and blubbering.

The chief stood inert for a moment, staring at his desk. "Now there, there," he finally said, offering her his handkerchief. "I didn't mean to make you go on and get all weepy. Why I—"

"I'm sorry. It's just a big change moving up here. It was all so sudden. I had a comfortable and uncomplicated life back in San Pedro. I worked five days a week as a bookkeeper, was always on time, earned enough to strike out on my own and take a room at Mrs. Holcomb's boarding house. Sure I ate from a hot plate, and my room was the size of a broom closet, but I did it all on my own. If I had a choice, I'd rather have my parents alive than have their money. But I don't have a choice," Penelope said, blowing into the handkerchief and becoming increasingly upset.

"Now my aunt has passed away too, and I have no blood relations save a sister who has no interest in me except for running my life the way she deems appropriate. So if you don't want to turn the electricity on at my place it's okay by me. I can eat from a can and read by candlelight and even go to the YWCA at Asilomar for a hot bath if I need to."

While Penelope bemoaned her plight, the chief rustled through one of his desk drawers and went about doing paperwork, seemingly oblivious to her tale of woe.

"Are you even listening to me, Chief Harrison?" she barked in frustration.

"Here you go, Miss Price," he said in a low voice, offering her a slip of paper.

"What is this?" she asked, sniffing back the last of her tears.

"It's your copy of the work order I'll be filing once

we're done here. I'll personally make sure your electricity gets turned on—today!"

"Thank you," she said softly, worrying the handkerchief in her hands.

"Now, would you like to set up your tearoom inspection while you're here, or wait for another time?"

"Inspection?" she said. "How did you know I wanted to turn the place into a tearoom? Only my best friend knows that. Do you know Zara?" she asked, her eyes widening.

"Who? No, Bernard Beekham, the lawyer you met with told me of your plans."

"Word travels fast in this town," she said aloud to herself.

"You have no idea," the chief returned under his breath, shaking his head.

Penelope took a deep breath. "To be honest, I don't know if opening a tearoom will even be possible. It's all so overwhelming," she said, her voice cracking as she spoke. Immediately, she regretted what she'd said. The gruff police chief was the last person in whom she would choose to confide.

"Steady on. You'll work yourself into a state again. If you do decide to convert Dee's antiques shop into a tearoom, you know where to find me," he said, his face again warm and inviting.

"Did you know my grandaunt?" she asked innocently.

Once more his tone and expression calloused. "I'm afraid I must ask you to leave now, Miss Price," he said, standing up and scooting his rickety chair back. "I have lots of other people to assist. You're not the only citizen in this town, you know."

Again confused, Penelope walked out of the office. "No, of course not. I didn't mean to—"

"Good day, Miss Price."

"Good day."

Though unsure as to what had just transpired, there was one thing of which she was certain—she would have electricity, and for the time being, that was good enough for her.

**\* \* \* \***

Standing outside City Hall, Penelope realized she hadn't thought further ahead in planning her day than the errand she'd just concluded—an errand that left her emotionally exhausted. She took another deep breath, positioned herself behind the wheel of her Model T, performed her ritual of checking left and right and rear again and again, then pulled out to visit to the antiques store.

As she unlocked the shop's front door, her hands still shaking from her encounter with Chief Harrison, Hubert Allen approached her.

"Ees eeverithinn to your sateesfaction, Mees Price?" he asked, startling her.

"Oh! Mr. Allen! You scared me," she said, trying to catch her breath as her corset strangled her ribs. "Yes, thank you. Everything arrived promptly and in perfect condition. I was very pleased with both your goods and service." As Penelope entered the boutique, Hubert followed her. "Is there something else I can do for you, Mr. Allen?"

"On thee contrareh, eet eez what I can do for you," he said, rolling his hands together and grinning.

"Oh? What would that be?" She was in no mood for games or surprises.

"I can take some of your late grandaunt's leess seellable articles off your hands. I am aware you want to opeen a tehroom and to beh frank, your store as eet now stands eez far too clutteered to beh attracteeve to customeers. You want to serve teh. I want to purvey colleectibles. It would beeneefeet us both."

She took her hat off and placed it on the entryway's hat rack. "Really, I don't know. I haven't had much of a chance to think, and I don't want to do anything that would put me in breach of contract. Mr. Beekham was very clear I had to keep selling antiques."

"Yees, I am quite aware," he said, nearly stepping on her heels as he shadowed her. "But you nedn't worreh. Your grandaunt had alreedeh ben seelinn much of heer stock to meh een order to make more space. Some of the veery pieces you purchased yeesteerday weere once sold een thees store."

"I see … I didn't realize …"

She was about to ask him to sit down, but thought better of it.

"No, of course not. Theere eez much for you to leern about the busineess … and thee town."

"So I'm finding out."

"Take your time. Theer eez no rush. I weel beh right neext door should you want to unload anehthing to make room to seet gueests and seerve food."

"You certainly have a point," she said, feeling her frame relax, though she'd been unaware how tense she was to that point. "Thank you, Mr. Allen. I truly appreciate your suggestions."

She offered him her hand. As he shook hers, she marveled at how fishlike his palm felt; the skin on top was chilled and moist while heat emanated from within. Surely, he was the most unusual man she'd ever met.

"Not at all, Mees Price. Weh small town businees owneers must aid one another. I thinnk you'll find the pehple of thee Grove to beh very heelpful and supporteeve."

"I hope you're right. I seem to have gotten off to a poor start with the police chief. I have no idea how."

"Weh all have bad days, Mees Price."

"True … wait, do you mean me or Chief Harrison?"

Just then the City Hall tower clock chimed.

"Time to seerve thee communeeteh," Hubert said.

"Oh, yes, goodbye," Penelope said, closing the door behind him.

Unsure what to do next, she gingerly hauled her carpetbag back to Aunt Dorothea's private office for safekeeping. She then went in search of paper and pen, ultimately finding them in the teller's cage where the cash register was kept. She stood mumbling for a few moments, gnawing on the end of the pen and unwittingly getting ink in her hair when she placed the implement behind her ear to lay out a large sheet of paper. After a moment of contemplation, she scribbled a sign:

## CLOSED TEMPORARILY FOR REFURBISHMENT

## WILL RE-OPEN SOON TO SERVE OUR FAIR COMMUNITY

She'd written the last part with Hubert Allen in mind. He appeared to be a successful businessman and respected member of the community. Certainly, Penelope had been impressed with his services in outfitting her home. While she was posting the announcement on the front door, a number of sconces and chandeliers suddenly illumined in the shop, startling her. She guessed Chief Harrison was somehow responsible, and she was grateful she had one less thing to worry about.

She then remembered she'd arranged for Dan Cooper to install her knew Kelvinator, and decided to telephone home to see how he was getting on. The only thing was, she had no idea what her new phone number might be. Tentatively, she lifted the phone receiver.

"Hello?" she spoke into the mouthpiece, wondering if anyone would be on the other end.

"Good morning, Dorothea. How's every little thing?" a

friendly voice cheeped.

"Oh, hello. This is Penelope Price, actually—Dorothea's niece."

The voice giggled. "Well aren't I a goose? Of course it is. Old habits and all. I'm Ethel Wilson, lead telephone operator here in Pacific Grove. It's a real pleasure to meet you ... so to speak."

"Thank you, Miss ehr Misses? ..."

"Misses."

"Mrs. Wilson. Nice to umm meet you too."

"Who can I ring for you today, dear?"

"Oh ... umm ... I don't suppose you know the phone number of my house ... the old Lacy place?"

"Franklin 9-1108. I'll connect you. Don't be a stranger now!"

Before Penelope could respond, she heard the clicks and rings suggesting the call was connecting.

"Hello? Miss ... Miss ... oh what's her name?" Dan Cooper said.

"Price?" Penelope said meekly.

"Price! Yes! Miss Price's residence. Dan Cooper here. Who may I say is calling?"

"Hello, Mr. Cooper. This is Miss Price."

"Yes, this is Miss Price's residence."

"No, I mean *I* am Miss Price."

"Miss Price? Is that you?"

Penelope chuckled. "Yes, Mr. Cooper. It's me, Penelope Price."

"Well whaddaya know. What are you doing telephoning your own house?"

"Looking for you actually. I just wanted to ring to see how the Kelvinator installation is coming along."

"Couldn't be better. The electricity was on by the time I got here. That sure made things easier. Your new machine is humming along and cooling down, and I was just about to put the old icebox on my truck. It's in good shape, and I should be able to get a fair price on it for you at the consignment shop."

"Why don't you stop here at the antiques store when you're done."

"Sure thing. See you shortly, Miss Price."

"That's fine. See you then, Mr. Cooper ... Oh! Mr. Cooper, are you still there?"

"Uh, yes? Hello? You there, Miss Price? I was just hanging up."

"Sorry to bother you, but do you know if Miss Zara is there by any chance?"

"Well ... yes ... I think so."

"Oh?"

"Let's just say, there's some loud snoring coming from her room at the moment. And earlier I could've sworn I heard two voices speaking ... I could be wrong, of course," Dan added, lest he tarnish Zara's reputation.

"I'm guessing you are not wrong, Mr. Cooper," she said sympathetically. "I'll see you soon."

Once off the phone, Penelope surveyed the never-ending collections of treasures and artifacts that jammed every nook and cranny of the shop. Pieces of obelisks from Egypt's Old Kingdom, Mayan relic replicas, modern jewelry, Ming-style vases, and worthless bric-a-brac were squeezed side by side and atop each other in grimy glass cases. Penelope doubted her grandaunt had ever dusted the place, and she wondered if Dorothea had had a firm grasp on the extent of her cache.

"Inventory," Penelope said aloud. "That should be my next step—take inventory and catalogue this place." She began making a list of categories under which she would enter each object, and looking down at the dozens of lines on the page, she remarked wistfully, "I'm going to need a lot more paper."

A few minutes later, she saw Dan pull up and park in front of the shop. Noticing her icebox was still in the back of his truck, she put down her paperwork and walked outside and question him. "Dan, I thought you said you were going to take the icebox to the consignment store."

"That I did ... and I am."

"But—"

Dan pointed up to the sign hanging over the adjoining store.

"*Pacific Grove Consignment*," Penelope read. "Well I'll be ..."

Dan gave her a friendly wink and set to unloading the icebox. Suddenly, Penelope was overwhelmed with a pang of sadness. Dan was charismatic and kind and, until Prohibition was instituted, he'd been one of the most esteemed men in town. Now he was—well she didn't know exactly what he was, but her heart went out to him. She feared her facial expression would betray her emotions, so she stole into the antiques store while he was occupied.

Within minutes, Penelope was once again deep into her list when she heard the jingle of the bells on the shop's front door. She looked up as Dan breezed in, beaming and holding up a handful of cash.

"Just as I expected—a handsome sum indeed," he said, offering the bills to Penelope.

She put her hands out to take the money, thought for a moment, then pulled them back. "Actually ... how about you keep it ... as a bonus for your hard work."

"Really?"

She nodded, smiling.

"Gee, that's swell of you, Miss Price. Thank you. You have no idea how much that will help my family."

Penelope choked up again. And then a brainstorm struck.

"Dan ... say, you wouldn't by any chance be available

to work here at the antiques store, would you? I want to turn the large back storage area into a tearoom—"

"What a swell idea!" he interjected enthusiastically.

"I'm so glad you think so!" She found his zeal refreshing and contagious. This was the sort of supportive person she wished to work with, the kind of person who put her instantly at ease, unlike Bernard Beekham, Chief Harrison or even Hubert Allen—though Hubert was beginning to grow on her. "The thing is, there's much more to be done than I could ever manage on my own."

"What about Miss Zara and Paolo?"

"Well …" Penelope stalled, her eyes darting around the ceiling as she searched for a polite answer. "Let's just say there's enough to do for all of us. Now, it would be a lot of physical labor, much like the last two days."

"Heck, I'm used to moving beer barrels for a living. Keeps me fit," he said, smiling and patting his emaciated abdomen.

"That settles it then. You'll be helping me organize things here and take the surplus to my home's carriage house. When can you start?"

Dan flashed another smile, clicked his heels and saluted. "Dan Cooper reporting for duty," he said.

He and Penelope both chuckled until interrupted by another jingle of the front door.

"Hellooooo … Anybody here?"

"Just us rats," Dan said, making rodent-like sounds and gestures.

"I knew I smelled something," Hank Edwards said, smiling broadly as he entered and put out his hand to shake Dan's.

Penelope gasped to see Hank. Not only had she forgotten all about Hank since she'd first met him, but she'd forgotten how impossibly attractive he was. "You two know each other?" she asked weakly, a look of disquiet gripping her face as she tugged to pull her tight collar away from her neck.

"Far too well," Hank said, tucking Dan under his arm in a headlock.

"I've tried to shake him, Miss Price, but he always comes back begging for more," Dan said, elbowing his friend in the ribs. "What brings you here, Hank? Nostalgia?"

"Nothing so sentimental, you old softy. Miss Price's friend, Miss Zara, asked me to stop by ... I'm not exactly sure why."

"I doubt she does either!" Dan teased.

"Anyway, wise guy, I came to see if Miss Price could use a hand with anything. This shop can be somewhat foudroyant."

"Foo-droi-whaa?" Dan asked, then leaned in to whisper to Penelope, "He's just showing off in front of you, Miss Price."

To Penelope's relief, she understood Hank's meaning, although she found his vocabulary to be somewhat lofty for a simple small town handyman. "Oh yes, Mr. Edwards, I admit to being overwhelmed wherever I look in this shop. I've never seen anything like it really. I can certainly use all the help I can get. You see, I wish to turn the back storage room into—"

"A tearoom, yes. Word gets around at the speed of light in the Grove," Hank said.

"I'll say," Penelope remarked to herself, marveling at the efficiency with which information spread through the borough.

"If you were smart, Miss Price, and I can tell you are," Dan said, "you'd lay out your vision for the place with Hank then let him loose. He has a knack for making things look good."

She nodded in assent as she gazed appreciatively at Hank in his tweed pants and tailored shirt. "I'll say," she muttered softly.

"What was that, Miss Price?" Dan asked.

Penelope realized she'd spoken her thoughts out loud and immediately she broke into a sweat of mortification.

"I ... uh ... what sort of things," she scrambled to say. "Are you some sort of decorator, Mr. Edwards?" she asked, looking away from him as she spoke.

"More like architect," Dan answered.

"Wishful architect. I didn't get too far with it," Hank said, uncomfortable talking about himself and shifting from one foot to the other as he ran a hand through his hair.

Penelope felt her breath catch and face flush. She had no idea why. It would become a condition that occurred with frequency in days to come.

# Chapter Six

"Really, I feel like I'm taking advantage of you, Mr. Edwards," Penelope said two hours into a productive session of sorting and cataloguing with Hank and Dan.

The comment caused him to look up quickly, and he locked eyes with Penelope for a brief, electrifying moment.

"I, I mean surely you have better things to do with your time," she said.

"Doubtful," Dan chaffed, flashing his disarming, trademark smile.

"I'm here for you as long as you'll have me, Miss Price," Hank said.

She listened intently to his words and thought she might lose consciousness.

"It's the least I could do for Dee's niece—volunteer to get the shop in order."

"Volunteer?! Heaven forbid, Mr. Edwards. I intend to pay you a fair wage," Penelope said, bouncing back from her near swoon.

"Then I suppose I'll have to quit," Hank replied, making a faux start to remove his tool belt.

"What? I don't understand!" she squawked, panic gurgling in her stomach.

"He means he'll only work for free, Miss Price. You really should let him. He was fast friends with your great aunt and knows every inch of this place," Dan said. "Besides, I'm not so sure if his work actually commands a 'fair wage,'" he added in jest.

Penelope stood smiling and saying nothing as she wrestled to catch her breath.

"Everything okay, Miss Price?" Dan asked. "Maybe you should sit down."

She nodded and lowered herself onto a back room chair Dan brought in, searching for something to say. Finally, she blurted out, "Mr. Edwards, I don't suppose you know where my aunt kept her inventory log. I've searched high and low, but haven't found anything in the way of records or paperwork."

"That's because Dee didn't keep any," Hank said, looking directly at Penelope, an amused, anticipatory grin on his face.

"Didn't keep any? But how is that possible? She must have thousands of items in this establishment. Did she at least maintain a financial ledger?" Penelope asked.

"Never … didn't believe in it," Hank said.

"But how did she do business?" Penelope asked rhetorically.

"Very well, actually," Dan said, unfolding a collapsible chair and nodding to Hank to do the same. "She was highly respected here in town and always had extra funds to share with those who needed them … and she was a good tipper."

"Pardon me? Ohhhhh, do you mean at your saloon?"

"Yes, ma'am. She came in every night, when she was in town, and always closed the place down. She was one heck of a good listener, putting up with me grousing night after night as Prohibition got closer and closer," Dan said.

"I thought the patrons were the grousers and the bartenders were the listeners," Penelope said warmly.

"We're a little backwards here in Pacific Grove, if you haven't noticed," Hank said.

The shop door jingled and Hank, Penelope, and Dan left off conversing.

"Customers?" Dan whispered hopefully.

"P … Ohhhhhh P," Zara called in a singsong tone.

"More like loafers," Penelope said with a shy smile. "Back here!" she cried as Zara and Paolo negotiated their way to the rear room. "Well good morning, you two."

"It is awfully early, isn't it?" Zara said, yawning.

Dan snorted. "Heck, we've been up and at it for about seven hours now."

"Well well, what an unexpected pleasure to see you here, Hank," Zara said, forgetting she'd asked him to come by.

"As requested," Hank said with a slight bow.

"Who's the forgetful one now?" Penelope said quietly to Zara.

"I'm not forgetful … just inattentive," she replied.

Hank turned to Paolo and extended his hand. "Hank Edwards."

"*Come?*" Paolo replied in Italian, looking baffled.

"*Nome* Hank," Zara said loudly, pointing to Hank.

"Hank, *bene*," Paolo said to Hank, then put his hand on his own chest. "Paolo."

"Oh, umm … *piacere di conoscerti*," Hank said.

"Paolo," Paolo repeated, pointing to himself.

"I didn't know you spoke Italian, Hank," Dan said.

"Apparently I don't," he replied with a chuckle.

"Stick to what you're good at, old sport," Dan said, slapping Hank's stomach with a clipboard and handing him a pencil.

\* \* \* \*

All looked to Penelope for direction, and it was at that moment she realized she'd never directed or supervised anyone. She'd been the lowest on the totem pole at her bookkeeper's job and was expected to do everyone else's bidding. Her family had a dog when she was very young, but she couldn't get it to mind her, and when sister Pauline was found to be allergic the pet had to go. When in Sunday School, she was once asked to lead a few desperate junior students down to the bathroom. Getting them there was easy. Getting them back was another story and not one that ended well. All told, asking someone to pass the butter at dinner was the extent of her management experience.

Mystified as to how to delegate she pulled Zara aside. "Help!" she gasped.

"I will! That's why we're all here ... even Paolo!" Zara said.

"No, I mean I need help telling everyone what to do. I have no idea how to!"

"Of course you do. I've seen you do it!"

"What? When?"

"On moving day—when you were directing Dan and Paolo, telling them where to put the furniture. You were brilliant."

"I was?"

Zara nodded.

"Well *that* was easy. I already knew where I wanted everything to go ... and it was just two of them."

"This is no harder, and you'll be fine. Just supervise us all the way *you* would want to be supervised."

Zara gave her friend a supportive peck on the cheek leaving a red imprint, then walked back to the group.

"Everything all right?" Hank asked.

Zara raised a thumb in affirmation as Penelope quickly

devised a plan. First off, she decided to play to everyone's strengths. Dan was energetic and good at moving things quickly and efficiently. Hank was a craftsman who could be depended on to bring style and an air of elegance to his endeavors. Zara was her ace when it came to window dressing—in every sense of the term. And Paolo would do whatever Zara asked of him, albeit begrudgingly—unless it involved food.

Something Penelope had not taken into account was the group's dynamic. Dan and Hank got on famously, as good friends do—same with Penelope and Zara. But Zara's flirtations with Hank were upsetting Paolo and he grew increasingly sullen, carping and moving the shop items roughly and noisily. Penelope thwarted the impending storm by limiting him to handling only non-fragile objects and running errands that required driving.

She put Zara in charge of deciding which bits should go on display and which into storage based on their eye appeal. Dan made sure everything got where it was supposed to go, and Hank set things up for ease of use and mobility, ensuring the cluttered space became comfortable to get around. Penelope simply supervised. She was at once exhilarated by her new role, but also felt guilty that she wasn't really *doing* anything, at least not in her estimation.

The little band of unlikely coworkers spent the remainder of the day categorizing, ogling, and marveling at Dorothea's merchandise, stopping only when the street lamps were lit. After all was said and done, Penelope had made for an effective delegator, and more was accomplished than she imagined possible.

Dan was the first to notice the late hour. "Well, folks. Time for me to get back to the family … dinnertime and all," he said, his previously happy-go-lucky expression now fading with concern.

Penelope got an idea. "Mr. Cooper, may I have a word?"

Dan followed her into the unkempt office cautiously,

his brown furrowing in worry. "Yes, Miss Price?" he said tentatively.

"Would you mind getting dinner for our crew here? I'd sure be grateful," she said, opening up her coin purse to produce a small bundle of bills. "This should cover it."

Dan exhaled audibly.

"Everything all right, Mr. Cooper?" Penelope asked.

"Yes … I thought you were sacking me, is all."

"Why on earth would you think that? Your work is exemplary!"

"Let's just say, luck and good fortune tend to run the other way these days."

"Well, those dark days are over."

He exhaled again and smiled. "What would you like for supper?"

"Oh, whatever you recommend is fine. You choose," she said, smiling kindly.

* * * *

Dan returned just over an hour later to find the shop deserted except for Penelope. His expression downcast, he raced over to her to apologize for his tardiness. "I'm sorry, Miss Price. I came back as fast as I could. Did everyone tire of waiting and go home?"

"Not at all, Mr. Cooper," she said, handing Dan an envelope.

"I don't understand," he said, accepting the envelope.

"The food is for you and your family."

"I … I don't know what to say."

"Don't say anything or your supper will get cold. Now get home. Shoo!"

He gulped and nodded to her, then turned and trotted out the door. As Penelope began the usual search for her keys, Dan burst back through the door. Peering into the envelope he asked, "How many days will this cover, Miss Price? I want to make sure you get your money's worth."

"That's just for today, Dan."

"But this is twice what we discussed … and three times more than the average wage."

"Well, you're three times more valuable than the average worker."

Dan looked at her speechlessly for a moment, then enfolded her in a bear hug tighter than her corset.

"Mr. Cooper!" she rasped.

"Please excuse me. It's just … you're an honest to goodness angel, Miss Price."

Penelope smoothed her skirt and hair, moved by Dan's display of emotion. "Thank you, Mr. Cooper. That's kind of you to say, though I doubt angels get as exhausted as I am now. Let's both go home."

Dan nodded and stayed long enough to help Penelope lock up and find her keys.

When she arrived home, once more she heard the bumptious sounds of Zara and Paolo's bedchamber activities—a connubial subject Penelope was far too tired to tackle at the time.

"I'll talk to her tomorrow," she said to herself as she slogged up the stairs, dropping onto her new bed, shoes and all.

* * * *

The next few days proceeded in the same productive and cordial manner. Penelope was in her glory making lists. Dan and Hank treated their labor as if it were play, joking and approaching every task as if it were a joy. Zara continued flirting with Hank, and Paolo continued glaring at her, frowning, and muttering under his breath in lieu of doing much in the way of actual work.

By the end of the week, every bauble and bibelot in the

entire store had been catalogued and boxed up, or incorporated into the front room displays. The containers along with the more cumbersome and bulky objects were moved to Penelope's carriage house; and the shop's large storage room was not only emptied, but scrubbed from top to bottom, including the previously blackened windows.

Come Monday morning, Penelope was the first to arrive at the shop. She stood in the vacant room, admiring her crew's accomplishments and stretching her sore back and arms when she heard the front door jingle.

"Good morning!" she called out.

"Good morninn!" she heard a voice say, a voice she struggled to recognize until the moment Hubert Allen walked into the room.

"Mr. Allen, what a pleasure. What brings you here this morning?" Penelope said, twisting her back for relief.

"I can hardly behlive my eyes," he said, gazing around the room. "Wheere deed eet all go?"

"The trinkets and small items were dispersed around the antiques shop. The large items are stacked to the ceiling in my carriage house," she said, eying the space with pride.

"Most eempreeseeve!"

"Thank you. It took a heck of a lot of elbow grease, I can tell you."

"Eexceelleent ... most eexceelleent eended," Hubert said, nodding as he looked around the room. "Mees Price, have you made arrangemeents for the deecorating of your tehroom as of yeet?"

"Now that you mention it, no. I've been so focused on clearing the place out, I never stopped to think about filling it back up. I suppose I'll need some furniture, won't I?" she said, thinking aloud.

"Oh yees, and a stove and sinnk ... and weell you beh wantinn anotheer Keelvinator?"

"Gadzooks! I forgot all about those things." For a moment she was tempted to panic, but she quickly decided to take control of the situation instead of letting it control her. She'd become better at that since arriving in Pacific Grove.

"Of course you'll ned tables and chairs, deeshees and leeneens, window coveerings, rugs."

Penelope's eyes widened at the thought of all she'd failed to take into account. She gulped down her worries. "But what I most need at the moment is a new list! Excuse me," she said as she trotted to the teller's cage to retrieve her clipboard and pencil. She returned, writing furiously. "Let's see, I'll also need utensils, serving platters, a large table on which to prepare food ... am I forgetting anything?" she asked, focusing on her list as a means of allaying her anxiety.

"Something weeth wheech to make thee teh peerhaps?" he replied.

Both chuckled at the obvious but neglected answer.

It felt good to laugh, and Penelope had been doing a great deal of it in the last few days. Her customary guilt and fear had begun to give place to contentment, along with a quiet faith that matters could and would work out well. New friendships were budding for her, and she was grateful for valuable allies such as Hubert.

"Yes, that would probably be a wise idea," Penelope said. "What would I do without you, Mr. Allen? I'm truly indebted to you. If there's anything I can ever do for you ..."

"Actually, theer is something I would like to ask you ... to at lest conseedeer ..."

"Oh yes, please ask."

"I don't know eef you've hired a shop cleerk yeet ..."

"I confess, the thought never crossed my mind," Penelope said, sitting on the red velvet banquette, trepidation gaining the advantage in her internal tug of war. "I fear I am in way over my head, Mr. Allen."

"Nonseense, you'll beh fine, Mees Price ... once

eeverihthinn has behn put in place."

"I don't think I'm suited to running a tearoom." Her lip quivered as she considered the extent of the vital details she'd overlooked.

"Have you applied for a reestaurant peermeet yeet?"

She shook her head no, put her clipboard down, and set her hands in her lap as her eyes started to fill.

"Whoa-ho, what's this?" Hank said, entering the shop to find Penelope on the verge of nervous prostration.

"I was just deescussing weeth Mees Price some of thee teekneecalitehs of opeening a food eestableeshment," Hubert explained.

"Are you all right, Miss Price?" Hank said, handing her his handkerchief.

"Yes … no … It turns out I'm not all right at all. I'm not fit to own a tearoom!" she sniveled.

"Allen, what did you say to her?" Hank said, shooting the man an accusatory glance.

Hubert jerked his chin defiantly and turned away from Hank, placing his fists on his hips and thrusting out his chest.

"Mr. Allen has been wonderful, actually … just wonderful," Penelope said, her lower lip waffling again.

"Why don't you tell me what happened, Miss Price?" Hank said, kneeling next to her and gently lifting her chin with his forefinger.

Dan walked through the open front door at that moment. "Who wants loganberry muffins? Baked 'em myself … Say, what's going on here?"

"Crisis of confidence would be my guess," Hank said.

"I don't follow," Dan said, offering Penelope a muffin.

She took it and began to pick at it, her eyes downcast. "This is quite good, Mr. Cooper," she murmured glumly.

"Dan," he replied warmly.

Penelope's slumped frame relaxed, and she took a larger bite from the muffin. "Dan … thank you … all of you. I apologize for my outburst. I don't know what came over me."

"Eet ees complettleh undeerstandable, Mees Price. Theere is much to do wheen opeening for beeznees."

Penelope sat for a moment studying Hank's handkerchief as she twirled it between her fingers, still too embarrassed to look up. "I thought I was on track, but boy, I haven't even left the station," she said quietly.

"Well not yet, you haven't. That's why we're all here, to help get the train rolling," Dan said encouragingly, handing her another muffin.

His indefatigable good humor and optimism made her smile, and she made a mental note to strive to adopt the same sort of sunny attitude. "Thank you, Dan. One breath at a time … Whew … Good thing we're not opening tomorrow, eh?"

"Wheen do you eenteend to opeen Mees Price?" Hubert asked.

"I think I should defer to you on that matter, Mr. Allen. It's clear I need a good deal of help if this business is ever to burgeon."

Hubert crossed one arm over his chest, stroking his chin with his other hand and paced about the room, taking long strides and muttering to himself. Penelope, Hank and Dan looked on in silence.

Whether it was the warm muffins or the selfless support of those around her, Penelope once again felt the sense of wellbeing and hopefulness that was part and parcel of her Pacific Grove experience. She lapsed now and again, but overall her confidence was definitely growing.

"Threh wekks!" Hubert blared suddenly, startling the three onlookers who all jumped simultaneously.

"Do you really think so?" Penelope said, discreetly dabbing her nose with Hank's handkerchief.

"I do," Hubert said.

She took a deep breath, determined to forge ahead. "Looks like I better get that restaurant permit right away. First things first. Then I suppose I'll need to find a cook. Mr. Allen, do you—"

"Ahem!" Dan said, crooking his thumbs under his arms and bobbing on his heels.

"He's making a not so subtle hint that he wants the job, Miss Price," Hank said.

"You, Dan?" she said in surprise.

"Cooking is a hobby of mine—making people happy by making them a delicious meal. I never wanted a saloon, to be honest. My dream was to open a hoity-toity restaurant. Creating the food at your tearoom would be just as good … better!"

"Turns out his cooking isn't totally inedible," Hank chimed in. "He used to make all the food at his saloon. He had quite a following, believe it or not."

Dan threw the napkin covering the muffin basket at him in response.

"Well if these muffins are any indication …" Penelope said, starting in on a third one.

"Mees Price," Hubert said, donning a pince-nez, then clasping his hands behind the small of his back. "Weh have work to do."

"We certainly do, Mr. Allen!" she said, rising and rolling up her sleeves.

# Chapter Seven

Hubert's advice was invaluable to Penelope, and she followed his directives to a T. He suggested she handle the issue of the restaurant license before getting carried away with tearoom décor, since without the former, there would be no latter.

This was a task to which Penelope did not look forward, as it required filling in legal forms, having them notarized, and then getting them approved by a city official. In the miniscule town of Pacific Grove, that meant dealing with both lawyer Bernard Beekham and Police Chief Walter Harrison.

In preparation of Penelope's impending city hall battle, Zara served as coach. Penelope had awakened early to dress, and Zara set up camp under the covers in Penelope's bed, unmaking it in the process.

"First off, ditch the pit of no return," Zara said, yawning and trying to open her eyes. "You can never find anything in that unwieldy bag, you can hardly carry it, and frankly, it looks awful. I wouldn't be surprised if it had fleas!"

"But it holds everything!" Penelope insisted. "Wherever I go, I have what I need."

"What you're gonna need is back surgery!"

"Harumph! As I was saying, I never think, 'Oh, if only I'd thought to bring this or that,' because I carry everything I could possibly need with me." She added a sweet smile to the end of her plea, hoping that would appease Zara.

"Not a chance," Zara said, hopping out of bed to go back to her own room. A moment later she returned. "Here. You can borrow a clutch from me."

Penelope recoiled in consternation.

"What?!" Zara said, handing her a shell-shaped, beaded eggshell bag decorated with hanging fringe and an ornate clasp. "How on earth can you object to this bag? I bought it at Gimbel's in Manhattan … and for a pretty penny too!"

"But Z!" she said, whispering loudly and looking around the room as if someone may hear them. "It looks like it belongs to a lady of the night!"

Zara laughed with abandon, getting back into Penelope's bed and kicking the covers into disarray. "Well … I suppose it does belong to one … or did. In any case, you're not lugging around that pit with you."

"Fine! I'll take my coin purse."

"And what about your keys?"

"I'll tie them to my coin purse ... somehow ... Oh fiddlesticks, I'll figure out something." Penelope said, becoming annoyed at the nuisance her plan presented.

"I don't see why you walk around with keys anyway. Or why you drive at all, for that matter. You look more like a jailor than a genteel lady clanking those keys about. And how will you ever avail yourself of the opportunity to have a man give you a lift when you practically run a taxi service of your own?!"

"You know darn well I like to be self-sufficient. Why would I wait around for a man to do something for me that I can easily do myself? I was most grateful to have learned the skills of an automotive mechanic during the Great War. I was able to repair Jeeps and serve the war effort. And I feel it is my duty to make use of that training and apply those abilities now ... It would be an insult to the brave boys who lost their lives to do otherwise."

"Well if you put it like that," Zara said, sliding deeper under the covers and pulling them up to her nose.

"Now that the handbag situation is settled, what do you make of my costume?" she said, smoothing her skirt, her head held high.

"I'm not sure. Give us a spin ... Very nice, actually, P. Businesslike yet feminine, and with a skirt you can walk in without looking like you're scuttling atop hot coals. A fine choice!"

"Glad you approve ... finally," Penelope said, angling her cartwheel hat atop her head and pinning it in place.

"Oh not that wooly mammoth!" Zara lamented.

"Now it's my hat that's too big?"

"You said it, not me."

Penelope glared at her, unpinning the great hat and brushing back her hair.

"Don't you have a cloche? Even a toque hat with a Mephisto feather or two would do."

Penelope shook her head *no*, unintentionally loosening her carefully pinned coiffure. "I suppose I shall just have to go naked," she said, dropping into the chair at her vanity table.

"That's it! The Lady Godiva approach. That should make an impression on that prig of a lawyer and the moody police captain."

"Chief," Penelope said absentmindedly.

"Fine, police chief … Oh snap out of it, P. If you don't have anything here, there must be something at Aunt Dee's shop you can wear."

"It's *my* shop now, thank you very much … but, say … I think you've come up with a marvelous idea."

"Of course I have … What idea is that?"

Penelope rummaged through her closet for a moment, then emerged holding a leather hatbox with brass clasps. When she opened it, Zara let out an awed gasp.

"Where on earth did you find such a divine creation?" Zara purred, reaching out her hands to take the elegant postillion hat. "What a beauty, and look at the lace on that delicate veil. A millinery triumph, to be sure. But where did it come from?"

"Aunt Dee's. When you mentioned the shop, I remembered I'd come across this lovely thing and hid it."

"But why would you hide such a gem?"

"I planned to give it to you for your birthday."

"Oh, P. What a thoughtful gesture."

"Well now the hat's out of the box, so to speak, it's yours. Happy Birthday, Z," she said with an elated grin.

"Ee gawd, I wouldn't be caught dead in that thing," Zara said, dropping the hat like it was infected with plague, and scooting it away with her foot.

"What?! I thought you said it was beautiful."

"It was! ... about five years ago. Really, P, I wouldn't consider wearing something from last season, let alone from last decade."

Penelope slowly put the hat away, sulking in silence.

Immediately Zara regretted her thoughtlessness. It was no secret Penelope was awkward when it came to both fashion and socializing, and Zara knew her friend could use all the bolstering Zara could provide. "I'm a fool ... and a haute couture snob. What can I say?" Zara began in apology.

"Oh you've said more than enough," Penelope replied flatly from within the walk-in closet.

"This is what happens when I'm awakened in the A.M.—which I have no doubt stands for *anti moral*—besides, I've not even had my coffee yet."

Penelope finished dressing in silence, looking everywhere but at Zara.

"Say ... what about that fetching hat over there," Zara said, pointing to the cartwheel hat she'd insisted Penelope remove. "Why, that looks just perfect! I don't know why you didn't model that one in the first place! Go ahead, put it on."

Penelope suppressed a grin and played along. "You mean this old thing?"

"Oh, P, that looks just swell on you. Yes, that's the ticket! Shame on you for not showing me that one first."

"Well, you know how forgetful I can be," Penelope said, glancing up at Zara for the first time since their spat began.

Zara put out her arms, inviting a hug. The two shared a warm embrace.

"Why do you put up with me, P?"

"Because apparently Costas won't," Penelope returned with a sneer.

"Why you devil!" Zara said, slapping at Penelope's hat.

"You really do look splendid, P., like a force of nature."

"Thanks, Z. Though nothing about this legal mumbo jumbo feels at all natural to me."

"Just remember how far you've come and how much you've done. This next step will be a breeze. Now go show those men what a thoroughly modern businesswoman is made of!"

Penelope once again poked a beaded pin through her hat, then slipped on her gloves, grabbed her coin purse and keys, and marched out the door. Zara slid further under the covers and closed her eyes. A moment later, Penelope barged back in.

"Shoes," was all she said.

\* \* \* \*

Three hours after opening her front door to tackle the tangle of red tape she was sure awaited her at city hall, Penelope returned, her hair disheveled and cheeks flushed.

"Helloooo," she called out upon stepping into the house's quiet foyer.

Hearing no response, she traipsed up to her room to change into her work apparel. There she found Zara, napping, a sweet smile on her slumbering face. The squeak of the closet door awakened Zara, and she stretched and sighed contentedly.

"Haven't you gone yet?" Zara said. "And why are you taking your hat off?" she protested. "I thought we agreed —"

Penelope removed the hat and held up a sheet of paper.

"What's this?" Zara said, sitting up in bed.

Penelope tossed the page onto the bed. Zara rubbed her eyes and began to read.

"Ya don't say," she mumbled, blinking at the page.

"We did it, Z."

"You mean _you_ did it, P."

"With your help. I don't think I could've faced those men without you."

"How did it go, by the way? You sure made quick work of it."

"Hardly. I've been gone a good three hours."

"My, my. Time flies when you're in someone else's bed."

Penelope looked at her askance.

"Oh you know what I mean. Now tell me what happened!"

She sat in her vanity chair to unlace her shoes and unfold the tale. "Well, I sauntered into Chief Harrison's office cool as a summer cucumber and ready to get down to business. I heard him call out in a friendly voice from a back room, 'I'll be right with you. Help yourself to some coffee and something called a Danish pastry. They were just delivered from the Butterfly Café. Never had one before myself, but they're not half bad!' ... 'Thank you, I will,' I said in reply. He then walked into the room and his friendly demeanor fell flat. 'Oh ... it's you, Miss Price. What brings you here?' he said. I felt about as welcome as the grim reaper."

"I wonder what this fellow has against you. Everyone says he's the most affable person in town," Zara said.

"Who's everyone?"

"Hank."

In Pavlovian fashion, the sound of that name caused Penelope to sit at attention, tingling as her heart rate elevated. She covered up her reaction by pretending to stretch her back. "Oww, this darn crick in my back! Anyway, I don't know what I may have done to insult the chief, but the upshot is he went over the forms with a fine-toothed comb and said, 'Well, I can't find anything wrong with your paperwork, not a single thing. Looks like I'll have to grant you that license.' And then he stamped each of the documents and handed them back to me. 'Will there be anything else, Miss Price? I have a whole town to oversee and can't spend all my time tinkering with lady businessmen.' 'No, that will be all. Thank you, Chief Harrison,' I said, and I walked out the door before he could change his mind."

"Brava, P!" Zara said, pulling a pillow to her chest and squeezing it. "Then what?"

"Then I strolled over to the office of Bernard Beekham, Esquire," she said, strolling across the room in an exaggerated manner and sitting on the edge of the bed.

"Good show! I bet he was surprised to see you so breezy and poised, the old slug."

"That's one way to put it."

"Oh? What would be another way?"

"Another way would be that by the time I got to his office—just two doors down from City Hall, by the way—I'd completely forgotten what I was doing there. I practically forgot my own name! That man is just so darn disconcerting!"

"Ugh!" Zara said, cringing and hiding under the covers.

"You're tellin' me!"

"I take it you eventually came to your senses and explained why you were there," Zara said, peeking from beneath a blanket.

"Not exactly. I babbled incoherently about the weather for a moment, trying to recollect why the dickens I might be there. He noticed the paper I was carrying and took it out of my hand. While he wordlessly processed it, I rambled on about the attractiveness of his office décor. I was in the middle of praising the cut of his armchair when he lifted me by the arm and walked me to the door. Again, not saying a word, he placed the document back in my hand and closed the door behind me."

"How excruciating! At least he notarized your paperwork."

"Yes. Thank heaven that's over!"

"What next?"

"Now we start setting up the tearoom," Penelope said, her voice cracking.

"What is it, P.?"

"It's just … those are words I never dreamed I'd have reason to say out loud. It's really and truly happening. I can hardly believe it. Thank you, Aunt Dee," she said, putting her fingers to her lips and blowing a kiss to the heavens.

"She'd be really proud of you … I know I am," Zara said, smiling. She yawned and stretched again. "I suppose I should consider getting out of bed eventually. Any sign of Paolo yet?"

"No, was he supposed to meet you here?"

"Meet me here? He's most likely still asleep in my room, the lovable lout."

Penelope felt instantly agitated and decided to broach the subject once and for all. "About that. Z, don't you think it's time for Paolo to go?"

"Go where? You mean back to Italy?"

"No, I mean … well I don't feel right about having him living in the same room as you. I'm a businesswoman now and trying to gain some respect in a new town."

"Why, Penelope Price. Since when do you care about gossip?"

"It's not that, not exactly. It's just … well this is my house and … and what you're doing does not sit right with me. It goes against my morals." There! She did it. She took a stand for her beliefs.

"Is that so?!" Zara sat upright in Penelope's bed, her tone bitter, and eyes squinting.

"What you do under your own roof is fine, but—"

"Oh, I see. Suddenly you're ashamed of me. I'm the good-time girl who you can take to the speakeasy but not to the tearoom. Well thank you very much, I don't need your charity or your judgment. Paolo and I are leaving!"

Zara jumped out of bed and headed for the door. Penelope got to it first and closed it.

"No, Z, please," she pleaded.

"Let me out!"

"Zara! Please. Just listen to me. I don't want you to go. But can't Paolo at least visit his own room once in a while?" she croaked, having difficulty speaking as her mouth dried up. "It's a very nice room," she added, trying to ease the tension.

Zara slid her back down the door and sat against it.

"I'm sorry, P. It's just … your whole career is ahead of you and mine … well mine is behind me … somewhere in Greece … I don't even think Costas has noticed I'm gone! I haven't received a single communiqué from him." She wiped a tear from her cheek. "You have the world by the tail and all I have is … well … Paolo."

Penelope sat next to her and patted Zara's knee. "Are you kidding? You have style, grace, wit, brains, beauty, charisma … and you have me."

Zara smiled through her sorrow.

"We're in this together. You know I can't do this without you," Penelope said.

"I'm not so sure about that," Zara said, looking at the floor.

"Well I am. Now come on. Let's go face the day … together."

Penelope stood up and extended a hand to Zara. Zara sat for some moments, trying to collect herself, then looked up into her friend's earnest eyes, and raised her hand to take Penelope's.

* * * *

By the time the twosome made it to the shop, it was late in the afternoon. Penelope, who lived by the clock during her days as a bookkeeper in San Pedro, had lost all sense of time since arriving in Pacific Grove. She'd become hard-pressed to know the day, let alone the hour, as she propelled through the juggernaut of her new venture.

"Nice of you ladies to drop by," Dan said, polishing the wood on the teller's cage.

"Hopefully you'll consider the wait worthwhile," Penelope said, holding up the tearoom permit.

"What've you got there?" Hank asked, walking into the room, cleaning paint off his hands with a rag.

The sight of him in his dungarees, his captivating smile, and tousled waves of hair caused Penelope's breath to catch. She grabbed her side as the corset pinched her ribs.

"You all right, Miss Price?" Hank asked, rushing to her aid.

"Just gas," Zara said, as if in confidence.

Penelope glared at her and handed the document to Hank.

"Well I'll be," he said.

"What is it?" Dan asked.

Hank handed him the paper and walked out of the room. Penelope feared it was the threat of intestinal vapors that had caused him to retreat.

"Congratulations, Miss Price!" Dan exulted. "This is a watershed moment for you. I remember the day I got my permit for the saloon. I felt like I could conquer the world. And *you* will!"

Hank re-entered holding a wooden plank. "I suppose now's as good a time as any to show you a little something I've been fiddling with." He turned the board around to reveal a hand-carved sign with gold letters that read: **AntiquiTeas**. "I hope you don't mind me taking the liberty."

"Mr. Edwards. I don't know what to say," Penelope

began, finding herself breathless again as a variety of heady emotions rode roughshod over her.

"It's the gas," Zara said in a mock whisper.

Penelope shot her another galled glance.

"I can redo it if you prefer," Hank offered.

"No, please. It's perfect," Penelope said, still clutching her side as she began to breathe normally. "Thank you, Mr. Edwards. That was very kind of you."

"Call it a business-warming gift, so to speak," he said, smiling. "It still needs to dry, but we have a full three weeks to get it up now that things are official. Congratulations on the permit."

"I seh you've come up weeth a name," Hubert said as he entered the shop's open door.

"Good morning, Mr. Allen! Good morning and good news," Penelope said, relieved to see Hubert who had become a stabilizing source for her when it came to business management. He made sound decisions and gently advised Penelope without berating her for her lack of knowledge or acumen. Having his store located next to hers assured her that help was only steps away, and following his example she'd begun to believe there was a feasible answer to every commercial dilemma.

Dan handed Hubert the permit.

"Weel weel thees eez good news eendehd, Mees Price. We can behgin construction on the tehroom at once!"

Just then Penelope noticed a teenage girl lurking outside the shop. "Hello there, may we help you?" she called.

"Oh, my apologiz. Steella. Steella come in her."

Hubert motioned to the girl who entered the room without her feet or eyes ever leaving the ground. She was a classic beauty with fine features and porcelain skin. Like Zara, she wore her hair in a bob, though Stella's looked as though it was cut impulsively with kitchen shears on a dare. Her deep blue eyes had a haunting quality to them, and she enjoyed staring at people for minutes on end, never blinking. She nearly always dressed in black, and wore fishnet stockings constantly, regardless of their condition.

"Thees eez my god-daughteer, Steella Parker. I thought peerhaps you would consideer heer when you behgin hirin. Sheh is sure to make a wondeerful shop geerl."

"Oh, I hadn't … how do you do, Miss Parker?" Penelope said, offering Stella her hand.

Stella merely put her hands behind her back and looked at Penelope blankly and unblinkingly.

"I see. Well, I am Miss Price, this is Miss … ehr"

"Zara, just Zara." Zara said, leaning indifferently against one of the display cases.

Stella looked up at Zara, perceptibly intrigued.

"This is Mr.—"

"Yeah, I know them," Stella said, disregarding Dan and Hank as her eyes remained fixed on Zara.

"How's tricks?" Zara asked casually, scratching her head and mussing her hair enticingly.

"Not bad," Stella said with a faint smile. "Say, what's a dame like you doin' marking time with these stiffs?" she added, testing Zara.

"I get a kick out of 'em … kind of like monkeys in the zoo," Zara said, sitting on the shop's banquette, her legs crossed and arms stretched along the top of the sofa. "So what's your story, little sister?"

"My god-awful god-father here says I have to get a job … actually, he seez I have to geet a job," she added, mocking Hubert's speech idiosyncrasy.

"Humph!" Hubert responded.

"What a sporting idea!" Zara said.

Stella's eyes widened. That was not the sort of response she expected from a cool customer like Zara.

"Think of all the things you'll do with the mazuma you'll earn. Why, the world's your oyster, just waiting for you to crack it open and seize the pearl that's yours. So tell me, what flips your pancakes, Stella?"

"Don't waste your breeth, Mees Zara. Sheh neeveer answeers queestions. Sheh is far too contrary. But sheh eez a very bright girl behneth all the ... black."

"Painting ... and Paris," Stella offered. "I want to move there one day, soonski."

Hubert stood agog.

"Ah, Montmartre, eh?" Zara responded coolly. "I've spent many a fabled evening at the Moulin Rouge. I was there the night the original theater burned down in fifteen. I had nothing to do with that fire, for the record," Zara said, reeling in the young flapper. "Taking a job here at AntiquiTeas would help you save up pennies for your grand journey to Paris ... but I'm sure you already thought of that, of course."

Stella turned to Hubert and gestured to him with her thumbs up. "Everything's Jake, Uncle Hubert."

"Who eez Jake?" he asked.

"I think she means she'll take the job?" Zara suggested.

"I'm glad someone here is hip to the jive and speaks English," Stella said, smiling and shaking Zara's hand.

"P?" Zara said, nodding to Stella.

"It's very Jake to have you on board, Stella," Penelope said, failing miserably at speaking in modern slang.

Stella stifled a laugh. Zara burst out into a hearty cackle.

"Weel, now that eez seetled, Mees Price, weh have much yeet to do."

"Stick with me kid. I'll show ya the ropes," Zara said, nodding to Stella.

"Don't forget to get a collar for your new pet," Penelope whispered as she walked past Zara on her way to the officially permitted tearoom.

# Chapter Eight

Progress on the shop continued at a steady pace, and as the business took shape, so did the relationships between all who were involved with the enterprise. Zara had gotten nowhere with her unabashed seduction of Hank, and as a result, had turned her gaze back toward Paolo. He was all too happy to take up where they left off, and they made up for their time apart by vigorously necking in public, much to the discomfiture of those around them. Only Stella seemed entertained by their primal behavior.

Dan and Hank were like a well-oiled machine combined with a comedy duo. They'd worked together for years, and each had a sixth sense when it came to the actions of the other, anticipating his next move and word. They joked and carried on and never seemed to get a thing done, until they stopped to view their handiwork, which was always far beyond what seemed possible to achieve in the time allotted.

Penelope spent much of her time conferring with Hubert. He proved to be instrumental and efficient when it came to outfitting the tearoom. Dan put in his two cents regarding kitchen equipment; and Zara shrewdly persuaded Penelope to eschew her color scheme choice of subdued beiges, light woods and ivory lace in favor of a bolder palette of burgundy and gold with dark woods and rich fabrics.

Four small brass chandeliers were installed around an enormous crystal chandelier outfitted with beads and tassels—Zara was an enthusiastic advocate of beads, tassels, feathers and fringe. The brocade curtains were fringed and tied up with tassels, and a veil of beads clattered in the doorway leading from the shop to the tearoom. Standing Chinese vases displayed both palms and peacock feathers in the corners of the dining room and were lit from within.

The focal point of the space was a large three-tiered fountain topped by a pineapple finial. Its clear gushing water gleamed along with the crystals of the massive chandelier that loomed above it. Four dining tables surrounded the fountain, each with tufted chairs, starched damask tablecloths, and rose-colored napkins folded into the shape of a blossoming flower. Centerpiece epergnes waited on shelves, at the ready to display fresh fruit and flowers on each of the dining tables.

Each corner section of the room bore a low coffee table, settee, and pair of armchairs. When at last open for business, these tables would each bear a dish of nuts, a small vase of flowers, and a dainty bowl of candied fruit.

In homage to the town's association with butterflies, Penelope chose a Limoges china pattern of colorful butterflies against a delicate white porcelain background. Cut glass goblets lined shelves in the serving area, and silver teapots, creamers and sugar bowls sat on sideboards against the walls adjoining the kitchen.

As Penelope had run through the bulk of her inheritance, she held off on hiring full-time wait staff. Ruby from the Butterfly Café offered to take a few shifts once the place was up and running, and Zara cajoled Stella into serving as a waitress for the time being. In turn, Stella talked her boyfriend Vincent Caruso into coming on board to assist with the grand opening.

Vincent was something of a celebrity-by-association owing to his kinship to famed tenor Enrico Caruso. Though Enrico's talent had by-passed his nephew, Vincent loved Italian opera, and was known to break out into song at the least provocation, and even when begged to refrain. A university student, attending Stanford through a correspondence course in pursuit of a Bachelor of Science degree in Criminology, he worked part-time as an unclassified assistant at Pacific Grove's police station in order to help pay the family bills. His father was a derelict whose only vocation was drinking to excess then taking out the failings of his life on his wife and eldest son, with his fists.

Aside from Stella, Vincent's mother and siblings were the center of his affections. The oldest of the Caruso offspring, twenty-year-old Vincent approached his role in the household pecking order with dignity and devotion. His career aspirations were more for his family's sake than his own. He was determined to be successful so that he could take care of his mother and the children. From his father's fiery example, Vincent had learned at a young age the value of watching and listening, as opposed to shouting and showboating. He'd also learned to run very fast in order to avoid the belt or a flying bottle, and had received a small scholarship as a result of his numerous track and field victories.

**\* \* \* \***

Penelope had been agonizing over the menu, driving everyone mad with her *absolutely final* versions that changed with increasing frequency as opening day approached. While Penelope wanted *simple food for simple tastes*, Zara had subtly coaxed her to inject a continental sensibility into the line-up. Penelope worked on the menu down to the deadline for ordering food supplies, eight days prior to the opening. All considered the *final* result a triumph.

With the preliminary organizing, decorating, and menu planning handled, Penelope accepted the fact that she would have to get out and publicize the tearoom's grand opening—a task to which she'd not looked forward. She was saved the effort of contacting the local newspaper when the local newspaper contacted her. Elsie Davies, Culture Columnist for The Butterfly Bugle, placed a surprise visit to the shop seven days before it opened. She'd learned about the budding business the way she always did, by snooping around at City Hall and sweet-talking Police Chief Walter Harrison.

Elsie had established herself as the *go-to girl* when it came to the news of who was doing what, and with whom. She had a bloodhound's nose for scandal, and if none existed, she was happy to stir some up.

"My, my, if this isn't a curious cross-section of Pacific Grove society," she said, standing in the open front doorway of the antiques shop, one hand resolutely placed on each side of the doorframe to ensure no one could bolt out the door upon seeing her, a situation that occurred routinely due to her brazen and indelicate manner of questioning. "Morning, Hank," she cooed, tossing her hair as she flounced past him. "Dan," she said curtly, not bothering to give him eye contact.

Dan's wife, Lily Cooper, was Elsie's best friend, and Elsie had been chummy with Dan during the days when he ran the Half-Way House Saloon. She frequented the place, viewing it as a goldmine for liquor-fueled gossip. It was a quarry she worked arduously and cunningly. When the saloon dried up, so did her source for indiscretion-laden fodder, and she showed open contempt for Dan once he was no longer wealthy and thus not able to offer Lily the comfortable lifestyle Elsie wished her to have—a lifestyle from which gal pal Elsie benefited greatly. Dan's change in finances meant Lily's change in social standing, and that was a scenario appearances-conscious Elsie could not abide.

"Ahh, Vincenzo," she said, putting on an exaggerated smile and sidling up to Vincent. "When are you going to introduce me to that uncle of yours?"

"Same answer as always, Miss Davies. Next time he comes to town, I'll make a point of getting you a few minutes with him," Vincent replied with good-natured patience, having answered the same question innumerable times.

"Such a clever young man," she said, pinching his cheek. "Now tell me, what brings you here to this work crew?"

"Her, of course. What else?" he said, nodding toward Stella with an adoring smile.

"Yes, of course," she said, turning to regard Stella. "Ee gawds, Stella, what happened to your eyes? Were you struck? Vincenzo, don't tell me your father—"

"His father has nothing to do with anything," Stella barked. "The smoky-eye look is all the rage, as I would think a society reporter would know."

"Steela, show some reespeect for your eeldeers," Hubert said as he entered the shop.

"I'm really not so much older than Stella, really," Elsie said, directing her comment to Hank.

"Good morning, Hubert!" Penelope said entering the shop from her office.

"A very good morning, it appears," he returned warmly, gesturing to the shop in general that had shaped up more beautifully than anyone could've imagined. As he strode to her side to chat, Elsie schmoozed both Vincent and Hank, the one for business, the other for pleasure.

"Just the person I wanted to speak to!" Penelope said. "I was thinking it would be nice to have some lace doilies on the sideboards and coffee tables ... to protect them from the tea serving sets. Do you carry those?"

Hubert stroked his chin. "Eet would take meh seeveeral wehks to acquire theem, and under thee ceercumstancees, that weell not do. But I behlive thee consignmeent shop neext door has a seet of twelve, Mees Price."

"Oho! So *you* are Miss Price," Elsie said, wheeling around to look Penelope over.

Since migrating to Pacific Grove, Penelope had approximated the life of the town's most beloved residents, the monarch butterflies. She'd taken the first imperceptible steps toward sloughing off her own non-descript caterpillar trappings so that one day she would emerge as a magnificent butterfly in her own right. But the moment Elsie Davies began interrogating her, Penelope retreated back into the safety of her cocoon, wrapping herself in timidity and confusion. It was like the first day in Bernard Beekham's law office all over again.

"As I'm sure you guessed, I'm Elsie Davies, Culture Columnist for the Butterfly Bugle," she said, poising an oversized pencil over a small notebook.

"How you do do?" Penelope stammered, wringing her hands.

Sensing Penelope's distress and impending doom, Zara swooped in. "What a pleasure to meet a female reporter. Your life must be so fascinating, full of galas and soirees," Zara gushed. "Oh how I envy you, Miss Davies." Zara added a dimpled smile to ensure her conquering of Elsie Davies.

Elsie stood silent for a moment, gawking flabbergasted at Zara who stood like a statuesque goddess, the incarnation of charm and elegance. "You … who …?"

"She's Zara and she's the cat's meow," Stella called from across the room, enjoying watching Elsie shrink before Zara's magnificence.

"Zara what?" Elsie sputtered.

Zara sat on the banquette sofa and patted the seat next to her, inviting Elsie to join her. As Elsie settled in, Zara discreetly motioned to Penelope to shut the doors to the tearoom to prevent Elsie from viewing it prior to opening day. Penelope stood up and attempted to act inconspicuous, meandering and softly humming as she slowly approached the tearoom doors. Not being adept at deception or subtlety, she drew the attention of Hank and Dan who had to cover their mouths and look away in order not to snicker as she looked around the room aimlessly, pretending to adjust her dress and touch up her hair while closing the doors.

"I am Miss Price's public relations director," Zara said, "and am delighted to answer any of your insightful questions. It would be an honor. Oh, what a fetching cloche. Is it a Molyneux? I do so love his new shop on Rue Royale, don't you?" Zara gushed, sending Elsie into a state of reverent overwhelm. "Excuse me, Penelope, didn't you say something about needing doilies?" she added, giving

Penelope an excuse to flee Elsie's prodding.

"Eef you'll eexcuse meh," Hubert said, exiting the shop.

"Oh yes, doilies. Of course. Doilies ... doilies doilies doilies," Penelope said, swinging her arms to appear carefree while backing toward the shop's front door.

Zara tilted her head, her eyes burrowing into Penelope's, exhorting Penelope to evacuate the premises.

Penelope walked the twenty steps to the consignment shop, stopping to look over the hodgepodge of items arbitrarily displayed in the storefront windows.

"How may I heelp you," a voice called from behind a clothing rack.

"Is that you, Mr. Allen?" Penelope asked, cheerily.

"Eet eez," he said, his mouth forming a thin smile and his left hand perfunctorily wiping oil off of his right hand—oil that that had come from his head when he'd smoothed back the scant crop of hair that clung to his scalp. "May I eenteereest you een some hand-tatted doilehs?"

"But ... I don't understand ... Do you own the consignment shop too?"

"Meh? Noooooo. The town owns eet. And eet is manned eentireleh by volunterrs ... such as myseelf.

"I had no idea."

"Her are thee doilez," he said, producing a stack of white starched linens tied together with a blue satin ribbon. "Note the intricate needlework ..."

* * * *

As Penelope stretched her hand to open the consignment shop door and depart, she heard Zara's voice. Peeking out the window, she viewed Zara and Hank escorting Elsie to her automobile while Dan held the car door open for her. Elsie put a hand out the window and waved as she drove off. Penelope regarded the scene as her cue the coast was clear, and followed the others back to the antiques shop.

"Zara, I've never witnessed anything like your handling of that newspaper woman. You really are something else. Smooth as honey. No wonder you were so successful as … in your career. You must've been a sight to behold."

"What career was that?" Stella asked, jumping at the chance to learn more about Zara.

"Don't you worry your pretty little bobbed head over it," Zara said, tousling up the crown of Stella's hair—an action Stella would have repelled if performed by anyone else. "Now … invitations."

"Awwww, do we really have to?" Stella whined.

"Yes, you *really have to*—all of us do. As AntiquiTeas' newly self-appointed public relations director, I command you," she said, brandishing her cigarette holder like a royal scepter. "I'm thinking we should break up into teams to cover the most ground. Vincent, you go with Dan."

"But why don't I get to go with Vincent?" Stella complained.

"Because you're coming with me," Zara answered.

Stella bounced up and down on her heels and clapped her hands.

"Looks like you're second fiddle, sport," Dan said, nudging Vincent's ribs with his elbow.

"You can say that again," Vincent replied.

"That leaves Hank and P. Now everyone grab a stack of invitations, and prepare to charm the socks off this town. We have one week to make AntiquiTeas' opening day the most memorable in Pacific Grove history."

"Amen!" Dan cheered.

"Wow," Vincent whispered reverentially as he picked up one of the cards. "These are the fanciest invitations I've ever seen."

The thick beveled pale grey cards were edged in silver and bordered with a silver art deco design:

*The pleasure of your company is requested*

*At the Grand Opening of AntiquiTeas*

*Tea Parlour and Home of Dorothea's Finds*

*Saturday, the twenty-second of May*

*At ten in the morning*

*Refreshments to be served*

"Not bad," Stella said, peering over his shoulder.

"We have your godfather to thank for those," Penelope said. "If it weren't for Hubert's guidance and ability to achieve the impossible, none of us would be standing here right now, preparing to go public with our little labor of love."

"And there he goes now!" Stella said, pointing to Hubert as he walked down the sidewalk from the consignment shop to his own store.

"Three cheers for Mr. Allen!" Penelope cried, drawing his attention.

"Hip, hip, hooray! Hip, hip, hooray! Hip, hip, hooray!" the group cheered as Hubert stopped to observe them.

When he realized the adulation was directed toward him, he palmed back his dwindling quantity of hair strands and bowed humbly, then continued walking toward his store, a spring in his step.

As the faithful ambled out the door, invitations in hand, Penelope searched for her keys, mumbling to herself and avoiding eye contact with Hank. She'd never been alone with him for more than a moment or two, and the thought of canvassing the town with him unnerved her. She was relieved that she found the keys in much less time than usual; even so, the invitations shook in her hand as she struggled to lock the shop doors.

"Miss Davies really got to you, eh?" he asked.

"Miss Davies? Oh, you mean the reporter? No, I mean, oh, uh."

Hank chuckled. "Why don't you let me carry those for you," he offered, relieving her of the jingling key ring she tightly clutched.

Both walked in silence for an awkward moment until saved by the near collision of a mother and toddler in a perambulator.

"Good morning, Mrs. Jenkins. Good morning, Timmy," Hank said, tipping his fedora to the mother.

"Hank," the lady said, smiling.

"Handyman Hank!" the little boy cheered, rising up out of his carriage.

"Mrs. Jenkins, may I present Miss Price? She's opening up a tearoom at Dorothea Tate's old antiques shop."

"A tearoom! How delightful."

"Thank you, Mrs. Jenkins. Here's an invitation to our grand opening next week if you're free. There will be refreshments and music and—"

"Can I come too?" Timmy asked, bouncing in his pram.

"Of co—" Penelope began.

"Oh no, Timmy. It's just for grownups," Mrs. Jenkins said. "Please, Miss Price, it would be my one chance to *alktay ithway ownupsgray*," she said, using Pig Latin so that Timmy wouldn't know she said, 'talk with grownups.'

"I hear you loud and clear, Mrs. Jenkins," Penelope said, adding an overt wink to show she was in on the ruse. "Another time, Timmy?"

"But, I wanna—" Timmy wailed.

"Good day, Mrs. Jenkins, Timmy," Hank said, putting his hand on Penelope's back to gently urge her on.

With all her might she resisted the shiver she felt coming on, occasioned by Hank's touch.

"One down, nine hundred ninety-nine to go," she said, attempting to pre-empt another awkward silence as they strolled.

"I beg your pardon?" Hank said.

"I figure if there are roughly three thousand residents in town, and we're in three teams of two, then you and I have about a thousand residents to contact … unless you break it into five hundred each, then—"

"Ahh, now I follow you," he said, placing his hands behind his back as he escorted her, making a point to adjust his pace to hers given that he was nearly a foot taller than she.

Within seconds, the dreaded awkward pause ensued. Penelope busied herself staring at the sidewalk and noticed there were a good many cracks in the pavement caused by sprouting tree roots. *I really should write to the city council about this. Someone could easily twist an ankle. I'll have to make a note of it when we return to the shop,* she mused, filling her head with any thought she could come up with to take her mind off the melting sensation she experienced walking alongside Hank.

The pair ambled on for several wordless minutes until they turned a corner right just as the cinema's latest show was getting out. A small little crowd emptied out of the theater, and once Hank called out the words, "Free food!" all were eager to hear about the new tearoom and grab an invitation to its grand opening. A half hour later, Penelope and Hank were out of cards and started back toward the shop.

Penelope was energized and elated by the crowd's enthusiasm, and began jabbering mindlessly to Hank, going on about what this and that person had to say about Aunt

Dorothea, and how so many were keen to have a tearoom in town. The pair arrived at the shop to find a robust, well-groomed matron leaning on a parasol and peering through the shop windows.

"May I help you, ma'am?" Penelope asked respectfully.

"You may ... if you are Miss Price, that is," the older woman said, turning around and producing one of the grand opening invitations.

"I am," Penelope said tentatively.

"How lovely to see you, Mrs. Morgan. You're looking well," Hank said cordially.

"As are you, Mr. Edwards. Now, young lady, what can you tell me about this tearoom business?" the woman asked.

"Well, you see ... my grandaunt ... I'm from San Pedro ..."

"Uh, perhaps you'd like to come in and sit down, Mrs. Morgan?" Hank suggested, unlocking and opening the door with the keys he still carried.

"Indeed I would, Mr. Edwards," Mrs. Morgan said, entering and taking a seat on the banquette, her hands again perched atop her parasol handle. "And a cup of tea, I should think, if this establishment is to be a tearoom."

"Of course, right away," Penelope said, turning to go to the kitchen.

"Tut tut, not you, Miss Price. I'd like a word with you," Mrs. Morgan commanded.

"If you ladies will excuse me, I suddenly have a craving for tea," Hank remarked, winking at Florence Morgan.

"Now tell me about yourself, Miss Price, and this tearoom of yours."

Penelope stumbled her way through her uneventful biography, explaining her work as a bookkeeper, her service in the war, her lifelong dream of operating a tearoom, and her duty to her grandaunt's legacy.

"In my day, marriage and children were our only dream, Miss Price—our only duty was to God and country; but war does strange things to civilization, and none more so than that abominable conflict that took so many to early graves," she said, kissing the locket that hung from her neck. "May I see your menu, Miss Price?"

"Oh, certainly," Penelope said, handing a gold-edged ivory card to her.

While Mrs. Morgan studied the menu, Penelope studied her. Florence Morgan was the recognized matriarch of the town. Old-fashioned, proper, and opinionated, when she spoke, others listened, and followed suit. Fortunately, she was fair and reasonable, as well as a good judge of character. She and her husband had raised their children in Maine, but once the nest was empty, the Morgans moved to California for the sake of Mr. Morgan's health. Ironically, he was often called back to the east for business, leaving Mrs. Morgan alone in California. She never lacked for company or activity, and was the most sought-after citizen in Pacific Grove.

# ANTIQUITEAS

**- TEAROOM MENU -**

### Hors d'Oeuvres
Miniature Vegetable Tart
Pistachio Apricots with Roquefort
Squash Blossom Canapés
Deviled Eggs

### Tea Sandwiches
English Cucumber with saltless butter and sweet vinegar from the Orient
Tarragon Egg Salad
Chicken breast with Cashew, Pineapple, mayonnaise and a dash of exotic Curry
Olive Cream Cheese roll
Welsh Leek and Cheddar

### Soup & Salad
Chilled Gazpacho
Lime Jell-O with Pear & Cream Cheese
Caribbean Cocktail with Shrimp, Grapes, Grapefruit, Celery, Avocado
& Russian dressing
House Salad du Jour

### Tea Entrées
Fruits of the Sea Newburg in Puff Pastry
Beef Stroganoff served in Crêpe
Chicken Divan served over Baked Potato

### Sweets
Petit Fours
Chocolate Pot de Crème
English Trifle with Lady Fingers, Custard, Fruit & Whipped Cream
Swan Cream Puff in a Raspberry Chocolate pool
Meringue Strata with Strawberries and Cream
Pecan Tartlets
Lemon Tart with Fresh Berries (in season)
Ice Cream Cakeball topped with Hot Fudge

### - Complimentary -
Apéritif of Consommé with Cheddar Crisp
Scone, Popover or Crumpet
European Cocoa Truffle
Teapot Shortbread Cookie
Tea or Coffee

111

"This is something of a provocative menu, Miss Price—rather continental in tone," Mrs. Morgan said.

Penelope felt her temples throb, and she mentally scolded herself for not going with the blander, safer offerings she'd initially planned. In a moment of startling inspiration she explained, "We'd hoped to come up with something that reflects the character of my aunt's collection of treasures ... something evoking far away lands and adventures while remaining approachable." She marveled at her own words, wondering where they'd come from.

"I believe you have succeeded, Miss Price," Florence said, placing the menu in her purse.

"I put extra milk and sugar in your cup, Florence, just the way you like it," Hank teased as he set down a tray devoid of sugar or milk.

"Oh, Henry, you fiend. You know full well I take my tea without additives—dilutes the brew, in my opinion."

He poured a steaming cup as Penelope sat insensible and stunned, still trying to process the knowledge that Mrs. Morgan had approved of the tearoom menu.

Florence took several slow sips then put her cup down. "Now, let's see that tearoom." She raised herself using the parasol for balance and strode toward the dining room entrance, the doors still closed following Elsie Davies' visit.

"Oh, really, we'd planned to keep the tearoom under wraps until the grand opening," Penelope said, worrying her hands as she scuttled behind Mrs. Morgan.

"It will be all right, Miss Price. I promise," Hank said quietly.

Penelope took a deep corset-compressing breath and separated the large sliding doors as Hank pulled a section of the beaded curtains aside to allow Florence to enter. Wordlessly, she strode around the room, employing a mother-of-pearl handled set of spectacles now and again in order to scrutinize the china and silver.

"I see your choice of décor is in keeping with your

menu," Florence said.

*Is that good or bad?* Penelope worried as she searched Mrs. Morgan's face for an answer.

"Did you design the space yourself, Miss Price?"

"I conferred with Mr. Allen who procured nearly everything for me. And my friend Zara was invaluable in preventing me from making the place too drab."

"Zara ... interesting name," Florence said.

"She's an interesting woman," Hank said with a slight smile.

Penelope felt her cheeks color, but she had no idea why, as she was in no way embarrassed. No, it was a different sort of feeling. She clasped her hands tightly.

"We hope to make Pacific Grove's tearoom a destination for out-of-town visitors, as well as a place of comfort and solace for residents," Penelope said, impressed by her own public relations pitch.

"I've seen enough," Florence said, returning her spectacles to her purse and snapping its clasp closed. She turned and headed toward the front door at a brisk pace.

Penelope's heart dropped, and she looked at Hank with pleading eyes. He put out a hand, gesturing for her to relax.

"Good day, Florence. I look forward to seeing you next week at the opening," Hank said.

"As do I, Henry. As do I. Miss Price?"

Penelope stood at attention.

"You have the makings of a blue ribbon enterprise in your hands, Miss Price. I trust you will treat it with care." Florence concluded. She then tapped the tip of her parasol twice on the ground and departed.

Hank closed the shop's front door after Florence was a good distance away. He turned to face Penelope and found her face frozen in a strange fish-like fashion, mouth wide and eyes bulging. "Are you all right, Miss Price?" he asked, half-amused, half-concerned.

"All right? *All right?!*" I'm euphoric! I'm beside myself! I can hardly believe what has transpired!" she said, once more adopting the same disturbing facial expression while leaning over with her hands on her knees. "I don't know what to do with myself."

"So it would seem," Hank said, entertained by Penelope's peculiar comportment.

Seconds later, Zara and Stella waltzed in.

"Copacetic," Stella said, giving the thumbs-up sign to Penelope then plopping on the banquette sofa, her legs spread out in front of her.

"Looks like you're in with the queen bee," Zara said, sitting next to Stella and pushing the teen's knees together.

"But how—" Penelope started.

"We ran into old lady Morgan on the street," Stella said. "She's the big cheese in town and basically, what she says goes."

"And what she *says* is that she 'sees a bright future for the enterprise.' Her words," Zara said.

"Truly?" Penelope asked longingly, clapping her hands together in front of her heart, a winsome smile on her face—a much gentler, more attractive expression than her previous tortured one.

"Mmm hmmmm," Zara said, removing her gloves. "Mrs. Morgan addressed us on the street and handed us the invitation to the grand opening. She adjured us to attend—"

"And said that she would be there too!" Stella interjected.

"'*O sole mio!*'"

"What on earth?" Penelope asked, looking anxiously out the shop window. "Is someone hurt?"

"Only if human eardrums count," Hank said, opening the door for Dan and Vincent who were singing opera together, loudly and badly.

"It sounds better if you speak Italian," Vincent said.

"Not really," Hank remarked.

"Speaking of Italian, where's Paolo?" Penelope asked.

"Well ... he and I needed a little break," Zara said.

Penelope raised an eyebrow. She had no idea what Zara was up to, but was sure she was up to something.

"All right, *I* needed a little break," Zara said. "Anyway, I know it's been hard on him being around all of us, hearing us whoop it up and carry on when he doesn't understand most of our jokes or what we're saying. So I told him he could take the Duesenberg and visit Carmel-by-the-Sea for the day. He's been dying to see the mission there, and I just haven't had the time to go with him—there's been so much going on here with the shop."

"That was awfully nice of you," Vincent said.

"Well he's been awfully nice to me," Zara said quietly.

An uneasy silence fell, and, unsure what to say, Penelope resorted to once again contorting her face in piscine fashion.

Inspired by Zara's words, Vincent slipped an affectionate arm around Stella.

Embarrassed in front of the rest of the group, she rebuffed him. "Get a coat hanger!" she snarled.

"I think we could all use something of a break at this point," Hank said, trying to ease the room's sudden and palpable tension.

"So what next, boss?" Dan asked, changing the subject.

"I don't really know. There's so much still to be done," Penelope said. "I suppose we should all just try to get through this next week without killing one another."

# Chapter Nine

Penelope's words were far more prophetic than anyone could have imagined. As the big day approached, nerves frayed and tempers flared. The morning before the grand opening, while potting flowers along the besidewalk in front of the shop, Penelope witnessed not one, but two scuffles. First, she noticed Dan and Hank shouting at one another in the tearoom. She couldn't make out what they were saying, but their body language indicated anger, and the situation became so heated Hank shoved Dan who then stormed out. Immediately thereafter, Vincent approached Dan who was endeavoring to cool off, and the two of them got into a brief confrontation.

Just minutes later, Zara and Paolo pulled up in the Duesenberg, but before Penelope could say hello to them, she saw that they too were arguing. In time, Vincent had Stella in tears, Dan and Hubert were at each other's throats, and Hubert stomped off in frustration after a fruitless attempt to converse with Paolo. At the time, Paolo sat smoking in the car while everyone else was working himself ragged. Later, Paolo snapped at Hank for talking to Zara, Penelope spotted Vincent giving Zara dirty looks, and even Stella and Dan had words!

Penelope knocked on wood—specifically, the new tearoom's cherry wood sideboard— in hopes of getting through the next day without running into a major altercation of her own. She and Zara had experienced a few minor spats, but she didn't count those, as best friends were bound to drive each other to distraction now and again. *If I have to get into a dispute, let it wait 'til after opening day*, she thought, trying to negotiate with God or herself or whomever might oversee such matters.

By the end of the night, the crew was too exhausted and excited to engage in disputations of any kind with each other or anyone else. One by one, the workers filtered into the tearoom upon accomplishing the last of their allotted tasks. When Zara noticed everyone was together and quiet, she dashed off to the kitchen, returning with a tray of small glasses and a chilled bottle of sparkling apple cider from the nearby Martinelli orchard in Monterey.

"What, no champagne?" Penelope said, smiling.

"Don't think the thought didn't cross my mind, but then again, so did the thought of you being put in jail on opening day for violating Prohibition. Enough about the libations, say something inspiring … or at least sappy," Zara added with a smirk.

Stella passed out the bubbling glasses while Penelope searched for the right words. Just then the front door opened.

"Oh, I hope I am not deesturbing you," Hubert said.

"Not at all. Your timing's perfect," Zara said, leading Hubert in to the fold.

Paolo, who normally would've glowered and growled at the sight of Zara on another man's arm, was in such high spirits he smiled and saluted Hubert.

"Yes, Mr. Allen, please, take a glass," Penelope said, handing him her own. "I was just about to say … well, I hadn't quite figured out what I was going to say actually."

The crowd chuckled.

"Hurry it up, P. These folks are thirsty," Zara cried, handing Penelope another glass of cider.

"Oh all right. All I can say is this tearoom represents a lifelong dream, a dream that is coming true thanks to each and every one of you. I'm so thankful for you all and look forward to many years of success together. Cheers to tomorrow and cheers to you!"

"Cheers!" all cried, downing their drinks.

"Now who's going to wash all these glasses?" Penelope asked.

Another communal chuckle ensued, followed by looks of dread as each pondered if he or she was to be the answer to the question.

"Let's see, it's just before ten now ... see you all in about ten hours," Penelope said, looking at her watch, her heart racing in excitement.

The workforce filed out the front door, their weariness matched only by their fervor to see the culmination of all their toil. Paolo and Zara walked off hand in hand, their affection rekindled after Paolo's visit to Carmel. "Paws off!" Penelope heard Stella object as the ever-tolerant Vincent walked her home.

Hank waited until Vincent and Stella were out of sight to bid Penelope goodnight. "Well, I suppose this is it. Goodnight then, Miss Price. And may the dawn bring with it the realization of your sweetest dreams," he said, kissing her hand gently.

Penelope gurgled unintelligibly in response, then succumbed to a bout of nervous giggles. Hank furrowed his brow in confusion, opened his mouth to speak, then opted to depart. Penelope called out after him, still talking in gibberish.

Dan hung back, refusing to leave until Penelope did so as well, fearing she'd fritter the night away at the shop, fidgeting with unimportant details instead of getting a much-needed full night of sleep.

"Yes, I'll go right home, Dan. Scout's honor," Penelope promised.

"Miss Price ... there's one other thing," Dan said quietly, rolling his cap in his hands.

"Yes, Mr. Cooper? Is everything all right?"

Dan sighed deeply, shifting from one foot the other. "I don't know how to say this ..."

"Oh Dan, don't tell me you're quitting already. I don't think I could bear it!"

"No, it's not that ... just the opposite, in fact ... it's just ... I wanted to thank you for what you've done for me ... and my family. We still have a long way to go, longer than my wife Lily deserves, I hate to say. But thanks to you, there's a light at the end of the tunnel now. By this time next year I think we'll be back on top. I just know it! I can't begin to tell you how much this job means to me."

"Mr. Cooper, if you go on like this I'll be blubbering from here 'til Sunday," she said, retrieving a hanky she'd tucked into her sleeve during the toast earlier, should she become weepy.

"Golly, Miss Price, I didn't mean to upset you."

"I'm not upset, Mr. Cooper. Just very moved … and grateful."

"Me too!" he said, smiling.

Penelope smiled in return, her smile turning into a yawn. "And very tired, it appears," she added.

"Me too!" he said enthusiastically.

Penelope giggled. "See you bright and early tomorrow, Dan. It's sure to be quite a day."

"Actually, I won't be in until later … that is if you still want me to go pick up those blocks of ice in Monterey."

"Oh that's right! I'd forgotten. Are you sure you don't want Vincent or Hank to go with you? Those blocks look awfully heavy."

"I'll be fine. Besides, I think you'll need as many hands on deck as you can get ahold of."

"Good point. The doors open at ten o'clock sharp, so try to get back around nine thirty. Too early and the ice will melt, and too late will be—"

"Too late!"

They both chuckled and set off for home. Everything would be different the next day.

**\* \* \* \***

Penelope slept briefly but soundly and awoke refreshed and expectant. With time to spare, she took advantage of the opportunity to sit in her bedroom's window seat and open the windows, appreciating the sights and sounds of the waves crashing beneath the warming sun's gradual ascent. She suspected she was still asleep and dreaming, so magnificent and serene was the scene, so auspicious were her prospects. Her thoughts drifted, and she wondered if she'd ever share such a moment with a husband. Surely, if a magical place like Pacific Grove could grant her wish of opening a tearoom, it had the power to provide her with romance. She shook the thought off as unattainable. "Let's not get carried away old girl," she said aloud to herself. "Just enjoy the day."

She rose from the window seat, stiff from having remained there for so long, then she donned her dressing gown and tiptoed toward the kitchen so as not to awaken Zara.

"Care for a cup?" Zara asked softly from the breakfast table.

"Aaaaaagggghhhhhh!" Penelope screamed.

"Does that mean yes? Or that you've had too much already?" Zara said, pouring a mug and handing it to Penelope, making sure to steady Penelope's juddering hands as she did so.

"What on earth are you doing up at this hour?!" Penelope asked, trying to catch her breath. "Thank the lord I hadn't put my corset on yet!"

"You're somethin' else, P. But to answer your question, I'm up at this ungodly hour because this is the biggest day of my best friend's life, and I wouldn't be late for it for all the tea in China!"

Penelope raised her coffee mug in thanks, her hand still unsteady. "What time is it anyway?"

"Half past six."

Penelope let out a languorous sigh. "Good, now we can savor our morning and not rush."

"Uh huh," Zara replied, looking askance at her friend.

"I'll bet you dollars to doughnuts you'll be rushing around tearing your hair out and nearly fainting in your corset within three quarters of an hour."

"Possibly," Penelope said, speaking into her coffee mug and peeking over its rim.

The two friends enjoyed a relatively leisurely breakfast of toast and coffee while Penelope tapped her foot and fiddled with the handle of her coffee mug. Eventually, they both went to dress.

"Where are you going?" Penelope asked as Zara walked down the hall. "Aren't you coming up?"

"After I wake Paolo. He slept down here last night … something about respect for both you and me and how kind you've been and that sort of rubbish," Zara said, smiling.

Penelope put her hand over her heart. "This is going to be a day to remember."

"It is at that."

**\* \* \* \***

Penelope took her time getting ready, not so much by choice as by circumstance in that as she was shaking in excitement to the extent she had difficulty doing up her buttons and arranging her hair. Fearing she was late, she didn't stop to chat with Zara and Paolo as she hurried down the stairs and out the door. She merely called out, "See you at AntiquiTeas," as she took up a brisk pace down the walkway toward her car.

"Let's see … keys, bag, coin purse … I think it's all here," she said aloud as she prepared to start the Model T.

Even in her rushed state, she made a point to look left and right and rear and left and right again before easing her car onto the road. "*Oh I am a tearoom queen! And it is, it is a glorious thing to be a tearoom queen!*" she sang, changing the lyrics to one of her favorite *Pirates of Penzance* songs as she drove toward the tearoom, *her* tearoom.

She arrived just before eight o'clock to find Stella and Vincent sitting on the sidewalk in front of the entrance.

"Aren't you two prompt?" she said as she unlocked the doors.

"Happy opening day, Miss Price," Stella said, handing her a tattered bunch of wild flowers.

"Stella, you shouldn't have," Penelope said, trying to hold onto the flowers and remove her keys from the lock at the same time.

"I didn't, actually. It was Vincent's idea," Stella admitted.

"Well then thanks to you both," Penelope said, tying her keys onto her coin purse and placing them in the drawer in the teller's cage.

"Prego," Vincent said, beaming.

"Ignore him," Stella said, rolling her eyes. "It's one of his Italian days."

"Well I hope you'll be back to English by the time we open in two hours," Penelope said, tapping her wristwatch.

"Si. Bene," Vincent replied with a nod.

"So where should we start?" Stella asked as Zara and Paolo entered, their arms wrapped around each other and lips meeting frequently.

"Ah, amore," Vincent said approvingly. "Buongiorno!"

"Buongiorno, Vincenzo!" Paolo said with a wide smile.

"Buongiorno!" Hank called from the entrance as he strode in.

"Can we all come back to America, please?" Penelope said genially.

"Yes, at your service, m'lady," Hank said with a slight bow.

Penelope tingled warmly, unsure if it was because of the thrill of the grand opening, or perhaps something else. She dismissed the feeling and took a deep breath. "Shall we?" she said.

"After you, Miss Price," Zara said, gesturing for Penelope to lead the way into the tearoom.

When Hank passed by, Penelope noticed that he was wearing a suit, a handsomely tailored suit that accentuated the breadth of his shoulders, his upright stature, his powerful arms and legs, the cool confidence in his gait, the waves of his luxurious sun-kissed hair, and the depth of his pale turquoise eyes. Yes, Penelope was sure his suit did all that.

"Mr. Edwards?" she said, still trying to rein in her jitters.

He stopped on the spot and turned to her as if he were a model effortlessly pivoting on a fashion runway.

"Thank you, for all you've done," she began. "To say you've gone above and beyond the call of duty does you no justice. And now, to think you'd stay on to help pour tea today … I'm most grateful."

"Well, you as a bookkeeper should understand, it's a simple matter of mathematics. You needed help. I like to help. Supply and demand," he said with a wink. "May I?" he added, crooking an arm for her to take.

She placed her hand on his forearm, and her breath caught, causing her corset to cramp. *Nerves*, she thought.

Once she entered the tearoom and saw the members of her disparate crew standing at their stations, all trepidation fell away, and she was ready to take command. "All right, everyone knows their places, but I think it would be a good idea for you all to know what each other is doing. The last thing we want to say to people today is, 'I don't know.' Now, Zara will handle seating, Paolo and Hank will pour tea, Stella and Vincent will serve the food, Dan will plate the food, and I, well, I suppose I'll put out fires."

"Say, where is Dan, anyway? Why did he get to sleep in?" Stella said.

"He went to Monterey to get a few blocks of ice," Penelope answered. "I didn't want him to go too early or the ice would melt. Not to worry, he has platters ready to go in the Kelvinator. He'll be back with the ice about half an hour before we open."

The crew set to work as if the events and demands of the day were second nature to them. Every member of the team understood exactly what they were expected to accomplish and how to go about doing it. About an hour before opening, Zara tapped Stella on the shoulder, a pair of garment bags in tow.

"No ... no ... no one said anything about wearing some hokum uniform," Stella protested.

"Not a word," Zara admonished. "Vincent, I have one for you too."

The young workers took their bags and slogged off, muttering under their breath.

"You want the bathroom or the office?" Stella asked resignedly.

"Lady's choice," he said.

"Neither?" she responded.

"You realize you don't stand a chance against both Zara and Miss Price."

"Oh all right, then. I'll take the office. There's no mirror in there so at least I won't have to look at myself in whatever ridiculous getup they're foisting on me. They keep this up and I'm going to form a union. We have rights too, ya know!" Stella said, bewailing her plight from the office doorway as Vincent passed by walking toward the kitchen. "Just where do you think you're going?! If I have to, so do—"

"Hold your water, Stella. I'm just going to the kitchen to change. The bathroom's occupied. Now close your mouth and close the door, and don't come out until you've changed both your outfit and your attitude. Is that clear?"

Stella stood for a moment with her eyes and mouth agape, then shut the door. She was unaccustomed to Vincent speaking to her so commandingly. Like Penelope, she began to tingle inexplicably and felt lightheaded. "I should have eaten breakfast," she reasoned aloud as she slipped off her favorite black cotton dress, faded from constant use.

"Whoa!" rang out from the kitchen.

Zara and Penelope giggled. A moment later, Vincent emerged in handsome livery, tugging on his shirt cuffs to show off his splendor.

"Magnifico!" Zara cheered, clapping enthusiastically as Vincent walked around in a circle for full effect.

"Absolutely radiant," Penelope said in a hushed voice as Stella entered the tearoom.

"Mama mia," Vincent whispered.

Stella tried to suppress a smile, but failed.

"Glad rags become you. Not exactly servant's attire now is it?" Zara said, twirling a finger indicating Stella should turn in place.

"Zara, it's absolutely beautiful," Penelope said.

"And absolutely flapper," Zara said. "Why should Stella pretend to be someone she's not? We flappers are the future, and we needn't be ashamed to show it."

Stella let out a squeal of delight as she spun in her black, knee-length, bugle-beaded, sheer-cap-sleeved dress. Black stockings, T-strap Mary Jane heels; and a matching necklace, earrings, and head-wreath set completed the ensemble.

Just then, a rapping on the front door interrupted the fashion show.

"Oh good, Dan's back a little early," Penelope said. She strode to the shop door and flung it open to find Elsie Davies and a photographer.

"Look sharp!" Elsie said, as a flashbulb popped and dropped to the ground.

"Oh Miss Davies, good morning. We will open the doors in about forty-five minutes," Penelope said, attempting to block the entrance.

"Don't mind us. We'll be quiet as mice. You won't even know we're here," Elsie said, barging past Penelope. "Roger, which spot do you think will be better for pictures? Here … or over here? I want to interview our more prominent citizens both coming and going. You made quite an impression on Florence Morgan, Miss Price. She's invited the entire garden club and symphony association to your little soiree today. Roger, go right on ahead and move anything that's in your way. Penelope won't mind, will you, Penelope?"

"Well actually—" Penelope began to say.

"Oh dear, are we too late to get a good seat?" a woman said, entering the shop through the open door. "Alice, Sophie, Mary come quickly or we won't get a seat!" she called back to her friends.

"Good morning, ladies. I'm afraid we're not quite open yet. If you'll give us another forty-five minutes—" Penelope said.

"Welcome, ladies. Elsie Davies from the Butterfly Bugle. What brings you to the grand opening of AntiquiTeas today?"

Realizing she stood a better chance of *joining* them than *beating* them, Penelope scurried to the tearoom, closing its doors behind her. As she did so, she heard two more parties enter the antiques shop, encouraged by Elsie Davies.

"Everyone, the floodgates have opened," Penelope said breathlessly. "I'm afraid we're going to have to start the show now."

"But what about Dan?" Stella said.

"We'll just have to go on without him. Do your best."

Stella, Vincent, and Paolo all panicked for a moment, running into each other in their discombobulated frenzy, behaving like the bungling characters in a Keystone Cops film. Zara and Hank remained nonchalant, manning their posts in preparation for whatever the day might throw at them.

"Come on, Dan. Get a move on," Penelope whispered, looking at her watch and rushing back toward the antiques shop. "Zara, can you cover the kitchen 'til Dan arrives?"

Zara nodded.

As Penelope cracked open the tearoom doors, she was greeted by a throng of guests, all ready to be seated, all ready to be served. "Good morning, and welcome to AntiquiTeas," she said, sliding the doors open wide. If you'd like to check in with me, I will be happy to seat you, one party at a time."

The mob paid her no heed and stampeded into the room. The women gasped and pointed and whispered. The men nodded in admiration and took their seats, ready for free food and attentive service. Penelope gave up acting as hostess and resorted to the kitchen to find Zara standing in front of the open Kelvinator, stupefied as to where to start.

"I'll take over from here, Z."

"Oh, thank God," Zara said.

"Where are Stella and Vincent?"

"Helping Paolo and Hank prepare the teapots. None of us were ready yet, you know."

"Oh believe me, I know," Penelope said, tying an apron around her waist and working at lightning speed to unwrap Dan's prepared platters for delivery to the waiting tables.

"Where's Dan when you need him?" Zara asked, taking the platters from Penelope and garnishing them with fresh vegetables.

"He should be here in no more than fifteen minutes."

"What should I do for now? I feel like a bump on a log," Zara said, placing a radish on a plate of cucumber sandwiches.

"Offer everyone sparkling cider and charm the pants off them … literally, if need be."

"Now *that* I can do."

Zara marched out of the kitchen to face the crowd as Stella and Vincent entered requesting food to serve. Everyone present had been given tea and was ready to eat. Penelope had just started to feel like she had a handle on the situation when she heard an unsettling hush fall over the tearoom.

She peeked through the kitchen door to see Florence Morgan entering the room. Hank gave her his arm and escorted her to a table situated between the fountain and floor-to-ceiling windows. Elsie Davies was hot on her heels, at the ready to scribble down every golden word Florence might deign to deliver, while Penelope hurried to arrange the platter designated for Florence's table.

Hank entered the kitchen and, upon seeing the unappealing pile of sandwiches, quickly reassembled them, standing some on their ends, leaning others against them at interesting angles. He then reached into his pocket, produced a switchblade, and rapidly carved the radishes into rose shapes, shaved the carrots into curls, and halved the grape tomatoes using v-shaped cuts to make them more attractive. He inserted the vegetables along with some herbs between the sandwiches and finished just as Vincent arrived in the kitchen requesting food for Mrs. Morgan's party.

A few minutes after Vincent presented the delicate comestibles to Florence, she asked him to fetch Hank, whom she then asked to summon Penelope.

"She's asking for you," Hank said, poking his head into the kitchen.

"She who?" Penelope asked, though she suspected she knew the answer.

With shaking hands, she removed her apron, then walked out into the tearoom.

Upon seeing her, Florence stood up and said, "I'd like to propose a toast—to Miss Penelope Price and her AntiquiTeas tearoom, both most welcome additions to Pacific Grove. Young lady, I believe your grandaunt would be quite proud. To AntiquiTeas!" she cheered, raising her teacup.

"To AntiquiTeas!" the crowd echoed, teacups aloft.

Penelope struggled to find the appropriate words to say, so filled with humble gratitude and emotion was she. She opened her mouth to speak, but all anyone heard was a blood-curdling scream.

And then her world came crashing down.

# Chapter Ten

"There's a dead man in the bathroom!" the young woman named Alice shrieked. "And blood … There's so very much blood!"

Hank sprinted to the scene.

"What?! Dead?! Who's dead?!" Elsie cried, more excited than upset. "Roger, follow me … and bring your flashbulbs!"

Zara went to calm Alice. Penelope ran to the bathroom. Hank tried to prevent her from entering.

"You don't want to go in there. It's not pretty," he said.

"Mr. Edwards, please let me by!" she demanded. "No … *Noooooo!* How can this be? How did—" she broke off, hyperventilating.

Hank automatically put an arm out and caught her before she could collapse to the floor.

Vincent rushed over to keep the crowd at bay. Stella and Paolo stood motionless in the hallway, holding trays and staring at one another, their faces white as the damask tablecloths.

"It can't be. It's not possible. Is he really dead?" Penelope asked, her weeping voice muffled against Hank's tear-soaked dress shirt.

"It looks that way. He's cold as a stone and lost a great deal of blood." Hank said, setting his jaw in an effort to fight back his own tears.

"What do we do now?" Penelope asked.

Hank let go of her and walked into the tearoom. "Party's over, folks. There's been a terrible accident."

"Is it true a man is dead?" someone called out.

"I'm afraid so," Hank replied.

"Who is it?" someone else shouted.

Hank took a breath. "Dan Cooper."

A buzz shot through the room as people vented their shock and disbelief. Paolo went to Vincent's aid and stood guard in the hallway to prevent lookie-loos from gawking at Dan. Hank telephoned the police station, and Zara handled Elsie Davies to keep her from sinking her gossip-grubbing claws into Penelope. Stella panicked and ran to a corner of the kitchen to cry.

Twenty minutes later, the crowd had dispersed.

**\* \* \* \***

As the staff sat huddled together waiting for the coroner, Hubert Allen arrived, dressed to the nines.

"I don't undeerstand. Eet eez now teen o'clock. Why has thee party not yeet beggun? And why do you all look so glum? Deed no one show up?"

"Dan Cooper is dead, Uncle Hubert," Stella said, sitting cross-legged on the floor in her expensive gown.

"What do you mehn *deed*? Is that one of your new slang teerms? Eet eez in veery poor taste, Steela!"

"No! Dead as in coffin nail dead!" Stella shouted.

"He had some sort of accident, and hit his head apparently," Penelope said, wiping her nose.

"How deed thees happeen?" Hubert asked, removing his hat.

"Nobody seems to know," Hank said, loosening his tie.

"Where eez heh now?" Hubert asked.

"In the bathroom, but really, you shouldn't go in

there," Penelope said.

Hubert strode in the direction of the bathroom. The crew watched in silence as Police Chief Walter Harrison drove up, followed by the coroner in the morgue's hearse.

Hank walked to the door to greet him.

"Hank," Chief Harrison said, removing his hat. "My condolences."

Hank nodded, and they exchanged a heartfelt handshake. "Right this way," Hank said, sniffling.

The rest of the group followed them to the bathroom and found Hubert washing his hands.

"I've neeveer senn so much blood," Hubert said, clearly unsettled by the scene.

"Hubert," Chief Harrison said with a nod.

"Chief," Hubert returned.

"Did you touch the body, Hubert?" the chief asked.

"Dan! His name was Dan! Not 'the body,'" Stella wailed.

"Yees. I was looking for signs of life, but—" Hubert broke off, wiping his trembling hands with a towel.

Instinctively, Vincent embraced Stella, Paolo embraced Zara, and Hank embraced Penelope. All were seeking comfort—and answers.

"I see ... did anyone else touch or move the body?" Chief Harrison asked, using a pen to move the hair from Dan's bloody brow."

"No, Vincent insisted no one touch anything," Penelope said.

Chief Harrison looked up, pleasantly surprised. "Good work, Caruso," he said, praising Vincent.

"Thank you, sir," Vincent whispered, the compliment lost on him under the circumstances.

"Walter, I checked his pulse, but that was about it," Hank said, his voice waffling.

"Thank you, Hank," the chief said, placing a comforting hand on Hank's shoulder.

The sound of rattling wheels informed the group the coroner was coming to collect Dan's body.

"Folks, I'll have to ask you all to leave this area now," the chief said.

They all moved into the deserted tearoom, some pacing, others mumbling to themselves, stifling sobs, chewing their nails. A few moments, later a sheet-covered gurney rolled out, presumably carting Dan to the morgue.

"No! Take that off him. He's not dead!" Stella shouted, lunging for the gurney.

Vincent caught her arm and pulled her back.

"Ehneh idehya what eexactleh happeened?" Hubert asked.

"Remains to be seen," the chief said.

"What a horrible accident," Penelope said.

"Remains to be seen," the chief repeated.

"What do you mean, Walter?" Hank said, growing uneasy.

"Hank, I've been in this game nearly all my life, and from what I've seen, things are rarely as simple as they first appear. The coroner will do a preliminary examination and then we'll determine what's what. For now, I would ask that no one who worked here last night or this morning leave these premises. I'll want to talk to you all before calling Lily. She deserves the full story. I'll escort the coroner back to the examination room then come back. That should give you all some time to collect yourselves. Miss Price, I suggest you make some tea ... strong tea."

"Yes, sir," she said quietly, turning to go to the kitchen. Zara followed her.

With shaking hands Penelope scooped some Darjeeling into a large teapot and put the kettle on. When Penelope's back was turned, Zara took the opportunity to infuse the tea leaves with the entire contents of her flask.

"Hey, whaddaya think you're doing? Get away from there!" Chief Harrison shouted from the street.

The crew ran outside to find Elsie Davies pulling back the sheet covering Dan's face, and giving instructions to her photographer. "Make sure to get some blood in the shot," she commanded, nearly salivating.

The photographer complied.

"You won't be needing this anymore today," Chief Harrison said, relieving the photographer of his heavy camera.

"Hey! What's the big idea?" the photographer complained.

"Evidence," the chief said, tossing the camera on the front seat of the squad car. "Nothing to see here, folks," he advised the small crowd that had formed. "As you were."

Penelope and company walked silently back into the shop, where she began to clean up the dirty dishes and disarray left by the abbreviated celebration. The others wordlessly followed her example, making quick work of the task as the party had been too brief to create much of a mess. Penelope reheated the water in the kettle and finished making the forgotten tea.

The group then pulled chairs from the tables in the tearoom and sat in a circle. No one said a word for some time. They simply sipped their tea and reflected. Hank took a large gulp of tea, sniffed the distinct aroma rising from his teacup, then looked at Zara to confirm his suspicions. She shrugged and smiled. Chief Harrison walked into the tearoom, and all eyes turned to regard him.

"I thought you'd like to know about our first findings. Now, understand they're far from conclusive."

Penelope refilled everyone's teacups as a brace against whatever news the chief might impart. She then sat down in the empty seat next to Vincent and clutched her teacup.

"It appears the cause of death was a blow to the head,"

the chief said.

"One lump or two?" Vincent quietly asked Penelope, holding a sugar bowl and pair of tongs over her cup.

"That's a very good question, Caruso. Fine police work," the chief said, assuming Vincent referred to Dan's assault.

Vincent and Penelope shared a bemused glance.

"One," she whispered to him.

"Two, actually," the chief continued.

"Two?" Hank said.

"Do I hear three?" Stella said, resorting to humor as a defense against shock.

Under the circumstances, no one reproached her.

"What exactly happened, Chief?" Zara asked, placing a gentle hand on Stella's shoulder.

"It will be some time before we have the whole thing worked out, Miss ehr …"

"Zara," she said.

"From what we can tell, there were two blows to the head—one to the back, and one in the front."

"Boy, that must have been some fall," Hank said.

"Yes, but the bump from the fall may not have been the cause of death."

"What do you mean, Walter?" Hank asked.

"Well Hank, I'll tell ya—Doc Greenway says Dan was dealt a severe blow to the back of his skull. When he fell in the bathroom, it looks like he banged his forehead on the sink. Doc needs to do a post mortem examination to determine the specific damage done by each injury."

"So then something fell on his head or something?" Stella asked.

"Or something," the chief replied.

"What's that supposed to mean?" Stella asked, sitting up straighter, her voice getting louder.

"I think it means that maybe something fell on his head … or maybe somebody hit him," Vincent said.

"Good deduction there, Caruso," the chief said.

"You mean like murder?!" Penelope shouted, her face flushed and words slurred.

"There's a chance, yes," the chief said.

Penelope downed the rest of her tea and lit into Chief Harrison. "Say, what do you mean coming in here spoiling my whole party and accusing my friends of murder? How dare you, sir! I'm afraid I shall have to ask you to leave! Good day," she said zig-zagging to the beaded curtain at the tearoom's entrance and parting the beads for the chief's exit. "Now will you leave quietly or will I have to throw you out? When did it get so hot in here?" she said, using her skirt to fan herself. "Zara, please call the police and have this man arrested!"

"Are you intoxicated, Miss Price?" the chief asked.

"I'm not intoxicated, I'm republican!" she bellowed, raising her arm and pointing to the sky, throwing herself off balance. She then turned at once both pale and green, and the liquid in her otherwise empty stomach pushed its way up past the constraints of her corset and erupted all over her new rug.

\* \* \* \*

"Please tell me it was only a nightmare," Penelope said, her sealed eyes battling the light. It took a few minutes for her to come to, but when she did, she found herself lying on a bench with her head in Zara's lap, facing the bars of a jail cell. "Where on earth?" she said, sitting up, the sudden change in position causing her head to throb.

"Some grand opening, eh kid? One for the history books," Zara said.

"What's going on here? Are we in jail?" Penelope asked, rubbing her temples.

"We sure are."

"But why … how?"

"Well, *you're* in for being intoxicated, obstruction of justice, and resisting arrest."

"Sounds like I've been busy … And what about you?"

"For possession and serving of hooch … and some very creative profanity."

"What a pair we are," Penelope said, massaging her forehead.

"Trio, actually," Hank said, leaning forward from the far end of the bench.

"Mr. Edwards, what are you doing here? Or I guess I should say, 'What are you in for?'"

"For defending your honor!" Zara said.

"Let's not forget punching the chief of police in the nose," he said, slouching back against the cell wall.

"One and the same, really," Zara said.

"I don't understand. What happened? What day is it? Ugh, I had the most awful dream that Dan was killed and the grand opening was a disaster," Penelope said, slowly getting to her feet, her head still dizzy.

Zara and Hank exchanged uneasy glances. "Darling, that part was real, I'm afraid," Zara confided.

"I need air," Penelope said, unfastening the top button of her high-collared blouse and fanning herself. "That still doesn't explain what any of us are doing here."

"Chief Harrison suggested you make tea, do you remember?" Zara asked.

"Yes, I recall," Penelope said. "But that doesn't explain—"

"Someone spiked the tea … that someone being me," Zara said, holding a hand up next to her face and wiggling her fingers in an endearing wave.

"What?!" Penelope shouted, immediately clasping her

head to ease the wooziness and pain.

"I thought it would help relax everyone … and it did … until Chief Harrison started talking about how Dan may have been murdered …"

Penelope groaned. "It's coming back to me now," she said, sitting down on the bench again and clutching her head.

"Well, one thing led to another and you lit into the chief, and he realized you were blotto, and he tried to arrest you, and then Hank stepped in."

"So did Zara," Hank said. "When Walter threatened to pull your restaurant permit for serving liquor, Zara confessed to lacing the tea without your knowledge."

"Imagine that … me using the truth to get us out of hot water," Zara said.

"Did everyone drink the tea?" Penelope asked. "What about Stella? She's underage."

"She had three cups actually," Zara said.

"Oh no … we're ruined," Penelope said.

"Not at all. The chief questioned her, and she passed with flying colors. Turns out the girl can really hold her booze," Zara said with a smile.

"Is that supposed to comfort me, Z?" Penelope whined.

"Henry Edwards? You're free to go," the police lieutenant announced, unlocking the cell.

"I don't understand," Hank said, standing.

"You made bail," the lieutenant replied, holding the door open.

"But how? I didn't call anyone. I don't have anyone to—"

"Beats me," the lieutenant said, using his nightstick to tap the cell's bars as a means of getting Hank to move along.

"You two sit tight. This isn't over yet," Hank said as he

exited the cell.

"It's not like we'll be going anywhere!" Zara called after him.

"Did he really slug the chief?" Penelope said.

"Mmmm hmmmm, you should've seen him—so chivalrous!"

"Why did I black out, I wonder?"

"You didn't *black* out … you *passed* out. I sometimes forget that your system is a stranger to the joys of alcohol."

"But not its woes," Penelope said, lying back down on the bench. "I still can't get over the fact that Dan is dead. Having a grand opening go bust is one thing … having a worker, a friend, die in the process is another. I don't know how I'll ever come back from this, Z. … any of it."

"And to think he may have been murdered."

"Do you really think so, Z? How could that be possible?"

"If there's one thing I've learned during my adventures and travels, *anything* is possible."

"Does Chief Harrison have any leads?"

"I have no idea. But he's sure got an uphill battle on his hands. From what Vincent said, the whole of the police department consists of the chief, a lieutenant, a constable, the coroner, and Vincent, the resident lackey. I wouldn't be surprised if they ruled the incident an accident, just to be done with it."

"We can't let that happen, Z. Dan deserves justice!" Penelope cried, grimacing at the fetid taste and stench emanating from her mouth.

"Hold on there, P. Chief Harrison hasn't made his final determination yet. It may very well have been an accident."

"With two bumps on his head? Doesn't seem likely."

"Oh there goes that logical mind of yours."

"We're going to get to the bottom of this, Z. Something's wrong. I can feel it in my gut."

"Oh, suddenly we're clairvoyant, are we?"

"Nothing of the sort. I have plenty of questions need answering is all. And frankly, if it does turn out it was murder, I want the culprit caught. Who wants to live around the corner from a killer?"

"Again with the logic."

"Well, it's called logic for a reason … because it makes sense."

"So, miss smartypants. Who are we gonna call to get us out of here. We can't call each other!"

"We're doomed."

"That would be the logical assessment."

Penelope shot her an unappreciative glance and groaned as a malodorous belch surfaced from her purged stomach.

\* \* \* \*

As the minutes ticked by, Penelope's hangover dissipated, and she and Zara made the best of their time in jail doing what best friends do, jabbering about any old thing and giggling—a lot.

"Shhhh Zara, we have to keep it down. What if someone hears us laughing? We don't want to be disrespectful of the departed."

"Oh come on, P. Do you really think Dan would want us boohooing, putting on ashes and sackcloth?"

"You're right … Ogh! I just want out of here so we can find out what happened to Dan!" Penelope said, adjusting the vexatious corset she'd slept in.

"I know you do … and we will."

Zara reached into her beaded clutch and removed a small sterling hairbrush. She then turned around in her seat next to Penelope on the cell's shabby cot and began to unpin and brush Penelope's long wavy hair.

"It's funny," Penelope said. "I've waited my whole adult life to own a tearoom. The hours I spent dreaming of it. But now all I can think of is Dan and doing right by him."

"That's probably just as well under the circumstances. As your director of public relations I can tell you, you're in a real pickle when it comes to community opinion," Zara said, braiding Penelope's locks.

"Well then we've got nowhere to go but up. I'm much more interested in the Dan Cooper situation anyway."

"Price, and no name," the police lieutenant shouted, opening the cell door. "You made bail."

"But how? Who?" Penelope asked.

"You'll have to ask him," the lieutenant said.

"Hank to the rescue again?" Zara said.

Penelope stood up, pinched her cheeks, and smoothed her skirt in anticipation of seeing Hank. She even adopted one of Zara's signature poses meant to show the female form to best advantage without being obvious. Unfortunately, when performed by Penelope, the pose made her look like a hunchback in need of assistance.

"You're free to go," Walter Harrison said, ambling up to the cell.

"Chief Harrison?" Penelope said, visibly disappointed as her face turned ashen and she backed up against the cell wall in trepidation.

"Is there someone else you were expecting, Miss Price?"

"No, not really. We, uh …" Penelope stammered, her cheeks turning pink again, this time from embarrassment.

"So we're free to go … just like that? … Without bail?" Zara asked.

"Hank Edwards paid your bail," the chief said.

"Oh, is he in the waiting room?" Penelope asked, craning her neck in the direction of the lobby.

"No, he's not. He went to Dan Cooper's place to

console Dan's wife, Lily. Why don't you two ladies go home now? You've had a long day."

Penelope nodded in agreement and relief. "Thank you, Chief Harrison."

"And take an aspirin or two, Miss Price. You don't want a hangover now, do you?"

"I'm afraid it's too late for that," she said, recalling the persistent ache in her head that she'd recently forgotten. "Thank you for letting us go, Chief. Really, we're so grateful. And you know—you'll get a kick out of this—I'm actually a teetotaler. Zara can tell you …"

Zara placed her brush in her purse, clapped it shut, stood up, wiggled her dress into place, and sauntered out of the cell, all while maintaining eye contact with Chief Harrison who held the door open, oblivious to Penelope's groveling and apologizing.

* * * *

The ladies got home to find Paolo sitting on the parlor sofa in the dark waiting for them. Upon seeing Zara, he ran up to her and enveloped her tightly, ravishing her neck and face with kisses. A moment later, he was down on one knee, delivering a marriage proposal that was part broken English, part pantomime. The ladies gleaned from his presentation that life was fragile, love fleeting, and he couldn't bear the thought of ever losing her.

Zara pantomimed the concept that she would *sleep* on it as a means of cutting the subject short—a subject that would have been her most cherished desire a few weeks prior, but at the moment it was one with which she wished not to be bothered.

"Bene," Paolo said, smiling and kissing her forehead and cheek and lips and neck and arm as they mauled each other on the way to the butler's bedroom.

Left alone in the parlor, Penelope realized she was hungry and hadn't eaten a thing all day. *All that beautiful tea food gone to waste*, she thought, but all she could stomach was a couple of Graham crackers and a glass of milk. She went over the day's events as she sat in the small kitchen, working to piece together when Dan may have been done in, and endeavoring to account for the whereabouts of those who'd visited the shop.

She focused her thoughts to picture who was at the tearoom when, and who could have seen anything that would be a clue as to what occurred. Four more Graham crackers helped her concentrate. What Zara said about Penelope being particularly logical was true, and Penelope hoped to use that skill to solve the riddle of what precisely happened to Dan Cooper. Too exhausted to bother doing the dishes, she put her glass and plate in the sink, then dragged herself up the stairs to prepare for bed. She'd just finished tying her hair in curling rags and was slipping off her dressing gown to crawl under the covers when she heard a knock rattle the front door.

She threw on a coat and hat and plodded down the stairs to the door, mortified to find Hank on the other side.

"Oh, I'm sorry," Hank said, noting Penelope's nightwear camouflaged under her hat and coat. "I didn't realize it was so late."

"It's not ... I was just bushed. I'd ask you to come in, but ..." Normally, if caught in her curlers by a handsome gentleman, Penelope would have spent a good minute stuttering her way through the two simple sentences she'd just uttered. But the day had not been a normal one, and she was too tired to feel nervous or self-conscious.

"No need to explain," Hank said, running a hand through his hair and looking to the ground, a weighty sigh escaping his lungs.

"Have you been to the Cooper home?" Penelope asked, clutching both the door and her coat.

He nodded in assent.

"I can't imagine how difficult that must've been."

He cleared his throat. "Yes, well we can discuss that another time. The reason I came here actually … You see, as you know, your grandaunt Dorothea and I were very close—"

"Oh yes, I know."

"And as such, the success of your business was very important to me."

"Was?" Her eyes began to sting with tears of dismay at the thought that not only Dan Cooper, but her tearoom had died that terrible morning.

Awash in melancholy of his own, Hank failed to notice Penelope's reaction. "My point is, I postponed a good many of my handyman jobs in favor of completing your tearoom in time for the grand opening. And now I need to make good on those appointments."

"I understand," she said, though she didn't fully comprehend his meaning.

"The next few weeks look to be somewhat hectic, but I'll do my best to check in on you all if I can and see how you're getting on. In any event, try to get some rest. Goodnight. Miss Price."

"Goodnight, Mr. Edwards," she said, watching him as he tipped his hat and walked away and wishing she could will him to stay.

She closed the door in something of a daze, unsure exactly what she was feeling, but sensing it was something akin to loss. It was then that the dam restraining her emotions broke, and she fell to the floor in the entryway and cried—big full-body sobs of sorrow and regret and loneliness. Her heart went out to Dan Cooper's wife and especially his children. She had no doubt he was a marvelous father.

It occurred to her she'd sunk her entire inheritance into the business and as a consequence was all but penniless. *Looks like it's back to bookkeeping. What was I thinking? Who am I to run a business?* She began running numbers in her head—

she was always good with numbers—and she started calculating the possibility of keeping the house versus the dreaded alternative—selling it and groveling to Mrs. Prescott, begging for her old spot at the Virgin Boarding house. She thought of Stella and how the shop's closure meant the rebellious teen would be out of a job; and she thought of Zara and how she would have nowhere to go. Counting costs rather than sheep, she fell asleep on the floor by the front door and stayed there until awakened by the sound of the Butterfly Bugle skidding onto her porch.

*I may as well start my day. It's not as if more sleep will make any of it go away,* she thought as she breathed in the salt air and retrieved the morning paper. She then trudged to the kitchen to make a pot of coffee. The stark brightness of the kitchen light caused her to pinch her eyes closed, and she felt around blindly for the coffeepot while waiting for her eyes to adjust.

She prepared a piece of toast with marmalade for solace. Her grandmother used to serve that to her in the mornings when Nana made her yearly visit from England to California. Penelope didn't take to marmalade right away. It was an acquired taste for her, and she suspected she enjoyed the jam more for its association with Nana than for its own merits. Taking a bite of toast, she smiled and unfolded the newspaper. The toast fell out of her mouth upon seeing the front page headline.

## Miss Price's Tearoom — Dead on Arrival

### Beloved former barkeep Daniel Cooper found deceased at the scene ~ Enterprise sets record for fastest failing business in the county

The photo below was worse, showing Penelope pulling a contorted face with her hands reaching menacingly forward making her look like the undead. She immediately slapped the paper closed and trekked upstairs to take a long hot bath.

It took some time for the old house's pipes to warm, and she filled the interval by running her hand in a swirling motion in the tub's water as its level and temperature rose. When she dipped a toe in and had to withdraw it due to the intense heat, she knew the bath water was just right. Her cares and woes seemed to float away with the soap bubbles as she languidly bathed, feeling calmer with each handful of water she scooped and let trickle down her back. She remained in the tub until the water started cooling, then automatically dressed to go to work at the shop, as had become her custom.

She searched for her keys, but found she was in no mood for the usual hide-and-seek nonsense, and so she up-ended the carpetbag and dumped the whole of its contents onto her bed. The size of the bag belied what it was capable of storing, and the mound rising from the queen bed threatened to spill over onto the floor. Going through the items was like going through a scrapbook full of receipts, old wrappers, even a photograph of her with her parents in front of their home in San Pedro. It all seemed a lifetime ago, yet she'd been in Pacific Grove for less than two months. She felt so different from the person she saw in the photo. She felt wiser, and somewhat war-torn.

There was so much paraphernalia in the pile that she satisfied herself by simply separating the items into smaller piles of similar articles. The putting-away would have to wait. At the moment, it seemed far too tedious. From out of the rubble, one petite item caught her attention—a delicate silver locket containing a faded tintype showing a strapping man with laughing eyes carrying a woman over his shoulder. Both were in gay nineties bathing costumes and appeared to be laughing heartily. Penelope let out a slight gasp. "Aunt Dee, is that you?" she said aloud, peering more closely at the image.

The chime of the city's clock tower alerted her it was time for her to face the tearoom. She dreaded going back, but at the same time felt compelled to return.

She arrived at seven thirty and quietly walked through antiques shop. It hinted at none of the trauma from the day before, and for a moment she thought—or at least hoped—it had all been in her head.

When she got to the kitchen, she absentmindedly opened the Kelvinator to find remnants of Dan's beautiful handiwork. The sandwiches resembled miniature works of art, and a lump in her throat arrested her breath at the sight. It was all so surreal. She began to perspire, working vigorously to discard the stacks of gorgeously prepared, uneaten foodstuffs, when she heard the jingle of the front door bells.

"Hello?" she called, wiping her hands on an apron as she walked toward the antiques shop. "Stella, what are you doing here?" she said compassionately.

"Showing up for work on time," Stella said, resorting to her former recalcitrant posture and tone.

Penelope had always been too self-conscious and shy to initiate physical affection, but before she realized what she was doing, she walked over to Stella and enveloped her in a heartfelt embrace. Stella resisted at first, but Penelope refused to let go, and it wasn't long before Stella put her head on Penelope's shoulder and began to weep softly.

"I know," Penelope said, rubbing her back. "I know … Come on, let's get you a cup of tea."

"Like the last pot of tea you made?" Stella said, a hint of a smile turning up the corner of her mouth.

"Ugh, don't remind me. The mere mention of it makes my head woozy … though I hear *you* certainly seemed to manage well enough."

"Sign of a true flapper," she said with pride. "Say, Zara gonna be in today?"

"I have no idea, actually. She—"

Just then the shop telephone rang. Penelope and Stella stared at each other, unmoving.

"I forgot we even had a telephone," Penelope said. "I don't think anyone's ever called it!"

"Well aren'tcha gonna get it? It might be Zara!"

Penelope lifted the receiver. "AntiquiTeas tearoom and home of Dorothea's Finds," she said clumsily. "... Yes, Mrs. Morgan, this is Miss Price ... Yes, I'll make sure to announce myself next time I answer the phone. You see, this is the first time anyone has ... I beg your pardon? ... You would? ... You are? ... Yes, Mrs. Morgan. That would be fine ... All right then ... Goodbye."

Penelope hung up the receiver slowly, a look of astonishment freezing her face.

"What is it? What happened? Is it bad?" Stella said, her voice rising.

"It's ... I don't know what it is ... but no, I don't think it's bad ... quite the contrary, possibly."

"Well what did she say? That was Florence Morgan, right?"

Penelope nodded, her jaw still hanging.

"Miss Price? ... Penelope!" Stella said, clapping loudly.

Penelope snapped out of her daze and put her hands atop Stella's shoulders. "Mrs. Morgan is bringing in three friends for a tea luncheon at eleven. She called to make the reservation."

"You're not pulling my leg, are you, Penelope?"

"I wouldn't even know how to pull a leg," she said, still reeling from the call.

"You mean we have customers? Paying customers?"

"It looks that way, Stella. We need someone to serve the food. Can you get ahold of Vincent?" Penelope said, walking toward the kitchen.

"Not a chance. Suspicious deaths are not something that happens in the Grove. The chief's got him working more hours than ever ... and he told Vincent not to fraternize with you or assist at the shop until Dan's case has been officially closed."

"Is that so?! Vincent is not allowed to *fraternize* with me, you say? Why I ought to give that police chief a piece of my mind!"

"Don't you think that ship has already sailed?"

"Oh ... that's right ... I hear I came on, shall we say, rather strong with the chief the other day."

"You let him have it with both barrels."

Penelope put her hands on her cheeks and shook her head. "My only consolation is that I don't remember most of that unfortunate incident. Now, it's half past nine. That gives us an hour and a half to prepare for Mrs. Morgan's arrival."

The front door jingled again and Penelope gasped. "Don't tell me she's here already!" She scurried to the front of the shop to find Hubert Allen waiting, his hat in hand.

"Mr. Allen, what an unexpected pleasure," Penelope said, exhaling in relief to see Hubert. She'd come to depend on his acuity and assistance, and felt a great deal of her brief success was owed to his collaboration.

"I came to offeer my condoleencees for the trajeek ehveents that took place her."

"That's very kind of you. I value your benevolence greatly, Mr. Allen. Thank you."

"Thee felling is rehceeprocateed, Mees Price," he said, his attempt to smile making him look like a braying donkey. "Eez eeverythin her in ordeer? You must teel meh eef you are in aneh sort of dangeer. I was told Mr. Coopeer's deeth has ben ruled suspeecious."

"So I keep hearing. In truth, I don't know much about what's going on. I've been incommunicado, I'm afraid.

"She was in the slammer," Stella added, a look of satisfaction on her face.

"Steela!" Hubert admonished.

Penelope wheezed and changed the subject. "Uh, Mr. Allen, while you're here, I do need your help."

"Eef eet weel heelp Danieel Coopeer reest in pess, I would beh humbled to heelp."

"Alas, it's nothing so noble. It's about Stella."

"Hey!" Stella objected.

"I fehr I can not heelp theer. I've ben tryinn for yehrs."

Penelope made a tight fist in an effort not to smile. "No, I mean with her wardrobe."

"Double hey! What's wrong with my wardrobe?!"

"Nothing … for going to the pictures, but today I need you to play the part of a waitress. We have just over an hour before Mrs. Morgan and her friends arrive."

"For cryin' out loud," Stella said, crossing her arms and huffing.

"I'll beh right back," Hubert said, exiting in the direction of the consignment store.

Penelope purposely ignored Stella's grunts and groans, confident in Hubert's ability to work magic. He returned in under a minute, carrying a garment bag.

"Whatever it is, I won't wear it," Stella said, turning her face from Hubert.

"What have you there, Mr. Allen?" Penelope asked as Hubert lifted off the bag to reveal an ensemble comprised of a mid-calf-length grey pleated skirt and delicate eggshell-colored long-sleeved sweater that extended down to the hips, accented with a V-neck outlined by a grey chevron.

Stella gasped a little.

"Mr. Allen, it's simply beautiful," Penelope said, clapping her hands.

"Well I don't know," Stella protested, though her twinkling eyes betrayed the fact she admired the outfit.

"Where did you get it?" Penelope asked, looking at the sweater's label. "Why, it's a Coco Chanel design!"

"It is?" Stella said, grabbing for the hanger.

"Eef you do not like eet, Steela, I can take eet back," Hubert said, clucking and pulling the ensemble away from her.

"No, no, I suppose I could force myself to wear it … for Miss Price's sake."

"To answeer your queestion, Mees Price. Your friend Mees Zara dropped eet off at thee consignmeent shop eaerleheer thees wekk. I had not yeet had time to log eet and put eet on deesplay."

Stella ripped the hanger out of Hubert's hands and ran toward the bathroom to change. When she got there, she saw a sign that read: **OFF LIMITS BY ORDER OF CHIEF WATER HARRISON. Apologies for any inconvenience. P.S. If you need to use the facilities, please try Allen's next door.**

Her breath caught and she stood static for several seconds before moving to the office to change. A moment later, she came skipping back into the antique shop, twirling in her finery.

"You look simply splendid, Stella!" Penelope cheered. "Mr. Allen, do you think Mrs. Morgan will object to Stella not being in proper maid attire?"

"Peerhaps. Sheh eez veery formal, but thees ees thee beest I can do for now."

"And I appreciate it. Dear me, will you look at the time. Excuse me, Mr. Allen, Stella and I have a tea luncheon to prepare and less than an hour in which to do it. Thank you for saving me … again. Don't forget to tell me what I owe you."

"Weh weel work that out later," he said, tipping his hat and smiling in his customary snake oil salesman fashion—a look he'd perfected, much to his detriment.

*The sparse oily hair strands and unusual manner of speech don't do much for him either,* Penelope thought as she hurried to the office to call Zara and Paolo for additional help. There was no answer, and Penelope reasoned if she took the time to drive to the house in search of the couple, it would take too long and defeat the purpose. She then strode to the kitchen and rolled up her blouse sleeves.

Soon thereafter, the tinkling of the front door bells indicated guests, and Penelope pricked her ears to divine who'd arrived. An instant later, Stella entered the kitchen. "They're here."

"Zara and Paolo? Oh thank the lord," Penelope said with a sigh of grateful relief.

"Huh? No. Mrs. Morgan and her friends."

"So soon? How can that be?"

"Well it *is* eleven," Stella said.

"But we're not ready. I've only prepared a few sandwiches. It will take me hours to— ... Stella, where are you going?" she whispered loudly as Stella exited the kitchen in the middle of Penelope's sentence.

Penelope turned the oven on, her hands shaking in panic. Neither she nor the kitchen was in a fit state to serve customers, especially, discriminating customers like Mrs. Morgan and her friends. Penelope heard Stella preparing tea and chose to view Stella's absence from the kitchen as a *no news is good news* omen. Every moment that clicked by without Stella coming in to place an order for something that was not yet prepared assuaged a little of Penelope's panic.

Penelope placed a small saucepan of consommé on a low-heat burner and checked the vast stock of desserts Dan had made. She was grateful that they all still smelled as fresh and delectable as the afternoon before last when he'd made them. "Thank you, Dan," she whispered.

Stella walked in smiling, and Penelope grasped the edge of the kitchen's stainless steel table to brace herself against whatever impossible food order Stella might sling at her.

"Four Daniel Cooper Memorial Specials," Stella said, a sad smile on her face.

"Four whats? I don't understand."

"I told the ladies that you're offering a special menu today in honor of Dan."

Penelope processed the information for a moment then said, "Stella, you're a genius!"

"So I've been trying to tell all of you," she replied with a sheepish grin. "Now get a wiggle on. I have tea to serve … Oh, Mrs. Morgan's friends love my outfit, by the way. Two of them asked where they can get one," she said, performing chaîné turns out of the kitchen.

"Four Daniel Cooper Memorial Specials … all right, Daniel Cooper. It looks like you're in charge of the kitchen after all," Penelope said aloud, pulling out the few menu items that were ready to serve and arranging them in as becoming a fashion as she could muster. "Your turn, Dan," she whispered. "…Oooh, great idea!"

Stella walked in just then.

"I'm not quite ready," Penelope said, sweat beading on her brow.

"Well you better get ready, because we have two more customers."

"What? How? … Who?"

"That four-flusher Elsie Davies … and Lily Cooper."

Penelope stopped what she was doing and looked up.

"Yep," Stella said, rocking back and forth on her T-strap Mary Jane heels and staring at her shoes.

Penelope gulped. "All right … no reason we can't get through this. Hold on just a minute. I'll give you something to take to Mrs. Morgan's party. No sense wasting a trip."

In days gone by, Penelope had a habit of becoming uncommonly scatterbrained when in deep thought over work. More than once she'd put her hat in the icebox, wore her gloves to bed, and answered her hairbrush instead of the telephone. Today's bungle saw her pour the consommé into eggcups that she then put on demitasse saucers garnished with cheddar crisps, all atop a silver tray. Stella looked at the tray, opened her mouth to speak, thought better of it, and took the soupçons out to Florence Morgan's table. By the time Stella returned to the kitchen, Penelope had prepared two more consommé and crisp set-ups, this time using the demitasse cups as originally planned.

Stella served the soups to Elsie Davies and Lily Cooper, a moment later returning to the kitchen still carrying the tray and broth. "Well, ten minutes in and we've already got our first problem."

"Oh, no! Don't tell me someone else has died in the tearoom!" Penelope spouted in alarm.

"Umm, no. Elsie Davies wants to know why Florence Morgan got her soup in eggcups, but she and Lily got little coffee cups."

"Eggcups? I have no idea what you're talking about," Penelope said, taking vegetable tarts and squash blossoms out of the oven and replacing them with pâte feuilletée shells.

Stella turned and left the room. Penelope simply shook her head at Stella's comment writing it off to youthful daftness. Shortly thereafter, Stella returned with a tray bearing the empty eggcups. Penelope gasped.

"Told ya," Stella said. "And now Elsie Davies wants the same thing."

Obediently, Penelope took two more eggcups off a shelf and poured broth into them. "Looks like we're going to need more eggcups!"

While Stella took the tray back to Elsie and Lily, Penelope tossed together a platter of pistachio-Roquefort-stuffed apricots, vegetable tarts, squash blossom canapés, and herb sprigs, intending to put the former on individual plates for Mrs. Morgan's party and using the latter to season a subsequent entree. While Penelope's back was turned, Stella retrieved the unfinished platter and dropped it off on Florence's table. Penelope hadn't noticed Stella come in, and assumed she herself had somehow lost or misplaced the hors d'oeuvres. Hence, she began a frantic search of the oven, cupboards, and shelves.

"I've lost the first course," she said in a near panic when Stella walked in.

"What are you talking about? I just served it."

"Good heavens! All on one platter?"

"Yeah, why?"

"But they weren't ready yet! Serving them all on one platter, Mrs. Morgan will think we're treating her party like a bunch of ranch hands."

"Keep your garters on, Penelope. I told them we were serving *family fashion* just like Dan used to do with his family. The old biddies ate it up ... all of it," Stella said with a grin.

"Oh this is a disaster," Penelope said, preparing two plates of appetizers for Elsie and Lily.

Stella walked out with the tray, just to return with it as quickly.

"Noooooo," Penelope said.

"Yep, they want it—"

"—the same way as Mrs. Morgan's."

Penelope reassembled the appetizers onto a platter and sent Stella back into the tearoom to deliver them and check on their guests. She then opened the oven to test the small pastry shells and found them to be only slightly done. Needing to stall for time—her confidence growing with each course successfully served—she decided to indulge one of her unorthodox brainstorms.

When Stella returned to collect whatever was to be served next, Penelope indicated she needed another minute and suggested Stella refill everyone's tea in the interim. A few moments later, Stella came back to the kitchen to find a tray on which were placed small dishes of lime Jell-O with Bartlett pears and a small ball of cream cheese dotting the cavity of each pear. The tray also bore four sherry glasses filled with sparkling apple cider.

"Okay, ya stumped me with this one," Stella said.

"This course will *perk up the palate*, more or less."

"I have no idea what that means, but it sounds much too filthy to say to Matriarch Morgan."

"It's something I've heard Zara say about fruit ices served in France. Well, we're not in France, and we have no fruit ices. So fruit, gelatin, and a sip of refreshing cider will have to do." Penelope waved her hands gesturing to Stella to shoo.

Though Penelope could not make out the conversation in the tearoom, she did hear a collective *oooh* when Stella presented the *palate-perker-course*. Penelope smiled as she re-checked the pastry cups in the oven, only to frown when she discovered they were now only half-done. She then took a multi-tiered crudité dish from off a shelf and looked at it for a long moment. Recalling Hank's quick and creative work with vegetable garnishing at the grand opening, she had a brainstorm.

When Stella entered to pick up the palate-refreshing course for Elsie and Lily, Penelope said, "After you deliver that, can you do me a favor and bring me one or two vases of flowers from the low tables in the tearoom?"

Stella nodded, picked up her tray, and returned a minute later with two vases. "They look a little wilty."

"They should be just fine," Penelope said, removing the flowers from the vases and pulling fading petals off of the roses to discard into the waste bin.

"Is this really the best time to be pruning the floral displays?" Stella asked.

"Hush, I'm creating."

Penelope had already assembled a selection of sandwiches on the three-tiered crudité dish and proceeded to strew some of the still-fresh rose petals atop the sandwiches, attaching two rosebuds along with some greenery to the metal stalk of the china dish, just below it's ringed handle. She stood in silent anticipation as Stella presented the display. Another and more enthusiastic round of *ooooohs* from the tearoom saw Penelope clapping her hands and bobbing on her heels. She looked to the heavens. "Thank you, Dan Cooper ... and Hank ... Thank you both."

"Scones then dessert," she decided, and placed six scones in the oven to warm. The pastry cups were beginning to behave at last.

She assembled sandwiches for Elsie and Lily just as she had for Mrs. Morgan, then dished out clotted cream, raspberry jam, and lemon curd into three-compartment relish dishes. She'd begun to enjoy using unconventional serving pieces and looked for ways to turn the culinary status-quo on its stylishly coiffed head—something she'd never dare even consider two months prior.

Before coming to Pacific Grove, she wanted nothing more than to follow the rules and avoid unpleasantness or controversy at all costs. Now that she was knee-deep in both, she found she rather enjoyed the recklessness of it all.

Her thoughts returned to Hank carving the vegetables that adorned the opening day food displays. She pictured his deft use of his knife, the swift strokes and sure hands, and she felt warm all over. It was that warmth that reminded her she had scones about to overcook in the oven.

After the scones left the kitchen, Penelope arranged petite portions of Dan's desserts in geometric patterns on a platter. Zara and Paolo waltzed in to find Penelope muttering to herself and combing the icebox.

"What's all this?" Zara asked, nodding toward the tearoom.

"It's Daniel Cooper looking down on us kindly from heaven," Penelope said.

"Here. I brought you something to lift your spirits, but now I'm not so sure you need it," Zara said placing an insulated container the size of a hatbox on the steel table.

"What is it?" Penelope asked, gasping in gratulation to find a bowl of ice cream on a bed of dry ice. "It's absolutely perfect!"

"I thought so too. And there's enough for the four of us, Stella included," Zara said, searching the kitchen hutch drawers for spoons.

Penelope had other ideas. She removed the puffed pastry cups from the oven, scooped a bit of ice cream into each of them, topped them with fresh berries, then placed them on saucers garnished with a cocoa truffle.

"Oi, that's my ice cream," Zara said as Penelope added the ice cream cups to the platter of petite desserts for Florence Morgan's table. "Oi, that's my dress!" Zara cried as Stella picked up the platter to deliver it.

"Not anymore!" Stella whispered over her shoulder.

Zara's jaw dropped in shock.

"Now that's an expression I've never seen on you," Penelope said to Zara.

"Bella, bella," Paolo remarked, admiring Stella.

Penelope asked Zara and Paolo to visit with the guests while she cleaned up the chaotic mess she'd made in the kitchen. When she was done, she paused to decide what to tackle next. The idea that came was not a prospect she relished. She untied her apron and walked out to the tearoom to speak to Lily Cooper.

What first struck Penelope was how different the two friends, Elsie and Lily, appeared. Elsie was light blonde, buxom, and brash—qualities Penelope thought would have made Elsie a hit as a saloon girl in the Wild West. Lily was thin and demure with long brunette hair and an attractive sort of bashfulness. Penelope would never have pictured them as chums and wondered if others thought the same of her and Zara.

Penelope steeled herself against whatever Elsie might say or do to disconcert her, and decided to come out talking so as to preempt Elsie's attack.

"Mrs. Cooper, I'm Penelope Price," she said warmly. "I just wanted to express my condolences for your tragic loss. Throughout our fugacious friendship, I found your husband to be a man of quality and character, with an infectious enthusiasm, and generosity of spirit I, for one, valued greatly."

"Thank you, Miss Price. Thank you," Lily said, grasping Penelope's hand so tightly the blood started to drain from Penelope's fingers, and they began to lose all feeling. "This job meant the world to Danny. You have no idea what you've done for our family. We'd sunk very low, and—"

"We really should be going, Lily," Elsie interrupted. "Miss Price, thank you for a most … *avant-garde* dining experience," she said with a reptilian smile. "Please tell your girl we'd like our check now."

"Oh that won't be necessary. There is no charge," Penelope said sweetly.

Elsie jutted her chin out and squinted, looking Penelope over with cold disdain and wariness.

"Thank you again. To think you named the meal after Danny—" Lily broke off, taking a handkerchief from a worn handbag.

"Most gracious of you, Miss Price," Elsie said disingenuously, standing up hastily.

"It's my pleasure."

"Come, Lillian," Elsie said, rushing the widow from the site.

"Miss Price, a word," Florence Morgan commanded.

Penelope smoothed her skirt and straightened her posture. *Thank the maker that Elsie woman's gone*, Penelope thought as she approached Florence's table.

"Mrs. Morgan, we're so very grateful for your support

at this trying time."

"It is the Pacific Grove way, Miss Price," she replied.

Florence's dining companions nodded in agreement, as they always did when the town's grand dame spoke.

"Well you're very kind to overlook our eccentric service style today," Penelope said.

"Rubbish! It was refreshing. To be served by a young lady accoutered in the latest fashion was most appealing … And the cuisine, a soporific sensation. Now, if you'll excuse us, I must get to my weekly auction bridge appointment with the mayor. I've not missed a game in eighteen years."

"Of course … Uh, Paolo?" Penelope said, nodding to encourage him to escort Mrs. Morgan to the door.

Penelope, Zara, and Stella followed Florence's party out in stately procession. Just as Mrs. Morgan exited the shop, a woman approached.

"Are they open for business?" the woman asked expectantly, peering in through the door past Florence.

"They most definitely are not!" Florence said, punctuating her words with the tip of her parasol on the ground. "Mrs. Gustafson, please show some respect for the passing of their fallen associate, Daniel Cooper. They will re-open after he has been laid to rest," she added, opening her parasol and looking back to give Penelope a nod and a smile."

Penelope smiled back, clasping her hands in gratitude.

The second the door closed behind Mrs. Morgan, Stella shouted, "Hot socks! Did you see how much cabbage they dropped?!"

Penelope regarded her blankly.

"She means they left a good deal of money," Zara translated.

Stella ran to the waitress station and returned with a large wad of cash.

"Good heavens!" Penelope exclaimed, taking the bills

and counting them. "Why, this is substantially more than anything we might have charged. "Here, Stella, this is for you," she said, handing the girl a five dollar bill.

"Holy cow! A fin? Who needs painting in Paris? I want to be a waitress in Pacific Grove!" she cheered, scrutinizing the piece of currency.

Zara and Penelope laughed. Eventually, Paolo joined in, looking lost. The gaiety ceased with the arrival of Police Chief Walter Harrison.

# Chapter Eleven

"Good afternoon, folks," he said, removing his hat. "I'd like to ask you all a few questions about Dan Cooper's final hours. Is there somewhere we can talk?"

"Of course, Chief. Please come in," Penelope said, gulping hard and beginning to shake as she locked the shop's door and hung the *closed* sign. She'd never been questioned by the police before, except for that one time when she was eight and a peach cobbler mysteriously disappeared from old lady Shaw's window ledge.

"Whaddaya wanna know, Chief?" Stella said.

"Not you, Stella. Your mother wants you home to help with the ironing," Chief Harrison said.

"I'm sure she'll understand. After all, what's more important—" Stella started.

"No chance, Stella. Home with you. If I need to ask you something I'll come to the house."

"Killjoy," Stella groused as she trudged out the door.

"Is it true Dan's death may have been deliberate?" Zara asked.

"Yes," the chief said, flipping open a small notebook and following Penelope and Zara into the tearoom.

"What exactly happened?" Penelope asked, trying to

appear relaxed.

"I'll be asking the questions, Miss Price," the chief barked.

"It looked to me like he simply slipped and fell and hit his head, but of course, I'm not a keen detective like you, Chief Harrison," Zara said, testing her powers of cajolery.

The chief looked at his notes and tried to hide a smile. He found her flattery charming, though on him it would be wholly ineffective. "You're correct that he fell and hit his head, Miss. But we now know conclusively that's not what killed him."

"No?" Penelope asked.

"What did I say about asking questions, Miss Price?!"

"But it looked so cut and dry … that lump on his forehead," Zara said.

"That was the second one, as you recall," the chief said. "He'd already been hit on the back of the head with a heavy blunt object. The first strike is the one that killed him."

"So he was struck here in the shop?" Zara asked.

"Yes, in the hallway or doorway to the bathroom," the chief said.

"But who would do such a thing?" Penelope asked rhetorically.

"For the last time, Miss Price!"

"Have you identified the object used, Chief Harrison?" Zara asked.

"No, not yet. We're still looking for it … Now, Miss Price, when was the last time you saw Daniel Cooper?"

"When the coroner wheeled him out on the gurney," Penelope said, sitting at one of the empty tables.

"Is this a joke to you, Miss Price?" the chief snapped.

"No … not at all …" she replied, her mouth becoming dry. "I thought—"

"The night before the grand opening was the last time any of us saw Dan. Isn't that right, Penelope?" Zara said.

"Thank you, Miss Zara, isn't it?"

"Yes, sir," she said simply. She sensed additional flirtation would most likely backfire with Chief Harrison who seemed too shrewd to fall for such a ploy.

"When did you see Dan Cooper last?"

"We all left the shop at just before ten o'clock the night before the grand opening," Zara said.

"You sure about that?" the chief said, his eyes on his notes.

"Are you accusing me of lying? Or of being empty-headed … or perhaps just wishy-washy?" Zara asked matter-of-factly, seeking to assess the chief's character.

He looked up, the slightest trace of a grin on his closed mouth. "Please continue, Miss Zara," he said, putting his pencil down to observe her as she spoke.

"We all shared a celebratory drink—sparkling cider, mind you—then went our separate ways. P—Miss Price, that is—mentioned that it was around ten and that she'd see us in ten hours. The tens stuck with me."

Penelope nodded wildly in concurrence.

"And who is *we all*?" the chief asked.

"Umm, it was me, Z—" Penelope started.

"I was speaking to Miss Zara," the chief admonished. "Believe me, you'll get your turn, Miss Price."

"Yes, your honor," Penelope said," sinking into her chair.

"Penelope and I, Paolo—he's my driver, Mr. Cooper, Mr. Edwards, Stella Parker, Vincent Caruso … and Mr. Allen dropped by to join us."

"And what about him?" the chief asked, pointing to Paolo who had remained happily insensible, smiling and nodding throughout the conversation.

"That's Paolo," Zara said flatly.

"You're Paolo?" the chief asked.

"Si, Paolo Rossi," Paolo said, pointing to his chest.

"Mr. Rossi, what can you tell me about the night before Daniel Cooper's death?"

"Si, Paolo Rossi," Paolo repeated, still smiling.

"Is he, uh, *touched?*" the chief said as an aside to Zara.

"Something like that," she replied with a smile. "He's Italian. He only knows a few words in English."

"I see ... Miss Price, I'd like to use your phone, please," Chief Harrison said.

"Certainly," Penelope said, escorting him to the office.

"Privately," he added.

She closed the door and slogged back to her seat in the tearoom.

"What was that all about?" Zara asked.

"You tell me," Penelope said.

The three sat in silence for a minute or two, unsure as to what to do.

"Now," Chief Harrison said, re-entering the room. "You say you all left at the same time. Is that your recollection, Miss Price?"

"Yes, exactly. Everyone left together," Penelope said.

"Very good," the chief said, scribbling in his notebook.

Just then a loud rap on the window caused Penelope to jump up and scream. Vincent stood outside pointing toward the front door, his cheeks flushed, and apparently out of breath.

"Caruso, good!" the chief said as Vincent entered the room, still breathing hard from running to the shop. "I want you to ask this Paolo fellow a few questions. He only speaks Italian."

"I'll try, Chief, but my Italian is pretty much limited to opera lyrics and terms of endearment."

"Just do your best, son. Ask him when he last saw Dan

Cooper."

"Umm … Quando è stata l'ultima volta che ha visto Dan Cooper?" Vincent stammered.

Paolo acted out his answer. "La notte," he said waving his hands to indicate the past. He then held up the fingers of both hands, and finally, made a slashing gesture across his throat to indicate death.

"La notte prima di morire alle dieci?" Vincent struggled to say in fractured Italian.

"Si," Paolo said holding a thumb up in affirmation.

"He says he last saw Dan at ten the night before his death," Vincent said.

"And how would he describe his relationship with the deceased?" Walter asked.

"Jeepers, that one may be beyond my vocabulary, Chief."

"Chief Harrison, I believe everyone you ask will tell you roughly the same—that Paolo and Mr. Cooper had little contact. They were on friendly terms," Penelope said.

"Uh huh," the chief said, taking notes.

"She's right, Chief. Because of the language barrier, Paolo doesn't engage in what you'd call deep discussion," Vincent said. "When he was working alongside Hank and Dan, he seemed to enjoy their company well enough, though he couldn't really keep up."

"Couldn't keep up with the work or with what they were saying?" the chief asked.

"Well …" Vincent began.

"Both!" Zara interjected. "Let's call a spade a spade. Paolo doesn't have much of a work ethic except when it comes to the gymnasium and the bedr—" Suddenly embarrassed, she changed the subject. "Let's just say, he was no match for Mr. Cooper or Mr. Edwards. They ran circles around us all. As for making out what they were saying, well you know how good friends are, it's hard for anyone to understand their conversation."

"It's true, Chief Harrison. When I talk to Zara even I don't know what I'm saying most of the time," Penelope offered haplessly.

"When Dan and Hank get on a roll, I have a heck of a time following those two characters ... *had*, not have," Vincent added, looking forlornly to the ground.

"And where did Paolo go after he left that evening?" the chief asked.

"He was with me," Zara said, placing a hand on Paolo's knee.

"Oh?" the chief asked, raising an eyebrow. "All night?"

"Every night," Zara returned unabashedly, determined to compensate for her momentary modesty.

"May I ask where you live, Miss Zara?" the chief asked.

"They live with me," Penelope answered. "Well, not *with* me. They have their own room ... rooms," she said with a nervous titter.

"I see ... and did you arrive home at the same time as Mr. Rossi and Miss Zara?"

"Just about ... a few minutes later, actually."

"Were you closing up the shop?"

"Yes ... and giving last minute instructions to Mr. Cooper," Penelope said.

"And did you see him talk to anyone else after that?" the chief said.

"No, I suppose not," Penelope said, fanning herself with one of her hands as she realized she was the last of her band to see Dan alive.

"Is something wrong, Miss Price?"

"It's just a little warm in here," she said, her mouth going dry and eyes blurring. She felt the first throes of hyperventilation coming on, and began pacing and mumbling to herself to stave off a fainting episode.

"Will there be anything else, Chief Harrison?" Zara asked, sensing her friend's distress.

"Not for the moment. But be sure you all stay in town, is that clear?"

Penelope and Zara nodded. Paolo copied them.

Chief Harrison put his hat on and exited. "Caruso!" he called, and Vincent trailed after him, miming the word *bye* as he departed. Penelope locked the door behind them.

"Am I ever glad that's over," Penelope gushed. "That was grueling,"

"P, you don't know from grueling. That was a cakewalk. If you were a suspect, that would be a whole different kind of interrogation."

Penelope exhaled loudly, having temporarily forgotten to breathe. "Thank goodness I'm not a suspect then. Do you really think there's a possibility Dan Cooper's death wasn't an accident?"

"I have no idea, but I'm betting that chief of police will get to the heart of the matter," Zara said.

Paolo yawned in boredom.

"Why don't you two get going," Penelope said. "I have some cleanup to do here, but should be home soon."

"No, we're here to help. We won't desert you," Zara said.

Penelope washed all the dishes, scrubbed the kitchen, and reset the tearoom tables. The help offered by her friends amounted to Zara pulling things out of the Kelvinator to nibble and making more of a mess for Penelope to clean up. Paolo helped by staying out of the way and sleeping on one of the tearoom's settees under the warming rays of the sun as it streamed through the majestic windows. Zara awakened Paolo just in time to leave, and the two walked Penelope to her car.

"See you at the house," Penelope said.

"Are you coming straight home?" Zara asked.

"You bet. I'm beat. It's been an exhausting few days."

Penelope drove mindlessly toward the house, finally familiar enough with the town to be get around without becoming irretrievably lost. As she drifted past a large Spanish Colonial home, Penelope noted a couple chatting on a front porch, and felt a lump form in her throat when she realized the man was Hank. She waved to him, but he didn't notice. The remainder of her drive home was occupied with thoughts of Hank, Hank's hair, Hank's stature, Hank's demeanor, Hank's humor, Hank's smile. In those moments, Penelope forgot she ever had a tearoom or that a friend had perished in it.

* * * *

Back at home, Paolo mixed cocktails.

"Paolo, you really mustn't keep doing that. It's illegal … *Prohibition*," Penelope said, whispering the last word lest anyone in the neighborhood catch wind of the house's forbidden activities.

Zara took the two lowball glasses from Paolo's hands and sauntered into the kitchen, returning with a pair of teacups. "Problem solved."

"Tea, that's more like it," Penelope said, imbibing the draft in her cup. Immediately, she began to choke. "What on earth?"

"Keeping up appearances, P. It's not what you do or say, but what others *think* you do or say that matters," Zara said.

Paolo drank his cocktail from its glass, then prepared a second one in a teacup.

"What an awful philosophy, Z," Penelope replied.

"No sense in rocking the boat," Zara said, sitting on the sofa and pulling her knees up under her. "Appearances and the … shall we say, *cultivating* of them have done more for me than cold hard facts ever did."

Penelope shook her head. "Tell me again, how is it that we're friends?"

"Because we're all we have," Zara answered with a bittersweet smile.

Penelope grabbed her hand in affection. Zara's point was a valid one.

"Mangia?" Paolo said.

"Yes, food, good idea, Paolo," Zara replied. "You hungry, P?"

"Famished … but far too tired to cook."

"Paolo, be a darling and go get us some Chinese food?"

"*Come?*" Paolo replied.

"Funny how he can't understand a word of English when it's something he objects to," Zara said.

"Chinese food? I don't know, Z. I think I'm with Paolo on this," Penelope said. "Can't we just get something from the Butterfly Café?

"Whaddaya say, Paolo? How about the Butterfly Café?" Zara shouted.

"Bene, bene," he replied. "Cosa?"

"What would you like, P? My treat."

"I could go for biscuits and gravy … or maybe some barbecued ribs," Penelope said, sinking into the parlor sofa.

"Or maybe both?" Zara asked.

Penelope raised a thumb in affirmation.

"Venga," Paolo said, beckoning Zara to accompany him.

"Oh all right, I suppose I could tolerate a sunset drive along the coast," Zara said, miming a kiss to Paolo. "Be back in a jiffy, P."

"Mmmm hmmmmm," Penelope returned, closing her eyes and settling deeper into the sofa.

\* \* \* \*

Zara and Paolo returned with a full barbecue dinner to find Penelope being escorted out of the house by Chief Harrison. Upon closer inspection, Zara noticed Penelope was manacled.

"Just what the devil is going on?!" Zara demanded.

"I'm afraid your friend here is the number one suspect in the murder of Daniel Cooper," the chief said, leading Penelope to the squad car.

"Suspect?! You must be joking," Zara said.

"I don't joke when it comes to murder."

"But how can this be?"

"She was the last person to see Dan alive."

"Zuh Z, I d-didn't, I didn't do it. I swear! You have to be-be-believe me!" Penelope wailed, abject fright causing her to shake and stutter uncontrollably.

"Obviously!" Zara said. "Chief Harrison, you can't possibly think—"

"I go where the evidence leads me, ma'am. And so far, it all points to Miss Price."

"This is absurd!" Zara huffed.

"Che cosa?" Paolo asked.

"What's happening?! I'll tell you what's happening, Paolo!" Zara yelled. "Penelope is being accused of murder!"

Paolo looked at her blankly.

Zara held up her wrists as if they were in handcuffs then pointed to Penelope and said, "Dan Cooper."

Paolo gasped. "Noooooooo."

"Well said, Paolo!" Zara responded.

"I'll ne-never forget you, Z," Penelope cried as Chief Harrison palmed her head to put her in the back of the police car. "You've been like a sister to me." Her lower lip trembled and her eyes filled as she gazed out of the squad car window at her beautiful home.

"Be strong, P. I'll get you out of this ... somehow!"

Penelope looked at her with pitiable eyes as the police car pulled away.

"Paolo, stay," Zara said, extending her arm, palm facing him. She then ran into the house to fetch Penelope's carpetbag. "Huh, not as heavy as I would've thought," she said to herself as she dragged it down the stairs.

Zara's appraisal of the satchel was astute. Penelope had recently thrown out half of the holdall's contents and stored another quarter of it. Even so, the bag remained ponderous. Zara and Paolo drove straight to the police station. Though Zara had no idea what to do, she felt certain there had to be something in Penelope's omnivorous carpetbag that could help. They arrived to find Penelope alone in a dark cell, its overhead light in need of a new bulb. Penelope sat rubbing her wrists to soothe the soreness from the cuffs.

"We're here!" Zara announced as a young constable unlocked the cell allowing her to enter.

"We?" Penelope asked, supposing Zara referred to her police escort.

"Me and Paolo. He's at the front desk where they're checking your bag for liquor and guns. How are you holding up?"

"Much improved since last you saw me. When they put me in the cell and locked the door, a strange sort of calm enveloped me, the kind they talk about in far eastern philosophies. I feel as if I'm looking at this whole situation as though I'm outside of it somehow. I don't quite have the words to explain, but if I didn't know better, I'd say this entire Pacific Grove experience has been a dream—just one big surreal dream," Penelope said, closing her eyes and smiling serenely.

"From dream come true to nightmare!" Zara said. "Does Chief Harrison really think you killed Dan Cooper?"

"Looks that way. I'm the last person to see him, supposedly," Penelope said calmly.

"His wife didn't see him after he left the shop?"

Penelope shook her head. "From what I've gathered, Lily awoke the day of the grand opening thinking nothing was wrong. Dan had forewarned her there was a good deal to do in preparation and that he'd likely get home late and leave early. So when she went to bed at her normal time and rose the next morning without seeing him, she wasn't worried in the least."

"Who told you that? How do we know it's the truth?"

"I overheard the chief and an officer talking."

"Well, did Dan actually go home that night? Maybe there was someone else who saw him. Somebody somewhere must've seen something!" Zara said, becoming atypically worked up.

"Your guess is as good as mine. I have no idea what transpired between the time I said goodnight to Dan and the moment he … his corpse … was discovered in the powder room."

"And yet, you're the one holding the bag …"

"A humongous bag …"

The two discussed the situation at length, going around in circles and getting absolutely nowhere. About thirty minutes later, they ceased conversing at the sound of lumbered steps and something dragging. They clutched each other in apprehension, their imaginations getting the best of them. A large shadow loomed, drawing closer. They held each other tighter. Soon Paolo came into view, cursing and hauling the carpetbag toward the cell. The two women exhaled and released their grip of one another.

"Paolo, I figured you left and drove home," Zara said, miming the action of driving a car. "What took so long?" she asked, tapping her wrist indicating the time.

He pointed down to the carpetbag, frowning and grumbling under his breath. Zara and Penelope broke into much needed laughter.

"Oh, constable," Zara called out.

In a flash, an eager young officer arrived, grinning.

"Oh brother, don't tell me you've got him under your spell already," Penelope whispered to Zara.

"There was no time to waste," she replied. "Constable Matlin, be a bunny and open the door so Miss Price here can have her things."

He chuckled the laugh of the smitten and did her bidding.

"Are you sure you don't have the kitchen sink in there?" Zara said as Paolo slid the carpetbag across the floor to Penelope.

"You should've seen it before I expunged most of the contents," Penelope said.

"There's something about a man in uniform, isn't there, P?" Zara said turning her attention to the enamored police constable and eliciting another goofy grin and nervous giggle from him.

Paolo noted the officer's reaction and folded his arms in protest, frowning and murmuring.

"Tell me, constable, how long does my undeniably innocent friend have to stay in this cold forbidding place?"

"I'm not at liberty to say, Miss. She first has to be arraigned, and Judge Houston won't be back from his fishing trip for a few more days."

"A few days! Why, that's nothing short of barbaric," Zara protested.

Penelope gulped and grabbed Zara's forearm for support.

"Is that even legal?" Zara asked.

"I, well, I don't really know," the officer said, his confidence starting to wane under Zara's questioning.

"Yes, Miss Zara, unfortunately it is," Vincent said, approaching the cell. "In California, a prisoner can be held up to 168 hours before being arraigned or charged."

"A full week!" Penelope cried.

"'Fraid so," Vincent said. "How're you getting on, Miss Price?" he added, his face full of sympathy and concern.

"I'm all right, Vincent. It's awfully nice to see you," Penelope said.

"Stella told me about how you won over Mrs. Morgan," he said encouragingly.

"Gracious, that seems like a lifetime ago. To be sure, Stella was a big part of the day's success. I can't wait to get back and get the business going," she said.

"That's not gonna happen just yet," he said. "I better go. I have strict orders not to—"

"Fraternize with me, I know. Wouldn't want you to be corrupted by the despicable influence of a tearoom-owning spinster, now," she said, frustrated.

"You won't be a spinster forever," Vincent said, smiling and raising a hand in farewell.

"I won't?" Penelope said, suddenly much more interested in Vincent's reply than the fact that she was in a jail cell on suspicion of murder. "Did you hear what he said, Z?"

"Easy does it, girl. You've got other things to think about right now," Zara said. "Now Paolo and I are going to go home and get a few of your things. We'll be back as quick as we can ... Oh, constable Matlin," she called out.

He stepped forward.

"I do hope you'll be here when I return."

"Yes, ma'am. Here all night."

"Good ... good ... And it's Miss."

"Pardon?"

"Miss, not ma'am," she said with a wink.

"Ohhhhhhh hahahahhah I gotcha, ma'am ... I mean miss ... uh—"

"Zara," she whispered as she lightly brushed against him when exiting the cell.

Penelope looked on in wonder. Zara grinned at her, kicked up the back of her skirt, and strutted down the corridor.

"What a tomato," Constable Matlin said under his breath, ogling her every move.

# Chapter Twelve

"Back so soon?" Penelope asked as Zara, Paolo, and Constable Matlin neared the cell, the latter two buckling under the cache of household items Zara deemed necessary for her friend's comfort.

"Don't forget that extra cot," Zara said to Constable Matlin, touching the end of his nose with her gloved index finger and smiling beguilingly.

Paolo gestured that he was going out for a smoke, and walked back down the hall, griping all the way.

"Extra cot?" Penelope asked.

"For me, of course," Zara said.

"Are you even supposed to be in here?" Penelope asked.

"It's a free country. And I should think the police would be more worried about people trying to break out of this place than breaking into it."

Penelope thought about Zara's comment and nodded in agreement.

"You seem awfully subdued. What have you been up to in my absence?" Zara asked.

Penelope held up a mass of tangled yarn. "Knitting!" she announced with unbridled pride.

"What in the world?" Zara said, turning the knotted mass in her hands.

"It does sort of look like a world, doesn't it?" Penelope said, admiring her handiwork.

"I didn't know you knitted."

"Neither did I. But one must start somewhere," Penelope said, her tongue creeping out of the corner of her mouth as she concentrated on producing another stitch.

"Get a load of you—cool as a cat. I would've expected you to be writhing on the floor in a frantic frenzy. What's gotten into you?"

"It's what I've gotten into … knitting."

"Oh I see, you've gone insane, that's it."

Penelope chuckled. "Have you ever been through something so awful that it doesn't even faze you because of how unreal it seems?"

"I was a courtesan for fourteen years, what do *you* think?" Zara said to Penelope in a low voice.

"Well, that's how I feel now. I started knitting and it dawned on me. It's just like knitting."

"What's just like knitting? Being accused of murder?"

"Sort of. Here's the thing. It's like the stitches when you knit. Each one of them looks inconsequential, unimportant. But when you put them all together they add up to something substantial … like a hat or even a sweater." Penelope put down her knitting and took her friend's hands in her own. "Z, I'm going to stitch together what happened to Daniel Cooper and get justice for him."

Zara searched Penelope's face for a long moment. "You know, I think you will at that … There's something that bothers me though, truth be told."

"What's that?" Penelope asked, trying to unravel the swarm of yarn she'd tangled.

"Why you?"

"Why me as in why do I want to get justice for Dan?"

"No, why are you the one who's been arrested?" Zara asked, her face showing concern.

"Apparently, it's because I was the last known person to see him. If you ask me, it's a matter of divine intervention. If I hadn't been arrested, I wouldn't be so keen to get to the bottom of his heartrending situation," Penelope said, her eyes clear and bright.

"I've never seen you so invigorated! You didn't squirrel away a flask did you?"

"I can't explain it, but I feel exhilarated in a way I've never known. It's thrilling, really."

"If you say so," Zara said, scoping out the hallway as she stole a swig from her own flask.

"You certainly made easy work of winding that young officer around your finger," Penelope remarked.

"Saying, 'Boo' would be enough to hook that little fish … which reminds me, he should've been back by now with the cot I requested. I'm going to see what's taking him," Zara stood up, smoothed her hair, and waltzed out the cell door that had been left open at her request.

Penelope returned to her thoughts and yarn, determined to make sense of both.

"Creating modern art, are we?" a male voice said.

Penelope looked up to see Hank leaning against the cell door and smiling.

She gasped and stood up quickly, causing her to experience tunnel vision and feel faint … a situation that often occurred when he was around.

"Mr. Edwards!"

"I hear you've been busy shaking things up in our quiet little town," he said, walking into the cell and toying with his fedora.

"May I … uh … offer you a seat?" Penelope said, motioning to the cell's small, weathered cot.

"Thank you, I can't stay long."

"Oh," she said looking at her knitting needles and fidgeting with them. "Well, it was good of you to come," she said, trying hard not to pout.

"Sick of me already?" he said with twinkling eyes as he attempted to perch on the edge of the cot's frame, upending it in the process and causing him to scramble to resume standing.

Penelope pursed her lips so as not to giggle.

"Careful or you'll hit the—" *Boom* "—wall," Zara called from the hallway.

Hank went to the aid of Constable Matlin who was beet red and dripping sweat from his battle with the metal-framed cot.

"Let me help you with that," Hank said, effortlessly lifting the cot and putting it against the wall adjoining the existing berth.

"Why, Hank, whatever brings you here?" Zara said, looking brightly at Penelope.

"I'd heard what happened to Miss Price and just wanted to offer my condolences," he said.

"Condolences?" Penelope repeated, her enthusiasm dampened by the sound of a word that brought to mind Dan Cooper's tragedy.

Realizing his blunder, Hank shook his head and looked at the ground. "Looks like I put my foot in it this time."

"P, you haven't looked at any of the things I brought for you," Zara said, changing the subject.

"You know how we knitters can be," Penelope said, taking up her needles and yarn in hopes of impressing Hank with her skills. Instead, she ended up getting yarn wrapped around her wrist so tightly that its blood flow was cut off, and she put both hands behind her back in order to extricate her wrist unobserved.

Zara rolled her eyes and began unpacking.

Hank said, "Looks like my cue to leave."

"Nonsense. Take the load off, Hank. I even brought cocoa," Zara said.

Penelope knelt on the floor next to Zara to unpack. The first thing Penelope pulled out was a nightgown that she immediately stuffed back into the box. "We really shouldn't keep Mr. Edwards, Z," she said, mortified at having her unmentionables on public display.

"Yes, I should get going," Hank said, equally abashed. "Ladies," he added as he pulled his fedora down over his brow.

Penelope just stared at him, saying nothing, still mulling over the nightgown incident.

"Don't be a stranger," Zara called after him.

\* \* \* \*

The two friends, along with harried Paolo, poured through the boxes and turned the cell into a cozy dormitory. They hung a curtain along the bars for privacy, and dressed the cots with feather beds, pillows, and linens from home. They even had a pair of Tiffany lamps and a radio that they plugged into an extension cord running to the front desk. For dinner, they enjoyed their take-away order from the Butterfly Café while seated in folding chairs at a card table outfitted with a cloth, utensils, a vase of flowers, and a small candelabra.

When Penelope began to doze off mid-dessert, Zara whispered goodnight to Paolo and sent him back home. An hour later, all was quiet in the jail cell, save the sounds of restful sleep in goose down comfort.

\* \* \* \*

Zara roused Penelope just after dawn so they could freshen up and dress prior to greeting any potential visitors. Zara never allowed a man to see her first thing in the morning without her going to great lengths to make it look like she woke up fresh and fabulous. Once the ladies had fixed themselves up, they returned to their bunks and chatted while waiting for Paolo to bring breakfast.

"How did you sleep?" Penelope asked.

"All right, I suppose," Zara replied. "I don't know the last time I slept without a man next to me. It felt strange, like something was missing."

"Sorry to hear that, Z. Though I'll have to take your word for it," Penelope said, punching her pillow to get it just right.

"I sometimes forget what an angel you are."

"I don't think angels are held on suspicion of murder, generally … other than archangel Michael I suppose."

"Buongiorno!" Paolo said cheerily as he entered the converted boudoir, carrying a picnic basket and the morning paper. "Ciao, amore," he added, kissing Zara passionately, the breakfast things threatening to elude his grasp.

"How did you sleep?" Penelope asked him, miming a gesture of sleep.

He frowned and feigned crying, putting a hand over his heart and nodding at Zara.

"Aww, he missed me too," Zara said, tucking an arm through his.

Penelope opened the newspaper and gasped.

"What is it?" Zara asked, rushing over to look. "Surely it can't be worse than what's already been printed."

# Tragedy to Triumph or Confection to Conviction?

## *Miss Penelope Price's tearoom and Daniel Cooper's legacy*

A select few of Pacific Grove's society elite congregated in secret yesterday at AntiquiTeas, the town's newest hot spot.

```
The  Daniel  Cooper  Memorial
menu     was     lavish     and
inventive,      served      in
avant-garde           splendor
rivaling  the  most  elegant
European cafes.

This  writer  was  among  the
privileged  set,  accompanied
by  Lillian  Cooper,  Daniel's
childhood  sweetheart  and  now
widow.  Miss  Price  is  assured
a   triumph-deluxe,   provided
she  escapes  the  noose  for
Daniel's murder.

On  behalf  of  the  Butterfly
Bugle,  this  reporter  will  be
keeping  a  close  eye  on  the
legal   proceedings   to   keep
our   readers   in   the   know.
Will  Miss  Price  receive  her
just  deserts?  Or  has  she
gotten   herself   into   water
too hot to escape?
```

Penelope looked up to see Chief Harrison standing in the doorway, surveying the cell. She jumped to her feet and froze, trying desperately to come up with an explanation.

"Bear claw, Chief Harrison?" Zara asked, offering the chief a pastry.

He accepted it and ate in silence, walking around the cubicle to scrutinize the contraband filling the space.

"It's much nicer now, don'tcha think?" Zara said, trying to appear nonchalant though she feared she'd gone too far with the decorating. "It just needed a woman's touch."

"Get comfy, you three," the chief said, walking out and closing the cell door without bothering to lock it. "I want to talk to each of you … Thanks for the bear claw."

Penelope dropped onto her cot, exhaling for the first time since the chief's arrival.

"Whew!" Zara said, dropping down next to her.

"Zara, you're a sorceress," Penelope said. "You saved us again."

"Holy cow, I thought we were sunk for certain."

"I can't make out Chief Harrison. He runs so hot and cold. One moment he seems unreasonable and rigid, the next, he's accepting breakfast pastries and leaving the cell unlocked."

"He's definitely complex. I find that fascinating."

"I find it unnerving," Penelope replied, pulling out her knitting and searching for the ends of the yarn.

"Is this how you plan to spend your day?" Zara asked.

"Knitting, or should I say *knotting*, helps me think. And I have a lot of thinking to do. But to answer your question, today we start to solve the case of what really happened to Dan Cooper," Penelope said, yanking a section of yarn and revealing its end.

"Oooooh, what should *I* do?" Zara said, excited by the prospect of playing detective and using her mind instead of her body.

"Take notes."

＊ ＊ ＊ ＊

The knitter and scribe started their investigation by making a list of everyone who was at the tearoom the last night Dan was alive. Paolo busied himself with calisthenics in the cell's only undecorated corner.

The sleuths then compiled a series of questions about

Dan they intended to ask the people they knew. What were his business and personal relationships like with the townsfolk? Was he really as beloved as he seemed? Did he have any skeletons in his closet? Did he have any enemies? Did anyone see where he went after leaving the tearoom that ill-fated night? What time was he killed, and most important, why?

"Now what?" Zara asked.

"Now we talk to people," Penelope said. "You know, if we were smart, we'd bone up on Chief Harrison's findings."

"Fortunately, we *are* smart," Zara said, chewing on the end of her pencil and smiling.

Penelope pontificated while Zara scribbled. Penelope's thoughts were a jumble resulting in Zara's notes being mostly indecipherable. As Penelope paced the room knitting, she created a labyrinth of yarn around the space that took several minutes to step over and around if one wished to extricate oneself and leave.

"I've got an idea!" Penelope suddenly announced.

"Good, because what we're doing now is a muddle. I feel like I'm living inside your carpetbag!"

Penelope wound up her yarn and pulled the table Paolo had brought from home into the center of the room. "There … we'll post our findings here," she said, nodding at the depressing, grey cinderblock wall.

"Okay …" Zara said, uncomprehendingly.

"Let's start by affixing to the wall pages bearing each person's name who may have seen or been involved with Dan the day he died. We can then use my yarn to show who was connected to whom."

Zara nodded, mulling the idea over as she wrote names on sheets of paper and handed them to Penelope. Within a few minutes they had a handful of names taped to their grid.

"Surely a likeable fellow like Dan knew more people than just our little opening day work band," Zara said.

"Exactly! That's why we'll need help. We need to know what the chief knows."

"Paolo Rossi, come with me, please. The chief would like to speak with you," Vincent called out, approaching the cell and avoiding eye contact with Penelope and Zara.

Paolo stood up, crossed himself, kissed his crucifix, and blew a kiss to Zara as he followed Vincent.

"Such a shame Vincent's not permitted to speak to us," Penelope said.

"But Stella is," Zara replied. "We can get Stella to run interference for us!"

"Oh you are good, Z."

"I do my best," she said, flashing her dimples. "I'm sure we can also get some information from dear young Constable Matlin."

"Did you call me, Miss Zara?" the officer said, jogging to the cell.

"My my, aren't we Johnny on the spot?" Zara cooed.

"Actually, my Christian name's Jimmy."

Penelope looked at Zara blankly, finding the constable's intellect less than promising.

"Tell me, Jimmy," Zara said. "What are you doing here so early? I thought you worked the night shift."

"I do. I just swung round to make sure you slept all right."

"Like babes in arms," Zara said. "Will we see you tonight then?"

"You bet you will! I wouldn't miss it for the world."

"Well then, until tonight, Jimmy Matlin," Zara said, dismissing the love-struck youth.

"Stella! Stella!" Penelope whispered to Zara, pointing at the officer.

"Oh Jimmy!" Zara called, "Before you go, would you do me the teensiest favor?"

"Sure thing, Miss Zara."

"Can you arrange for Stella Parker to come visit us? We have a few questions for her."

"Gee, I don't know …"

"You don't know Stella or you don't know if you can ask her to come see us?" Zara said, controlling the conversation.

"I … it's just … the chief says I need to be careful around you ladies and not let you 'ensnare me' … Those were his words."

Zara chuckled good-naturedly. "Your chief is sharp! But not to worry, Jimmy, I won't be ensnaring anyone, I assure you. Now, be a good boy and fetch Stella, won't you?" she said, batting her eyes and inching up her skirt to adjust her garter.

"Yuh … yeah … sure thing, Miss Zara," Jimmy said, bumping into the cell door before racing out of the precinct.

"Won't be ensnaring anyone, Z? Now we both know that's a lie."

"No it's not … all the ensnaring I need to do has already been accomplished."

"Oh? You mean you've already wound Chief Harrison in your web?"

"No, and I don't intend to. He's a man of integrity. Those types don't fall for my antics … rather like Hank."

"Hank!" Penelope said, jumping up in astonishment at the mention of the name.

"Did I strike a nerve, P?" Zara said, returning to her worktable and notes, casting a knowing sideways glance at Penelope.

"Don't be silly … I just had an idea is all."

"Oh I bet you have all sorts of ideas when it comes to Hank," Zara teased.

"What I *mean* is, I think we should talk to Hank first.

He was Dan Cooper's best friend and all."

"Uh huh … Perhaps you'd prefer to interrogate him alone."

Penelope threw her wad of yarn at Zara.

"Oh look. You knitted a ball," Zara said.

"Hush, you. Let's get back to it … Now what can our wall tell us? You, me, Paolo, Stella, Vincent and Hank—I think that's everyone who was part of our little team."

"Should we add Hubert Allen?"

"Good idea. And we should probably include Florence Morgan, Lily Cooper and that Elsie Davies woman."

"Surely you don't think any of them were involved in Dan's death."

"No, but they may have a kernel of information that can help us start to unravel this case."

"Case?" Zara said, surprised.

"Yes … Being in the clink really helps put things in perspective. I am no longer just a tearoom and antiques shop owner—"

"Well, you have yet to really be either one—"

"Nonetheless, I am going to dedicate my spare hours to serving this community as the voice of truth … as a truth sleuth!"

"Isn't that the job of the police?"

"They can't do it all … especially when they are bound by jurisprudence and legal procedures. We are bound by nothing other than conscience and truth!"

"Surely, the newspaper satisfies that need."

"For dispensing the truth?!"

"You're right, what was I thinking?"

"Zara, we have the opportunity to be of benefit here, far more than we could be by just pouring tea."

"That's where I think you're wrong, P."

Penelope looked at her questioningly.

"Think about it," Zara said. "Think how people share the most scandalous private details with their hairdresser."

"Yes, so?"

"So, imagine what confidences people might divulge when plied with a pot of tea and a sympathetic ear."

"Tea and sympathy—Zara, I think you're right!"

"Oh I know I am!"

"So what do we do first?"

"Get cards printed, I should think. The Tea and Sympathy Investigative Agency," Zara said, fanning her hand out in panorama.

"We sleuth for truth!" Penelope added.

The friends giggled.

Paolo returned to the cell in silence, followed by Chief Harrison.

"Miss Zara, I can't tell if your friend here doesn't know anything or really doesn't know *anything*," the chief said.

Zara suppressed a smile as Paolo sat, wiping the sweat from his brow. "He doesn't speak much English."

"Or much of anything," the chief replied. "Granted, Caruso's Italian isn't the best, but still, Mr. Rossi was like a … It was as if … Has he ever undergone any medical procedures … perhaps a partial lobotomy?"

She pinched herself hard to keep from laughing. "Well, conversation is not his strong suit."

"I certainly hope *you* can be of more help. Will you follow me, please?"

"Certainly, Chief Harrison," she said, tidying her hair and re-applying her lipstick. "Paolo, be a dear and get us lunch."

He looked at her in bewilderment.

"Mangia," she said, miming the gesture of putting food in her mouth as she followed Chief Harrison to his office.

Paolo wasted no time in departing the precinct in

search of sustenance.

Penelope stood staring at her wall of witnesses for some time, getting nowhere in her ponderings. Despite her knack for logic, the circumstances of the situation clouded her sense of reason. She decided it would be helpful to reflect on the days leading up to Dan's death, but found it difficult to do so. Every time her thoughts went down that path, she became too emotional to continue.

She likened her inner turmoil to the idea of making toast with a toaster that keeps short-circuiting. Her grief continually short-circuited her ability to rationally work through the events of Dan's final days. If anyone had been watching her, they would have witnessed Penelope at turns weeping, chuckling, mumbling to herself, talking to Dan, and for all intents and purposes, carrying on like a madwoman. Yet for all her erratic conduct, she was no further along in her thought process. Eventually, her inertia was relieved by the arrival of Stella.

"Here she is, Miss Zara, just as you asked," Jimmy Matlin said, reeking of catchpenny cologne and holding a daisy intended for Zara.

"Nice digs!" Stella said, nodding in approval as she surveyed the posh cubicle.

"Thank you, Constable Matlin. Zara's with the chief. I'll let her know you were here," Penelope said, holding a napkin over her nose to mask the overpowering odor of the cologne and taking the flower from the crestfallen constable.

"Thank heavens you're here," she said, hugging Stella, much to the young girl's discomfiture.

"Sure. Umm … how are you?"

"Never better!" Penelope said, her eyes bright and tone buoyant. "Stella, how would you feel about being a junior inquiry agent?"

"What's that?"

"You've heard of the legendary Pinkertons?"

"Who hasn't?!"

"Well that's what it is," Penelope said, her mood having shifted to the joyous end of the emotion spectrum—the part bordering on ecstatic insanity, she feared.

"Holy smoke! You mean a female detective like Kate Warne?"

"Precisely!" she said, pacing hurriedly and unwittingly plucking the petals off Jimmy's daisies.

"I'd be all in, of course! Why do you ask?"

"Because we are going to figure out who killed Dan Cooper!"

"Before the police figure out you did it?"

Penelope stopped in her tracks and glared at her.

"That didn't come out right," Stella said.

Penelope noted the mass of petals marking her steps and put the remaining flowers in a glass on the table before resuming pacing. "We have a great deal of work ahead of us, naturally," she muttered, thinking aloud.

"So whaddawe do now? Do I take some sort of oath or something?"

"What was that?" Penelope said, returning to their conversation. "An oath? No, no, that won't be necessary." Noticing Stella's look of disappointment, she immediately amended her answer. "Oh where's my head today? I meant to say I believe an oath to be absolutely necessary! Uh ... here, put your hand on this teapot and repeat after me: I, Stella Parker, do pledge myself to the ideals of the Tea and Sympathy Investigative Agency as a truth sleuth."

Stella did so. Penelope continued. "I promise to serve tea and justice to all who call on me for aid and to ferret out—"

"Maybe we should quit while we're ahead, Penelope."

"Good idea. Consider yourself duly sworn in. Now, I want you to take a look at the *sprawl wall.*"

"The what?"

"That's the name I came up with for this wall of information. The grid we've created shows all of the people who we know were involved with Dan Cooper. Catchy name, don't you think?"

Stella waffled her hand in a *so-so* gesture.

"In any event, we're trying to pinpoint who was in contact with Dan that fateful night. We'll want to establish what sort of relationships Dan had with these people in order to come up with motives they may have harbored for wanting to do him ill. We already know he was killed with a blow to the head by a heavy blunt object. But we need to know who may have been in the shop that night ..."

"And why," Stella added.

"Yes! Oh I can tell you're going to be a marvelous detective."

Stella beamed.

"Mees Price, I came as soon as I heerd," Hubert Allen said, holding his hat in his hands as he stood outside the cell, his plaintive countenance making him appear softer and kinder than usual. "This alleegations are reedeeculous, of course. Eez theere anihthinn I can do to beh of aid?"

"Mr. Allen, what an unexpected pleasure!" Penelope said, striding over to him and shaking his hand energetically. "You're a breath of fresh air, to be sure. May I offer you something? Coffee? A bear claw?"

Stella grinned to see the expression of flummoxed shock on her godfather's face as Penelope welcomed him into the cell as if she were receiving him for a celebratory social call at home. "What's wrong, Uncle Hubert? You look like someone just goosed your keister."

"No, I ... Meess Price, I've ehteen, thank you," Hubert said, trying to compose himself and disregarding Stella's comments as he eyed the table adornments and food spread. "I seh they are trehtihn you weel?"

"One makes do," Penelope said with a smile, sitting and gesturing for Hubert to do the same. "Mr. Allen, there are a good many things we require, and you, of course, are just the man to get them for us. First and foremost, I'll need a sign for my cell."

"A sign? For your ceel?! I don't undeerstand."

Penelope grabbed a sheet of paper and quickly scrawled the words: *Tea & Sympathy Investigative Agency ~ We Sleuth for Truth.*

He looked at her in puzzlement.

"You, Mr. Allen, are looking at the first female detecting agency in the land," Penelope said with unbridled delectation, gesturing around the jail cell with sweeping arms.

Stella posed next to the *sprawl wall* as if she were a merchandise model showing off the latest new and improved product. "And I'm a junior inquiry agent ... like Kate Warne of the Pinkertons!"

Hubert stammered in a failed search for a response.

"Of course, we require a number of tools for our trade," Penelope went on. "Would you like to write these down, Mr. Allen? ... Mr. Allen?"

# Chapter Thirteen

"Well hello, Hubert," Zara called as she passed him in the hallway when returning from her questioning session with Chief Harrison. "Were you expecting him?" she asked Penelope as she entered the cheery cell.

"No, but per usual, he was absolutely invaluable. How ever would I get on without him?"

"Hiya, Zara," Stella said casually, hiding her giddiness about her appointment to the detective team.

"Will ya look what the tied washed in," Zara remarked to Penelope, wagging a thumb toward Stella.

"I'll thank you not to mock my junior enquiry agent,"

Penelope said.

"So she dragged you into this too?" Zara said to Stella, taking a seat and lighting a cigarette.

"Yessiree. Took an oath and everything."

"Impressive."

"How did the interrogation go?" Penelope asked, fiddling with her fingernails in nervousness.

"I had a ball. Did you know he is an avid gardener? He grows his own fruits and vegetables and blue ribbon flowers. He even sings in a barbershop quartet! Isn't that the quaintest thing?" Zara said, smiling wistfully.

Penelope stared at her, dumbfounded. "You do know I was referring to your talk with Chief Harrison."

"Mmmm hmmmm," Zara vocalized as she took a long drag from her cigarette wand.

"As in grumpy, curt, volatile Chief Harrison," Penelope said.

"Actually he's exceptionally jovial and convivial," Zara said, her dimples fully activated.

"Everybody in town loves him. He's just unpleasant with you," Stella told Penelope.

Penelope sunk into her tufted armchair. "How did I get so fortunate?"

"Miss Price?" Vincent said, approaching the cell and gesturing for Penelope to walk with him.

Penelope stood and smoothed her skirt. "Time for the Spanish Inquisition. Wish me luck."

"Luck!" Zara said, still smiling.

"She'll need more than luck," Stella whispered.

To Penelope, the walk down the short hallway to the chief's office was never-ending. She found the fall of her feet to be uncommonly loud, and she noticed her steps kept time with the rhythm of her pulse. The pounding of her heart became ever louder, and she was certain Vincent could hear it too. She wondered if it made her appear guilty.

The story of Edgar Allen Poe's *Tell-Tale Heart* came to mind, causing her heart to race ever faster, and she convinced herself she was headed straight for the firing squad.

Unable to corral her crazed fear, she came unhinged and dropped to the ground screaming. "Vincent, I didn't do it! I swear on my parents' graves! Tear up the floorboards in my house and you'll see ... there's nothing there!"

Cringing with embarrassment, Vincent lifted her by the arm and spoke quietly. "Of course not, Miss Price. No one thinks—"

"Chief Harrison does," Penelope blathered, backing up against the wall in the foyer and working her tongue to produce saliva so she could speak. "But I didn't chop up Dan and bury him under my floor. You have my word. God strike me dead if I'm lying!"

"Thank you, Mr. Caruso," the chief said, coming out of his office to subdue Penelope. "That will be all."

"Yes sir," he said, walking away quickly should Penelope undergo another outburst.

"Actually, one more thing, Caruso," the chief called out, holding open his office door for Penelope. "Won't you take a seat, Miss Price," he said gently to her. "I'll be right in."

Vincent stood up straight and turned around, nervous as to what might be asked of him. "Yes, sir?"

"I think we'll be needing some tea ... and some of those little English biscuits I like ... Do you like English biscuits, Miss Price?"

She nodded from her chair.

"Extra biscuits, Caruso ... and chocolate. I recently read that dark chocolate can pacify any crisis. Perhaps our soldiers should have shot chocolate balls instead of cannon balls in the war. I dare say we'd be a sight better off today."

Vincent smiled. "You got it, sir."

Chief Harrison's calming tone and light remarks

helped Penelope to breathe normally again. He was an enigma in her eyes, soothingly warm one minute, icy cold the next, and she never knew whether to expect—a Jekyll or Hyde—when she faced him.

He waited for Vincent's return before entering the room in order to give Penelope time to compose herself.

"I see you've been making the most of your stay with us, Miss Price," he said, carrying the tea tray delivered by Vincent. In the absence of a clear space to set it, he placed it precariously on a tall stack of papers on his small desk. "You're sure to win the Department of Corrections' blue ribbon for most attractively decorated cell," he joshed, endeavoring to put her at ease.

"You really think so? Why that's the best news I've heard in, well, far too long," she said, the timber of her voice rising in joy.

He smiled sympathetically at her—the way one does when dealing with the gullible and clueless.

"The credit goes to my dear friend, Zara," Penelope explained, considering herself exceptionally cunning for shifting the blame for the unconventional cell décor to Zara since the chief and Zara appeared to have established a rapport.

Chief Harrison opened his mouth to respond, but decided against it. Instead, he took to reading and flipping pages in a folder labeled with Penelope's name. For the first time, she really looked at him. He was middle-aged, balding, had a bulbous belly, and his eyes laughed rather than smoldered—not at all Zara's type, and yet, he had made Zara smile in a way Penelope had not seen in a very long time—maybe ever. By all accounts, Walter Harrison was one of the most admired and beloved citizens of Pacific Grove, the man who played Santa Claus at the yearly Christmas festival and took in stray animals.

He never married, as the love of his life had broken his heart, and for years he'd devoted himself to his beloved widowed sister who lived in town. Just a year prior, she came down with an extreme case of dropsy that rendered her bedridden for months until she succumbed to congestive heart failure. The chief took off work to be by her side, nursing her, feeding her.

Since arriving in Pacific Grove, Penelope had heard nothing but worshipful praise for Chief Harrison. So then why was he always so gruff and nasty with her?

"Do you know why you're in jail, Miss Price?"

"Because Dan Cooper was the last person to see me alive."

"Excuse me?"

"I mean, I was the last person to see Dan Cooper alive … As far as you know."

He lowered the file and looked at her over the rims of his reading spectacles. "Tell me again about your last conversation with him."

"Well," she said, clearing her throat exaggeratedly as she tried to recall. "Everyone had just gone home the night before."

"The night before what?"

"Our grand opening. We'd all had a long day and knew we had another one ahead of us come morning."

"Fascinating. Pray tell, is there more?"

"Well … Mr. Cooper hung back to go over the plan for him to pick up ice in Monterey the next morning …" Penelope stopped, remembering their conversation, her nervousness turning to sorrow.

"Anything else, Miss Price?"

Penelope gulped back her emotions. "He told me how thankful he was for the job and how much it would help his family get back on track."

"Just what do you mean by 'back on track?'"

"I believe he had been having difficulty finding work following the closing of his saloon."

"Is *that* what you believe?" the chief said, his words

colored with mistrust.

"Yes, sir. That's all I know. I've only been in town for about two months—"

"Sure have stirred the pot a whole lot in only two months. Tell me, why did you have to leave San Pedro? Did you run into trouble with the law there too?"

"No! Just the opposite!"

"Are you suggesting you were above the law?"

"Not at all! Chief Harrison, I think we've gotten off on the wrong foot. You seem to have a view of me that couldn't be farther from the truth."

"That's too bad. I viewed you as a respectable businesswoman. Are you saying that's not the case?"

"No, I'm saying I … I plead the fifth amendment of the United States of America," Penelope declared in desperation.

"Chief?" Vincent said, knocking on the office door and poking his head in.

"What is it, Caruso?"

"Mrs. Jarvis called. Little Georgie got his head stuck between the bars of their wrought iron fence again."

"Can Bill at the firehouse handle it?"

"His wife said he's taking a nap."

The chief looked at his wristwatch. "Like clockwork," he said with a chuckle. "Tell Mrs. Jarvis not to worry. I'll be right there … oh and tell her to rub some lard around Georgie's neck and ears."

"Yes, chief," Vincent said, closing the door again.

"Looks like duty calls," the chief said. "I would ask someone to escort you back to your cell, Miss Price, to ensure you didn't try to escape, but with that Taj Mahal setup you've got going, I doubt you're in a hurry to leave."

He then opened the door and walked out, leaving Penelope in his office. She yearned for nothing more than to rifle through the paperwork on his desk in search of clues, but she knew she'd just be digging her own grave if she were caught doing so. After glancing around the room hunting for clues, and finding none, she trudged back to the cell.

"Isn't he a teddy bear?" Zara gushed.

"A real sweetheart," Penelope said sarcastically, more confused than ever by the paradox Walter Harrison represented.

"Did he ask you about your hobbies and what books you like?" Zara said.

"Didn't he ask you about Dan Cooper or the night of his death at all?" Penelope responded.

"Sure he did! He asked me how I knew Dan, how I know you ... how I know Paolo and how Paolo knew Dan et cetera ... and all the other things he'd tried to ask Paolo but couldn't because he got fouled up by the language barrier."

"And what did you tell him?" Penelope pried.

"Stella, be a peach and grab me a glass of cool water from the station's icebox?" Zara said.

"Sure thing, Z," she answered, skipping from the cell.

"Whaddaya think, I told him, fraidy-cat?!" Zara said quietly. "I told him we've been like sisters since we were toddlers. I told him how I came to know Dan when you employed him at your shop a month ago or whenever it was. I told him that I didn't see Dan after I left the night before the grand opening. I told him how I met Paolo in San Francisco a few weeks before coming to town and how he and I literally bumped into one another in Little Italy and how he offered to buy me a drink to make up for running my stocking ... how Paolo had just arrived in America days before I met him and since he was looking for work and I was looking for a driver, we pooled our resources, so to speak, and have been together ever since."

"I didn't know that's how you met Paolo."

"It's not," Zara said with a sweet smile.

"But that's perjury!" Penelope whispered loudly.

"More like banana oil … Okay, so maybe I embellished the truth a little regarding Paolo, but the real story is no one's business, and it really has no bearing on Dan's murder."

"Incredible," Penelope said, shaking her head. "Did the chief ask you anything else?"

"Yes, he also asked me how well I knew Hubert Allen and Elsie Davies, you know, the gossip gal from the local paper. I found that odd."

"Uncle Hubert *is* odd!" Stella said, delivering the water.

"Thanks, doll," Zara said, accepting the glass.

"Stella, if you don't mind my asking, what exactly is the source of his accent? I've never heard anything quite like it," Penelope said.

"Simple. It's not an accent at all," Stella said.

"Coulda fooled me," Zara said, handing the glass of water to Penelope.

"It's like this—Uncle Hubert was deaf as a kid, and when he learned to talk he got the sounds *ee* and *eh* ferhoodled. When he was older he got hearing aids, but he'd already locked in the weird way he talked and it stuck. Just a few years ago some doctors fixed him up with some sort of new surgery and now his hearing's better than a bat's. Gotta be careful what you say around him; he hears everything!"

"Interesting," Penelope said, pondering. "I wonder if he's heard anything that can help us determine what happened to Dan … Did you two get anything out of Vincent?"

"Not a blasted thing," Stella said, pouting. "He's so annoyingly professional—such an eagle scout."

"How are we ever going to find a suspect in this town of fine upstanding citizens?" Penelope fretted.

Stella snorted. "Are you kidding? There are more dirty secrets in this town than tea leaves in China."

"Really? Do tell," Zara said, pulling a chair close to Stella and handing her a bear claw.

"Not until after you're sworn in as an agent," Stella said with a puckish smile, tearing a large bite off of the pastry.

**\* \* \* \***

Having grown up in Pacific Grove, Stella had a lifetime of opportunities to become privy to the confidences and scandals of the town's residents. Zara and Penelope were so rapt by Stella's tittle-tattle, neither thought to take notes, which was just as well since the information was too damning to risk leaving in print, casually laying around.

First off, the neophyte junior detective had plenty to say about Dan. "He was one real egg. And things were just ducky for him and Lily before Volstead. They were hittin on all sixes alright. Then everything got all balled up and he more or less went the way of a bindle punk and Lily threatened to take the ankle biters and blow. It's not like Dan was a lollygagger—not at all! He just couldn't find anything to bring in kale the way he used to, to keep Lily sitting pretty. It was that high hat Elsie Davies who gummed up the works—she was always grungy when it came to Lily. Lily practically got the bum's rush for running up PG tabs without scratch. That's when Dan became grummy but bad. And so, finally, he started up a drum to bring in the clams."

Zara nodded, taking it all in.

Penelope sat motionless for a moment or two, then at last said, "I beg your pardon?"

Stella mentioned a few more details and Penelope asked for an aspirin. Zara explained to Penelope the gist of what Stella shared: that Dan Cooper was just as fine a fellow as they believed him to be. When Dan's livelihood dried up with Prohibition, and he was unable to find steady work, Lily threatened to take the children and move in with her parents back in Missouri if he didn't do something—

not just anything—but something that brought in enough money for her to live the quality of life to which she'd become accustomed. She refused to economize and charged up outrageous debts with the local vendors—especially Allen's General Store. Everyone knew that Lily's attitude was a product of Elsie Davies' insidious influence. Lily wasn't greedy or uppity, but she was weak, and fell prey to Elsie's machinations. Desperate, Dan did the only thing he could think of to save his family. He opened a speakeasy.

"Are you certain all of this is true?" Penelope asked. "Or just frivolous clishmaclaver?"

"Of course, I'm sure! I used to sneak into The Pig—"

"The Pig?" Penelope interrupted.

"The Blind Pig," Stella and Zara said in unison.

"The Pig was what he called his speakeasy," Stella said.

"Whatever for? That's an awful—"

"It's a common term in the trade," Zara said as Penelope looked at her with concern. "I'll explain it all later. Go on, Stella."

"Like I was saying, I used to sneak into The Pig every Saturday night after my parents knocked off for the night. What was Dan gonna do? Tell 'em he'd caught me at *his* illegal drinking hole?"

"Bootlegging, that's a serious charge!" Penelope admonished.

"So's murder," Stella deadpanned.

"Touché, Stella, touché," Penelope said.

In Stella's estimation, what was perhaps most upsetting to Dan was the fact that someone had died at his speakeasy from the lethal effects of home-distilled alcohol that was smuggled into the club unbeknownst to him. Though Dan was in no way culpable, the memory of a 22-year-old flapper expiring in his arms haunted him. Stella was there that night and witnessed the tragedy.

"White lightning killed that dumb Dora, pure and

simple," Stella opined.

"Lightning? Indoors?" Penelope said. "How is that possible?"

"Ya know, coffin varnish, busthead," Stella clarified.

Penelope looked at her vacantly.

"Come on … horse liniment … strike-me-dead?" Stella continued, becoming exasperated by Penelope's lack of comprehension.

"She means dangerous, probably homemade, bootleg liquor," Zara translated.

"At first I thought she'd just had a few too many belts and was blind," Stella recounted.

"Good heavens! Dan served liquor to a blind girl?" Penelope said.

"No … blind as in bent … ya know … zozzled?"

"Drunk," Zara told Penelope.

"But then she just up and croaked," Stella said. "Butt me, Z?"

"Not a chance. Chief Harrison would most likely throw a fit if he caught you with a cigarette in your hand under his roof."

Stella folded her arms and scowled.

"And no doubt he'd blame me," Penelope added.

Zara and Stella both nodded in concurrence, and Zara turned her cigarette wand toward Stella. "Just one puff," the seasoned flapper said to her subordinate.

Stella took a long drag, then divulged how after the fatal incident with the girl at the speakeasy, she had ongoing rows with Dan every time she showed up on site. Dan feared for Stella's safety and was insistent she stay away from the place.

In the course of Stella's report, it came out that Florence Morgan had been drinking on the sly for years—more so since the constitutional ban on intoxicating beverages passed. Florence had enjoyed a glass of wine with dinner from the time she came of age and wasn't able to get to sleep without it—and didn't intend to try. The wine drinking in itself would not be deemed reprehensible were it not that she had been a vociferous advocate for the temperance movement, and that sort of hypocrisy would seriously undermine Mrs. Morgan's standing as matriarch of the community.

Stella further revealed that Elsie Davies suffered from a condition called bulimia, though Stella had never heard it discussed. She'd simply witnessed Elsie emptying her stomach on several occasions without Elsie's knowledge. As for Elsie's relationship with Dan Cooper, she had been his chief champion when he owned the saloon. He made a lot of money at the time and was able to provide nice things for Lily, along with footing the bill on extravagant dinners and outings for Lily and her best friend Elsie.

Additionally, he was able to provide the reporter an ongoing supply of loose-lipped, liquor-induced confessions from late night patrons—just the sort of thing a gossipmonger like Elsie thrived on. But when the saloon closed its doors, and Dan was no longer a top businessman or of use to her, Elsie changed her tune and reviled him, encouraging Lily to leave him for her own sake and reputation. Elsie's behavior was, in short, superficial and self-serving.

Throughout the course of the conversation, Stella mentioned that Vincent had inadvertently become a track star when in high school. She divulged that his incentive to run fast had nothing to do with excelling in sports and everything to do with escaping the clutches of his hot-tempered, violent father.

With each new seed of information Stella shared, Penelope and Zara inched their chairs closer toward her until they were practically sitting atop her.

"What can you tell us about Hank?" Zara asked when Stella ran out of things to say.

"That Joe Brooks plays it close to the vest," Stella said.

"What about how he's dressed?" Penelope asked.

"All right, little bearcat, what say ya bring it down to a flat tire level, so Penelope can follow along, huh?" Zara suggested.

"Posilutely," Stella said, giving Zara a knowing nod and wink.

Penelope sensed she may have been insulted, but didn't want to bring it up and risk diverging from the topic of Hank.

"Most of the women in town are in love with him, but he hasn't pursued any of them," Stella disclosed. "If ya ask me, he has some sort of sadness hanging over him. I've never found out what it is. Your grandaunt Dorothea Tate most likely knew. They were thick as thieves."

Penelope perked up. "Oh?"

"Yep, he talked to her more than he talked to anyone else in town ... and of course they were in the Bohemian Club together ... don't tell him I said that. He doesn't know I know. The club supposedly doesn't exist."

"The what?" Zara asked, her eyes alight with interest.

"It's a local thing."

"My sweet old grandaunt was in a secret club?"

Stella guffawed. "I don't know what sweet old lady you're talking about, but in Pacific Grove, your grandaunt was known as an explorer and adventurer. She was a real darb. Women were intimidated by her, and men wanted to be like her. That dame was one tough cookie! And boy, the stories she could tell! What a life she lived."

"But I always thought those stories were pleasant fictions ... works of her fanciful imagination," Penelope said.

"Boy, you really didn't know Dorothea at all, did ya," Stella said.

"I knew there was a reason I always liked Aunt Dee," Zara remarked, jumping up to ravage a bear claw as excitement coursed through her veins.

"Aunt Dee an adventurer? … And part of a secret society? …This is all too much to take in," Penelope said, holding her head in her hands.

"Well better unloose that corset of yours, Penny. The road ahead is unpaved," Stella proclaimed.

Penelope's chin dropped, and Zara burst out laughing. No one had called Penelope *Penny* since she graduated high school. Penelope too began to giggle, and Stella joined in and laughed along with them, though she hadn't the slightest idea what was so funny.

* * * *

Paolo returned from the Butterfly Café bearing a relish tray, Waldorf salad, grilled ham-and-cheese sandwiches, and triple berry pie just as Zara and Penelope were winding down their hysterics. He laughed along too, as he was used to doing whenever he didn't understand what was being said. Hubert Allen walked in shortly thereafter, bearing the sign Penelope had requested.

"My goodness, you're efficient," Penelope said, her mood ebullient after all Stella had imparted. "The sign looks marvelous, Mr. Allen. Won't you join us for lunch? There's plenty to go around."

"That would beh spleendeed, Mees Price. I haven't ehteen all day," he said, taking advantage of the opportunity to keep company with Zara.

"But earlier when I offered you a bear claw, I thought you said you'd just eat—" Penelope began.

Zara cut her off so as not to embarrass Hubert. "Stella, go grab another chair from the waiting room, won't you?"

Paolo dug in before Penelope had a chance to parcel out the food, while Zara supervised Hubert's hanging of the Tea and Sympathy sign.

"Simply smashing, Hubert!" Zara said, clapping in approval.

Hubert gave her a pleased but uninviting grin, licked his palm, and smoothed down his few remaining strands of hair.

"What is it, Stella?" Zara said quietly as Stella returned with a chair, looking to the ground and wiping her eyes with her sleeve.

"Men," Stella said under her breath.

"Did something happen between you and Vincent?" Zara asked.

"He says we're making a mockery of the law," Stella answered.

"I knew all of this decorating would get us into hot water," Penelope remarked, getting up to strip the room of its ornaments.

"You know what Eleanor Roosevelt said," Zara told Stella. "'A woman is like a tea bag—you can't tell how strong she is until you put her in hot water.'"

"No, it's not that," Stella said, sniffing.

"No?" Penelope asked, ceasing her décor removal.

"Vincent says setting up shop as female detectives is an affront to the men and laws that protect our streets … and that we'll just get in the way and officers will have to drop important work to ensure our safety."

"Oh does he now?!" Penelope fumed, standing defiantly.

Zara burst out giggling.

"Just what's so funny, Zara? He meant you too!" Penelope said.

"P, if I had a nickel for every time a man told me I couldn't do something … We'll get far more bees with honey than vinegar, trust me. Let 'em think we're weak and ineffectual. That'll make our jobs all the easier."

"How so?" Penelope asked, sitting back down and

taking a bite of her sandwich, the other half of which had been appropriated by Paolo when Penelope wasn't looking.

"The men will let their guard down around us and possibly even do our bidding if they don't view us a threat. Isn't that right, Hubert?"

"Yees, Mees Zara. No man could say no to you," Hubert said.

"Ya see, P?"

"All you have to do is appeal to their egos and they'll sing like canaries and jump when you call … Say, Hubert, I just noticed what a fine suit you're wearing today. Why, the cut makes you look so … ooh, what's the word … virile … P, I'm having a sudden craving for an egg cream. Do we have the makings?"

Penelope shook her head *no*.

"Not to worreh, Mees Zara. I know wheere to geet one. I shall rehturn shortleh."

"Aww, you really are a knight, Hubert. Thank you … and better make it four!" she cried out as he rushed from the building. "… See what I mean?" Zara said, leaning back in her chair with her hands behind her head.

"Remarkable," Penelope whispered.

Stella applauded.

"Now, back to that secret society you mentioned," Penelope prodded, eager to hear more about the town's mysterious subculture.

"Oh yes, let's hear more about that. Spill!" Zara said.

"Can't right now. The warden at home will wring my neck if I don't get back to do my chores. But I'll come 'round tomorrow. There's loads more to tell," Stella said, ecstatic to know she was able to impress the ladies with her knowledge.

"Can't you stay 'til Hubert returns with the egg creams?"

"Nah, but that's okay. I pass by the Butterfly on the

way home and I'll extort one from Uncle Hubert while he's picking them up."

"Smart girl," Zara said to Penelope, nodding in the direction of Stella who disappeared down the hall.

"Smart and informed," Penelope said, jotting down notes on the day's conversation as Paolo quietly snatched the rest of her sandwich.

The intelligence Stella shared provided Penelope more questions than answers. From the time Penelope arrived in Pacific Grove and received the antiques store keys from Bernard Beekham, she had been on the go nonstop, never really taking time to assess or reflect on her new life or the new people in it. The conversation with Stella gave her much-needed insight into the inner-workings and motivations of the folks she'd been laboring alongside, and she desperately yearned to find out more, especially about the Bohemian Club and her grandaunt—and Hank.

A loud thud roused Penelope from her contemplation. Paolo had dozed off in his chair and fallen to the floor. He cursed under his breath as he stumbled to retake his seat.

"Poor thing. He's not used to me getting him up before mid-day ... well, not dressed anyway," Zara said.

Penelope gurgled in disgust at the lascivious implication.

"Paolo, why don't you go on home. I know this must be awfully dull for you," Zara said in the loud voice she always used with Paolo, whose hearing was just fine.

He looked at her quizzically and raised his hands to signal he didn't understand.

"Tu," she said, pointing to him then pantomiming the steering of a car. "Casa."

"Casa," he repeated with a smile and hearty stretch. "Ciao, bella." He grabbed the car keys, kissed her mouth rapaciously (as was their custom) then swaggered out the jail cell.

"Well if that isn't catawampus," Penelope said. "Paolo's

going home to our house to sleep while you and I spend the night in a jail cell."

"And what a cell it is!" Zara cooed, jumping backward to sit on her cot, its featherbed enveloping her on either side.

"I'm with Paolo. I'm spent," Penelope said, curling up on her cot and closing her eyes.

"Miss Price!" a woman's voice boomed.

Penelope jumped with a scream and an involuntary flailing of limbs to see Florence Morgan standing at the cell door, her parasol firmly planted.

"I expected more of you, Miss Price!"

Penelope smoothed her skirt and hair. "Mrs. Morgan, I assure you, I had absolutely nothing to do with the demise of Dan Cooper."

"Pull yourself together, Miss Price, and focus on the issue at hand. Your innocence is obvious—at least to me. I'm certain you understand I cannot patronize an establishment run from prison and owned by a felon convicted of capital crimes and facing the gallows."

"Not to worry, Mrs. Morgan, I'm sure to be released eventually."

"Eventually is not good enough! I will not have the proprietress of the town's only tearoom incarcerated when she should be preparing for a coming-of-age tea dance I intend to host for Daniel Cooper's eldest daughter, Margaret."

"But isn't she only twelve?" Penelope asked sheepishly.

"The fact that the reception will be held four years hence is not the point, Miss Price! The fact that I require your exoneration is the point. Now, I understand you are moonlighting as an investigative agent," she said, tapping the Tea and Sympathy sign with the tip of her parasol.

"Yes, but I assure you it won't interfere with the tea—"

"*If* I may be permitted to finish?"

"Yes, of course, Mrs. Morgan."

"You may have gleaned that your grandaunt, Miss Tate, and I disagreed on many points … many, many points."

"No, I had no idea—"

"*But*, we were both staunch promoters of the fair treatment of women. A single woman or widow should have the right to earn a living as much as a man."

"Yes, ma'am?" Penelope said, having no idea where Florence was going with the conversation.

"That said, I would like to employ you and your Tea and Sympathy agency to investigate the death of Daniel Cooper, which I am aware has been determined conclusively to have occurred as a result of murder … Murder … here in Pacific Grove!"

"Don't you think Chief Harrison is up to the task?" Zara asked, goading Florence into proffering her opinion of the man.

"I insinuated no such thing, young lady! I have nothing but the highest regard for Chief Walter Harrison. He is a man of uncommon decency, uprightness and charity. It is for that very reason I wish to employ you ladies."

"I don't understand," Penelope said, her eyes glazing over.

"P, I think what Mrs. Morgan means is that Chief Harrison must uphold the letter of the law and adhere to strict rules of conduct … whereas … well … we, as civilians, may take far greater liberties."

"But what—" Penelope interjected.

"Penelope was suggesting much the same thing just before you arrived," Zara told Florence.

"Ohhhhhhh," Penelope said, nodding slowly as comprehension dawned on her.

Florence opened her dignified pocketbook and produced a check already made out to Tea and Sympathy Investigative Agency.

"Oh, Mrs. Morgan, that's very generous of you, but I can't take your money, really," Penelope said.

"Nonsense! I have made my thoughts on single ladies in business quite clear. And I fully intend to be your first paying customer. In fact, I insist on it. It's the Panglossian in me, you see," she said, holding out the check.

"I really don't know what to say, Mrs. Morgan."

"Say *thank you*, and that we'll solve the case, P," Zara said as she gracefully took the check from Florence's outstretched hand and passed it to Penelope.

"Yes, thank you, Mrs. Morgan. We'll get you out of jail just as soon as we can," Penelope said, her mouth going dry.

"I beg your pardon?"

"Not to worry, Mrs. Morgan," Zara said calmly. "When she's on the verge of a brilliant thought her mind outraces her mouth and she makes no sense."

"Oh … I see," Mrs. Morgan said, looking sideways at Penelope.

"Sign of a true genius, they say," Zara added, escorting Florence from the room.

"One more thing," Florence said, turning and facing Penelope.

"I am aware Judge Houston will be back in two days and that he will determine your bail. Rest assured, I will cover that cost, to ensure you are released and can vigorously attack the case. Until that time, we must see to it you have all that you need to work from here. I note your creature comforts have been handled," Florence said, looking around the cell that increasingly resembled a bordello. "I will be here promptly at eight tomorrow morning for you to question me. At that time, I hope you will give me a list of the others you wish to interrogate and I will see them brought to you."

"Oh … yes … that would be very helpful … uh … would you like any sort of refreshment?"

"Miss Price—"

"No, you're right. A murder investigation is no place for tea and scones."

"On the contrary. We are not huns, Miss Price. I suggest you wield some of your esculent magic and produce something worthy of my faith in you. I wish to inform my circle of your ongoing success, even while caged. Now I really must go."

"Playing auction bridge with the mayor?" Penelope asked with a jaunty smile.

"Hardly. I will be reading to our incapacitated boys at the veteran's convalescent home. They're keen to hear what happens next to Mr. Pickwick and Sam Weller … and so am I," she said as she tapped her parasol twice on the ground and perambulated off.

"My my, who woulda thunk it," Zara said.

"Do you ever feel like you're living in a fool's paradise?" Penelope said.

"Only every day of my life since I left San Pedro at eighteen … So, what can we expect in the way of interrogation edibles tomorrow?" Zara said, lying on her stomach on the cot and pulling a pillow under her chest.

"I have no idea! You know I can't cook!"

"You certainly bamboozled Florence Morgan. She believes you possess *esculent magic*," Zara said with an amused grin.

"All I did was combine things already prepared by Dan Cooper. The closest I ever came to actual cooking was making macaroni over my hot plate!"

"Well you better think of something fast. You're a tearoom owner now."

"Whose cook is dead … How in heaven's name could anyone think I killed him? I'm lost without him!"

"Leave everything to me," Zara said casually.

Penelope snorted. "But you're even more inept at cooking than I!"

"Depends what you mean by cooking … What *I'm* cooking up is a plan. I'll be back in a minute," she said, gamboling off her cot and strutting down the hall with a hitch in her step, the way she always did when she felt on top of the world.

In Zara's absence, Penelope looked over the notes her partner had taken during their meeting with Florence Morgan.

"These are dreck!" she said aloud, turning the page this way and that, trying make out recognizable words and phrases. She then transcribed the bits and pieces of information as best she could, filling in the gaping holes while the material was fresh in her mind.

A few moments later Zara returned, still in full swagger.

"These notes on Mrs. Morgan are woefully wanting!" Penelope said.

"Never mind that. Culinary help is on its way."

"Z, I need to learn how to do this on my own. Mrs. Morgan is expecting it. I can't call in a ringer."

"Who said anything about a ringer?"

"Zara, tell me what's going on!"

"Oh, hold your water. You'll thank me later."

Several minutes later, Constable Jimmy Matlin arrived, walking slowly and carrying three egg creams. "Mr. Allen said to tell you it will take him a couple of hours to get everything on your list," he relayed, looking adoringly at Zara instead of at the egg cream dripping down his sleeve.

"Good boy, Jimmy. And one other thing," Zara said.

"Anything!" he said, putting the drinks down clumsily and creating a puddle of cream on the table.

"I'll need your keys," she said, gliding over to him and gazing dreamily into his eyes as she unclipped the key ring from his trousers' belt loop. He opened his mouth to remonstrate, but she put a finger to his lips. "We girls need our privacy. You wouldn't want some lout creeping in here in the middle of the night and doing God knows what, would you, Jimmy?"

"Golly, no!" the infatuated constable protested.

"Now you run along and wait for Mr. Allen. Toodle-oo!"

He jogged off, whistling.

"Hubert Allen? I don't understand," Penelope said, becoming agitated.

"If Mohammed can't come to the kitchen, the kitchen will come to Mohammed," Zara said with a smile.

"A whole kitchen?!"

"Just a few things to help you whip up something for Florence Morgan in the morning."

"And just what is it I'll be 'whipping up?'"

"Kanelbulle, if you must know."

"Canalbool? I don't even know how to say it, let alone know how to make it … whatever it is!"

"You'll be fine. It's the original cinnamon roll, originated in Sweden."

"Another something you learned from that Swedish telephone inventor you mentioned?"

"From his housekeeper, Alva, actually."

"But I don't have a Swedish cookbook … and even if I did, I don't read Swedish!" Penelope said, pacing and wringing her hands, her breath labored.

"Easy, girl! You're working yourself into a state! I've left instructions for Hubert to bring a copy of Mrs. Beeton's, the book your mother used to swear by."

Penelope looked at her blankly for a moment, then opened her arms to embrace her. "Oh, Z, you remember that?"

"How could I forget?" Zara said sentimentally. "Hanging around the kitchen baking with your mother …"

"You mean dipping our fingers into the batter and having them whacked with a wooden spoon while Mother did all the baking," Penelope corrected.

"Exactly," she said, disengaging from their hug. "Now, what do we do in the interim?"

"Well … I suppose we should go over the treasure trove of information Stella supplied."

Zara set the jail keys on the table.

"Say, what was that all about?" Penelope asked, nodding at the keys.

"Last night I caught sight of young Jimmy hovering over me in my sleep."

"Saints preserve us!" Penelope exclaimed, standing up to peer down the hall and close the cell door.

"No reason to call in the saints. I know the type. He's harmless … a tad creepy, but harmless."

Penelope shuddered and sat down to make notes on Stella's testimony, all the while, keeping a wary eye on the door. "Let's discuss Stella's disclosures, shall we?"

They tried to recount all Stella had said, often coming back to the topic of Pacific Grove's secret society. Both were intrigued and couldn't wait to find out more. Soon enough, Hubert Allen arrived bearing baking supplies.

"What's all this?" Penelope asked, her eyes lighting up.

"You're a prince, Hubert," Zara said, blowing him a kiss.

He snickered salaciously as he unpacked boxes from a hand-pulled wagon.

"Oh, Z, look! There's even a hotplate!" Penelope gushed.

"Of course!" Zara replied casually.

"But why did you have poor Mr. Allen bring all these unopened ingredients? We could've just had Paolo collect things from home."

"I rang him first, but he didn't answer. I forgot how terrified he is of answering the telephone."

"Yees, heez language leemeetations are a probleem," Hubert said.

Zara bit her lip to keep from laughing.

Hubert made quick work of the unpacking and prepared to leave.

"Thank you, Hubert—sincerely," Penelope said.

He put his hat on and bid them goodnight.

"Say, Hubert. You wouldn't know anything about a secret society called the Bohemian Club, would you?" Zara called as he walked down the hall.

He stopped in his tracks and stiffened, then returned to the cell.

"Wheere deed you her of that?" he said in a low, tense tone.

"Your goddaughter, Stella, mentioned it," Penelope said.

"Sheh shouldn't have done that," he said.

"So, then you *do* know of it," Zara said, pulling out a chair for him.

"Yees," he said curtly.

"Is it true that my grandaunt was part of it?"

"Yees," he said, looking unconsciously around the empty cell as if to see if someone were listening.

"And Hank?" Zara asked.

"You would have to ask heem."

"Hubert," Zara said, gently placing a hand on his forearm. "Stella was not the first person to tell us about the Bohemian Club. Aunt Dee's personal notebooks are full of details on the club's activities, and history ... and members. Isn't that right, P," she said, encouraging Penelope to play along.

"Yes," she said, sitting up straighter. "My grandaunt left me copious notes on the subject."

He scrutinized her face for a long moment. "I find that

hard to behlehv," he said, sitting back in his chair and folding his arms.

Penelope looked to Zara for help. Zara gave a negligible shake of her head to indicate she had nothing to say to persuade Hubert. Penelope took a gamble and went on the offensive.

"Mr. Allen, I assure you I take this matter quite seriously. Frankly, I hadn't even mentioned the B.C. to Zara. Your goddaughter did. My grandaunt Dorothea stipulated I maintain the antiques store for a reason. That reason has much to do with the B.C."

Zara leaned forward, engrossed by Penelope's oration. Penelope glanced up at Hubert and saw him stroking his chin. Her tenacity increasing, she pushed on. "There are a great many artifacts housed in the shop that are particular to the club. My grandaunt entrusted them to me … and expected me to follow in her footsteps as a member. I trust you will honor her wishes."

Zara's mouth dropped wide open as she gawped at Penelope's boldness. Hubert continued to stroke his chin, scrutinizing Penelope's expression and carriage.

"Why have you not brought thees up sooneer?" he asked.

"Good heavens, Mr. Allen! First I was trying to launch my business and now I'm trying to get out of jail … for murder!"

He sat silent again. "Your meembeership would have to beh approved by thee leddeership counceel—"

"May I join too?" Zara cooed.

"There eez only room for new meembeers wheen one passees, as is your friend Mees Pricee's case."

"He's right, Z," Penelope said, talking out of her hat.

"You undeerstand that your meembeersheep—eef approved—would beh of an honorareh nature. You would not have thee same preeveleegees as males weeth full-fleedged meembeersheeps."

"Yes, yes, Mr. Allen, I am well aware," Penelope answered, feigning annoyance. "However, I don't think we should discuss this further while in the company of ..." She tilted her head toward Zara, hinting to Hubert that they should cut the conversation short in front of her.

"Leet meh seh what I can do," he said, getting up to leave. "Again, goodnight. Thee ehveenin has benn, shall weh say, eenlighteeneng."

Penelope gave him a stately nod, her face stoic. Zara got up to pull closed the drapes she'd had installed in the cell. She then crept down the hall to confirm Hubert had gone. When she saw him exit the building, she ran back to the cell. There, the two friends took to jumping on their flimsy cots in giddy amazement.

"Penelope Price, you missed your calling!"

"As a thespian?"

"As a poker player! Never have I seen such bluffing! You were sensational!"

"I don't know what came over me, actually," Penelope said, descending from the cot.

"Maybe you were channeling Aunt Dee."

"Maybe ... I've never felt like that ... I rather liked it," she said, pacing as her heart raced.

"Brava, my friend ... Brava!"

"Whew, I feel like I just won the sweepstakes. Look, my hands are shaking ... What should we do now?"

"I would say let's eat dinner, but I think it's a little late for that," Zara said, consulting the clock figurine on the scarf-draped end table by her cot.

"I don't think I could eat anyway," Penelope said, still pacing in figure eights and trying to catch her breath.

"What about nibbling some of the leftover tri-berry pie?" Zara enticed.

"That's a different story."

Zara held up a pair of forks and the friends dug in, giggling, whispering and nibbling the night away.

# Chapter Fourteen

"Pssst, Miss Zara … Psssst … Psssssssssssssst."

Penelope awoke to the sound of Jimmy Matlin hissing.

"Who let the air out of that tire?!" Zara groaned as she put a pillow over her head.

"Wakey, wakey … Yooohooooooo."

"We're awake, Constable Matlin, thank you," Penelope said. "We'll be up in just a minute … Come on, Z. Time to get a move on."

"For cryin' out loud. It's the middle of the night," Zara whined.

"No it's not. It's morning—the time of day when most people wake up."

"But I'm not most people."

"Do you want Florence Morgan to catch you pouting in that whisper of lace you call a nightgown?"

"I dunno. Might do her a world of good," she said, smiling at the thought and rousing from her drowsy daze.

Penelope dressed quickly, then began assembling the items brought by Hubert. "Z, there's no milk or eggs. How can I make those cannibals without milk or eggs?" she said, her anxiety rising.

"It's too early for a panic attack, and besides, they're called kanelbulle," Zara said, walking to the door. "Oh Constable Matlin, we need youuuuu," she called in a melodious tone.

She'd scarcely gotten the words out of her mouth when Jimmy Matlin skidded up the hallway.

"Be a pet and get the eggs and milk Mr. Allen delivered, won't you?" Zara said, poking her head between the cell's curtains. "I believe they're in the station's icebox. There's a good fellow."

He ran dutifully to fulfill his charge.

"See? Another problem solved. That's what I do, solve

problems," Zara said, changing out of her nightgown and into a celadon, sleeveless drop-waste tunic, and wrapping herself in a fringed Oriental shawl before sliding open the draperies and unlocking the cell door.

Jimmy was back in an instant, lithering into the cell and hitting the bowl of eggs against the bars of the door.

"Careful! You'll break them!" Penelope shouted.

"She's a little on edge," Zara confided to Jimmy.

"Heck, I would be too if I was on trial for murder," he replied.

Penelope snatched the bowl of eggs from him and said, "No one's on trial yet. And even if I were, one is innocent until *proven* guilty."

"Can I help?" Jimmy asked. "I still have two more hours left on my shift and sure wouldn't mind having some of whatever it is you're making for breakfast."

"No, thank you," Penelope said. "Yes, we'd love your help," Zara said simultaneously.

"Hot dawg! Where do I start?" the constable asked.

"With this," Zara said, seductively tying a ruffled apron over his coat shoulders and around his waist as he wilted in pleasure at her touch.

"Oh, all right," Penelope snapped. "Just make sure not to get in the way."

"Yes, miss," he said.

"P, don't forget the flower petals on top like last time. That was a big hit with the ladies," Zara added. "A splash of lavender would look lovely, don't you think?"

"What I *think* is that I first need to bake something on which to sprinkle them," Penelope snapped.

"Coffee … that's what's missing," Zara said, turning to make a pot.

The coffee pot percolated, filling the cubicle with its aromatic welcome to a new day as Penelope tossed ingredients into a bowl, grumbling to herself and checking and rechecking the recipe. "How can this be? It doesn't say how long to let the dough rise," she worried.

"That's because it's a yeastless recipe. You just roll it out and throw it in the oven," Zara said.

"Z, you're a mastermind!"

Zara raised her coffee cup in acknowledgement.

"All right then—I think that's everything. Time to make some cannonballs," Penelope said, mopping her brow.

"What can I do?" Jimmy asked.

"How about you stir it all together while I make myself a cup of coffee," Penelope said, starting to relax.

"Builds strong arm muscles," Zara said with a wink.

Jimmy began stirring furiously, and shortly thereafter proudly announced, "It's all mixed together."

"Good, now just roll out the dough, making sure to sprinkle a little flour on the board as well," Penelope directed, sitting down and putting her feet up on a spare chair.

Jimmy carried out his instructions just as he heard them, and sprinkled *a little flower* on the board—specifically, the tiny petals from a sprig of lavender. "Done!" he exclaimed.

"That's fine. Now just spoon out that bowl of cinnamon filling on top of the dough … nice and even, please," Penelope said, enjoying her temporary respite from care and labor.

"You're doing beautifully, Jimmy—a real natural," Zara said, smiling and crinkling up her nose in a beguiling way.

"Okay, now what?" Jimmy said, working up a sweat in his heavy uniform and apron.

"Now we roll it up and cut it," Penelope said, finishing her coffee and getting up to wind the dough.

"Good heavens! What have you done?!" she shouted, noticing the lavender bits on the bottom of the dough as she rolled it.

"I did just what you said," Jimmy pleaded.

"But what is this?!" she said, pointing to the lavender.

"You said to be sure to sprinkle a little flower onto the board ... and Miss Zara suggested using lavender," he explained, perspiration dripping from his temples.

Penelope looked aghast at Zara.

Zara burst out laughing. "It's true, P. We both did say that."

"We don't have enough ingredients to start over," Penelope said as she frantically looked through the items on the table. "I'm ruined," she said, dropping into a chair.

"Baloney. Just say you meant for it to turn out like that. I'll tell Mrs. Morgan I've seen it done that way in Paris. *Cinnamon lavender buds*, we'll call them."

"Why buds?" Penelope asked indifferently.

"Because when you roll them they look like a flower bud. They'll be a smash, you'll see."

"I hope you're right," Penelope said, returning to roll the dough.

"Aren't I always?"

Penelope lifted an eyebrow in response.

"I notice you didn't try to refute me—'cause you can't," Zara said with a grin.

"So then everything's gonna be okay?" Jimmy asked, wiping his worried brow.

"Of course it is," Zara said, patting his knee.

Penelope rolled up the lavender-crusted dough, sliced it, and tucked the rounds in a pan then placed the pan on the hot plate Hubert provided, covered the pan, and turned on the heat.

"Is that it then?" Jimmy asked, eager to be done.

"Just need to make the icing," Penelope said, pouring confectioner's sugar into a bowl.

"Would you like some coffee, Jimmy? You look like

you could use it," Zara offered.

"Never touch the stuff. Stunts your growth," the below-average-height constable answered.

"I believe Mr. Allen brought some fresh orange juice as well. It should be in the ice box if you'd like some," Zara said.

"Yes, ma'am," he said, trudging down the hall still wearing the ruffle-edged apron.

"I think you wore him out," Penelope said, smiling as she cut bits of butter and cream cheese into a bowl.

"Well if that's all it takes," Zara said, winking. "You doing all right, constable?" she asked as Jimmy slogged back into the room holding a frosty glass bottle of orange juice. "Here, let me pour you some. Why don't you sit down?"

"This cooking is hard work," he said, dabbing the moisture from his sideburns. "I don't know how you womenfolk do it?"

"Neither do I," Zara said. "How do you do it, P?" she said with a wry smile.

"With a very large wooden spoon," Penelope said, threatening Zara. "Now where did I put the vanilla?" she said quietly, looking around the table.

"Here it is," Jimmy offered enthusiastically, reaching to grab it and inadvertently toppling his orange juice flute into Penelope's mixing bowl.

"For crying out loud, Jimmy!" Penelope barked. "Now you've wrecked the icing with your orange juice!"

"There was only a little left. I can try to spoon it out," Jimmy said apologetically.

"Breathe, P. Breathe."

"I'm fine," she said with a huff, pushing the bowl away. "I don't have my corset on yet."

Zara giggled. "Well, you know what they say, 'If you have a lemon, make a lemonade.'"

"Yes, but this is an orange," Penelope replied, pouting. After a moment, she leaned forward and continued mixing the icing, sampling a little from a spoon when all the ingredients had been incorporated. "Not half bad," she said, her eyes widening. "Try some."

Zara put a finger in and licked the icing off salaciously for the benefit of Jimmy on whom she took pity. "Scrumptious! Try some, Jimmy," she said, handing him an icing-coated spoon.

"Wow, this really is good!" he said, smiling brightly.

"Cinnamon lavender buds with orange icing ... Yes, you're sure to have Florence Morgan eating out of your hand ... literally," Zara said with a dimple-accented smile.

Jimmy and the jailbirds enjoyed a casual conversation as the buns baked on the hotplate, filling the stationhouse with their warm and inviting aroma. By and by, Penelope excused herself to the bathroom to don her corset. The table was cleaned off and a fresh cloth lain, and all was in readiness for Florence Morgan's visit.

The tap of a parasol on the bars of the cell door indicated she'd arrived. Penelope and Jimmy jumped up, and Jimmy saluted, still wearing the apron.

"As you were, constable ... Is this a new addition to your uniform?" Florence asked dryly, lifting the apron with the end of her parasol.

"No ma'am, I was just ... My shift is over actually," he said, removing the apron and tugging down on his coattails. "You won't tell the chief, will you, Mrs. Morgan?"

"I don't see there's anything to tell," she said matter-of-factly. "Now what is that enticing smell I noticed upon entering the building?"

\* \* \* \*

The interview with Florence Morgan went relatively smoothly, owing in great part to the beneficence and determination of Mrs. Morgan herself who spoon-fed

Penelope the questions she should ask. Zara was tasked with taking notes, and Penelope was in charge of interrogation. Neither was particularly competent in her position. Zara became far too engrossed in Florence's answers to write anything down, and Penelope lacked diplomacy, often asking questions that were indelicate and making statements that were blunt and off-color. All was forgiven thanks to the success of the breakfast buns.

"Miss Price, you are a savant!" Florence said as she accepted the basket of leftovers Penelope wrapped up for her to take. "Lavender ... and orange! Who would've concocted such a pairing with the humble sweet roll. I am mightily impressed.

"The board of the YWCA is meeting at my house this morning to vote on a matter close to my heart, and I believe your pastries may be the very thing needed to swing the vote in my favor. In fact, I think I shall use them as tools of bribery, or would it be blackmail?" She tittered to herself, shocked at her audacity, then whispered, "Not the thing one should say in these environs." She then saluted with her parasol and snuck out of the cell, still giggling.

A few moments later, she returned. "One more thing—a piece of advice, if you'll allow me. Miss Price, I am aware you've been employed as a bookkeeper and have an eye for detail when it comes to facts and figures."

"Yes, Mrs. Morgan?" Penelope queried.

"And you, Miss Zara, while I don't know if you have ever been employed, or in what capacity, I notice that you possess tact along with keen and subtle powers of persuasion ... especially where the opposite sex is concerned."

Zara nodded tactfully.

"I believe you, Miss Zara, would be best suited to asking the questions and Miss Price to logging the answers. That is my advice ... as a paying client. Good day, ladies," she said, tapping her parasol twice on the floor and turning on her heel.

Penelope and Zara stamped their feet and squealed in celebration until they heard the words, "Good morning, Mrs. Morgan," from a male voice down the hall.

"Oh no! The chief!" Penelope said, feverishly trying to hide the evidence of their breakfast meeting.

Chief Harrison read the Tea and Sympathy Investigative Agency sign hanging on the cell door, looked to the ground, and covered his mouth for a moment, striving with all his might not to laugh.

"Good morning, Chef Harrison," Penelope said as she stood at attention, looking painfully guilty.

"Chef? Looks more like *you're* the chef," he said, taking in the myriad changes in décor since his last visit.

Zara handed him a pastry and a cup of coffee laced with a splash of milk.

"You read my mind," he said, accepting the treats. He then looked into the cup and asked, "How did you know how I take my coffee?"

Zara shrugged enchantingly and sat down, acting more modest and demure than she normally did around men.

"*Chief* Harrison, I can explain—" Penelope began.

"Save your breath, Miss Price. You'll get to do plenty of explaining to Judge Houston. He'll be returning from his fishing trip mid-day."

Penelope took a deep breath, stood tall, and extended her wrists for shackling. "I'm ready."

He chuckled. "Well Judge Houston is not. He'll see you at his bench at nine tomorrow morning."

"Yes, sir," Penelope said, placing her unmanacled wrists behind her back before the chief changed his mind.

"You'll need a business permit for that you know," he said, raising his coffee cup toward the Tea and Sympathy sign.

"For the sign?" Penelope screeched.

"I believe he means for the business, P," Zara said.

Chief Harrison nodded while taking a swig from his coffee cup.

"Yes sir, right away," Penelope said. "Shall I make an appointment with you now?" she added nervously.

"Just come down the hall when you're ready ... which reminds me, do either of you have Jimmy Matlin's keys?"

Zara produced the key ring and held it out for the chief.

"Why don't you hold onto them, Miss Zara. You probably keep better track of them than he does ... Ladies," he said, holding his cup aloft and moseying back down the hall.

Zara sat down and began touching up her makeup and hair.

"Whew, that was a close one," Penelope said, fanning herself with a tea towel.

"Not at all, I told ya he's a teddy bear."

"More like a grizzly, if you ask me ... Where are you going?"

"To get that business permit, of course. We want to prove we're conscientious businesswomen who handle things promptly, don't we?" Zara said, dropping her shawl just below her shoulders and sashaying down the hall.

Penelope looked on in bewilderment, then set to cleaning up the multi-purpose table that served as a kitchen, dining area, and detective office. A few moments, later Stella showed up.

"What's cookin'?" the junior detective asked, inhaling the lingering scent of the baked goods.

"Cinnamon lavender buds with orange icing," Penelope said absentmindedly, handing one to Stella.

"Whats? ... Say, where's Zara," she asked, her mouth full as she devoured the pastry and helped herself to another.

"In with Chief Harrison."

"He giving her the third degree?" she asked as she poured a mug of coffee and sat Indian style in one of the folding chairs.

"Beats me."

"I was kidding. I don't even think he knows what the third degree is."

"I can't figure him out," Penelope said, shaking her head bemusedly.

"Don't you have other things to figure out … like who killed Dan?"

"Good point, Stella. You know, you're a very level-headed young lady."

"I am? Gee, no one's ever called me that before," she said, smiling through a mouth ringed with orange icing. "So … where do we start?"

"I'm guessing *you* start by going to school. Aren't you late for class?"

She shrugged. "It's a science class and since our teacher Mr. Gould says *time is relative*, I decided to take him at his word."

"You're too clever for your own good," Penelope said, folding a piece of paper into an envelope on which she wrote the words: *Mr. Allen.* "Here's something you can do—take this to your godfather, please."

"What is it?"

"It's sealed, that's what it is," Penelope said, giving Stella a cautioning look.

"And what do I do after that?"

"You go to school. You may come visit after all of your classes today, if you like. I should have something that will be of interest to you by then, but not before then. Do you understand?"

"Yes, commander," Stella said half-heartedly, holding the envelope up to the light to try to make out its contents.

"Stella," Zara said with a nonchalant nod as she

entered the cell, fanning herself with a folded sheet of paper.

"Zara," the girl mimicked.

"Stella was just leaving for school," Penelope said.

"Get her!" Stella said, pointing to Penelope.

"Good!" Zara said.

"Don't tell me you're becoming a fire extinguisher too!" Stella said to Zara.

"Nothing of the sort. We need eyes and ears at the school. Take note of anything unusual your classmates say about the night Dan perished."

"Oh … well when you put it like that …" Stella said.

"Remember, anything unusual," Zara said, swiping her forefinger across her nose in solidarity.

"Gotcha," Stella said, returning the gesture and departing.

"Mrs. Morgan was right," Penelope said. "You have a knack for this work. What was that you were fluttering in your hand, by the way?"

"Oh, nothing—just the business permit for the Tea and Sympathy Investigative Agency," she said with an exaggerated air of superiority.

"So fast? How did you—"

"Nothing to it. I told Chief Harrison what I wanted, he filled in the paperwork, we chitchatted about this and that, and voila!"

"Voila, indeed!" Penelope said, viewing the document with admiration. "Excellent work with Stella, by the way. I think she believed every word."

"So did I! Once I said it, I realized it actually made sense!"

"Now, let's see who we can interview today. I want to get as much done as possible before I appear before the judge tomorrow."

"P, you do realize he's only going to set your bail tomorrow. It's not your trial."

"Yes … I just want to be prepared is all."

"Cara mia!" Paolo gushed as he breezed into the cell and covered Zara with kisses.

"Not in front of Penelope," she said awkwardly.

"Dove … tu?" he asked, holding his hands in the air and shaking his head in confusion.

"Where have I been?" Zara translated. "Why here, of course. I couldn't get home. You have the car, you know."

He looked at her enquiringly. She pointed to him and then made the gesture of steering a car, "Tu … auto."

"Ohhhhhhhh," he said, at last comprehending she'd been stranded at the police station without him or the car. "Bacio," he said, placing a finger on his cheek, requesting a kiss.

She kissed his cheek in what Penelope regarded as a sisterly sort of way.

"Notizie?" he asked.

"Notizie? I'm afraid I don't know that word. Non capisco," Zara said loudly.

"Uh, informazioni?" he said.

"I think he's asking if we have any news … new information?" Penelope said.

"Si!" Paolo said, pointing to Penelope in confirmation.

"A little," Penelope said.

Zara made a hand gesture with her forefinger and thumb to indicate a small amount.

"Chi," he said, then made a slash across the throat gesture, "Dan?"

"Who killed Dan? We have no idea," Penelope said, shaking her head.

Paolo pulled Zara in close to him and squeezed her, indicating he would keep her safe. She stood rigidly in his arms.

"What say we get back to work, eh?" Zara said.

"Yes, let's. Now, who's on our list of interviewees? ... Zara, I can't read these notes at all."

"All the more reason you should be the scribe and I the voice."

"Why do I suddenly feel like Watson to your Holmes?"

"Because I smoke a pipe, would be my guess."

**\* \* \* \***

The ladies worked diligently to piece together what they knew about whom and how it all tied together. They didn't get far.

"We need to get our questions down pat," Penelope said. "We want to ask where each person was between the time I last saw Dan and the time he was found dead at the tearoom."

"I wouldn't lead with that," Zara cautioned. "You'll make people defensive out of the gate."

"Fair enough. That's where your diplomacy comes in. We should also ask how each person knew Dan, what their relationship was like, if they knew of any reason anyone would want to harm him or if he had any enemies."

"I'm with ya."

"We should really practice. Shall we start with Paolo?"

"We can try, but I wouldn't expect too much."

Zara did her best to pantomime the questions to Paolo as Chief Harrison noted when returning his empty coffee cup to the cell. He took his time, remaining for a moment to observe her entertaining antics as she mimed wildly and to no avail.

"He knows bupkis," Zara finally said, collapsing in a sweat from her inquiries and attendant gymnastics.

"Mangia?" asked the ever-hungry Paolo.

"Yes, si, mangia, why not!" Zara said in frustration.

"Z, why don't you and Paolo swing by the tearoom and collect the perishables. We'll see what we can throw together here on our hotplate."

"But what if you need me? We can just send Paolo, and I can stay here with you."

"No, no. I'll be fine. I'd like to have some time alone to cogitate anyway."

"All right … if you're sure."

"Yes, I'm sure. Now you two lovebirds run along. I have lots to work out."

"Venga," Zara said, beckoning Paolo to follow—more in the manner of a master commanding his dog than a lover inviting her paramour to steal away with her.

As Zara and Paolo exited, Penelope gleefully took out her yarn and knitting needles. "I'm going to figure you out, and I'm going to figure this case out. Mark my words," she informed the spool.

Penelope pondered a variety of topics as she sat and knitted. The ones that kept creeping to the forefront of thought were the Bohemian Club and Hank. She hadn't seen much of Hank in recent days, following weeks of seeing him daily, and she unreasonably feared that during the interim he might have forgotten who she was altogether. Her stomach knotted, and she presumed she was in need of food. Her contemplations did nothing for her knitting that began to take the shape of a short twisted ladder of haphazardly woven overworked wool.

'Knit one, pearl two … more like knit two, unravel one," Penelope said aloud as she wrestled with her project, pulling it this way and that in an effort to flatten the stitches into submission.

"Back so soon?" she asked as she heard Zara and Paolo approach.

"We've been gone well over an hour," Zara said. "I tried to explain to Paolo that he could go home if he'd like since you and I will just be talking shop and he'd be bored to distraction. But whether the language issue or the lure of a hot meal, it looks like he's staying."

"Tu … cucina … mangia … Italia?" Penelope said to Paolo in very broken Italian. "You cook Italian food?"

"Italia?! Si!" he cheered, his eyes lighting up at the prospect. Immediately he tied on an apron and began peeling tomatoes.

"Looks like you're not the only problem-solver in this company," Penelope crowed.

"Not bad, P," Zara said approvingly. "So, any revelations in my absence?"

"Yes, I can't knit," Penelope said.

Both chuckled.

"While I was gone I did some thinking as well," Zara said. "And I believe the sooner we get to the bottom of this business with the secret society, the better."

"I agree. I wonder who else in town is a member."

"So far we know about Aunt Dee, Hubert, and Hank. We should really interview Hank," Zara said.

"I wonder if Dan Cooper was a member," Penelope said, trying to change the subject to hide her excessive interest. "Perhaps his death has something to do with the club."

"You mean maybe he let leak that they sacrifice virgins or something of that ilk?"

"I certainly hope not! *Euuuff!* You gave me the chills!"

"Sorry, P. I'm just being dramatic."

"Unless they actually *do* do that sort of thing."

"We definitely need to interview Hank … and soon."

**\* \* \* \***

After preparing a Bolognese sauce, Paolo made pasta noodles from scratch, kneading the dough, cutting it, twisting it and pulling it into long tendrils that he dropped into boiling water. He then prepared a simple salad of greens, cucumbers, and cheese with an oil and vinegar dressing he carelessly tossed together. When he was done with the preparations, he lit the candelabra, laid the food out, and drew the curtains in order to cut down on the amount of light in the room, beckoning the ladies to join him at the table.

"Oh Paolo, this is beautiful!" Penelope said. "I wish I had a photograph."

"I wish I had a jug of wine," Zara said wistfully.

After the meal, Penelope surreptitiously collected her toiletries and said, "I know you two haven't had much time together the way you're accustomed to. I apologize for that. Why don't you enjoy some privacy and the candlelight. I'm going to take a bath."

"Don't let us run you out, P," Zara called out as Penelope walked down the hall to the bathroom.

The police station boasted several showers in one room and a single bathtub in another. Penelope was grateful to have some real privacy away from the steady stream of visitors and even Zara. She knew she should be worried that she was in jail and about to be arraigned on murder charges, but somehow, it didn't faze her. What weighed far more heavily on her mind was the thought of the Bohemian Club and their rituals—rituals in which Hank may have participated.

When Penelope returned to the cell she found Paolo had gone.

"What, no dessert?" she joked.

"Not tonight," Zara replied. "I told Paolo my head was killing me and sent him home. I don't think he was too happy about it."

"Everything all right, Z? You haven't seemed like yourself the last couple days."

"I must be catching something. I feel a little off …

Like I said, headache and all. Mind if we call it an early night? It's been a long day."

"Oh … ehrm, by all means. I forgot you're not used to getting up when the clock points to the single numbers in the morning."

"That's when I'm used to getting my night started," she said with a wan smile.

"I'm actually rather tired too. Will you want to sleep in late tomorrow morning to get back on your usual slugabed schedule?"

"No. I think it's time for me to try a new regimen. Besides, your arraignment is at nine."

"It certainly is," Penelope said with an apprehensive sigh.

After performing their evening constitutionals, both crawled into their cots and turned off the lights.

"Aren't you forgetting something, Z?"

"Ah yes, that's right," she said, getting up to draw the curtains for maximum coverage, and locking the door of the cell.

A few minutes later, Penelope spoke. "You still awake?"

"… Maybe."

"I just wanted to tell you … I love you, Z."

"You're okay in my book too, P."

The friends closed their eyes and enjoyed the silence.

About ten minutes later, Constable Matlin arrived on the scene, trying the cell door. "Pssst, Miss Zara … are you in there? … Yoohoooooo."

They both held their breath until his fading footsteps suggested he was gone, then burst into a short fit of giggles. Soon they were quiet again and both drifted off to a deep sleep.

# Chapter Fifteen

They awoke the next morning to find a newspaper slid under the door with a daisy atop it—clearly the work of Jimmy Matlin.

"Looks like you made the headlines again, P," Zara said, squeezing onto the tiny cot with her and unfurling the paper.

## Jailbird Diva Transforms Brig into a Drawing Room

If there's no rest for the wicked, then suspected murderess Miss Penelope Price has been working overtime. Turning the lockup into a lounge, her cell is decorated with more comforts than most readers' homes. When not knitting or cooking up new taste sensations such as Cinnamon Lavender Buds with Orange Icing, she can be found serving lavish meals to guests and holding court at the newly permitted Tea and Sympathy Investigative Agency. Expect more on this mercurial lady of business after her arraignment tomorrow.

"Don't these people have anything more interesting to write about?" Penelope blustered.

"Not likely. It's a small town. That usually means small minds, or at least small news. Your activities may very well be the most excitement this hamlet's seen in years."

"How is that possible when they're the home of a secret society?!"

"Ahhh, but that's just it; the society's a secret. Not exactly the thing they splash across the front page of the public paper. As you recall, you didn't find out much about the Bohemians at the library."

"What's a bearcat, by the way?" Penelope asked.

"A celebrated and successful woman—the type who gets what she wants."

Penelope gasped. "Did they mean me?"

"Looks that way, hotshot. The way others see you in this town is a sight different than how you see yourself."

"Apparently," Penelope said, floored by the way she'd been depicted in the newspaper and the fact than she'd been mentioned in it repeatedly. "Where are you going?" she asked as Zara scrambled out of bed.

"To start the coffee, of course! You have a big day … and a matinal one at that."

"I still can't get used to you being coherent before noon. It upsets the natural order of things."

"Well you know how I love to upset the natural order," Zara said with a smile. "Now, tell me, what will you be wearing to court today?"

Penelope pointed to an ensemble she'd hung on the cell bars the night before. It included an ecru and taupe striped skirt, ecru high-neck collared blouse with eyelet accents, button-up ivory shoes, kid gloves, and a toque hat accented with ivory ribbon roses.

"Don't tell me … too dowdy," Penelope said.

"Just dowdy enough!" Zara said.

"I would say, 'thank you,' but I'm not sure it was a compliment."

"It was. Your wardrobe is perfect—tasteful, proper … so very very proper."

"Hmmm," Penelope said, pulling her mouth to one side incredulously.

**＊ ＊ ＊ ＊**

After dressing, Penelope set to tidying up the cell on the outside chance the judge might happen to drop by unexpectedly. Zara dressed quickly then sat down to repose with coffee and the newspaper while nibbling leftover bits of the now famous cinnamon buds from the day before.

"Aren't you going to eat anything?" Zara said. "You really should. Don't want you fainting in court … although that could curry sympathy …"

"I'm far too nervous to eat anything," Penelope said, starting to pace in a circle around the table.

"You really need to relax, P. What's the worst that could happen?"

Penelope stopped and glared at her.

"Okay, aside from the electric chair …"

"So many things, Z. Life in prison … never getting the chance to get justice for Dan."

"Point taken," Zara said, licking the last of the orange icing off her finger.

A quiet knock on the wall of their cell attracted their attention.

"It's time, Miss Price," Chief Harrison said.

Penelope smoothed her skirt and drew back the curtain shrouding the cell.

"I'm ready, Chief Harrison," she said, placing her hat on her head and unsuccessfully trying to pin it with shaking hands.

"Let me do that for you," Zara said, getting up to assist.

"Miss Zara," Chief Harrison said with a polite nod.

"Chief Harrison," she returned with a demure smile and slight bend of her knee.

"Did you just curtsy?" Penelope whispered as Zara scooted her toward the door.

"You're becoming delusional ... Now chin up. I'll be in the courtroom cheering you on. And if things get really ugly, I'll create a diversion, Paolo will throw you over his shoulder, and we'll all make a run for the border."

Penelope smiled despite herself, and the friends embraced. The chief held the door open as Penelope straightened her shoulders and began walking down the hall as if attending a funeral. He then escorted her to an antechamber and instructed her to sit quietly until he came for her.

The dark windowless vestibule was no bigger than three feet square and stripped of all ornamentation. Penelope shuddered to picture herself living in such a confined space if convicted. A side door opened, and the bright light from the room beyond blinded her for a moment.

"Come with me, Miss Price," she heard the chief say as he gently took her arm and led her into the courtroom.

She squinted wildly, trying to see where she was going, and ended up stumbling into the witness box. Chief Harrison stopped and turned her around. The sound of clanking metal and the feel of discomfort on her wrist told her she was being fettered.

"Is that really necessary, Chief Harrison?" she whispered.

"No, but it is the law here in Pacific Grove," he said quietly.

As Penelope's eyes adjusted, she saw that she stood in a small, sequestered box containing a wooden armchair, and that she was fenced in by wrought iron railing, to which she was shackled. Looking around the courtroom, she noted it was jam-packed, and that all eyes were fixed on her. She'd just begun to sit when she heard the words: All rise for the honorable Francis Houston.

She froze and gulped.

A short man with robes far too long for his stature took the bench. His face was inordinately sunburned save for two round white circles surrounding his eyes.

"All may be seated," a disembodied voice said.

"Now what do we have here?" the judge asked, followed by a sneeze and loud blowing of his nose.

"Bless you, judge," someone called out.

"Thank you, Mrs. Prescott," the judge said.

Penelope shrank at the sound of her former boarding house landlady's name and the thought that the woman would be seeing her on trial.

"You catch a cold, Judge Houston?" another asked.

"Well Frank, let's see. I caught a cold, I caught a sunburn … only thing I didn't catch was a fish."

The courtroom erupted in an easy chuckle.

"So you're the Miss Price I've been reading about," the judge said, turning his gaze to Penelope.

She jumped up, hurting her wrist as it pulled hard on the short handcuff chain. "Ouch. Yes you're honored … I mean, I'm honored. You're your honor." She was at that point of nervousness where her mouth went dry and severed its connection with her mind. This was not the time for her to jumble her words. She swallowed hard rather than risk speaking again.

"Do you know why you're here, Miss Price?" he asked kindly.

She took a deep breath, hoping to synchronize mouth and mind. "I believe it is because I was the last person to have admitted seeing Mr. Cooper before his tragic demise."

He looked at her for several seconds before addressing her. She rubbed her sore wrist and worked to breathe normally.

"You are charged with the murder of Daniel Cooper," he said, reading the document before him. "How do you plead, Miss Price?"

"Well innocent, of course."

"It would be best for you not to speak. This is where your lawyer does the talking for you."

"But I don't have a lawyer," Penelope said, fretting.

"My client pleads not guilty, your honor," Bernard Beekham said, standing up and buttoning his overly tailored suit.

Penelope regarded him in stupefaction. Bernard Beekham had treated her with nothing but contempt when she met with him to settle her grandaunt's affairs; and his subsequent conduct wasn't much better when she visited him to obtain his notarized signature for the tearoom's business permit.

"Ask and ye shall receive. Looks like you *do* have a lawyer, Miss Price," the judge said merrily.

"The state requests the prisoner be held without benefit of bail, your honor," a smug young prosecutor said from his chair.

"Does this poor woman look like a public threat to you, counselor?" the judge asked, wiping his eyeglasses with one of his overly long sleeves.

"Based on what I've read about her, yes!"

A low murmur of laughter washed over the audience.

"Sensationalistic journalism notwithstanding, I will grant Miss Price bail. The amount is set at one thousand dollars. Who here will put up the bond? Please stand if you are willing to do so."

Penelope looked out at the crowd to see an assortment of people standing: Zara and Paolo, Florence Morgan, Stella, Hubert Allen, Chief Harrison, and Hank. She was overwhelmed by the number of people who stood, and bewildered by the identities of some of those who had chosen to do so.

"This court will reconvene in one week at this same time. You are free to go, Miss Price," he said, concluding the court session with a rap of his gavel.

"But I like it here," Penelope lamented.

"Nonetheless, you must go home," the judge said kindly, walking back to his chambers and trying not to trip on his robe.

Chief Harrison unfastened her restraints and gestured for her to walk ahead of him.

"Do I really have to go?" she asked him.

"You sure as hellfire do! The station house has been a three-ring circus since you set up camp. Go home, Miss Price. You have a busy week ahead."

A small group lingered in the courtroom to speak with Penelope. As she walked toward them, they applauded. She noticed Hank hanging back by the exit door and wished desperately to talk to him, but she didn't know where to begin. She raised a hand to wave to him, and he raised his fedora in response.

Florence Morgan began speaking, and Hank disappeared from view. "This is but a first step and very small victory, Miss Price. I expect you to make the most of your liberation and buckle down in earnest this week."

"Oh, I shall, Mrs. Morgan. You can count on it."

Among the many who stood in solidarity to greet her, there was one to whom Penelope wished to speak most. Without warning, she grabbed Stella and hugged her tightly. Stella wailed in agony briefly, but then gave in and returned the hug.

"This isn't becoming a habit it with you, is it … this cuddling business?"

"I can't believe you offered to post bail for me. I'm overcome. Where would you get that kind of money?"

"Well I do have a job now, ya know," she said with a smile. "Besides, I figured I could always squeeze the dough out my godfather Hubert, or get it from you if things got desperate."

"I really don't know how to thank you."

"Mees Price," Hubert said, holding out a long, thin box to her.

"This isn't a dagger, I hope, Mr. Allen. I'm in trouble enough as it is."

The little group chuckled.

"Opeen eet," Hubert beamed. "Eet eez just as you rehqueesteed."

Penelope untied the ribbon around the box and lifted the lid to expose three sets of cards. She picked up one from the first group and read it silently:

### Miss Penelope Price
### AntiquiTeas Proprietress
### and
### Tea & Sympathy Investigative Agency
### Truth Sleuth

"Oh, Mr. Allen, these are magnificent!" she gushed. "And to think you offered bail—"

"Give us a peek," Zara said, elbowing her way next to Penelope.

Penelope handed her a card and Zara read it aloud: Zara, Tea and Sympathy ... Chief Inquirer ... My first business card," she whispered reverently. "You even, left off the *Miss* ... Thank you, P! ...Say, Stella ..."

The girl looked up excitedly then hastened to Penelope's side. Zara rolled her wrist and presented her with a card.

"Miss Stella Parker, Tea and Sympathy Investigative Agency, Junior Inquiry Agent—Did you hear that? I'm a genuine junior inquiry agent!" she announced to all within earshot. "Hot socks!" she cheered, jumping toward Vincent and straddling him mid-air as he steadied himself and put his arms out to catch her.

"Vincent, I didn't expect to see you here," Penelope said.

"I'm off the clock, and now that you're moving out of the police station, when I'm off the clock, I'm on your side," he said with a smile.

"Well done, Mr. Allen," Florence Morgan said. "All is coming apace nicely."

"Miss Price, what will be your first order of business during what may be your last week of freedom on this earth?" a voice inquired from behind the remaining stragglers.

Penelope looked up to see Elsie Davies, pen and paper in hand, a malevolent grin on her painted lips.

"Good morning, Miss Davies. I should think my answer would be obvious—to uncover the truth about what happened to Daniel Cooper." As she spoke she reached out a hand to Lily Cooper who was standing beside Elsie.

"God watch over you, Miss Price. I pray you catch Danny's killer and bring her to justice," Lily said impassionedly.

"Her?" Zara repeated.

"Pardon?" Lily replied.

"You said 'bring *her* to justice.'"

"Did I? I'm afraid I've not been paying much attention to what I've been saying lately. If you'll excuse me," she concluded, wiping her eyes and hurrying toward the exit.

"Miss Price, is it true that you illegally—" Elsie began.

"All right, folks. Let's move this out of doors. The courtroom is now closed," Vincent said, attempting to squelch Elsie's inquest.

Florence then grabbed Penelope's arm and pretended to engage in serious conversation with her as an additional ploy to stave off Elsie's leading questions.

Once outside the courthouse, Penelope bid adieu to Florence, Stella, Vincent, and Hubert. Then she, Zara, and Paolo walked back into the cellblock to begin packing up their ad hoc home.

"I'm going to miss this place," Penelope said wistfully, glancing around the festooned cage.

"Me too," Zara said under her breath, gazing in the direction of the station's offices.

"Be at my place of business the day after next to discuss your defense, Miss Price," Bernard Beekham said, standing in the doorway of the cell.

"Mr. Beekham, I don't know what to say. I had no idea you believed in me, or my innocence. To think you would offer to defend me … I'm very humbled and thankful."

"Miss Price, I was appointed by the court as the town's only public defender. I have pledged to assist and advocate for all who need representation, no matter how reprehensible I may find them. Degenerates, profligates, murderers such as yourself, I am duty-bound to serve them all. Good day."

"We need to solve this case and fast!" Zara said, sneering at Bernard Beekham and packing up quickly.

* * * *

As they entered the Queen Anne Victorian, Penelope viewed the place as though it were unfamiliar to her. It appeared cold and without sentiment to her, and at that moment, she preferred her cozy jail cell.

The three housemates unpacked in relative silence, casually putting things back in place.

"Why does it seem to be taking so much longer to put this stuff away than it did to put it all up at the jail?" Penelope said.

"Because that was an adventure—this is a chore."

"I'll say!"

A short while later, the boxes from the jail were emptied and everything returned to its rightful spot.

"You hungry?" Penelope asked.

"Peckish," Zara replied.

Paolo nodded fervently.

"No language barrier where food is concerned," Zara japed.

Penelope trudged into the kitchen and opened the door to the Kelvinator. Its pristine white walls and empty shelves gleamed. "Looks like we'll be going out to eat."

"I can't bear the thought of getting back in the car," Zara moaned. "Can't we entice someone to get food for us," she said, pointing covertly to Paolo.

"Don't you think poor Paolo's been our Man Friday long enough? I say we give him a respite."

A knock at the door caused them to look at one another in surprise.

"Cibo ... prontissimo?" Paolo joked, looking quite pleased with himself.

Zara chortled.

"What did I miss?" Penelope asked, walking to the door.

"Paolo actually made a joke ... suggesting the door knock meant food was here already."

Penelope offered no response.

"It was funnier when he said it."

Penelope opened the door. "Stella, what are you doing here?"

"It's good to see you too, bosslady," Stella said, not waiting for an invitation before walking in. "Fancy flophouse ... kinda aseptic though. You need to inject some life into this mausoleum. Maybe a shindig would warm the place up."

"Shouldn't you be in school?"

"Yep ... so should all the other kids. Unfortunately, someone pulled a fire alarm and school's been closed down for the rest of the day."

"What a lucky break for the Tea and Sympathy Investigative Agency," Penelope said earnestly, smiling.

"Yeah, lucky," Zara said, walking past Stella and lightly smacking the back of her head.

"So where do we start?" Stella asked, dropping onto the parlor sofa and putting her feet up on the coffee table in front of it.

"We start by behaving like professionals," Zara said, swiping Stella's feet off the table.

"Who sucked all the fun out of your sail?" Stella said.

"We also start with lunch," Zara said, producing several bills from her purse. "Your choice, whatever you want ... as long as there's enough for all of us."

Stella nodded, counting the money greedily.

"Paolo, do you mind?" Zara asked, miming the motion of driving.

"To the Butterfly Café, Paolo," Stella directed.

"Si!" he said, racing Stella to the car.

While Stella and Paolo were out, Penelope and Zara began a list of people to interview. Since they'd already talked to Florence Morga, they settled on Stella, Vincent, Hubert, Hank, and each other.

"Think we should include Chief Harrison on the list?" Zara asked nonchalantly.

Penelope guffawed. "Whatever for!"

"Well ... maybe he'll divulge something we didn't know or perhaps would never have thought of. He's bound to say something we can use."

"Fair point. Please tell me we don't have to talk to that insufferable gossip hound."

"Elsie Davies? I should say not! I envision more harm than good coming out of that conversation."

"What about Dan's wife, Lily?"

"If we can do so without upsetting her. I can't imagine losing a husband," Zara said.

"I can't imagine having a husband," Penelope said absentmindedly.

Zara broke out laughing. Once Penelope realized what she'd said, she giggled too.

"While we're waiting, what say we question each other?" Zara suggested. "I suppose we should first decide what our goal is with each interviewee."

"Our goal is to get to the truth, Zara."

"I still can't believe Dan Cooper was murdered. He was such a charming man ... and a looker, too."

"And a fantastic worker. He was a real gem. Funny how you can come to care so much about someone you've hardly known.'

"I know whatcha mean," Zara said, gazing off into the distance.

The pair grilled each other on what they knew about Dan and the specifics of the day before his death. Neither was able to think of anything they hadn't mentioned a dozen times already and were relieved when Stella and Paolo arrived with lunch to break the stalemate.

"I told Ruby to give me whatever tasted good and they had plenty of," Stella announced, opening the door for Paolo who carried a crate of Butterfly Café cuisine.

"Meatloaf!" he announced enthusiastically.

"Told ya he could speak English if it involved food," Zara said to Penelope.

The foursome unloaded the baking dishes and linen-swathed baskets to unearth a whole meatloaf fresh from the oven, along with icebox rolls, a bowl of mashed potatoes, green beans, and rhubarb-peach pie.

"Mangia!" Paolo announced once the table was set and everyone seated.

"Mangia, indeed!" Zara said, lifting a forkful of meatloaf and mashed potatoes to her mouth.

"Unh unh," Penelope said, folding her hands.

"Good God!" Zara grunted, rolling her eyes and putting her fork down.

"Precisely. Now, everyone will you bow your heads with me. Our Father, for this day, for our friends, for this food, we thank thee. Amen."

"Amen," the others repeated—Zara did so with a full mouth.

The dinner conversation was boisterous and scattered, and Stella could not stop talking about how Zara's decorating of the jail cell was the cat's pajamas, how Penelope's launching of a detective agency was the gnat's whistle, how being a junior inquiry agent was the elephant's eyebrows, and how the arraignment had been the eel's hips. In short, she thought everything about Penelope's arrest was marvelous as described in a variety of animal appellatives.

"That's all well and good, but we still need to get P out of this jam," Zara said.

"And find the killer," Penelope added.

"Easy as eating pie, for the Tea and Sympathy Investigative Agency," Stella said, taking a large swig of milk and smiling with a white moustache.

"That's the spirit!" Zara cheered, raising an arm in triumph.

"Pie!" Paolo cheered, also raising an arm.

The ladies giggled and Penelope cut and served the rhubarb-peach pie.

"Whadda we do next?" Stella asked eagerly.

"Next, our junior inquiry agent sets up appointments with those on our witness and information list," Penelope said.

"Oh," Stella said sans her previous zeal.

"Is something wrong, Stella?" Penelope asked.

"It's just ... so you're going to be interviewing these people, you say," Stella said.

"Yes?" Penelope said.

"In hopes of getting something out of them?"

"Of course," Penelope said.

"Actually, *I* will be interviewing them," Zara said.

"Oh, that's different. Pie!" Stella cheered, raising an arm.

Zara chuckled. Paolo smiled and nodded and took another bite of pie.

"I don't get it," Penelope said.

"Yes, P, I know—believe me, I know," Zara said, flashing her a sympathetic smile and patting her on the head.

"Uh, moving on ahead," Penelope said, "Stella, is there anything more you can tell us about the Bohemian Club? I'm hoping there's a connection to the club and Dan's murder."

"Sorry, I told you everything I know."

"Our first dead end," Penelope said.

"Why don't you just go look it up at the library?" Stella asked through a mouthful of pie.

"You have one of those in this little town?" Zara asked.

Penelope choked. "You mean to tell me a secret society is actually documented ... and in the library?"

"I think so," Stella said. "The Bohemians own land in town, so there must be something on them."

"Count me out. Those places give me the willies," Zara said.

"But then what will you do, Zara? You don't want to just stay here and stare at the walls, do ya?" Stella said.

"More like stare at the ceiling," Penelope said under

her breath with a wicked smile.

"Penelope Pearl Price!" Zara exclaimed.

"Oh I get it," Stella said with a knowing smile and mouthful of pie.

"You see, she and Paolo have been apart for an extended time," Penelope explained.

"She said she got it, P! … Besides, I thought I could go over to the police station and interview Chief Harrison while you're at the library. Double our efforts, so to speak."

"But who will take notes?" Penelope said.

"I'll be fine, P. Anyway, having you there may make things worse."

"You're probably right. Stella, would you care to join me on an adventure to the library?"

"I'd rather go with Zara—"

"I won't be long," Zara said. "And I'm sure P could use additional eyes with all those books."

"You don't have any overdue library books, do you, Stella?" Penelope said, chuckling at what she considered to be a witty joke.

"No," Stella replied blandly.

"Good for you!" Penelope said.

"I've never set foot in the library before," Stella said.

Zara broke out laughing.

Paolo laughed along, raised an arm and asked, "Pie?"

"Then you actually are *overdue*, Stella—if you'll forgive the library pun," Penelope said, once again amusing herself.

Zara and Stella groaned.

Paolo dejectedly asked, "No pie?"

"Shall we sally forth, junior inquiry agent?" Penelope said, rising and crooking an arm for Stella to take.

"Indubitably," Stella said, feigning an upper-crust British accent.

"Paolo, per favore," Zara began, making a motion of washing dishes.

"Siesta!" he replied, depositing himself on the parlor's chaise and closing his eyes.

"Just as good," Zara said, collecting her clutch and applying fresh lipstick.

# Chapter Sixteen

They stood outside the lovingly maintained Mission style building, erected just 12 years previously, and surveyed its arched portico and welcoming arched windows.

"Do I really have to go in there? What if someone sees me?" Stella protested.

"You may as well get used to it now. Research is a big part of an inquiry agent's duties, junior or otherwise."

The moment they entered the edifice, they were greeted by the apple-cheeked, smiling face of Mrs. Hume, the town's librarian. She'd held her post since the first library was opened in 1886 as part of the Reading Corner of the Old Parlor, just a few blocks from the library's newer Central Avenue location. She nodded to them with lively eyes, her hands folded on the counter before her.

"How do you do?" Penelope whispered reverently. "I'm Miss Price—"

Mrs. Hume's eyes widened and her lips flapped without producing sound. Penelope's reputation had preceded her.

"... and this is my assistant, Miss Parker."

"Just Stella."

The woman tapped her nametag and adjusted the sweater draping her shoulders.

"A pleasure to meet you, Mrs. Hume," Penelope said nearly inaudibly.

Mrs. Hume put a finger to her lips, adjuring Penelope

to be quiet.

Penelope nodded in understanding. "We're looking for information on the Bohemian Club," she said in the tiniest whisper possible.

Mrs. Hume cupped her hand around her ear.

"We're looking for information on the Bohemian Club," she repeated, just a fraction more loudly.

Mrs. Hume tapped her forefinger to her lips several times and scowled, indicating Penelope was being too noisy.

When Mrs. Hume failed to give an answer, Penelope tried again, in a voice as low as the first time. "We're looking for information on the Bohemian Club."

Again, Mrs. Hume put a hand to her ear.

Stella turned her back to Mrs. Hume and stared at a gum spot on the ground in an effort not to laugh.

Finally, Penelope wrote down the request on a scrap of paper.

"Yes, I heard you the second time," Mrs. Hume whispered deafeningly. "Right this way. You'll find what you're looking for in the newspaper section. We pride ourselves on the accuracy of the Butterfly Bugle."

The patrons seated in the library covered their ears as Mrs. Hume passed.

Remembering how she herself had been depicted in that publication, Penelope whispered faintly, "Are there any other sources we could consult? Perhaps a book or two?"

Mrs. Hume raised her finger to her lips. "Just one. *Bohemian Jinks* written by Porter Garnett in 1908," she rasped.

Penelope nodded affably, following Mrs. Hume as she wound a serpentine trail around the library stacks.

"Here it is," Mrs. Hume shouted, her voice reverberating through the aisles.

"Thank you," Penelope mouthed silently.

Mrs. Hume frowned and furiously tapped her

forefinger to her lips.

Penelope found a table at which to sit and gestured for Stella to do the same. As Penelope flipped through a few pages to determine if the book might be of merit, Stella fidgeted in her chair, pulling her eyebrows out as a show of dissent. Finally, Penelope turned the book toward her to get her to stop wiggling.

"Look, Stella! A description of a place called Bohemian Grove, where the club's clandestine meetings are held. What do you think? Should we borrow the book?"

"Does it mean we'd be getting out of this mortuary?"

"Yes."

Stella grabbed the tome and sprinted to the front desk.

"Your library card, please." Mrs. Hume bellowed so loudly Penelope heard her from back in the study room.

"My what?" Stella said.

Penelope strode to the desk, producing one of her new calling cards. Mrs. Hume opened drawers, wrote in notebooks, and engaged in a variety of clerical tasks that were requisite to complete the copious amounts of paperwork needed to obtain a Pacific Grove library card.

"Would you like me to get that notarized?" Penelope asked sarcastically, putting a finger to her lips thereafter to preempt Mrs. Hume's shushing of her.

Mrs. Hume looked to the heavens to ponder the notary question for a moment, then shook her head no.

Several minutes later, Penelope and Stella emerged from the building, book and library card in hand.

"That wasn't so bad, now was it?" Penelope asked.

"The worst!" Stella objected. "I'm scarred for life."

"Nothing a fruit phosphate can't cure, I should think."

"I have heard tell that phosphates may contain much needed medicinal properties," Stella answered drolly.

Penelope regarded the exchange as a victory in getting Stella to warm to her.

A short walk later they were seated at the local soda fountain. They sat elbow to elbow in rapt silence, sipping their drinks as they scanned for interesting passages in the *Bohemian Jinks* book.

"Looks to me like a bunch of grown men pretending to be gods and fairies and putting on plays in the forest," Stella said.

"They do seem to do a lot of that," Penelope responded, flipping ahead through the pages. "I find it fascinating how it all began with men in the arts. I wonder how my grandaunt fit into it all."

"You really think you can learn enough about the club to figure out who killed Dan before your trial next week?"

Penelope shook her head. "No, definitely not. I sense there is a great deal more to this club than Mr. Garnett may have described in his book," she said, closing the volume with a discouraged sigh. "Come on. We better get you home before your mother objects."

**\* \* \* \***

"How did it go?" Penelope called as she walked into the house. "… Hello?"

"Huh? Oh, ciao," Paolo said, rousing from a deep sleep on the parlor chaise.

"Zara?" Penelope asked.

Paolo shrugged.

"Zara, you here? … Probably taking a bath," she said to herself as she walked up the stairs in search of her friend. "Where the deuce can she be? Certainly it can't take that long to ask a policeman a few simple questions."

Her search proving fruitless, she went to her own bedroom to change out of her courtroom attire. She was about to put on a casual day skirt and blouse when she decided to go straight to her nightgown.

She didn't realize she'd fallen asleep while reading

*Bohemian Jinks* until she heard the front door close. Bleary-eyed, she careened down the hallway and stairs to see who had come or gone and what she'd missed.

Zara stood in the entryway, removing her cloche, tousling her hair, and swinging her fringed shawl off her shoulders and onto the hall tree.

"Surely it can't be as late as that," she said, noting Penelope's bedwear.

"I couldn't bear the thought of putting in the energy to change twice. I'm simply exhausted from this whirlwind we've been caught up in. Where's Paolo? Did you two go out?"

"Wasn't he here when you arrived?"

"Yes, but that was hours ago. Are you two not just getting home?"

"From where?"

"From wherever it is you've been."

"I was interviewing Chief Harrison. Remember?"

"Yes, but that was eons ago. What have you been doing since?"

"Nothing. I just got home."

Paolo knocked over an empty bottle as he rolled over on the chaise where he'd been sleeping unnoticed by Penelope and Zara.

"Should we wake him so he can go up to bed with you?" Penelope said.

Zara sat on the hall tree's seat and removed her shoes, stretching her feet and moaning appreciatively. "Actually, we had a talk, and Paolo agreed that he should sleep downstairs for now ... Don't want to risk the appearance of impropriety while you're fighting for your life."

"That's very thoughtful of you two," Penelope said, picking up the empty bottle and inspecting it. "Looks like Paolo already broke your pledge of propriety."

Zara got up and took the bottle from Penelope, giving

it a hearty sniff. "Whewy that is strong! I'm betting he'll be out 'til morning."

Paolo let out a long whistling snore and rolled over the other way. Penelope motioned for Zara to follow her into the kitchen.

"You mean Paolo wasn't with you?" she said, opening the Kelvinator to take out a bottle of milk. "I'm confused."

"You know for someone so smart," Zara said, sliding into one of the kitchen chairs. "I went to interview the chief … and just got home. That's all."

Penelope's eyebrows elevated. "Oh? Based on the hour, I take it he had a lot to say?"

"Not so much really," Zara replied, gazing far off and playing with one of the crystals that dangled from her ear as Penelope retrieved a tin of dark chocolate powder from a cupboard and placed a saucepan on the stove to prepare hot cocoa. "We laughed most of the time … and talked about our favorite moving pictures and music. He even sang to me a little," she added, tilting her head and clasping her hands to her chest, a look of innocent delight softening her glamorous features.

"Why, Minnie Clark!" Penelope exclaimed, leaving off stirring the cocoa to regard her friend.

"Oh hush … and keep stirring," she replied, adopting her usual world-wise demeanor. "Now tell me how you made out with Stella."

"You mean Stella who has dispensed with her last name, just like you?"

"Has she now? I knew I liked that girl."

"*That girl*, as you call her, idolizes you. So you better mind your Ps and Qs and set a suitable example."

She poured the cocoa in a pair of mugs and put them on the kitchen table, making sure to check she'd turned off the gas burner. She then sat down, then got up to re-check the stove, twice.

"I'm trying," Zara said with a demure smile, holding

the cocoa mug in both hands and blowing on the dark creamy liquid to cool it.

Penelope narrowed her eyes and stared at her oldest friend, convinced Zara was up to something.

"Now, tell me, did you find anything at the library?" Zara said.

"Surprisingly, yes! A book about Bohemian Grove."

"Ooh, Bohemian Grove—I like the sound of that."

"It's a secluded area in the redwoods where the artistically-inclined members of the club stage theatrical presentations."

"P, you just *have* to get me into that club!"

"I have to get myself in first … or I should say, I have to ensure I'm not going to prison, first." Involuntarily, Penelope yawned.

"You're awfully blasé about going to prison!" Zara jested.

"Hardly. I just don't think I can keep my eyes open any more."

"Let's turn in then," Zara said, getting up from the table as Penelope checked the stove burner one final time.

"Have you made any plans yet for tomorrow?" Zara asked as they ascended the stairs.

"I thought we'd head into the tearoom. It feels like years since we've been there. I hoped we could conduct our interviews there. Unless you think it odd."

"Makes sense to me. I don't know if you were planning on opening the tearoom back up for regular business—"

"No, I don't think that would be a good idea until the case is settled."

"Good to hear, because Walter said you're not allowed to under the circumstances."

"Who said that?"

"Walter … Chief Harrison."

"I see. You know, you needn't cozy up to the chief of police on my account, Z."

"Who says it's on your account?" Zara said with a grin, turning on her heel to enter her bedroom.

**✳ ✳ ✳ ✳**

Just as Zara had predicted, Paolo was still asleep on the chaise when the ladies met downstairs for breakfast the next morning.

"Should we wake him?" Penelope asked.

Zara nodded. "Absolutely. I'm betting we could use his help at some point. And I don't want him to drink the day away." She then called to him, gently nudged him, shouted at him, and roughly shook him.

"Incredible," Penelope said, looking at the unfazed sleeper.

"I know what will work," Zara said. "I'll be right back."

She put on a pair of mule slippers and walked out the front door, still wearing her red silk kimono robe.

"Zara, you can't go out dressed like that!" Penelope cried.

Zara slid the kimono off a shoulder.

Penelope gasped and covered her eyes. When she heard the door close she opened her eyes again and turned to regard Paolo "Still asleep."

While waiting for Zara, Penelope prepared a pot of coffee and started composing a list of food items to purchase for the house. Zara walked in a minute later.

"Frying pan, please," Zara said, smiling mischievously. "This should do the trick."

"Don't tell me you're going to hit him with it!" Penelope said.

"Hit him with it? The way your mind works … You *sure* you're not a murderer?" Zara said, slapping into the skillet half a dozen rashers of bacon that she'd *borrowed* from the house next door.

As the meat began to sizzle and its odor fill the downstairs, Paolo stirred and made wake-up sounds. By the time the bacon was fully cooked, he was fully awake.

"Buongiorno!" he said, rubbing his eyes and smiling as he entered the kitchen to pour some coffee. "Mmmmm, bacon."

"Now there's an English word he knows," Penelope said.

"Not exactly. It's the same word in Italian," Zara corrected.

Penelope chuckled and shook her head. "What are you going to do with this fellow?" she said jokingly, looking on as he burnt his fingers in his haste to extract the still bubbling bacon from the pan.

"I've been thinking a lot about that lately," Zara said, her tone serious.

"Oh! I didn't realize …"

"Ow! Ow! Ow!" Paolo yelped as he sat down at the kitchen table, tossing the searing bacon from one hand to the other.

"I've also been thinking about what you said about our living arrangements," Zara said.

Penelope sipped her coffee wordlessly, wondering where Zara was taking the conversation.

"Now that I'm going to be a businesswoman," Zara continued, "my lifestyle will be very different from the one Paolo signed on for. Poor thing is so bored, but he never complains. Still, it really isn't fair to him …"

"Well, it's nothing you need to solve today."

"You're right. The case is the thing we need to solve. Once that's settled we can … reassess other things."

"How very sensible of you, Z."

"Don't get excited. This doesn't mean I'm going to run

off and join the temperance league or lower the length of my hemline."

"The thought never crossed my mind," Penelope said, marveling at the unexpected changes in her friend.

# Chapter Seventeen

Walking into the tearoom felt like walking into a twisted dream from the past for Penelope. There were so many intense memories, both good and bad, created in a very short period of time. The venue was the place she earned Mrs. Morgan's endorsement, where she met Hank—the quiet masculine presence who had disappeared from her life as quickly as it had entered—and it's where the effervescent Dan Cooper had breathed his last.

It was less than three months prior that she and Zara first walked into the place and got the idea for AntiquiTeas. Now, they walked arm in arm toward the bathroom, bracing themselves for what they might find as the shop was still roped off and labeled a crime scene. To their relief, there were no stains, no evidence of any kind that would indicate a cold-blooded murder had taken place there. Instead, an inviting cascade of sunrays peeked through the organza curtains covering the room's window.

As Zara made use of the water closet, Penelope headed to the kitchen. She opened the Kelvinator and gazed at its contents, not moving or speaking for minutes on end.

"Something in there have you transfixed?" Zara asked upon entering.

"Hmmm? Oh, yes, actually I was looking to see what food had spoiled in our absence so I could throw it out. I guess my mind must've wandered."

"Shouldn't you two be getting ready to interview witnesses instead of staring into the icebox?" Stella said, sauntering into the kitchen.

"Shouldn't you be in school? Really, Stella, I must insist you go to school at once ... either that or I'll have to dismiss you," Penelope said.

"Hang on to your bonnet. School's closed today," Stella said, helping herself to a pear from the still open Kelvinator.

"Don't tell me you triggered the fire alarm again. Chief Harrison is going to hold me—"

"Yep, school's closed today, and there's nothin' you can do about it," Stella said, jumping up to sit on the kitchen prep table, taking a large bite of the pear and grinning contumaciously at Penelope.

"Z, are you just going to stand there and say nothing? Don't tell me you approve of her truancy?"

"Well, as I recollect, there was a significant amount of truancy when the two of us were in school."

"Yes, but that was all on *your* part. I never skipped class."

"Oh ... that's right. And now here I am, up and it at bright and early, and by choice, no less."

"Zara, say something to her!" Penelope pleaded.

"Stella, you have my blessing to *not* go to school today. In fact, why don't you take tomorrow off as well."

"Zara!" Penelope shouted, turning red with perturbation.

Zara and Stella broke out into laughter.

"That's it! ... You're both ... *fired!*"

The pair laughed all the harder, and Penelope slammed the Kelvinator shut and stormed out of the room.

"Stella, heat the kettle. Looks like someone needs tea," Zara said quietly before following Penelope out to the tearoom where Penelope sat on one of the settees, looking out the window, her arms crossed in displeasure.

"Now there's no need to sulk, P," Zara said, taking a

seat across from her. "We were only clowning around. Today's Saturday, so there is no school."

"Well I don't find it very …" Penelope stopped and thought, then smiled. "All right, you two got me."

"Kettle's on," Stella said, entering cautiously.

Penelope sighed. "I must remember to keep my wits about me when I'm with you. You're far too clever for me."

"Aw, don't feel bad," Stella said, perching on the arm of a chair. "I'm too clever for most everyone."

Zara swatted Stella's leg. "Since you know so much, tell us who we'll be interviewing today and when."

Stella produced a small notepad from the top of her stocking.

"Since when do you wear stockings?" Zara asked. "I thought you only wore tattered fishnets … or went defiantly bare-legged."

"You've shown me how handy they are for hiding things … especially from my parents."

Penelope threw up her hands in mild exasperation.

"And my mother is thrilled to see me being more *ladylike*, as she puts it."

Penelope nodded in approval.

"But to answer your original question, Lily Cooper is coming in at ten, Vincent's at eleven, and Hank will be in around noon or whenever he takes his lunch break. My godfather said just to stop by anytime you're ready for him. He'll be in his store next door all day."

"Excellent work, Stella!" Penelope praised. "Z, is there anyone we're forgetting?"

"Not that I can think of," Zara said.

"Very well." Penelope stood up and walked around the room, viewing it from different angles. "I think we should seat the witnesses here," she said, pointing to a settee near the tearoom's entrance. "This area gets lots of light. I'll sit in this chair to take notes. Zara would you prefer to sit or stand?"

"I suppose I'll find out when the time comes."

"What about me? What do I do?" Stella asked.

"We'll want to offer the witnesses some refreshment to put them at ease. So tea would be good, for starters," Penelope said.

"Let George do it!" Stella said, waving her hand in irritation.

"Who's George? Is he a member of the Bohemian Club?" Penelope asked.

"I'm talking about the noodle juice!" Stella said petulantly, putting her hands on her hips and huffing.

"She means she's not thrilled about pouring tea," Zara said.

"What detective would be thrilled about being demoted to waitress?!" Stella said, grimacing with arms folded.

"Looks like this one don't know from nothin,'" Zara said, wagging a thumb toward Stella.

"Hey! What gives?!" Stella retorted.

"Dontcha get it? You're our ace in the hole," Zara said.

"Oh? Howdja mean?" Stella asked, dropping her arms and inching closer to Zara.

"Think about it," Zara said, sneaking a wink at Penelope. "I'll be searching for questions to ask in order to glean as much as possible from our interviewees. P will have her nose buried in her notes. We'll need you to reconnoiter."

"What's that?"

"Your job will be to study each person, look for signs of nervousness or discomfort, ticks or tells … to determine whether they're on the level or …"

"Or whether they're feeding you a line?" Stella added enthusiastically.

"Now you're on the trolley! While unobtrusively serving tea, you'll be able to observe much more than P or I will. People will most likely let their guard down around you."

"So basically, I'm a spy."

"Basically, yes."

"This job just keeps getting better and better," Stella said, twisting her hips forward and back in celebration and causing the fringe on her dress to dance. "Can I add *spy* to my business cards?"

Penelope opened her mouth to deny the request, but Zara spoke first.

"Come now, would a spy actually advertise the fact?" Zara asked.

"You've got a point," Stella admitted. 'Stella, girl detective—hum drum waitress by day, super sleuth by night.'"

Zara chuckled. "Something like that."

The bells hanging from the front door jingled.

"You know what to ask? And you'll stick to the list of questions we discussed?" Penelope said to Zara, her hands quaking as she held a pencil over her notepad.

"I know how to get information out of people, P. Trust me."

"Right this way, Mrs. Cooper," Stella said respectfully, escorting Lily into the tearoom.

"Good morning, Mrs. Cooper. I'm Miss Price's business companion, Zara," she said, gesturing for Lily to sit. "May we offer you a hot cup of tea?"

"Yes, that would be nice," Lily said, her gloved hands clutching her purse like a talisman. "Miss Price," she said, noticing Penelope as she sat.

"Lovely to see you again, Mrs. Cooper," Penelope said, a range of emotions fluctuating from woe to guilt to outrage threatening to crumble her composure.

Zara sat across from Penelope in the chair adjacent to Lily. "Mrs. Cooper, as you know, Miss Price here is determined to get justice for your husband. Do you mind if we ask you a few questions? It will help us begin to piece the puzzle together as to what actually befell him."

Lily nodded.

"Dan was such a likeable man, always ready to help, always cheerful," Zara said. "I can't imagine anyone wishing him ill, but it appears someone did. Do you have any idea who may have been at odds with Dan—perhaps a disgruntled patron or supplier from his days owning the saloon? ... Or maybe ... someone unhappy about his more recent business dealings?"

Lily looked up at Zara in surprise at her last remark. Penelope struggled to keep her gaze on her notepad, fearful that she'd suffer an outburst of emotion should she lock eyes with Dan's widow.

Lily gulped before speaking. "You're right in every aspect, Miss ..."

"Zara."

"Miss Zara. Danny was beloved by so many. But when you own a saloon or ... anyway, you're bound to make a few enemies, whether drunken customers you remove against their will, or shady characters you refuse to do business with."

"And regarding Dan's career since the closing of the saloon?"

"Your tea, Mrs. Cooper. I brought milk and sugar just in case. Oh and lemon too!" Stella said, scrutinizing Lily while depositing the tea tray on the table.

"How thoughtful, Stella. Thank you," Zara said.

"Yes, thank you," Lily said, looking into her teacup for a moment before answering. "When the saloon closed, we lost everything—no one more so than Danny. He lost his dignity. After all, what value does a man have if he can't provide for his family?"

Penelope's mouth opened in objection. A look from Zara discouraged her from speaking.

"I can't imagine how hard that must have been for him," Zara said. "As I understand, he took up ... a *variety* of jobs since then?"

"Yes."

"Mrs. Cooper, I'm afraid I must ask you, in your opinion, were there people who expected—perhaps even demanded—that Dan continue purveying liquor, *after* Prohibition went into effect?"

"Yes," Lily said quietly, sipping her tea and staring intently into the cup.

"What can you tell us about the Bohemian Club?" Penelope blurted.

"The what?"

"May I refresh your cup for you?" Zara asked, redirecting the conversation.

"Oh, uh yes, thank you."

"I believe you told Chief Harrison that you expected Dan to be out late the night before the grand opening here, and up early the next morning to go get ice. Is that correct?"

"Yes, that's correct."

"And you have no idea whether or not he actually slept at home."

Lily shook her head.

"And no reason to suspect he slept anywhere else," Zara asked gently.

Lily looked pitifully up at Zara, tears filling her eyes. "No … never … Daniel was a faithful husband and father."

"No one could doubt that. It was obvious he doted on you all," Zara said, offering Lily a tea napkin to dry her eyes.

"He was a good man," Lily said, her emotions bubbling over.

Zara instantly went to Lily's side and enfolded her in a hug, mouthing the word *fudge* to Stella. Stella looked confused for a moment, then bolted from the tearoom. Penelope sat paralyzed, feeling helpless and blameworthy and doing her best not to cry. In less than a minute, Stella returned from her godfather's store with a slab of dark fudge.

"Here, Mrs. Cooper, take this. It's the most effectual curative known to man," Zara said, breaking off a piece and handing it to Lily.

Lily smiled and put the candy in her mouth.

"There, what did I tell you? Feeling better already?" Zara asked.

"Yes, actually," she said, breaking off another piece of fudge and following it with a sip of tea. "You ladies are very kindhearted. I'm most grateful for all you're doing for my Danny."

"It's our pleasure," Penelope said.

"And duty," Zara added.

"We're truth sleuths, Mrs. Cooper," Stella said. "We'll get to the bottom of what happened. Don't you worry."

Lily smiled wearily.

Penelope discreetly tapped her watch, alerting Zara that their time was up.

"It's been an honor to meet you, Mrs. Cooper," Zara said. "I hope we didn't detain you too long."

Lily shook her head *no* and primped to compose herself before departing.

"Just one more thing," Zara said. "Has a date been chosen for Dan's funeral?"

"Not yet. We're waiting for Miss Price's awful court case to be concluded. I know you didn't do it, Miss Price. Every bone in my body tells me as much!"

"Thank you, Mrs. Cooper. Your trust and confidence mean very much to me," Penelope said, becoming verklempt.

"I'll walk you out," Zara said, looping her arm gently through Lily's.

Penelope finally dared lift her eyes and glanced at Stella who was already looking at her in eager anticipation of what Penelope might say.

Before Penelope could form words, Zara returned to

the tearoom and sprawled out on the floor. "That was exhausting!"

"Zara, you were absolutely magnificent! Oh, better than that you were ducky, nifty, the cat's whiskers!" Penelope exulted. "And Stella, you were … well … stellar!"

"What a fabulous nickname!" Zara said, lifting her head from her prostrate position.

"Stellar … I like that," the girl said, nodding in approval. "I did what you asked, by the way, and observed Lily closely. My take is that she suspects Dan was involved in bootlegging. She may not know the specifics, but she sure suspects something."

"I agree," Penelope said.

Zara nodded. "I think you're spot on! P, did you get anything we can use?"

"No, not really, but interviewing her was invaluable in a larger sense; and she was the perfect person to start with, to get our feet wet, so to speak.

The bells on the front door clanged and a voice called out, "Buongiorno!"

"Is that Paolo?" Penelope asked.

"Doesn't sound like him," Zara said.

"It's just Vincent," Stella said. "We're back here!" she shouted.

"Ladies," Vincent said, walking to the tearoom and bowing slightly, a buoyant smile on his face.

"Well if it isn't the enemy," Zara joked.

"Hardly, more like your inside man," Vincent said, putting his hands in his trouser pockets and trying to look formidable.

"Oooh I like that!" Zara said. "So Mr. Inside Man, what can you tell us, or should I say, what are you *allowed* to tell us without losing your job?"

"Well I can tell ya right off the bat no one at the precinct thinks Miss Price did it."

"What?!" Penelope shouted, rising from her chair. "Then why on earth—"

Vincent shook his head and cut her off. "I have no idea, really. I can't figure the chief out on this one. You must've really done something to get on his bad side. Actually, he doesn't have a bad side. But whatever you did, it must've been a doozy."

"But I didn't *do* anything!" Penelope began to pace and nibble her fingernails. "I've hardly ever spoken to Chief Harrison. He was gruff with me from the first moment we met! This is outrageous!"

"It is, P, and we will crack that nut one of these days. But for now, isn't it comforting to know that the Chief doesn't think it was you?" Zara said.

"Not when I'm scheduled to go to trial in less than a week!" she said, wheeling around to confront Zara.

"Well I'm determined to look at this as good news," Zara said.

"Fine! You do that," Penelope said, dropping into a chair and brooding with her arms folded.

"Vincent, I'll be the one conducting our little chat, if that suits you," Zara said.

"Fine by me," he said, settling into an armchair.

"Aren't you going to take notes?" Stella asked Penelope.

Penelope glared at her hard, her arms still folded.

"Okay, mental notes then," Stella said to herself. "P, if it's all right with you, I'm going to forego the usual questions with Vincent and just let him tell us what he knows."

"Sure, why not? It's only my neck that's on the line," Penelope said, tossing a pencil in the air.

"Pay no attention to the prime suspect," Zara said to Vincent. "Now, tell us what you can."

"Okay, well, the chief has pieced the forensic evidence

together—that's the information they deduce from the state of the crime scene. According to the coroner, whatever hit Dan was larger and more blunt than a gun handle. And when the chief asked if the weapon may have been an object from one of the shelves in the antiques store, the coroner said, yes, that was very likely."

"Did the chief come up with a time that this attack might have taken place?" Penelope asked, her interest in the conversation growing.

"Yep, between eleven and midnight, about an hour or so after we all left."

"And did the chief posit a motive or perhaps a scenario," Penelope plied.

"He thinks somebody may have broken in to steal something and Dan walked in on them and they jumped him."

"They, meaning more than one person?" Stella asked.

"Fine question, Stellar!" Zara said.

"Stellar?" Vincent said.

"That's me," Stella said, beaming.

"Uh, okay, and no, I'm pretty sure the chief thinks it was just one person," Vincent said.

"We need to do an inventory," Penelope said, getting up from her seat.

"Looks like all of your nitpicky recordkeeping is going to pay off," Zara said.

"We bookkeepers are born detectives," she replied, smoothing her hair in mock smugness.

"I don't think I have time to help you look through everything right now. I have to get to work," Vincent said.

"I didn't know you worked at the police station on Saturdays," Penelope said.

"I don't. I took a weekend job—it's just temporary—to help Mom and the kids," he said, sitting up straight and shuffling his feet as he looked to the ground.

"We're almost done here, Vincent," Zara said warmly. "Just one last thing, for the time being. What do you know about the Bohemian Club? Did the chief mention it at all?"

"I know the same stuff everyone else does, I guess. It's a bunch of artists and rich businessmen who get together in the woods and put on fancy pageants and feast like kings and sleep in luxurious cabins."

"The chief didn't bring it up in connection with P's case?"

"Not that I recall."

"Thank you, Vincent, you've been a wonderful help," Zara said.

"Yes thank you, Vincent. I really value your assistance," Penelope said. She then awkwardly approached him and hugged him. "It's very good to see you."

"Uh, thank you, Miss Price. It's good to see you too. And don't worry, I'll be back here at the tearoom soon enough. "

Penelope held her breath to avoid sniveling.

"Goodbye, ladies," Vincent said.

"I'll ankle out with you," Stella said.

"What was that hugging business all about?" Zara asked Penelope, taking Vincent's seat.

"I don't know. I just suddenly became so emotional. To think Chief Harrison believes I'm innocent gives me hope, whatever his gripe with me might be."

"That was some meaty information from Vincent, huh?"

"I'll say! My head is swirling!"

"Your next appointment is here," Stella announced in a sing-song manner.

"Who's next?" Zara asked Penelope.

Before Penelope could consult her notes, a voice called out, "Good afternoon, Miss Price, Miss Zara."

"Hank! What a pleasure!" Zara said, walking up to him and offering him her hand in business-like fashion, her flirtatiousness with him a thing of the past.

Penelope froze in place at the sound of his name, just when she was bending over to grab her notebook.

"How are you holding up, Miss Price?" Hank said, noting her hunched-over crone-like bearing.

"Uh ... fudge?" Penelope said, regaining her mobility and holding out the candy dish toward him.

"Oh, umm no thanks. I'm just about to have lunch," he answered, his warm eyes twinkling.

"Fine weather we've been having. Do you think we might rain any time soon?" Penelope said, bereft of rational thought, her hand shaking violently as she put the candy dish down.

"Oh P, you and your nutty sense of humor," Zara said, feigning laughter as a means of glossing over Penelope's social clumsiness. "Hank, would you like to have a seat? We just have a few mundane questions for you, nothing too provocative."

"What can you tell us about the Bohemian Club?! What did my grandaunt have to do with it?! And how does it factor into Dan's murder?!" Penelope spouted.

Zara opened her mouth to cover Penelope's impulsive inquiry, but was rendered speechless by the blunt litany.

"Those are answers that may take more time than we have today," Hank said diplomatically. "I'd be happy to discuss the club, another time. For now, wouldn't it be most helpful to talk about Dan's death? As I understand, you only have six days until your trial."

"So then the Bohemian Club was not involved with Dan's murder?" Zara asked.

"I can't see how it would be," Hank said.

"But you admit you're a member?" Stella asked.

"Yes, I'm a member."

"Tea?" Stella asked, eying him carefully, pouring him a cup without waiting for his response.

"And so was my grandaunt?" Penelope said, her flusteredness yielding to fascination.

"Yes, she sure was—a beloved member, actually—and one of the few women the club's ever allowed in."

"Is there anyone you can think of who would want to do Dan harm?" Zara asked.

"Yes," Hank said, deftly lifting the teacup to his lips.

"Oh?" Penelope said.

"It's nothing I can discuss around, Stella, I'm afraid," he said.

"If you're talking about The Pig, I've been there plenty."

"Is that a fact?!" Hank replied.

"Yessiree, and I saw you there a couple of times to boot!" Stella said.

"Oh really!" Zara said.

Penelope gasped, dumbstruck.

"It's not what you think," Hank tried to assure her.

"I don't know *what* to think," Penelope thought aloud, stunned at the notion that Hank would patronize a speakeasy.

"Miss Price, if Dan were here to speak for himself, I'd say, 'Go talk to him,' but since he's not ..."

The three women leaned in, anxious to hear what he might disclose.

"You must understand ..." Hank began. "Dan was under an unbearable amount of pressure. He'd been a successful businessman with a wife and four little ones. When he lost the saloon, he lost his ability to keep his family in the lifestyle he'd always provided. Even Lily was under pressure to keep living high on the hog to maintain her status in society."

"Pressured by whom?" Penelope asked quietly, riveted by Hank's testimony.

"By society women," Zara said. "Am I right, Hank?"

He nodded.

"P, you have no idea how vicious those women can be. When you have the latest frocks and finest furnishings they clamor to sit at your feet. The instant you falter, they desert you, and hurl venomous aspersions—happy to ruin your reputation in a heartbeat," Zara said.

"But surely you don't mean the women of polite society," Penelope said. "I would think that sort of thing would be ... well ... more like what would go on in the, how shall I say, courtesan ranks."

Zara looked at her incredulously, swallowing to hide the pain Penelope's remark induced. Stella, astute enough to pick up on any change in the emotional environment, was too focused on Hank to notice Zara's wounded reaction.

"Zara's absolutely correct," Hank said. "I've seen society women tear each other apart like rabid dogs on a duck. The nouveau riche are the most vicious and have no regard for their victims' families."

"Surely, you don't think any of that catty social warfare was involved in Dan's death," Penelope said, oblivious that she had aggrieved her most cherished friend.

"I don't know enough about the circumstances to proffer an opinion," Hank said.

"The coroner determined Dan was hit on the head with a large object here at AntiquiTeas between eleven and midnight," Zara said plainly, shaking off Penelope's unintended slight. "It's been suggested that Dan may have walked in on someone who was in the act of stealing something from the antiques shop. Do you consider it feasible that the item may be somehow associated with the Bohemian Club?"

"Yes," Hank answered.

"Indeed?" Penelope said, trying to fathom the gravity

of Hank's words.

"Based on what you've told me, very much so," Hank said.

"But why specifically the night before the grand opening?" Stella chimed in.

"Excellent question, Stella!" Penelope said.

"That's Stellar, if you please," she replied.

"Look, if it really did have something to do with the club, then I would think that whoever stole whatever they stole would want to do it before your store opened for business," Hank said.

The novice detectives looked at him blankly.

"… to ensure no one bought it!" Hank explained.

"Ohhhhhh/Ahhhhhh" the ladies said in unison.

"We really must conduct that inventory!" Penelope said, standing up and scuttling to the office to fetch her ledger.

"Can't that wait 'til after Hank leaves?" Zara called after her.

"It's gone!" Penelope shouted from her office, running back into the tearoom. "The ledger's gone!" she shrieked, her skirt fluttering as her knees began to knock together.

"Calm down, P. I'm sure there's a logical explanation," Zara said.

"Of course there is. Someone stole it!" Penelope said, pacing and chewing her thumbnail. "You don't suppose the thief struck again!" she said, her eyes wide in terror.

"Did you look in the pit of no return?" Stella said calmly.

"The what?" Hank asked.

"My carpetbag? No! Why would I look there?!" Penelope squawked. She stood for a moment, her eyes darting in thought; then she hurried back to the office to retrieve the massive tote. "I haven't used this bag much lately. My goodness, it's even heavier than I remembered!

But if that ledger is in here I'll eat my …. Well whaddaya know," Penelope said, producing the logbook.

"You'll eat what?" Zara said.

"… My pride … and maybe some dessert," Penelope said, flipping through the book's pages without realizing what she'd said.

"Well, ladies, I have to be going, so I'll let you get to it. Glad you found the ledger. If you have any other questions, please don't hesitate," Hank said, putting his fedora on and tugging on the front of the brim in salutation.

By the time Penelope realized Hank was leaving, he'd already gone.

"Brilliant suggestion about the carpetbag, Stellar!" Zara said.

"Neh," Stella said with a shrug. "All in a day's work for a junior inquiry agent."

"I would say let's go visit Hubert next, but I know you want to—" Zara began.

"Do inventory!" Zara and Penelope said together.

**\* \* \* \***

The three investigators combed the antiques store, with Zara searching through the floor displays, Stella up on the library ladder examining the hard-to-reach items, and Penelope comfortably seated with her ledger in her lap, rattling off item descriptions and their supposed whereabouts.

"I owe you an apology, P," Zara said.

"Just the one?" Penelope scoffed.

"The horrible things I said about you in my head when you made that ledger list, logging which shelf we put what on. Today, we'd be up a creek without it."

Penelope simply smiled, licked the tip of her pencil, and ticked items off in the ledger.

\* \* \* \*

"Well that's the last of it," Penelope said, closing the ledger and stretching. "And the findings are intriguing, in my estimation. Two things are unaccounted for."

"A brooch in the shape of an owl and a bust of Mozart," Stella declared.

Penelope gasped. "Exactly right ... Stellar."

Stella smiled, thrilled to hear her nickname as well as to know she was right.

"Are you thinking what I'm thinking?" Zara said, joining Penelope on the banquette sofa and stretching her back.

"I doubt it. My mind has never dipped to those depraved depths," Penelope joked.

"Wisenheimer! What I meant was that—"

"That the thief hit Dan over the head with the statue and made off with the owl pin," Stella cut in, getting down from the ladder.

"P, why do I get the feeling you and I have been rendered redundant?"

"Because great minds think alike; and because I wholeheartedly concur with Stella's hypothesis."

"We may as well just retire now and turn the business over to this stellar upstart."

Stella beamed under the praise.

"Mees Price?" Hubert said, poking his head through the shop door.

"Hello, Mr. Allen. We owe you a visit this afternoon don't we?" Penelope said.

"I'm afraid thee afteernoon eez long past," he said.

"Oh gracious, look at the time!" Penelope said, jumping up as she checked her wristwatch.

"Yees, and now I must atteend to otheer matteers," he said, looking at his watch.

"How thoughtless of us, Hubert. Please accept our apologies," Zara said, sidling up to him and unleashing a modicum of her substantial charisma. "Can we offer you a cup of tea before you race off? What's your favorite type?"

"Ireesh Breekfast?" he said.

Zara feigned a gasp. "Mine too! And that's just what we were about to serve. Isn't it, Stellar? Do sit down, Hubert. The tea will be right out," Zara said, artfully lowering herself on the banquette sofa and patting the seat next to her.

"Weel, peerhaps just one cup," he said, slicking back his few dozen hairs and smiling thinly as he accepted the invitation to sit beside Zara.

She nodded to Stella who turned and strode to the kitchen. Penelope retrieved a high-backed stool from the teller's cage and sat with notebook and pencil at the ready.

"As you are aware, Hubert, our dear innocent Penelope has been charged with a murder we all know she didn't commit. We believe we have determined both the means and the motive for the crime," Zara said.

"Mees Zara, eef I were not impreesed with your taleents beffore ..."

Zara rose and began to amble around the room, pausing and posing for maximum dramatic effect. "We further believe there might be a connection between the item stolen and the Bohemian Club."

Hubert gulped loudly.

"My exact sentiments," Zara said.

"But how?" he whispered, peering around the room for eavesdroppers.

"We don't know just yet. That's what we were hoping you could help us with."

"I'm afraid I rehlly can't," Hubert said, standing. "Thee sancteeteh of thee club must beh prehseerved. I took a vow to—"

"Please, Hubert," Zara said, placing a hand on his chest, "for Penelope."

He shivered at her touch and sat back down.

"You see, your tea has arrived," Zara said as Stella brought in yet another tray of tea accoutrements. "Milk? Sugar?" Zara asked, her hands dancing bewitchingly as she poured and prepared the tea. "Now what can you tell us … without breaking your oath?"

"I … you seh … Peerhaps if you told meh what has benn taken," he asked, accepting the teacup from Zara.

"A brooch in the shape of an owl," Penelope said.

"Covered in little diamonds with two big diamonds for eyes," Stella added. "Thing's gotta be worth a crate of clams."

Hubert's hands twitched, spilling his tea.

"You know this pin?" Zara asked.

"Of course. Weh all do. Eet eez priceleess."

"Expensive, I'll grant you, but priceless?" Penelope said.

"Mees Price, eets significance far outweighs the mathehrials from wheech eet was forged."

"Go on, Hubert," Zara said, removing a handkerchief from the lacy top of her stocking and blotting the tea driblets from Hubert's thigh.

"Weel," he began cautiously, his voice cracking as Zara applied her hanky. "Thee owl is thee reecognized symbol of thee Bohehmian Club and Bohehmian Grove."

"Of course! I knew something about that owl seemed familiar!" Penelope exclaimed. "I saw a photograph of it in the *Bohemian Jinks* book I was just reading."

"Thee club eez not jinnxed, and that book eez rubbish!" Hubert said jumping to his feet.

"That is why we need *you*, Hubert," Zara said, placing a hand on his, "to give us the straight dope on the club and what might have transpired in relation to Dan."

"And why," Penelope added.

Hubert sighed, resumed his seat, and sipped his tea. "Thee brooch was geeven to Harry Eedwards, one of our most eellustrehious founding meembeers on thee occasion of heez dehparture to thee esst coast een pursuit of heez choseen vocation as a Shakesperreyan theespian."

"I read about a Henry Edwards. Is that who you mean?" Penelope asked.

"Yees, Harry was the neekname by wheech weh all reefeered to heem. The date the peen was preeseenteed to heem was June 29, 1878—the same day Bohemmian Grove came eento eexeesteence."

"Well if he went east, how did the pin end up back here?" Stella asked, eyeing him intently from behind the fragile display case on which she leaned.

"Another excellent question, Stellar!" Zara cheered.

"Heh deed not take eet weeth him. Heh entrusteed eet to thee club's preeseedeent, stating heh would come back and colleect it later, as a way of promeesin heh would rehturn to the Bohehmians one day, you seh. It was keept for yehrs at the Club's offeecees off Union Square."

"In San Francisco?" Penelope asked.

"Prehcisely," he said. "Harry made good on heez promeese and een 1888, on thee way back from conducting business in Australia, he came to Caleefornia to veeseet heez feellow Bohemmians. Eet was at that time heh gave thee peen to Mees Price's grandaunt, Dorotheya Tate, thee club's feerst fehmale member—honorareh meember, naturalleh."

"Naturally," Zara said, playing along.

"Jeepers," Stella whispered.

"Are you getting all this, P?" Zara asked quietly.

"Not a lick," Penelope said, leaning on her hand with her elbow digging into her thigh as she hung on Hubert's every word. "I do have a question, though," she said, snapping out of her awe-inspired reverie. "Why now? Why wait until I owned the shop to steal the brooch? Why not steal it years ago?"

"No one knew wheere Mees Deh kept it. Sheh deed not share your taleent for organeezation, Mees Price."

Stella snorted. "Have you seen her carpetbag?"

"I am gueessing you put thee pin on display with thee reest of your aunt's reeleecs, unaware of eets heestoreec value?" Hubert said.

Penelope nodded.

"Mees Price, eet eez of great importance to meh, as a Bohemmian, that thees objeect eez found. I weell asseest your seerch een any way I can."

"Thank you, Mr. Allen. Your camaraderie means a great deal to me," Penelope said.

"Mees Zara, eef theere eez anythin I can do for you … day or night," he said, standing and looking her over from top to bottom in one long ravenous gaze.

Zara arched an eyebrow and nodded her understanding. Hubert exited, and Penelope locked the door behind him.

"Ladies, I do believe we're getting somewhere," Penelope said, clapping her hands.

"Yeah, but where?" Stella asked.

"Closer, Stellar, ever closer," Penelope said, pacing and gnawing her thumbnail.

"So now what?" Stella asked.

"Phosphates, obviously," Zara said, smiling.

Stella's eyes lit up.

"A capital idea, Z. Ladies, collect your coats and hats. We're going out to celebrate," Penelope said, lugging her carpetbag over to the banquette in order to search for her keys.

"Celebrate what? We still don't know who the killer is. We don't even have the murder weapon!" Stella said, pulling a cloche hat down low over her eyes and donning crocheted gloves.

"Small victories, my dear," Zara said, sliding her fingers into kid gloves.

"Ugh! This thing is heavier than ever!" Penelope complained. "And I just cleaned it out recently … What in blue blazes? Is that a rock?" she asked, her arm deep into the bag. "Is one of you playing some sort of joke on me?"

Zara and Stella shook their heads and looked to one another.

"Why, it's enormous!" Penelope said.

"P! Watch your language in front of Stella!" Zara quipped.

Stella chortled.

"If only I could grab … There!" Penelope said, removing a bust statue of Mozart.

The three sleuths stared at one another, all too dumbfounded to speak.

**∗ ∗ ∗ ∗**

Stella was the first to form words. "It's the weapon!"

"It looks that way," Penelope said, excitedly inspecting the bust.

"And it also looks like you're the one who used it, P. It's in your bag!" Zara said, worry cracking her voice.

"Maybe the police can find some finger impressions on it to tell us who handled it," Penelope said, turning the object in her hands.

"Yeah, and they'll all be yours," Stella said.

Penelope put the piece on a display case and backed away from it.

"You want me to get rid of it for you? Smash it to bits and scatter the pieces?" Stella asked.

"Yes," Penelope said.

"P!" Zara said. "I'm surprised at you."

"Well that is what I *want*. It doesn't mean it's what I think we should do."

"You think we should turn it over to the police, don't you?" Zara asked.

Penelope nodded, walking around the display to view the statue from all sides. "I don't see any blood on it."

"Probably wiped off ... along with the finger impressions," Zara said.

"Probably," Penelope said automatically. She scurried over to the phone in the teller's cage and lifted the mouthpiece. "Hello, this is Miss Price, from the AntiquiTeas shop ... Yes, jail was very nice, thank you so much for inquiring. Why yes, I would indeed like to call Chief Harrison's office. Thank you kindly ... Yes, thank you, I hope I don't hang also ... Hello? Chief Harrison? This is Penelope Price. I believe I found your murder weapon ... in my carpetbag."

# Chapter Eighteen

"Does this mean I'll be going back to jail?" Penelope asked as Chief Harrison took out his handkerchief to lift the bust and inspect it.

"I'm afraid not, Miss Price. That has proven to be too distracting for our personnel," he said, giving a knowing look to Zara.

She smiled modestly and tucked her hair behind her ear.

"No, you remain out on bail; and your turning over this bit of evidence is a good faith gesture of your cooperation," he said.

"But not of my innocence," Penelope lamented.

"Unfortunately, no. Bag the evidence please, Caruso."

Vincent put on a pair of white cotton butler's gloves and deposited the statue in a drawstring canvas bag.

"Would either of you like some tea? It should still be hot," Zara offered.

Penelope glared at her. As far as she was concerned, the sooner Chief Harrison left, the better.

"I thought we were going out for phosphates!" Stella cried.

"I do love a good phosphate," the chief said, putting his hat on. "Shall we?"

"I don't understand what is happening here," Penelope said.

"Just go with it, P. This is one of those *present moments* we discussed," Zara whispered, swaying through the door as Chief Harrison held it open for her.

Vincent gave Stella a peck on the cheek that she rubbed off in feigned disapproval. In retaliation, he took her hand and led her out.

"I still need to find my keys," Penelope murmured, plunging her arm back into the carpetbag. In the absence of the bulky statue, she found them in seconds, and locked up.

"Don't dawdle, Miss Price," the chief called back to her as he strolled alongside Zara.

* * * *

At the soda shop, Penelope sat in silence, sipping a chocolate soda and watching in wonder as Walter Harrison joked and laughed with Zara and the young couple.

"Cat got your tongue, Penelope?" Stella asked.

"Blink if you can hear us," Zara said.

Penelope opened and shut her eyes several times as she continued to sip. After an exceptionally long shlurp, she worked up the nerve to address the lawman. "Chief Harrison, do you really think I killed Daniel Cooper? And if not, why are you painting me as public enemy number one?"

All other conversation stopped.

Walter took a long drag on his phosphate and responded, "Why, Miss Price, you know I can't discuss the case with you."

"But—"

"But nothing, Miss Price," he replied.

Zara inconspicuously extended her hand in a *stop* gesture, admonishing Penelope to drop the subject.

"Ahhhh, that hit the spot," Walter said, finishing off the last of his drink. "Caruso, you and I need to get back to the station. Ladies, will you excuse us?"

He scooted out of the booth from his seat next to Vincent and lay down a dollar bill, covering the cost of all five phosphates as well as a hefty tip.

"Awfully generous for a civil servant," Penelope commented once the men were out of earshot.

"He's always been generous like that. That's how he got the nickname Santa," Stella remarked.

"Curious," Penelope remarked, sliding out of the *girls' side* of the booth to sit across from Zara and Stella.

"One needn't be a Rockefeller to be generous, P," Zara chided.

"So what's the plan now, P?" Stella asked.

Zara snickered loudly at hearing Stella address Penelope by only her first initial.

Penelope lifted an eyebrow in response. "Well, I'm not exactly sure, to be honest."

"We've gotten a lot of answers today. That must be of some comfort," Zara suggested.

"Yes, it is. Though I seem to have more questions than ever! I want to look through that book from the library on The Bohemian Club ... and we should probably consider expanding the scope of our interviews ... as well as revisit a few—Mr. Edwards, for starters," Penelope said.

"Oh really!" Zara said, smirking.

"Yes, really," Penelope said, not daring to make eye

contact. "He was the most forthcoming, and, as you recall, he offered to tell us more about the club."

"What about Lily?" Stella asked, leaning in.

"I sense she's told us about as much as she knows," Zara said.

"Let's leave her be for now," Penelope said.

"I had a thought … and it's not a particularly pleasant thought," Zara said, also leaning in. "Shouldn't we batten the hatches and take a crack at that reporter Elsie Davies?"

"I've been thinking the same thing," Penelope whispered, huddling with the others. "But I'd rather not unless it becomes absolutely necessary."

"Best watch your back around her. She's a real snake in the grass," Stella slurred, using her tongue to tie a maraschino cherry into a knot.

"Agreed," Zara said in a low voice, "on both counts."

"You're not sitting down on the job, are you Miss Price?"

All three turned to see Florence Morgan standing beside the booth.

"Mrs. Morgan? I didn't know people like you drank phosphates," Stella said, surprised to see the matriarch of Pacific Grove at a soda fountain.

"Miss Parker, I would venture to say there is a great deal you don't know about *people like me*. But I am not the person you should be investigating, now am I?"

"No, ma'am," Stella said.

"Is this how you're spending the money I paid you, ladies?"

"No, Mrs. Morgan," Penelope said. "This is not … we were just … my apologies, Mrs. Morgan. It won't happen again."

"Miss Price, you really must learn to discern when someone is speaking in jest … especially those with dry humor," Florence said.

"Oh … I …" Penelope stammered.

"We've made some headway, Mrs. Morgan," Zara began. "We believe we've found both the murder weapon and the motive for the crime. A valuable object was taken from the shop."

"Excellent, Miss Zara. This news pleases me greatly. I imagine you will now want to revisit that last critical day before the tragedy. You're sure to find something in the way of a clue leading up to Daniel's demise."

"That's actually our next step, Mrs. Morgan," Zara said.

"It is? I thought we were going to interview Elsie Davies," Penelope said.

"Dry humor," Zara said to Florence, attempting to override Penelope's statement.

"I see you're catching on, Miss Price. Do be careful when it comes to questioning Miss Davies. She's a member of the press, you know. Chances are she'll get more out of you than you will out of her," Florence warned.

"Yes, Mrs. Morgan," Penelope said.

"Now if you ladies will pardon me, I'm quite in the mood for a chocolate malted," Florence said with a trademark double tap of her parasol.

The trio collected their things and began walking back toward AntiquiTeas.

"Where do you want to go from here, P?" Zara asked. "Do you want to interview Elsie Davies? Or Hank? Or read your Bohemian Club book? Or try to work out a timeline of what took place the day before the grand opening?"

"Yes," Penelope answered.

Zara chuckled. "Well, it's getting late—"

Penelope stopped and shook her head.

"What is it?" Zara asked, halting and turning to face her.

"I never thought I'd see the day when Zara the goodtime gal would call eight in the evening *late*."

"I meant late for the people we might interview, of

course," Zara said, resuming walking, "So we should probably pick up the interviews tomorrow."

"Nuh unh," Stella commented, trailing her.

"Why not?" Zara asked.

"Tomorrow's Sunday," Stella and Penelope said in unison.

"And?" Zara asked.

"And civilized people don't do things like interview murder witnesses and suspects on the Lord's day," Penelope said.

"No, I suppose not. They most likely go to church and have dinner with their families, don't they?" Zara thought aloud.

"Yep, dullsville," Stella said, extracting a cigarette from the top of her stocking.

"Stella, really!" Penelope said. "Put that thing away!"

"Relax, P. I don't usually light 'em unless I've got some hooch to go with it," Stella said.

"I'll never understand you flappers," Penelope replied.

"Here's what I suggest," Zara began. "Let's all go home and get a good night's sleep. Stella, no speakeasy for you tonight. Agreed?"

Stella nodded reluctantly.

"That reminds me, what's become of The Blind Pig in Dan's absence?" Penelope asked.

"Beats me. Guess I'd have to go visit it to find out," Stella commented satirically.

"Good point," Zara said.

"Very well, but no drinking liquor!" Penelope said.

"Why not?!" Stella protested.

"Because first off it's illegal, and second, you're underage," Penelope said.

"Never stopped me before. Ya know, if I wanted another mother—"

"Because you're on duty," Zara interjected. "You'll need to be extra keen ... especially since you'll be engaged in an undercover operation and all."

"Ohhhhh ... okay ... makes sense," Stella said, tucking her cigarette back in her stocking.

Zara crinkled her eyes at Penelope. "As I was about to say ... P, tonight you can bone up on the Bohemian Club, and tomorrow we can have a nice family dinner at home. I'll cook."

"You'll *what?!*" Penelope balked.

"Oh, how hard can it be?" Zara retorted.

"What has this town done to you?" Penelope said, shaking her head in dismay.

"It'll be nice," Zara said, disregarding her friend's taunts. "And it will give us time to talk through the events that took place on the day before *it* happened."

"And it will give us time to get our stomachs pumped, you mean," Penelope moaned.

"Hush, you. Stellar, I'm sorry we'll have to miss you tomorrow. I'm sure your mother will want you at home on a Sunday," Zara said.

Stella frowned and nodded.

"Count your lucky stars," Penelope whispered.

Zara glared at her. "Your humor? Not so humorous. By the way, Stella, before I forget, does Chief Harrison attend church?"

"Mmm hmmm, every Sunday."

"Protestant or Catholic?" Zara asked.

"Methodist. Vincent almost turned down the job at the police station because of it. You know how those Italian Catholics are."

"Oh no!" Zara shouted.

"What is it, Z?" Penelope asked, her heart instantly racing in concern.

"Poor Paolo!" Zara said, holding her hat on her head as she began to run the last block toward the antiques shop. "I forgot all about him. I really must do something about him. We can't … I need to get home, P. Drive me?"

"If I ever catch up to you!" Penelope gasped, her petite legs racing as Zara pulled away into the distance.

"The end," Stella said in farewell as she trotted home.

\* \* \* \*

Once they'd parked at the Victorian, Zara dashed into the house in search of Paolo. By the time Penelope got to the parlor, a full-scale argument had broken out behind closed bedroom doors with a great deal of shouting in both English and Italian.

Penelope quietly took a bath and dressed for bed. She'd just burrowed under the covers and cracked open *Bohemian Jinks* when Zara tapped lightly on the door, opening it without waiting to be invited in.

"Z, what's wrong?" Penelope asked, scooting up in bed and noting Zara's tear-streaked face.

"We had an enormous row," Zara said sniffling.

"Oh? I didn't notice," Penelope said.

Zara smiled. "You're an awful liar, you know."

"Tell your pal Chief Harrison that! But for now, tell me what happened with Paolo."

Zara got into bed with her. "Amazing what anger will do for your communication skills. Somehow we got across what we wanted to say loud and clear."

"What is it *he* wanted to say?"

"That I never spend any time with him or pay any attention to him and basically, that he's leaving."

"And what is it *you* wanted to say?" Penelope asked, lying on her side to face Zara.

Zara turned over on her side as well. "That I was sorry for being so distracted, but that surely he must understand that your life is at stake here."

"And did he understand that after my case is settled, one way or the other, things can get back to normal for you two?"

"No ... I don't know ... You see ... I didn't give him a chance to even discuss that ... When he told me he wanted to leave I told him that was fine with me and that I wanted him to go."

"Surely he must know you only said that because you were hurt and upset and that you didn't really mean it."

"Didn't I?" Zara said, looking dolefully into Penelope's eyes.

"Z, I've never seen you like this. Something's really wrong, isn't it?"

Zara looked away and rolled out of bed. "I suppose I'm just overly sensitive, leaving the lifestyle behind and all ... and settling into hometown USA. I'll be fine. Goodnight, P," she said as she walked toward the door.

"Minnie Clark, don't think for one moment I'm buying that malarkey. Something *is* wrong. Now spit it out!"

"That's just it. I don't know what it is ... truly," Zara said, exiting the room and weeping softly as she walked down the hall to her room.

**\* \* \* \***

Penelope slept in later than she would have liked. "Darn! How the devil did I miss church?" she said aloud as she stumbled through the motions of making coffee.

"Buongiorno," Paolo said sheepishly, walking into the kitchen.

"Good morning, Paolo. What has you up so early in the day?" she asked, pointing to the kitchen clock.

He thought for a minute then gestured, making the

sign of the cross.

"Ah, good man. I was supposed to be at church myself. Think God will forgive me?" she said with a smile.

He looked at her vacuously.

"I really have to work on my sense of humor," she mumbled to herself. "Coffee?" she asked, holding out a fresh pot.

"Si," he replied, smiling as he took a mug off the shelf.

"I wish you would think twice about leaving. Zara really is awfully fond of you, you know. She's just consumed with my situation at the moment. She's a very good friend, you see."

Paolo sipped his coffee, staring absently into his cup.

"You probably don't understand a word I'm saying, do you?" she said.

Paolo looked up and gasped. "Ritardo!"

"I beg your pardon!" Penelope said. "I called you no such thing!"

He hurriedly drank the rest of his coffee and pointed to the clock.

"Ohhhhh, do you mean you're late?"

"Ciao," he said, giving her a kiss on the cheek and racing out of the house to attend mass at San Carlos Cathedral in neighboring Monterey, the closest Catholic church in the area.

Penelope held the side of her cheek, a twinge of melancholy overcoming her as she watched him leave. She prepared a pair of poached eggs and rye toast and let her mind wander, pondering the vastly different paths she and Zara had trod since their school days.

Zara had seen far off countries, exotic peoples, and several of the famed wonders of the world. Penelope had seen little more than a never-ending procession of balance sheets and a handful of motion pictures. Zara had known physical intimacy with a variety of men, whereas Paolo's peck on the cheek was one of the few kisses Penelope had ever experienced. Zara lived each day like it might be her last on earth, Penelope lived each day carefully so as not to jeopardize the future.

She'd noticed a change in Zara recently though—a mellowing, a domesticating. Zara truly seemed ready to settle down, whereas Penelope's life was just getting started. Unintentionally, her thoughts drifted toward Hank, and she again caressed the side of her cheek where Paolo had planted his friendly kiss. She sighed and got up to wash her breakfast dishes, not even realizing she'd eaten.

After dressing, she grabbed *Bohemian Jinks*, which she'd failed to read the evening before, and descended the stairs to the parlor, determined to dive into the book at last. Just then the front door opened.

"Good morning, lazy bones," Zara said, smiling with flushed cheeks.

"Good morning to you too! Are you all right? Your cheeks are red. Do you have a fever?"

"Not at all. I feel marvelous. I just walked briskly home from church is all."

Penelope shut her book and regarded Zara in astonishment as Zara removed her hat and gloves.

"I don't know which terrifies me more—to hear you went to church or that you walked all the way home."

"All the way there too."

"It's settled. This has all been one very long bizarre dream. Aunt Dee never died and I'm home in my bed in Mrs. Holcomb's boarding house back in San Pedro. My best friend, Zara, is off in Europe somewhere living the life of a duchess."

Zara pinched her hard.

"Oww! What was that for?!"

"Proof you're not dreaming. Now, tell me how to make a pot roast."

# Chapter Nineteen

Penelope was only slightly more experienced than Zara when it came to cooking, but at least she had the advantage of being able to identify the various implements occupying the kitchen drawers. Plus, she owned a cookbook. It took the pair two hours to put together a simple dinner and another two hours to clean up the mess they'd created.

"I thought you knew how to do this sort of thing," Zara said. "You were such a triumph when Florence Morgan came to the tearoom."

"That wasn't actually cooking though. That was just sort of mixing ... and matching. That was much easier ... at least for me."

"Well you're a mix-match master, to be sure. And if that scrumptious aroma is any indication, we're no slouches in the cooking department either."

"We shall see. The proof is in the pot roast."

The friends giggled and sat down to relax in the parlor. Penelope tossed her unread book on the coffee table and let out a satisfied sigh.

"I'm craving tea but am too lazy to get back up and make it," she said. "You must be exhausted, being unaccustomed to both walking and puttering around the kitchen."

"I feel fantastic, revitalized! Besides, I've always kept myself in fighting shape, just in the bedroom versus the kitchen."

Penelope shook her head. "Oh, Z, what a storied life you've led. I would think your new lifestyle here must be horribly dull in comparison."

"Not in the least. I don't find it dull at all—just different ... You're different too, you know."

"Me? You must be joking."

"My humor's not *that* dry," Zara gibed. "It's true though.

You've changed since coming to Pacific Grove. You're like the monarch butterflies that flock here every year."

"Kaleidoscope."

"Gesundheit?" Zara replied.

"A group of butterflies isn't called a flock. It's a kaleidoscope."

"Don't try to change the subject. You're blossoming, and you know it."

"Well, I *will* say that I'm enjoying Pacific Grove—death row notwithstanding."

"Ah yes, the ubiquitous case. I suppose we should get back to it."

"I'm still trying to muster the energy to get up and make tea!"

The doorbell rang and Zara momentarily panicked. "Don't tell me he's here already," she said, jumping up to adjust her dress and hair.

"Paolo only went to mass in Monterey. He must have forgotten his key," Penelope said, making a start for the door. "Stella, what are you doing here?"

"Good to see you too, P," Stella said, letting herself in.

"Oh … it's you," Zara said, relaxing from her staged pose on the settee where she pretended she was reading.

"What gives with you two?" Stella asked, turning Zara's book right side up as she meandered by. "And what's that smell?" she said, sniffing.

"It's pot roast. At least that's the hope," Zara said.

"Not bad," Stella said, opening the oven and inspecting its contents.

"Things improved dramatically once we thought to turn the oven on," Penelope said, returning to her seat and collapsing. "Drat! I forgot to put the kettle on. Stellar, be a dear …"

"Yes, boss," Stella said, dutifully filling the tea kettle with water and placing it on the stove.

"Say, how did your reconnaissance mission at The Blind Pig go last night?" Zara asked.

"Umm …"

"Don't tell me you got caught!" Penelope said.

"Not exactly." Stella said, returning to the parlor.

"Then *what* exactly?" Zara said.

"Well … I was waiting for my parents to go to bed so I could sneak out."

"And …?" Zara prompted.

"And … I fell asleep," Stella said nearly inaudibly, looking everywhere in the room other than at Penelope or Zara.

"Bully for you!" Zara said. "Oh thank the lord!" Penelope said at the same time.

"You don't mind?" Stella said.

Zara shook her head *no*.

"Mind?! I couldn't be more relieved!" Penelope said.

"Whew! Glad to hear it," Stella said, going back to the kitchen to check on the tea kettle. "What about you two? You make much headway since I saw you last?"

"Not me. I've made a few well-intended attempts though," Penelope said.

"And you, Z? You get anything out of Chief Harrison this morning? I saw you licking his boots outside of church. Clever way to get on the good side of a God-fearing man like the chief."

"Is that right," Penelope said, looking warily at her friend.

"Nothing to report. But let's get back to our young rebel," Zara said, changing the subject. "How is it your mother allowed you over here on a Sunday?"

"Or did you steal away without telling her?" Penelope asked, certain the investigative agency's activities would eventually land Stella in Juvenile Hall.

"I'm here with her blessing, actually," Stella said, pouring three cups of tea and carrying them in on a tray.

Zara narrowed her eyes in response.

"It's true. Mother said that helping Miss Price with her case would be the *Christian thing to do*. She all but insisted I come over."

Zara burst out laughing. "Didn't I tell you our young friend was extraordinary?" she said to Penelope, standing up and kissing Stella on the top of her head. "Now, if you two will excuse me for a moment, I should get changed. I must reek of flour."

"Flour doesn't really smell," Stella said.

"No?" Zara said, exiting the room.

"But your excuse to leave the room sure stinks!" Penelope called after her.

"I invited Vincent for dinner too. I hope that's copacetic," Stella said to Penelope, passing her the sugar.

"Will his mother spare him on a Sunday as well?"

"You kidding? She was over the moon to think she'd have one less mouth to feed at dinner. In fact, I was thinking ... if there are any leftovers ... maybe ..."

"Yes, Vincent can take them, of course. Are things really so bad at his house?"

Stella looked to the floor and nodded.

"What about Dan Cooper's family? Have you heard anything about how they're making do? Do they have enough to eat?"

Stella downed her tea in one long gulp. "Florence Morgan's looking after his girls—just like she always has."

"What do you mean?"

Stella made herself comfortable on the chaise, lounging with her hands behind her head. "She took them under her wing years ago. Dan used to do a lot for the town before Prohibition. And Mrs. Morgan was involved in most of the civic groups he benefited. She wanted to thank him somehow, but he wouldn't let her. So she decided to become the unofficial patron of his daughters, paying for them to have piano lessons, English horse-riding lessons, ballet lessons, you name it."

"How altruistic of her."

"If you say so. I personally wouldn't take kindly to having some old biddy stick her nose into *my* family life if I were Dan. But he wanted to keep Lily happy, and Lily wanted all of that hogwash for their girls. She insisted on it really. She didn't used to be like that. She used to be so down-to-earth, not into money and appearances like she is now."

"What do you think changed her?"

"You mean *who*."

"Don't tell me … Elsie Davies?" Penelope said, sipping her tea in satisfaction.

"Who else?" Stella answered.

"I wonder if that's who Hank was referring to …" Penelope said, her interest piqued.

"When Dan's saloon started to become a success, Elsie started pressganging Lily to improve her social standing—you know, by dressing fancy, buying expensive stuff they really couldn't afford. If you ask me, Elsie did it so she could feel important and wealthy by proxy. She's a barracuda, that one, ever since she got jilted."

"I'm sorry to hear she was jilted. Can you tell me what happened or is it too personal?"

"Too personal? It made the headlines! She was left at the altar, and when the reverend and her maid of honor went looking for the groom, they found him with his best man … in the altogether."

"You mean in flagrante delicto?"

"If you mean altogether together, yeah," Stella said.

"Good heavens!" Penelope gasped.

"Yeah, they ran off together that night. Last I heard

they opened a racy cabaret in San Francisco."

"That poor woman."

"Poor woman, nothin'!" Stella shouted, rising in agitation. "I bet she drove him to it. Everything is about appearances with her. It doesn't matter what the truth is as long is it *looks* good. Even when Dan lost his business, did she show a moment's compassion? Nope. She kept pouring poison in Lily's ear, telling Lily she should leave Dan if he didn't start making more money. That's how he ended up with The Pig—Elsie talked him into it—*yelled* him into it is more like it. She railed on him when he was at his lowest, saying that if he were any sort of man he'd do whatever it took to keep his family living at the level people expected. She shamed him into bootlegging."

"How do you know all this?" Penelope asked.

Stella moved closer, taking a seat in the chair by Penelope.

"I'm a bored high school girl in a small town. I know my onions and pretty much everything that goes on around here. … Ya see? I was born to be an investigative agent," she said, putting her feet up on the coffee table.

"Investigative agents know better than to put their feet on the table," Penelope said, pouring another cup of tea. "You make a superb pot of tea, I'll give you that."

"So do you really think you can get all this jazz sewn up by Wednesday? I'm all for a whizbang thrill same as the next gal, but …"

"Not to worry, we have until Friday."

"Wednesday," Stella corrected.

"But the judge said Friday!" Penelope yelped.

"Judge Houston's goin' out of town," Stella said, retrieving an unopened newspaper from beside the front door and dropping it Penelope's lap.

"*What?!*" Penelope cried, opening the paper and reading the headline.

# It's a Bouncing Baby Boy for Proud Grandpa Judge Houston

```
He and the misses will be
heading out to Salinas on
Thursday to visit daughter
Mindy and her husband Josh,
and to meet their first
grandchild. Congratulations
to the whole Houston clan.
```

She crumpled the newspaper, her eyes darting in erratic thought.

Zara descended the stairs, her hair and makeup flawless, to find Penelope pacing in figure eights and muttering.

"Uh oh, looks like she found out about Judge Houston," Zara said.

"You mean you knew?!" Penelope shouted, leaving off pacing to fume at Zara.

"I just found out this morning," Zara said. "I was going to tell you."

"When?!"

"Today, this evening, I don't know, before the bells chimed midnight. It simply slipped my mind."

"*It slipped your mind?!*"

"Uh, maybe I should go," Stella said, standing up.

"She'll be fine. Just give her a few minutes to let off steam," Zara said, putting a hand on Stella's shoulder to keep her from fleeing.

"Looks like there's more than a few minutes worth of steam there," Stella said.

"Z, I'm a goner," Penelope said, collapsing onto the couch. "What could we ever hope to accomplish in the next two days?"

"More or less what we could accomplish in the originally allotted four days, if we stay on track and work efficiently," Zara said.

"It's impossible," Penelope said, her face in her hands. "This whole thing is impossible. I should make a will. Yes, that's the thing to do. Drop all this sleuth play-acting and do the sensible thing and make out a will. I'll call Bernard Beekham first thing in the morning. He's good at that sort of legal tommyrot."

"You'll do nothing of the kind," Zara said.

"Of course, I'll make sure you're taken care of, Z. And Stella, I'll include enough to get you through college. Please promise you'll go to college ... for me?"

"Yeah, umm sure, boss."

"I'll want to leave something for Vincent as well. I know he could most decidedly use it. Be good to him, Stella. Be so very good to him. We never know how much time we have on this orb we call home."

The front door opened and Vincent walked in.

"Vincent, it's so good to see you," Penelope said, walking swiftly toward him and flinging her arms around him in a tight embrace.

"You too, Miss Price," he croaked, gasping for air.

"Are you alone, Vincent?" Zara asked nervously.

"No, ma'am. Come on in," he called out once Penelope had released him.

"So glad you could make it," Zara began. "Oh ... Paolo ... it's you."

"Signorina," he said, unsure as to whether he would be welcome.

"Of course it's Paolo. Who else would it be?" Penelope said, holding the door open and gesturing for him to enter.

"You're right, yes," Zara said, walking toward Paolo and hugging him perfunctorily while peering out the still-open front door.

Paolo produced a red rose he'd concealed behind his back, then kissed it and handed it to Zara.

"That was very thoughtful, Paolo. Grazie," she said stiffly.

"I'm so glad you're all here," Penelope said. "I cherish every moment with you. Please make yourselves comfortable. Dinner should be ready in a quarter of an hour," she continued, walking around to each person and affectionately touching his or her arm or head.

"What's all that about?" Vincent said under his breath to Stella.

"She read about the judge going out of town."

"Ah," he responded, nodding. "Looks like the heat's been turned up on your case, Miss Price. If there's anything I can do ... within the law ..."

"Penelope. Call me Penelope, please. I think we're beyond all pretense at this point, don't you?"

The phone rang and Penelope wandered in its direction. Zara hoped the call was intended for herself, and made up an excuse to answer the phone.

"You're in no fit state," Zara said, striding past Penelope and picking up the receiver.

"Price residence, Zara speaking ... Why, I'm glad I answered too," she said twirling the phone cord around her index finger. "Oh really? ... That's a shame ... I'm sorry you ... no I understand ... another time then ... Yes ... all right ... You too."

"Who was that, P?" Penelope asked.

"Walter. He won't be joining us after all. Something about a busted water main on the way here. I fear he ruined his suit," Zara said, slowly sitting and gazing out the window.

"Walter? Who's Walter? A friend of yours, Vincent?" Penelope asked.

"Walter's my boss. Chief Walter Harrison?"

"What in the Sam Hill was he coming here for?" Penelope asked.

"Dinner would be my guess," Stella said.

"Well it doesn't matter now, does it," Zara said, swallowing her emotions. She turned toward Paolo and smiled brightly, "How was church?"

He looked at her perplexedly.

"Chiesa," Vincent translated.

"Ahh, choorch," Paolo said, smiling, then kissing his hand and raising his eyes toward heaven.

Penelope glanced at her watch and announced, "Friends, I do believe our pot has roasted."

All chuckled.

"Oh, you know what I mean. Let's go in to dinner, shall we?"

"You sure you're up to this Miss—" Vincent began.

"Uh, unh," Penelope admonished.

"... *Penelope*," Vincent continued. "If you'd rather work on your case, we can just—"

"No, Vincent, thank you. This is exactly what I want to do tonight. No talk of the case. I don't want to hear a word about it. I want to hear about all of you. Now you get seated. Z, would you like to help me in the kitchen?"

Zara followed her in and asked indifferently, "What would you like me to do first?"

"You sure you're all right?"

"Of course. Why wouldn't I be?"

"Just checking ... Very well. Would you get drinks for everyone?"

"I'd love to," Zara replied, affecting fervor.

"And if you want a bottle of wine ... well, I won't tell," Penelope said in an attempt to perk up Zara's spirits.

"No, no. That's quite all right ... Besides, we don't

want to put Vincent in an awkward position."

"You have a point there."

**\* \* \* \***

Within a few minutes, dinner had been dished out—pot roast with potatoes, carrots, pearl onions, lots of gravy, and Brussels sprouts on the side.

"Who would like to say grace?" Penelope asked.

Just then the doorknocker struck.

"Now who could that be?" Penelope said.

"God?" Vincent quipped.

Stella snorted.

"Come on in," Penelope hollered.

"Anyone have a towel?" a voice called as the door creaked open.

"Walter?" Zara said, rushing to the door. "Look at you, soaked through. Paolo, do you have anything Chief Harrison can wear to get him out of his wet clothes?"

Paolo looked at her unresponsively.

"Uh, vestititi … vestiario," Vincent said, trying to interpret for Paolo.

Paolo huffed, made a fist, and muttered as he walked to his room, all the while glaring at the chief.

A few minutes later, Walter emerged from the bathroom wearing Zara's cherry blossom kimono robe over his undershirt, shorts, and gartered socks. Paolo burst out laughing and all joined in—the scene made all the funnier since it featured the chief of police. Good-humoredly, Walter strutted into the room and did a turn, one hand on his hip, the other by his ear, posing like a saloon girl.

"Paolo's clothes are made for his fit physique, not this bowlful of jelly," he said, patting his ample mid-section. "You should all thank me for wearing this robe. It covers much more, believe me."

"You look splendid, Walter. It's so nice to have you with us," Penelope said.

"Thank you, Miss Price," he said, eyeing her skeptically as he took the table's empty seat. "She isn't drunk again, is she?" he whispered to Vincent.

Stella snorted again and Vincent shook his head *no*.

"We were just about to say grace. Would you like to do the honors?" Zara said.

"I'd be ... well ... honored!" Walter said with a chuckle. He then bowed his head and folded his hands. "For food that stays our hunger, for rest that brings us ease, for homes where memories linger, we give our thanks for these ... Amen."

"Amen," all said.

Vincent and Paolo crossed themselves.

"This looks delicious," the chief remarked as Zara placed a plate in front of him.

"Looks can be deceiving," Penelope said sagely.

"Pay no attention to her. She's waxing doomed," Zara said.

"She read the paper today, did she?" Walter asked. "Mmmm mmmm you ladies make a fine pot roast ... mighty fine," he said, taking a large bite and smiling benevolently.

**＊ ＊ ＊ ＊**

The evening proceeded as though no one had a care in the world, and not at all as if the lady of the house was facing certain death. At Penelope's insistence, no talk of the case was conducted, and all agreed the pot roast was *entirely edible*.

When time came for dessert and coffee, Zara lamented that they'd forgotten to make dessert. Without a word, Walter toddled out to his car and returned with a devil's food cake. Stella made coffee, and the ragtag group genially caroused for hours. Even Paolo had a good time and laughed along with the others, whether or not he had any idea as to what they were laughing about.

Walter insisted on staying to do the dishes, and Zara was all smiles when tying a frilly apron around the floral dressing gown he still wore. The sleeves kept unrolling and dipping into the dishwater, much to Zara's amusement, and Walter blew a handful of suds at her as retribution for her jeering. Penelope noted she had never before seen Zara dry a dish. Then again she had never before seen Zara so happy. Penelope looked at Walter—whom she estimated to be twice Paolo's age as well as girth—and then she looked at Paolo whose good looks could stop traffic. Yes, under Walter's influence, Zara looked to be settling down, but in no way settling for second best.

Paolo and Vincent busied themselves crooning Italian songs, and Stella insisted on teaching Penelope how to Charleston.

"If you're going to the electric chair, you may as well dance your way there," the young flapper counseled.

A short time later, another knock came at the door. Penelope answered to find the uniformed Jimmy Matlin. "Constable Matlin?"

"Good evening, Miss Price. We had a complaint from a neighbor regarding a noisy party taking place here. They suggested that the drinking of liquor was going on. I'm afraid I'll have to search the premises and your guests for alcohol. Is Miss Zara here? I can start my search with her," he said, craning his neck to look for her.

"What seems to be the problem, constable?" Walter said, drying his hands on the frilly apron as he approached the door.

Jimmy looked him over and was rendered dumbstruck.

"Nothing to worry about here, constable. I have everything under control," Walter said, striking a heroic stance with his feet apart and fists on hips.

Jimmy merely gaped in silence. The others exploded in an outburst of mirth.

"Go on back to the precinct, constable. You have my word we have not been drinking," Walter said.

"Then how do you explain—" Jimmy began.

"Devil's food cake, son, devil's food cake."

The revelers in the parlor burst into additional peals of laughter.

"It's the devil's work!" Stella howled through tears of hilarity.

Walter closed the door then turned to the group. "Well folks, looks like that's my cue to get going. Thank you for a splendid evening. I don't remember the last time I enjoyed myself so thoroughly."

"Ah, c'mon, Chief, you have fun wherever you go," Vincent said.

"It's true, Walter, you're more or less the official life of the party here in Pacific Grove," Stella said, wiping the remnants of mirth-induced tears from her eyes and spreading her smoky eye-makeup into even larger, darker circles.

"Well, nonetheless ..." he continued, untying the apron to expose his imposing belly that had escaped the confines of the kimono.

No one dared laugh ... until he did ... then none could stop laughing.

"Life of the party or court jester?" he joked as he donned his shoes and hat, still wearing the dressing gown, with his damp clothes thrown over his arm. "I'll return your robe tomorrow, if that's all right, Minnie," he said to Zara.

"Who's Minnie?" Stella asked.

"I meant *Zara*," Walter corrected. "Good night all ... oh and Miss Price, I'll be in Monterey tomorrow morning, testifying in a case, but when I get back, we should have a conversation."

"If you'd like," Penelope answered blithely.

She was beyond the point of regarding any news or development as either good or bad, but rather resigned to her fate and determined to live out her days as an exemplary prisoner. A life in lockup would give her time to read and even master the art of knitting. Yes, she was ready for the hoosegow.

"Looks like we'll be going too," Stella said. "Zara said we have a big week and need our rest."

"Zara said that?" Penelope asked, astonished at her friend's responsible advice.

"Told you I was a good influence," Zara said, smiling and dipping a finger into the last of the cake's frosting.

"Zara, per favore," Paolo said, pulling her aside and whispering.

"Good night all. Buona notte," Vincent said, opening the door for Stella.

"Oh, just a minute. Will you do me a favor and take this?" Penelope said, grabbing a basket full of leftovers and holding it out for Vincent.

He frowned. "Thank you, no. I don't need your charity, Miss Price."

"No, I … uhh …" Penelope stammered, at a loss as to how to respond.

"Please, Vincent, for me?" Zara said. "Penelope knows I can't bear to look at leftovers the next morning … makes me retch … It's awfully wasteful and over-indulgent I know … Just one of the deplorable habits I picked up living abroad. If someone doesn't take those victuals I'll just throw them in the waste bin."

"Oh, I see … Well, it would be a shame to see such delicious food thrown away. I'll be happy to dispose of it for you so you don't have to face the trauma of waking up to leftovers," Vincent said, taking the basket in hand.

Zara pinched his cheek. "You're a doll."

"And you'll see Stella safely home?" Penelope said, trying to re-enter the conversation after her blunder.

"I always do," Vincent said, putting an arm around his girlfriend.

"Sorry, Mac, bank's closed," Stella said, ducking his embrace as she always did in front of others.

"Good night, you two," Penelope said, closing the door after them.

"Belle donne," Paolo said, bowing chivalrously. "Ti amo, Zara," he added, retiring to his room without requesting her to follow.

"Everything all right?" Penelope asked Zara as they once again sat in the parlor and put their feet up.

"Never been better," Zara said, looking intently at the last of the cake which she consumed pinch by pinch.

"I mean with Paolo," Penelope said.

"Oh! Yes! Of course. What makes you ask?"

"Well he went to his own room for starters ... without you! And you two looked to be deep in discussion earlier, or as deep as one can be with Paolo."

Zara smiled. "Yes, everything's fine there too. We discussed—at least I think we did— giving our relationship a serious look after your trial is over ... to see where we stand."

"He really cares about you, you know," Penelope said.

"You think so?"

"Of course! Why else would he put up with all of the nonsense we've put him through ... and without anyone to talk to."

"Free room and board?"

"I highly doubt it. You know as well as I that an Adonis like Paolo could find free room and board wherever he liked ... but he *chooses* to be with you."

"Have you been eavesdropping on us?"

Penelope looked at her curiously.

"Paolo mentioned, or rather mimed, much of what you just said. Poor lamb seems so forlorn. You don't think he'll do anything drastic do you?"

"How so?"

"Well, he asked if he could borrow the car tomorrow to drive to San Francisco. You don't think he'll …"

"What? Jump off a cliff?"

"The thought did cross my mind. You know how dramatic he is … short on words but big on gestures."

"I'm sure he'll be fine. Probably just wants some time away to think, and get some perspective."

Zara nodded.

"Speaking of perspective, I've made my peace. I'm ready for the gallows," Penelope said calmly, closing her eyes and breathing deeply.

Zara erupted in a spate of sniggers.

Penelope opened her eyes, her mouth agape.

"I'm sorry, P. It's just … You're not going to the gallows, not if I have anything to say about it, that is. I won't allow it."

"Don't tell me you've been sidling up to Chief Harrison just to keep me from hanging."

"What a heinous thing to say!" Zara snapped uncharacteristically. "He's the finest man I know and if I've been *sidling up* to him, as you say, it's because I enjoy his company and feel privileged that he seems to enjoy mine. Really, P, that was not only uncalled for, but cruel."

"Z, I … I am sorry … truly … I didn't realize … You really care for him, don't you?"

"Well of course I do! Everyone in town does. What's not to like?"

"I suppose you're right. He seemed very different tonight than when I first met him. Maybe someday I'll find out what I did to anger him at the outset, but you're right, the man I dined with tonight was wonderful. Accept my apology?"

Zara nodded, wiping an errant tear from her chin.

"And another thing, as long as I'm ranting," Zara continued, "no more of that fatalistic talk, ya hear? You may not give a fig if you live or die, but I do! You're all I've got in this world and I'm not about to lose you. Are we clear?"

"Yes, ma'am," Penelope said.

"Good. Now tomorrow we're going to get up at the crack of dawn and go to the shop to recreate the day before Dan's death, as planned. We can stop by the Butterfly Café on the way to get breakfast take-away. Paolo will be gone ... and eventually return, God willing ... Stella will be in school until mid-day, Vincent will be at work, and Walter will be in court in Monterey. It will be just you and me."

"That's all we need," Penelope said, smiling.

"Darn tootin'," Zara said, finishing off the last pinch of cake and licking her fingers to punctuate her words.

The two walked up the stairs to turn in.

"Just what time should I expect dawn to crack tomorrow, by the way?" Penelope asked as they ascended.

"I should think around nine o'clock?"

"You'd make a terrible farmer, you know that?"

"Good thing I'm a professional investigator then, eh?"

# Chapter Twenty

Good to her word, Zara was ready to go the next morning at the allotted time with seconds to spare.

"I ordered an egg and bacon pie from the café. If we leave now it should be just out of the oven, ready for us to pick up," Penelope said, taking a deep breath.

"You okay, P?"

"The situation's just catching up to me. We have today and tomorrow and that's it."

"And each other. Don't forget we have each other."

"Thanks, Z. You're the best sister I could ever ask for," she said, pinning on her hat.

"Well compared to the sister you've got, I'm not so sure that's much of a compliment," Zara quipped.

Penelope chuckled. "I'll go get my keys."

"I'll go take a nap."

"There will be no time for your jibes. I already have my keys out, see?" she said, jingling them.

"Looks like we're already off to a fabulous start. Keep the faith, P. Keep the faith."

The friends rolled down the windows in Penelope's modest car, taking in the invigorating fresh air.

"Aunt Dee sure picked a beautiful spot, didn't she?" Zara said.

"She really did. This town is something special."

"The kind you could live out a lifetime."

"Which may be a short one, in my case."

"No negativity. Not today, P."

"I'll do my best. Besides, who could be negative in such a setting?"

**\* \* \* \***

About a quarter of an hour later, the investigators opened the door to the antique shop and unpacked their things along with the breakfast pie.

"I'll start the tea," Zara said. "I'm thinking we should go with something bold this morning—what would you say to some Russian Caravan?"

Penelope nodded and opened her notebook. "Where to start. Let's see, it says here you're to request an interview with Elsie Davies. Be careful with that one, she's slippery."

"I can handle the Elsie Davieses of this world while putting on my lipstick with my eyes closed," Zara called from the kitchen.

"For now, let's take advantage of the quiet and try to recreate that day before the opening. Did anything suspicious happen? Fuses were exceptionally short as I recall."

"Understandably so. We'd been working 'round the clock and still had so much to get done." Zara said, entering the tearoom with plates, silverware and napkins.

"And no one worked harder than Dan," Penelope said, her voice faltering as she clumsily dished out the breakfast pie.

Zara stretched out a hand to steady Penelope's. "He was a good man. And his death had nothing to do with you. You know that, don't you?"

"If you say so," Penelope said unconvincingly. "Okay … I'm ready to take notes."

They walked through the occurrences of that fateful day, recounting as best as they could all that happened, at turns laughing and weeping as they shared anecdotes of Dan's industriousness and good humor—especially when it came to his antics with Hank.

"Those two were quite an entertaining pair," Zara said.

Penelope nodded and sighed.

"He'll be back," Zara said.

"Who? You mean Dan? Do you think he's going to haunt us?"

"No, ninny. Hank!"

"Who said anything about Hank?"

"You did. Your body language did. Your heart did. Don't forget, I know you inside and out, P."

"Well then perhaps you know something I don't. In any event, let's get back to it."

They made a verbal tour of the tearoom and antiques

shop, trying to recollect if they'd seen anyone unusual canvasing or lurking. They ended up no further along than when they'd started.

"The main thing I remember about that day was all the squabbles," Penelope said. "I recall Dan and Hank shouting at one another in the tearoom. I couldn't make out what they were saying, but their mannerisms indicated anger, and the situation became so tense that Hank shoved Dan, and Dan stormed out."

"That doesn't sound like the two of them," Zara remarked.

"And there's more! After that, Dan got into a brief confrontation with Vincent … That's when you and Paolo drove up, and I noticed you were arguing. Later in the day, Vincent had Stella in tears."

"Zowie!"

"There's still more. Dan and Hubert were at each other's throats, and a moment later, Hubert approached Paolo only to stomp off in frustration after a fruitless attempt to converse with him while Paolo lounged in the Duesenberg. Everyone was working himself to the bone and Paolo sat in the car, smoking as the rest of us toiled. I couldn't hear what Hubert said to him but I bet he gave Paolo a piece of his mind for loafing. A little later, Paolo snapped at Hank for talking to you. And even Stella and Dan had words!"

"Sounds like we were lucky to have only seen one fatality!" Zara said. "You think we should ask everyone about these incidents to see if we can find a thread? We have nothing else."

"It looks that way. We already know what weapon was used, as well as the suspected motive, but maybe one of our opening day crew knows more than he or she realizes … something that can point us to the killer's identity."

"You'll never take me alive," a low voice rasped loudly.

Penelope and Zara screamed.

Stella snickered. "Relax, it's just me," she said, coming out from the behind the tearoom doorway where she'd hidden.

"Stella! You almost gave me a heart attack!" Zara said.

Penelope stood wheezing, trying to catch her breath, on the verge of keeling over.

"We've got to get you out of corsets once and for all, P," Zara said. "Slow, deep breaths."

"I saw you two deep in conversation through the window so I opened the door slowly enough not to jiggle the bells."

"Why aren't you in sch—" Penelope began as Zara scribbled a note.

"Lunchtime," Stella said, reclining on one of the tearoom's settees.

"They let you leave the school grounds at lunch?" Penelope asked.

"What do you think?" Zara said sarcastically, handing Stella the note she'd written. "Here. Make use of your time. We want to see all of these people again, this evening, if possible. It will be brief, you can assure them."

"Affirmative," Stella said, taking the paper and racing out the door.

"Good thinking," Penelope said, still trying to normalize her breathing.

"Now, what is it exactly we want to ask tonight's interrogees?"

"Well, I suppose what everyone was arguing about, mostly."

"I can tell you what Paolo and I were fighting about. He accused me of flirting with Hank."

"You *were* flirting with Hank!"

"Well … I'm not anymore … I'm not flirting with anyone."

Penelope raised an eyebrow.

"Walter Harrison doesn't count. That's not flirting … not for me, at any rate," Zara said.

"Fair enough. Speaking of Hank, I suppose we should ask him why he and Dan were arguing … and why it came down to shoving. Vincent and Dan exchanged words briefly, so we'll want to uncover what that was about. I find it especially interesting that Hubert, who is always so calm and collected, got into a tiff with Dan and then accosted Paolo. We can ask both Hubert and Paolo what went on there."

"Hank, Vincent, Hubert and Paolo. Do you really think any of them will have anything to say that they haven't told us already?"

"Maybe not. But perhaps you and I will get more out of what they tell us, given that we now know why and how Dan was killed."

"Or at least *think* we know."

"Well, if the theft theory is good enough for Walter Harrison, it's good enough for me," Penelope said.

Zara clasped her hands to her heart. "Thank you," she whispered, then leaned across the table and gave Penelope a kiss on the cheek.

"Pfft, I've had better," Penelope jeered.

"You don't say! From whom?"

"Paolo, if you must know. Just yesterday."

"Is that so!" Zara said, feigning jealousy before her tone turned melancholy. "I wonder how he's getting on in San Francisco. I do worry about him, you know."

"My guess is he's having a marvelous time. Probably in Little Italy right now confabbing with his countrymen, sneaking glasses of wine, and consuming any number of dishes made with noodles, garlic, and olive oil."

"I hope you're right," Zara said, smiling faintly.

They whiled away the afternoon jumping from one topic to the next—from the case to Paolo to the meaning of life and even Penelope's sister, Pauline. At length, they were interrupted by a visitor.

"Good afternoon, ladies," Florence Morgan said, her hands poised atop her parasol as she stood in the tearoom's entrance. "The door was open. I do hope you're not being careless when it comes to security."

"Mrs. Morgan, what a pleasure. I'm afraid we don't have much to report," Penelope said. "We'll be conducting one last round of interviews this evening ... or at least we hope they'll be the last."

"I am not here to discuss the case, Miss Price. I am here to discuss a tea party for the Horticulturists Society. It's scheduled four weeks from Friday and I am expecting forty guests. That is your maximum, I believe?"

"Yes, but shouldn't we wait until after my trial to—"

"I have every confidence you will be acquitted, Miss Price. And you should too!"

"I'll go freshen the tea," Zara said, excusing herself. "P, your notebook," she whispered as she walked to the kitchen.

"Yes, I should take notes. What exactly did you have in mind, Mrs. Morgan?"

"Something substantial enough to satisfy the men and dainty enough to please the ladies. I look to your creativity to sort out the particulars. Good day, Miss Price." Two taps of her parasol later, Florence departed the shop.

"The water should be done in a minute or two," Zara said, walking back in with a tray of tea accessories. "Don't tell me you sent her away."

Penelope shook her head. "Why on earth would Mrs. Morgan plan a party before I've even had my trial."

"Perhaps that's her way of saying she has faith in you?"

"She's said it in many ways already."

"When will you get it through that thick noggin' of yours that people are on your side and rooting for you to succeed?"

"But why should they? I'm nothing special."

"Are you saying I'd choose someone ordinary as my best friend?"

Penelope smiled appreciatively. "Perhaps *you* should be my lawyer."

"Perhaps I should! … What say you lock the door while I finish with the tea."

As Penelope walked to the front door to lock it, she espied Hank across the street. Her heart caught in her throat and she stood immobile. She tried to avert her eyes so as not to stare at him, but couldn't. Before she could make herself look away, she'd caught his eye. She nodded and locked the door, but then noticed he was walking toward the shop. At least she thought he was. *What if he's just crossing the street? What do I do? Zara, help!* she thought, smiling at him as he approached.

He raised a hand in salutation and she dared open the door for him. "Good afternoon, Mr. Edwards. How nice to see you."

"You as well."

"… Do … How … They say it's unseasonably warm here this time of year," Penelope offered feebly.

"Hank, thank you for coming in so quickly," Zara said, extending her hand in a friendly shake.

"Happy to oblige," he said, shaking her hand amiably. "I don't know what help I can be …"

"We just have a few quick questions to ask you. Tea?" Zara offered.

"Yes, I'd love some."

"P? Would you like to play mother?" Zara asked as the three walked into the tearoom to sit.

"I'm not nearly old enough to be his mother!" Penelope whispered to Zara.

"I meant would you like to be in charge of pouring the tea!"

"Oh! Hahahaha," Penelope responded, laughing loudly and nervously.

"Are you sure you're up to this?" Hank asked, noting her peculiar behavior.

"Oh yes, I'm right as rain. You know, speaking of rain—"

Zara cut her off before she could get any further into her meteorological ramblings. "Please, take a sink, Hank," Zara said, motioning to an armchair as she dropped comfortably onto the settee.

Penelope sat in the chair across from Hank and wordlessly gazed at him.

"P?" Zara urged.

"Huh?" she said, still staring at Hank.

"The tea?"

"Oh yes, of course," she said, coming to her senses.

Recalling Zara's graceful and fluid movements, Penelope tried to emulate her, making birdlike motions and rolling her hands and arms unintentionally comically. Zara and Hank both fought to stifle their laughter.

"Hank, to get right to the point," Zara said, looking away from Penelope lest a snigger escape. "What can you tell us about the spat you had with Dan the day before the grand opening … When Dan shoved you?"

"*I* shoved *him*, actually," Hank said, accepting the sloshing teacup from Penelope's shaking hands. His fingers brushed against hers, making hers shake all the more.

"Oh?" Zara said.

"Dan and I rarely quarreled, and when we did, it was always about the same thing—the speakeasy."

"You didn't approve of his new venture?" Zara asked.

"I didn't approve of him doing anything that went against his conscious, and the speakeasy did just that. I shoved him to try to get him to wise up. I was angry with him for risking so much for so little."

"What do you mean, Mr. Edwards?" Penelope said, her nervousness turning to intrigue.

"He was doing it just for the money."

"Don't most people work *for the money*?" Zara said.

Hank ran a hand through his hair. "This was beyond that, far beyond. He was getting on fine with odd jobs … and he had a bright future here with you, Miss Price. He told me as much."

"Then what are you saying?" Penelope asked.

"I'm saying that he kowtowed to Elsie Davies' ludicrous greed for status."

"Whose status?" Penelope said. "Elsie's or Lily's?"

"Both! When Dan first started doing well, it took him no time to become a respected member of the community, and of course, his business success made Lily a society success by default. Lily never cared about that sort of thing, but Elsie sure did. He'd promised me he was going to quit the bootlegging, once he'd started working here with you. But I found out he was still at it. That's when we argued and I shoved him … I shoved him for being stupid."

"But he told me he was so happy here. Why would he continue to bootleg?" Penelope said.

"He told me he couldn't get out. That 'they' wouldn't let him. That if he tried to stop bootlegging, 'they' would report his activities to the police and ruin his life," Hank said.

"So he was being blackmailed," Zara said.

Hank nodded.

"Who is this *they* to whom he referred?" Penelope asked.

"I wish I knew. I've racked my brain trying to figure it out, but never made any headway. Dan and I agreed we would finish our conversation after the grand opening. And I vowed to help him extricate himself from the speakeasy and blackmail mess—only, he was gone before we ever got a chance to have that talk."

Hank took a deep breath and then sipped his tea, his eyes on the table.

"Mr. Edwards, you were a good friend to him. You must know that," Penelope said, placing a hand on Hank's, her flusteredness having given way to compassion.

He looked at her hand and smiled. "Thank you, Miss Price. I hope so. He was the best friend I ever had, actually. He knew all about me, but never minded. He accepted me just the way I am."

He took another breath and they sat in silence for moments. The only sound was that of teacups meeting saucers as they drank their tea and contemplated.

"Will there be anything else, ladies?" Hank said when he'd finished his tea.

"No, thank you, Hank. You've been most helpful," Zara said.

"Actually ... just one more thing, if you don't mind, Mr. Edwards," Penelope said.

Zara looked at her inquiringly.

"Your name, Hank, is short for Henry, correct?"

"Yes?"

"So then your name, Henry Edwards, is the same as Henry Edwards who was one of the founders of the Bohemian Club ... and you both being members ... May I ask ... are you related to him? Was he your father perhaps?"

"No, we are not related," Hank said, standing abruptly. "Good day, ladies; and thank you for the tea."

He pulled his fedora over his brow and walked briskly out of the tearoom and shop, leaving Penelope and Zara in wonder.

"Did I say something wrong?" Penelope asked, a lump in her throat.

"I don't know ... I doubt it."

"I did, didn't I," Penelope said, hanging limply over the arm of her chair.

"So Dan was blackmailed. Do you think that had anything to do with the theft or his murder?" Zara asked.

"I don't see how it could, but who knows. I sure don't," Penelope said sullenly.

"Don't pout, P. It doesn't become you. I wonder who the blackmailer could be. What if it's someone we know?"

"You've read too many dime novels. I'm betting it's someone from Monterey. That's where his saloon was located. Pacific Grove has been a dry town since its inception. They've never allowed the sale of spirits."

"Interesting … where are you going?" Zara asked as Penelope got up and smoothed her skirt.

"To make a stronger pot of tea. I think we're in for a doozy of an afternoon, and frankly, I could use a stiff drink!"

Zara followed her into the kitchen. "What do you think Hank was talking about when he said Dan knew all about him but accepted him anyway?"

"I have no idea. Perhaps he just meant how friends know each other's foibles and about the skeletons in one another's closets, but they remain loyal chums nonetheless."

"What sort of skeletons do you think Hank Edwards has in his closet?"

"Not Henry Edwards of the Bohemian Club apparently."

"Is he still alive?"

"Heavens no. He died back in '91, in New York, I believe."

"Well I have no idea how Hank may be connected to this Bohemian Henry Edwards fellow, but your asking about him struck some sort of nerve with Hank."

"Agreed."

"Look what this cat dragged in," Stella called out, pushing Vincent through the shop ahead of her. "And no funny business, Caruso."

"Someone may be taking her job a little too seriously," Zara said, walking back into the tearoom. "I'll handle him from here. Come on in, Vincent."

"If that is your real name!" Stella said as she followed them to the same sitting area where the ladies had chatted with Hank.

"Any idea why you're here?" Zara asked, gesturing for Vincent to sit.

"Because my girlfriend told me to be?"

"Wise answer," Zara said.

Stella sat on the arm of the settee, her arms folded and grin smug.

"Vincent, what can you tell us about your relationship with Dan?" Penelope asked, taking her previous seat and opening her notebook. "I saw you too at odds the day before the grand opening."

Vincent sat for a moment, straightening his posture and rubbing his hands on his thighs. At length, he spoke. "I think you know that my family is … once in awhile, we find ourselves strapped for cash now and again. I do what I can to help Mom, taking small jobs here and there … to work around my job at the precinct …"

"And school," Penelope added.

"Yes, around school too."

"Well …" he cleared his throat. "You see, Dan … after the saloon closed … well he … ummm"

"They know about The Blind Pig, Caruso," Stella said.

"Oh … what a relief," he said, his posture relaxing as he wiped his brow. "Well then, you should know that I asked Dan for a job … at The Pig."

"You mean the speakeasy," Penelope said.

"Yes ma'am."

"Is that what you two were fighting about?" Zara asked.

Vincent nodded. "I'd begged Dan for a job a few

weeks prior. All we had in the house at the time was some souring milk and a little lard. It was before you brought me on here to help out. I was desperate to make some money to buy food ... but Dan wouldn't give me a job."

"That doesn't sound like bighearted Dan," Zara said.

"Sure it does," Stella said. "Think about it."

"Dan didn't want Vincent to do something illegal and risk his future. Isn't that right, Vincent?" Penelope said.

He nodded again. "He offered me money. He offered me food, but—" he broke off, disquieted.

"But your Italian ego got in the way, and you refused his help," Zara said.

"Yes. That same night, when I got home after work at the police station, I found out someone had anonymously dropped a crate full of food on our doorstep. Mom said it was from God. I knew straight off it was from Dan."

"So what made you argue with him the day before the opening?" Penelope said.

"I asked him again about a job. The extra money from working here really made a difference, and I knew you wouldn't need me anymore after the grand opening. So I went to Dan again."

"And again he said no," Zara said.

"Yes, ma'am."

Zara shuddered. "Promise me you'll never call me that again."

"Yes, ma'-uh-m'lady."

All chuckled.

"Vincent, just one last question before you go. A serious one," Penelope said, putting down her pencil and looking at him intently.

Vincent shifted in his seat.

"We have reason to believe Dan was being blackmailed. Do you have any idea who may have been behind such a scheme?"

"Empirically? Or intuitionally?" he said.

"Either," Zara said. "Both," Penelope said in tandem.

Vincent thought for a moment. "Empirically, I have no idea ..."

"And intuitionally?" Zara pressed.

"... Mr. Allen."

"Hubert?" Zara asked in surprise.

"Vincent, that's a very serious charge to levy at Stella's godfather!" Penelope admonished. "Apologize to her at once!"

"It's okay," Stella said, unfazed. "Just disregard his ravings. He's always had it in for Hubert."

"There's something about him I don't trust. Have you heard the way he talks?" Vincent said.

"Vincent, you should be ashamed of yourself!" Penelope cried.

"I'm used to it," Stella said. "Vincent takes exception to people all the time. You should've heard the things he said about Zara at first."

"Oh?" Zara said, crossing her arms over her knee and wagging her foot in amused interest.

"I was wrong about you, Miss Zara. I'm not ashamed to say it. When I first met you I thought you were a bad influence on my Stella ... that you'd lead her down a path that would take her away from me ... Then ... well, now I think you're pretty swell. And I'm really sorry."

Zara blew him a kiss, hoping to embarrass him.

It worked.

"Anyone else on your watch list?" Penelope asked.

"Elsie Davies, of course," he said.

"Why Elsie Davies?" Penelope asked.

He looked at her askance. "Is that a real question?"

"P's been practicing her dry humor," Zara joked.

Vincent and Penelope both furrowed their brows in

puzzlement.

"Did I miss something?" Vincent asked.

"Nothing worth explaining," Zara said.

"He didn't care much for Hank when Hank first came to town," Stella said.

"Hank Edwards?" Penelope asked, gripping the arm of her chair.

"That's not exactly true. I just felt like he had some sort of secret," Vincent said.

"Do you still feel that way?" Zara asked.

"Don't get me wrong, Hank's a real standup guy," Vincent said.

"Vincent ... that's not what I asked."

He took a moment. "Yes, yes I do think he carries a secret ... But gee whiz, who doesn't?"

Penelope and Zara shared a look.

"Thank you, Vincent, you've been a tremendous help," Penelope said.

Vincent nodded and put his cap on.

"Move along, Caruso—Beat it!" Stella said, pushing him out of the room. "I'll be back in a blink," she called as she exited the antiques store.

"What do you think?" Penelope said once she and Zara were alone.

"Honestly, I'm not sure what to think," Zara said.

"You don't believe what he said about Hubert Allen ... do you?"

"Of course not ... do you?"

"Noooooooo ... though I do think Vincent is most likely a good judge of character. He sure had you dead to rights," Penelope said, smirking.

"Another of your attempts at humor, P?"

Penelope smirked again and made a show of licking her pencil as she prepared to take notes.

"Last one," Stella said, escorting Hubert into the tearoom.

"Hubert, delighted as always," Zara said. "What a handsome suit. You must wear it more often."

Penelope frowned and rolled her tongue around her mouth in distaste. When she looked at the pencil she's licked, she found it was a fountain pen.

"Ladehs," he said, smiling and standing tall, pulling on his shirt cuffs. "How may I beh of asseestance?"

Penelope opened her inky mouth to speak, but Zara cut her off.

"Hubert, we're trying to gain a better understanding of Dan's activities during his last day. We know he was agitated. He and Hank had a rather heated exchange, in fact. And we know he had words with you. Can you share with us what you discussed? It might be of invaluable help," Zara said.

Hubert straightened his tie then said, "May I seet?"

"Of course. Where are our manners?" Zara said, gesturing toward the armchair.

"Thez are matteers beest deescussed weethout my goddaughteer preezeent."

"I already know about The Blind Pig, Hubert," Stella said, taking her spot on the arm of the settee.

His mouth fell open.

"Weel ... een that case ... Danieel Coopeer was a veery good man, an honorable man. Eet eez eemportant you understand thees," Vincent began.

"Oh yes, we're quite aware," Penelope said.

He cocked his head and stared at her, noting her blackened tongue.

"An honorable man ... like you, Hubert," Zara said, smiling demurely and lightly touching his knee.

He stiffened and grinned, moving his hand to cover Zara's just as she casually pulled hers away.

"Thees eez a deefeecult subject," he said.

"Difficult for us all," Penelope said, trying to insert herself into the conversation.

"What I mehn eez … I am not comfortable behsmeerchinn such a man's characteer … eespeecialleh wheen heh eez no longeer her to dehfeend heemseelf …"

"We appreciate that, Hubert," Zara encouraged. "Go on. You're among friends here."

"You seh … thee day before Danieel's passing … heh and I quarreeled."

"What about?" Penelope asked.

Zara gave her a look indicating Penelope should leave the talking to her.

"I heezeetate …" Hubert said.

"Go on, Hubert. It may help uncover the truth as to what happened to Dan," Zara said.

"You seh … Dan had come to meh to borrow moneh … again."

"Again?! Had he done so before?" Penelope asked.

"More times than I care to say. Eet was neeveer for heem though, you seh. Eet was for heez wife and heez daughters. Fine frocks and museec leessons do not come chepp … and Dan had deets … I told heem I could no longeer kep bailing heem out … that heh would have to coortail heez eenjudeecious, wasteful speending."

"Do you think that's why someone was blackmailing him … perhaps Elsie Davies … or even the mob?" Penelope interjected.

Zara and Hubert looked at her in astonishment.

After a moment he spoke. "I was not aware Danieel was behing blackmailed … but yees, what you say about thee mob sounds correect. Bootleeggeers are a seddy and dangeerous bunch. They may veery weell have threeteened Danieel een some way. I told heem to close thee spekkehzeh … on many occasions … but heh was too stubborn and proud."

"That doesn't sound like Dan," Penelope said.

"Madam, I assure you, I knew Danieel Coopeer far longeer than you—for many, many yerrs. And wheen a man can't provide for heez family and beccomes deespeerate, heh weel rehsort to deds more teerrible than you can eemageene."

"You tried to help him, Hubert. If he didn't choose to accept your help, that's no fault of yours," Zara said. "I just have one last question. If you can spare another moment."

"Eet would beh my pleezure."

"After you and Dan squabbled, you approached Paolo who was smoking in the Duesenberg, if I understand correctly. Can you tell me what prompted your exchange?"

"Gladly! Eet was two-fold. Feerst off, I had noteeced heem watching meh and Dan as weh spoke. Paolo was lerring. I walked straight oveer to heem and suggeesteed heh not leeseen een on thee conveersation of otheers."

"And second?" Zara nudged.

"I chideed heem for lazin een the car while thee reest of you weer eenside weerking like wheerling deerveeshees ..."

"He is a bit of a dewdropper, I'll admit," Zara said.

"Veery lazeh eendedd," Hubert said, nodding. "I theen rehalized heh deedn't spekk Ennglish and had no ideh what I was saying, so I walked away."

"Did you feel just a little bit better for reading him the riot act?" Zara asked, smiling.

"Yees ... a leettle beet."

Hubert and Zara chuckled.

"Thank you so much for coming to chat with us, Hubert. We can always count on you," Zara said.

"Good luck to you, Mees Price. You rehmain een my prayers."

"Thank you, Mr. Allen. Your encouragement means a great deal to me," Penelope said.

"I'll walk you out, Hubert," Zara said, rising to escort him.

"He was the last on my list. We're done then, right?" Stella asked Penelope.

"Looks that way. Zara and I want to talk to Paolo again . . ."

"But that doesn't really count," Stella said, grinning.

"Precisely."

"I'm bushed," Zara said upon reentering the room. "Let's call it a night."

"So soon? We're just getting started!" Stella protested.

"Playing interrogator is taxing. I could use a drink," Zara said.

Penelope looked up at her in concern.

"But I won't," Zara assured her. "Regardless, I really do want to get going, if it's all the same to you, P."

"Of course. You've earned a break. That was an impressive display, Z. How you got so much from everyone so effortlessly," Penelope said.

"It was far from effortless, trust me."

"You were like a prima ballerina," Stella said, attempting a pirouette and nearly knocking the tea things off the table. "Dancers always look like they're floating on air, but really, they're hard-as-nails athletes."

"Well put, Stella!" Penelope said.

"Well this ballerina's taking her tutu and hitting the road," Zara said, walking back to the antiques shop to collect her hat and gloves.

"Come on, Stella," Penelope said, getting up. "Our star needs her rest."

"But we only have one more day," Stella whined.

"We know, Stella, we know all too well," Zara said.

"See you at lunch tomorrow?" Stella asked.

"Does it matter if I say no?" Penelope asked, lifting

her carpetbag to find her keys beneath it.

"Not a chance," Stella said, jogging backward out of the door and smiling.

"See you at lunch," Penelope said, pinning on her hat.

**＊＊＊＊**

Zara dropped into the passenger seat of Penelope's Model T and closed her eyes.

"Let's get you home," Penelope said.

"Actually, can we joyride a little? I'd love to take a drive along the coastline ... feel the wind ... smell the ocean."

"But my flivver's not a breezer like yours," Penelope said with a subdued grin.

"Why Penelope Price! Was that jazz jargon I heard come out of your choir girl mouth?"

"And so's your old man," she said smiling proudly.

"You have no idea what that means, do you?"

Penelope's smile faded instantaneously.

"For a minute, P, you were right there. Now, now you're back to ... being ... well ... you!"

"I was trying to say that my Model T isn't a convertible," Penelope said with a discouraged huff.

"Yes, P. I know. Remember, while you were back in Pedro perfecting your shorthand, I was off sneaking into juice joints and perfecting my flapperspeak. You'd be surprised how much gibberish was cooked up by me and my roaring jazz-lovin' rabble of cronies, just to keep the older generation in the dark as to what we were saying." She yawned. "As for your automobile, the windows down will be just fine."

"You hungry?" Penelope asked as she leaned past Zara to crank down her window.

"Ravenous."

"Me too. What say we tour the coast until we find a

place to eat."

"What I say is 'that sounds wonderful.' I'm just going to close my eyes ..."

**＊＊＊＊**

"We're here," Penelope said softly, turning off the engine and engaging the parking break.

Zara yawned and stretched. "Mmmmmm how long was I out?"

"About ten minutes."

"What? That's impossible. I feel like I slept for ages."

"Oh you were out like a used flashbulb, I can tell you."

"What is this place?" Zara asked as they stepped out of the car.

"No idea. I don't see a sign, but I do see a pie in the window."

"That's all the sign I need!" Zara said, quickening her pace.

They opened the door to find the eatery deserted. The only evidence of business activity ever having taken place was the number of tables loaded with dirty dishes.

"Anywhere ya like," a voice called from the kitchen.

Penelope sat down and scooted into a booth. Zara immediately pulled her out of the seat and began swatting at her backside.

Horrified, Penelope tried to wriggle away. "If you're trying to make it look like we're lesbians again, I don't appreciate the humor."

"I'm afraid you're not my type, P," Zara deadpanned, "and what I'm *trying to* do is brush the dust off your dress. You're covered in white powder."

"What on earth?" Penelope said, craning to examine the back of her skirt.

Zara took an unused napkin from the table next to

theirs and began wiping down the seat of their booth.

"Why, it's all over. What do you suppose it could be?" Penelope said, using her hanky to whisk her side of the booth.

"Cocaine most likely," Zara kidded, taking her seat.

"Cocaine! If I didn't know better, I'd say you're determined to land me back in the pokey," Penelope whispered, shaking her handkerchief to clean it and choking on the cloud of dust that sprung from it.

A moment later, a round woman dressed all in white walked up to the table, flour covering the bulk of her exposed skin and hair. "Now what can I get for you ladies?"

"Menus, for starters, if you please," Zara said.

"Seeing as we're about to close, there's not much left. You can take your pick of beef, chicken, cherry or lemon," the woman said, inadvertently applying even more flour to her face as she attempted to put a stray strand of hair behind her ear using the back of her hand.

"Beef or lemon what?" Penelope asked.

"Pie, of course! What else ya think we'd sell at a pie stand?" the woman said, shaking her head and causing a gentle fall of flour to rain over them.

"We'll take them all!" Zara announced.

"Now that's more like it!" the woman replied, smiling and taking from her apron pocket a flour-covered rag that she then used to wipe down their table, covering the clean surface with a fresh film of flour.

Drained from the day's heady interviews, the friends sat in relaxed silence as the pie lady busied herself, clanging cookwear and singing to herself and kicking up clouds of dust.

"So who wants which?" she asked, bringing them glasses of water covered in floury fingermarks.

"Umm, I guess I'll take the one in your right hand," Penelope said.

Zara shook her head at her friend's lack of comprehension. "She's referring to the pies, P."

"Oh ... in that case, we'll take the savory ones now to split between us, and the sweet pies to go, if that's all right with you," Penelope said.

"Peachy by me ... There's a little pie funny for ya— free of charge," the woman said, snorting and shrugging her shoulders repeatedly as she amused herself. "I'll just heat those up for you and be back in a jiffy ... Coffee?"

Both nodded.

She walked back to the kitchen, a trail of flour in her wake.

"I hope I can keep my eyes open until the coffee arrives," Zara said.

"Z, really, I am so proud of you. You were unstoppable today. Never have I witnessed such powers of persuasion."

"Diplomacy is a key skill for the courtesan. Nice to find it has other applications."

"I'll say. You had them all exactly where you wanted them."

"That's all fine and well, but what did we learn?"

"That Dan was being blackmailed, for one thing."

"Do you really think he ran into trouble with gangsters?"

"It seems to make the most sense."

"Even more so than Elsie Davies?"

"Unfortunately ... But what would a gangster be doing in my shop late at night?" Suddenly Penelope gasped.

"What is it, P? What's wrong?"

"Zara ... you don't think ..."

"I take exception to that. I often think."

Penelope disregarded the comment, a look of dismay crossing her face. "You don't think Dan stole the pin do you?"

"Of course not! Why would he .... Ohhhhhhhh you think perhaps he stole it in hopes of selling it to pay back the blackmailers?"

"It's just a thought ... a terrible one, I know ..."

"And the mobsters followed him and caught him in the act? Killing him and stealing the brooch for themselves?"

"It sounds more plausible than anything we've come up with so far ... more so than Elsie Davies clobbering him."

"It certainly does," Zara said, gulping down some of the cool water.

"Z, I get the feeling ... I don't want to get my hopes up, but I think there's a chance I'm not guilty!"

Zara choked on the water. "Pardon me? Being guilty or not is something one knows from the get-go, P. Is your innocence just dawning on you now?"

"No, of course not. What I'm trying to say is I believe our hypothesis may be enough to exonerate me and turn suspicion elsewhere. After all, the police have no actual proof that I killed Dan, and both you and Vincent said Chief Harrison doesn't believe I did it. Do you know what this means, Z?"

"I'm afraid to ask."

"It means I may live!" she squealed. "Miss?!" she shouted to the pie purveyor, "a glass of milk for me and my friend here, please! This calls for a celebration!"

"If you want to go completely wild, we could make it chocolate milk," Zara added with a wink.

Whether it was due to the superiority of the fare or the likelihood of solving the case, the friends agreed they had never tasted better pie, and they attacked their feast with abandon. By the time they were finished, they found themselves inexplicably covered in flour, and once they'd exited the pie shop, they wiggled and shimmied to dislodge the particles from their hair and clothing. In so doing,

Penelope inadvertently loosened her coiffeur and her locks cascaded elegantly around her shoulders.

Zara gasped to see Penelope with her hair down. "Penelope Price, you're nothing short of exquisite."

"We'll see about that!" Penelope said, smiling gleefully and shaking her hair into disarray.

The friends giggled and skipped arm in arm to the car. Despite the lumberjack portions of pie they'd ingested, Penelope felt lighter than she had in weeks.

**\* \* \* \***

On the way home, they kept the windows down, and the wind blew through their manes as they sang favorite songs from their youth, each singing in a different key.

"Maybe some day they'll put radios in automobiles," Penelope shouted wistfully.

"Maybe, but for now, it's you and me, sister!"

Once they'd arrived at the house, Zara knocked softly on Paolo's door. "Paolo, come out, come out. We brought pie. Your favorite flavor."

"Which is his favorite?"

"Pie."

The pair dissolved into fresh giggles.

"He's not here," Zara said, opening his door.

"Just a moment," Penelope said, walking to the front window. "Your car's not here either. He must still be in San Francisco."

"Of course. I wasn't thinking. You know how those Italians are when they get together," Zara said, approaching the stairs.

"True ... but we don't actually know if he's in Little Italy or where he is exactly ... other than San Francisco," Penelope said, working her way up the stairway.

"You're right. Well wherever he is, I hope he's having a

rollicking good time. He deserves it. Lord knows I haven't shown him much of one in quite a while."

"Z, you mustn't be so hard on yourself when it comes to Paolo. You've been nothing but wonderful to him."

"Thanks, P. Makes me feel like less of a heel." Zara yawned as they reached the landing. "I'm all in. Mind if I say goodnight?"

"I'd prefer if you *sang* goodnight. 'Good night, my love, the shadows gently fall; The stars above are watching over all. The dying embers glow; The winds are whisp'ring soft and low,'" Penelope sang, dancing a soft shoe toward her bedroom.

"'Goodnight, goodnight, Goodnight,'" Zara sang, finishing the song.

# Chapter Twenty-One

"Wake up, P. We have to go!"

"Huh? What time is it? Am I late for court? I'll hang for sure!" Penelope said, bounding from bed and putting on her shoes in a somnambulant stupor.

"No, court's tomorrow! It's Paolo!"

"You're not Paolo. You're Zara. And I'm going back to bed," she said as she crawled under the covers and closed her eyes, still wearing her shoes. "You'd have to get up pretty early in the morning to fool me."

"It *is* pretty early, and I'm not trying to fool you, you fool. I'm trying to wake you up!" Zara said, shaking Penelope hard.

"Z, what's come over you? Go back to bed!" Penelope said, now fully roused.

"We have to go find Paolo!" she said, pulling the covers off Penelope.

"Why?"

"He never came home."

"He's a grown man, Z. He can take care of himself," Penelope groaned, pulling the covers back up. "He probably tied one on and then did the sensible thing by staying put rather than risk driving home in a haze of liquor."

"No, P. Something's wrong. I feel it. I've been worried ever since he left—worried he may do something drastic … that he may hurt himself."

Penelope sat up to pay closer attention as Zara continued.

"I have visions of him throwing himself from the Cliff House precipice as a dramatic gesture of love. He's threatened to do so before, and he was heartbroken when he left. If I knew how to drive, or where the devil to find your keys, I'd just go myself, but I can't," Zara broke off, sitting on the edge of the bed and sobbing.

"Z, you're really upset, aren't you?"

Zara nodded, dabbing her eyes with Penelope's bedcovers.

"I'll be ready to go in two shakes," Penelope said, crawling past Zara to get out of bed. "Can you make some coffee while I dress?"

Zara nodded again and blew her nose on Penelope's pillowcase.

**\* \* \* \***

Moments later, the two were back in the Model T and pulling out on the road, a thermos of coffee and the dessert pies from the night before in a basket placed between them.

"So where exactly is it we're going?" Penelope asked.

"Little Italy and the Cliff House."

"You do realize San Francisco is a good three hours away."

"Is it?" Zara said, fretfully.

"And this is the last day before I go to trial."

"You're right. We should just go back," Zara said, her voice trembling.

Penelope glanced at Zara and noted how distressed she was. "No, we should go to San Francisco. If anything were to befall Paolo ... well I don't want two deaths on my hands, now do I?" Her hand clasped Zara's for one tender moment before Penelope realized what she'd done and quickly returned her hand to its designated position on the steering wheel.

Zara smiled and sniffed back her tears. They motored wordlessly for the next half hour.

Penelope's thoughts were a jumble, going from Zara's inordinate fear to her own fears about her impending trial, to thoughts of the tea parties she may never get to present for Mrs. Morgan, to thoughts of the walks she may never get to take with Hank, to her childhood with Zara, to her parents and sister Pauline. She lingered on the thought of Pauline, wondering how her life was progressing, wondering if they'd ever speak again. *I should write to her ... the instant we arrive home ... just in case.*

Her mental meanderings were brought to a halt when Zara leaned over and placed her head against Penelope's shoulder.

"Z ... if you don't mind my asking," Penelope said, breaking the silence. "I've never seen you so distraught. What's going on? I know you're worried about Paolo, that he may do something rash, but ... well, it seems like it's more than that."

"You're right, P ... It is." Zara took a long breath. "You know, we've never talked much about our careers."

"What was there to tell? I spent my days on a Burrough's calculating machine and my nights eating soup at Mrs. Holcomb's noisy Boarding House. That sums it up ... if you'll excuse the bookkeeping pun."

"Well ... there's lots I didn't tell you about *my* career."

"I can imagine! The stories you've shared so far have been whoppers. I'm sure there are dozens more. What an exciting life you've led."

"Exciting, but lonely."

"You? Lonely?" Penelope guffawed. "From what you've said, you had society at your feet, out at parties nearly nightly, and with a steady stream of suitors lining up to court you."

Zara exhaled. "Yes, if one looked at it from the outside, that was all true. But it was still a very lonely life. Costas wasn't the first to *dismiss* me as it were."

"But you always found someone new. And from what I gathered, you were never really in love with any of them."

"Actually, you fall a little bit in love with *all* of them. And even if your heart isn't fully invested, it still always hurts to be dismissed … discarded."

"Being thrown over is never easy for anyone."

"But there's something about it when relationships are your livelihood. The rejection threatens to undermine your self-worth as well as perceived value among those in your circle. The attendant depression and self-doubt is something I'd never wish on anyone—especially not Paolo."

"But Paolo's not a … umm … are they called chevaliers?"

"A cicisbeo is the Italian equivalent, and yes, he is, or at least was," Zara said, looking out the window.

"I had no idea … Z, you've never told me, how exactly did you and Paolo meet?"

"It was in San Francisco actually."

"In Little Italy perhaps?"

Zara sat silent, looking out the window.

"Or was it at the Cliff House?"

Zara wept bitterly. Penelope pulled the car over to the shoulder of the road.

"Zara, look at me. What is it you're not telling me?"

Zara took a moment to curtail her sobs. "Yes, I met Paolo at the Cliff House."

"Did he ... was he ... suicidal?"

"No," Zara said softly, looking away.

"Thank God."

"I was."

"What? Why didn't you ever tell me?" Penelope whispered, holding Zara's hands in her own.

"I never told anyone. Besides, what was I supposed to say? That I was vain and aging? That I was too old and no one wanted me anymore? That I'd lost both my looks and my career?"

"Tell me about what happened at the Cliff House."

"I was a mess, and I'd been drinking. I was at my lowest ebb and looking for something, *anything*, to brighten my dreary existence. I'd been to the Cliff House over the years several times and had loved every iteration it had gone through in its storied history. This newest version, built six years ago, boasted the best cuisine and dancing in town; so I primped and painted myself and took a taxi from Nob Hill out to the spot.

"When I got there, I found the area desolate. Turns out the President had signed some sort of legislature banning liquor from any establishment within half a mile of a military installation—that included the Cliff House. I was so tired, P. So tired of it all. So tired of having to put on a face, not just the makeup, but the persona. I felt too weary to go on ... so ... I stepped out onto the edge of the cliff ..."

"Did Paolo rescue you?"

Zara took to bawling again and nodded. "I heard a gentle voice say, 'Signorina,' and I turned around to see this gorgeous Italian god smiling kindly at me and holding his hand out to me. He later told me ... well, as best he could ... that he too had come to the Cliff House looking for some fun, and just happened to notice me when he was leaving. He sensed what I intended to do and chose to stop me."

"He saved your life."

Zara nodded fiercely.

"Z … I had no idea … this explains, well, a great deal."

"I owe him my life, you see."

"Well I don't know about that … though, I've always wondered … How was Paolo able to just drop everything and follow you here?"

"He's an actor who'd recently come to San Francisco looking for work … He'd struck out at every audition he attempted—"

"No doubt the language issue had something to do with that."

"I invited him to stay with me … he'd exhausted all his funds and …"

"Then how could he have afforded a night at the Cliff House?"

"He couldn't."

"I don't understand."

"He was hoping some lonesome matron would succumb to his charms and pick up the tab. When you have looks like that, charity is offered you freely."

"I see …"

"A week or so later I learned about Aunt Dee and that you'd be coming north. I told Paolo I wanted to move to Pacific Grove—to get a new start—and that I was looking forward to trying the quiet life in a small town … Dear Paolo cheerfully agreed to come with me. And now I've broken things off with him, and he's in a strange country where he doesn't speak the language, with no family, no money, no job."

"I'm so sorry, Z. I feel dreadful."

"Why on earth should *you* feel dreadful?"

"For not paying more attention—for not asking more questions. I've been so wrapped up in my own concerns, with Aunt Dee, the antiques shop, opening a tearoom, this whole Dan thing … It never occurred to me that someone like you could have a care in the world."

"Someone like me? What's that supposed to mean?" Zara snapped.

"Someone so perfect, with everything going for her," Penelope answered kindly.

Zara sat speechless for a moment, searching Penelope's eyes. "Is that how you really see me, P?"

"Of course. I always have—even when you were Minnie Clark. To me you've always been absolutely perfect."

Zara broke down in heaving sobs, clutching Penelope in a tight embrace.

"Come on, let's go find Paolo," Penelope said as Zara blubbered.

"In a minute," Zara said, not yet ready to let go of her friend.

Penelope stroked Zara's hair and rocked her until her snivels subsided.

"Shall we?" Penelope asked softly.

"Yes, please … Want some pie?"

"Is that a rhetorical question?"

As Penelope was unwilling to let go of the steering wheel, Zara handfed her chunks of pie, resulting in the bulk of the crust crumbling all over Penelope's lap and the car's upholstery.

The remainder of the trip was far less somber than its outset and brought the friends even closer together. Zara said she felt like an enormous weight had been lifted off her chest by confiding in Penelope, and Penelope realized a little bit more clearly that Zara was really just a regular female with regular problems—they were just better dressed problems, but regular problems nonetheless.

**\* \* \* \***

"Welcome to San Francisco. Where do you want to go first?" Penelope said as they'd crossed the city's border.

"The Cliff House, if you don't mind … I'd feel much more relieved to find, well, nothing."

A few moments later, they arrived at the jagged cliffs overlooking the beach. The day was cloudy and the winds whipped up from the sea, bringing stinging spray with them.

"No signs of police or a disturbance," Penelope said. "In fact, no signs that anything has gone on here for quite some time."

"Mercifully," Zara said with a thankful sigh, her eyes bright and hopeful. "Shall we head to Little Italy?"

"I hope you know how to get there, 'cause I sure don't."

"I have a general idea, and if we get lost …" Zara slid her skirt up one thigh and winked.

"Oh how I love your ingenuity, Z."

"I still have a few tricks up my … skirt," she said, giggling.

"Z!" Penelope exclaimed, blushing.

Their navigation skills proved wanting, and they took so many wrong turns that there were no streets lefts for them to travel save those in the city's Little Italy section. The shops and restaurants were just opening their doors, and shopkeepers lined the streets—brooms in hand—to sweep the sidewalks before greeting customers. Zara employed the scant fragments of Italian she knew to inquire as to whether anyone on the street had seen Paolo. The answer was unanimous—*no*. She introduced a photograph, still no one recognized him.

"Maybe you should look for some women to ask. It's all men out sweeping the streets, and I have a feeling a woman would remember Paolo far better than a man,"

Penelope said.

"Good thinking, P! I'm ashamed I didn't come up with it myself!"

They walked into a small café and upon seeing a young waitress, Zara said, "Buongiorno. Per favore, siete a conoscenza di Paolo?"

"Paolo?" the young girl repeated, her eyes twinkling.

"What did you say?" Penelope asked.

"I said 'are you acquainted with Paolo' … At least that's what I hope I said."

"Paolo?!" an older woman repeated, running from back in the kitchen, her white apron stained with tomato sauce.

"Show them the picture," Penelope said.

"Paolo!" the young girl squealed, taking the picture and stroking it dreamily.

"Amica di Paolo?" the older woman said.

"Friend? Yes, I'm a friend of Paolo," Zara said. "Do you know … Dove Paolo?"

"Non lo so," the older woman said, shaking her head.

"Non lo so," the girl repeated, kissing the photograph.

"Ha pranzato qui ieri," the woman said, miming the motion of eating. "La notte scorsa."

"What did she say?" Penelope asked.

"I think she said Paolo was here yesterday."

"Ask about his mood."

"E … was he happy … felice?" Zara said, searching for words.

"Felice? Paolo?" the older woman said, smiling broadly. "Si, molto felice!"

Zara exhaled in relief. "Grazie, signora. Grazie mille."

"Prego," the woman said, smiling and heading back to the kitchen.

"Signorina?" Zara said, putting out a hand to retrieve

the photograph the young girl was clutching to her chest.

"Amo Paolo … I loff heem," she said in an Italian accent.

"Oh I have do doubt you love him," Zara said, prying the photograph from the girl's grasp.

Penelope and Zara exited the restaurant and strode back to the car.

"You have no idea how relieved I am, P. Look, I'm shaking."

"Do you want to keep looking for him?" Penelope asked, looking at her watch.

"Oh, P! Your court case! It's in the morning, and I sent us out on this trip for biscuits."

"Biscuits? I only brought pie. I don't under—"

"Sorry, wild goose chase, I mean," Zara said.

"It's not a goose chase if you found peace of mind along the way … Did you?"

"Yes, very much so. I don't know why I was so out of sorts earlier, but I feel much better now."

"Perhaps the time had come to share a burden you could no longer carry on your own."

"I think you're right. I've wanted to tell you so many things for so long … and now you know the worst of it … the worst of me."

"Don't be a silly goose … or a biscuit, Z. I'm sure there's far worse to learn about you."

"Why, you rascal!"

Penelope turned on the ignition with a smirk and began her pre-driving mirror ritual.

"Let's get back to Pacific Grove and solve your case," Zara said. "My head is finally clear, and I have a feeling we are very close to getting to the bottom of things."

"I'd like to make one stop along the way, if it's all the same to you," Penelope said, driving past Union Square.

"Shopping at a time like this?"

"Hardly ... look ... Do you see that building?" Penelope said, applying the brakes, and pointing to a brick structure on the corner.

"Yes?"

"That's the city clubhouse headquarters of the Bohemian Club," she said, parking the car. "I recognize it from the photo in that *Bohemian Jinks* book."

"P, how brilliant! Did you have this up your sleeve all along?"

"I only thought of it after we went to the Italian restaurant and heard that Paolo had been sighted and things appeared to be all right."

"What do we do now?"

"I hadn't gotten that far. I suppose we go in and tell them who were are ... specifically that I'm Dorothea Tate's grandniece—that should curry some favor—and that we're looking for information on anyone who may have stolen the owl brooch. Given that it's something along the lines of the club's Holy Grail, I think they'd be only too keen to assist us in retrieving it."

"Fabulous plan ... but let me lead, eh?"

Zara exited the car, rolled her shoulders back and swept into the lobby, her hips doing a good deal of the talking for her. "Good afternoon, gentlemen," she said to the desk clerk and lobby guard. "We're here to discuss some urgent yet delicate business with whomever is available from the board of directors here."

"Where is it you think you are, Miss?" the desk clerk asked.

"Why, le club de bohème, of course," she said coyly.

"Beg yer pardon?"

"The Bohemian Club," she whispered as Penelope crept in behind her.

"Never heard of it. I'm afraid I'll have to ask you to

leave. Guard, show these ladies out."

"Have you ever heard of Dorothea Tate?" Penelope asked as the guard opened the door to escort them outside.

"'Course I have. I'm not an idiot, ya know."

"That remains to be seen," Zara said under her breath.

"Well I am Penelope Price, her grandniece, and proprietress of her antiques shop. You know, the one with all the *rare and priceless artifacts*?"

The clerk looked at her for a moment then lifted the receiver on the desk's telephone and covered the mouthpiece as he spoke. A moment later, he addressed Penelope. "Go right on up, Miss. Second floor, third door on the left."

"Thank you, sir," Penelope said. "Zara, after you."

"Nuh unh, that one stays here," the desk clerk said. "Just you."

Penelope nodded, and Zara shrugged her shoulders, perching on the edge of the clerk's desk. "Bum a gasper?" she said.

The clerk handed Zara a cigarette and lit it for her as Penelope walked upstairs to enter the inner sanctum of the mysterious club's headquarters.

\* \* \* \*

Just as Zara was putting out the butt of her cigarette, Penelope returned to the lobby.

"Let's go, Z," Penelope said curtly.

"That bad?" Zara asked, alighting from the desk.

"Can I get yer number?" the desk clerk called after her.

"Toodle-oo, Stanley," she said, waving as she strutted away. "Slow down, P. What happened?" Zara whispered loudly, trailing Penelope as she trod out of the building and toward the Model T.

"In the car, please," she said quietly.

They got in the car and closed the doors. "Locked, please," Penelope said, pushing down the lock button on her door and surveying the people on the street.

"Are you gonna tell me what happened or not?" Zara said, locking her car door.

"Z, you'll never believe it."

"Well how can I if you don't tell me?"

"There's not much to tell," Penelope said, trying to catch her breath.

"Then spit it out!"

"All right, here goes. The long and the short of it is that a man was in their office yesterday … trying to sell the pin!"

"*The* pin?"

"Yes, the owl pin!"

"Incredible! Did they call the police?"

"No, they had no idea the brooch was stolen. The man who claimed to have it said it had been a gift, and that he would be willing to part with it for a fair sum, noting that the diamonds alone would be worth a small fortune, let alone the sentimental aspect of the piece and its history with the club."

"I'm stupefied! Was there more?"

"Just this—the club's secretary, a Mr. Wilcox, the man to whom I spoke, instructed the fellow to return today at one o'clock. Mr. Wilcox said he would talk to the members of the board to arrive at a fair settlement amount that Mr. Wilcox would pay in cash in exchange for the brooch. He has the cash with him now and the seller should be here at one o'clock."

Zara grabbed Penelope's wrist to read her watch. "Why, that's in less than twenty minutes!"

"I know! Keep an eye out for anyone who looks suspicious."

"Did they give a description of the man?"

"Yes, come to think of it—average height, average build, dark hair and a New York accent."

Zara gasped. "So then it really is the mob! They killed Dan!"

"It sure looks that way."

"P, we may have solved the case!"

Penelope's mouth dropped open, and the two friends caterwauled for minutes on end, holding hands and bobbing up and down in their seats in elation. Stares from passersby who'd noticed the jostling car terminated their frivolity.

"We should try to keep a low profile," Penelope said, pulling her large hat over her brow and sliding down into the driver's seat.

Zara nodded, donning a pair of dark glasses. "What do we do once we find the man?"

"I hadn't thought of that. Perhaps the guard in the lobby can help?"

"Doubtful. He only had a billy club, and I'm betting those mob types carry pistols ... Well can ya beat that ..."

"What?"

"Look!"

Penelope gasped. "What's Paolo doing here?"

"Isn't it obvious, P?" Zara said, her voice quivering. "He's trying to help with the case—as a gesture of his affection. Oh, P, I feel like such a louse."

"Steady on, Z. The gangster may be here any minute."

"We have to warn Paolo. What if he were to get caught in the crossfire?" Zara said, bounding from the car.

"No, Z! It's too dangerous!" Penelope cried after her, exiting the car to pull her back.

"Paolo! Thank heaven, you're all right!" Zara said, running up to him and covering his face with kisses. "I know why you're here and what you're doing, and may I just say, I'm very moved by—"

"Whaddaya doin' here? How'd ya find out? Who told ya?" he said sharply in his native New York dialect. "Don't think you can cut in on my action."

"Paolo? You speak English? I don't understand," Zara said, whimpering in confusion.

"That's cuz yer too wrapped up in yer own self ta notice anything but yer reflection in the mirror, and too busy talkin' about your *glamorous* life all the time, talkin', talkin', don't ya ever shut that yap of yours?" he said, pulling a switchblade from his pocket and flipping it open.

Zara backed toward the wall as Paolo approached her, his striking face now a mass of hatred and malevolence. "Paolo, what are you doing?"

"What I been itchin' ta do for months. Cuttin' out that waggin' tongue once and for all."

Zara screamed as Paolo lunged at her.

Just then Penelope made a roundhouse turn with her carpetbag and knocked Paolo out cold.

Penelope stood panting and clutching the bag tightly by the handles. "Is he dead?"

"No," Zara said, seething with clarity as she kicked the knife from Paolo's hand. "He's breathing ... for now. But if I have any say in the matter—"

The thunder of someone racing down the stairs caught their attention and a man burst through the doors toward Penelope.

"Get back, I warn you!" she cried.

Before she could swing the carpetbag, the man grabbed her and lifted her in the air.

"Thank God, you're all right," Hank said, holding her in a stifling embrace. "If anything had happened to you ..." his voice faltered.

"Mr. Edwards!" she exclaimed, struggling for a brief moment, then melting into his arms.

He let out a slight wince as she dropped the carpetbag

on his foot.

Several euphoric seconds later, she said, "You can put me down now."

"I apologize," he said, releasing her and grasping her hands as he looked into her eyes. "You must tell me, are either of you hurt?"

Penelope shook her head and gazed up at him, her thoughts a whir.

"What about you, Miss Zara?" he said, letting go of Penelope's hands to put a comforting arm around Zara's shoulder.

"Only my pride," she said, her heel on Paolo's chest to hold him down.

"Mr. Edwards, what are you doing here?" Penelope suddenly gasped, once more grabbing the handles of her carpetbag. "You're one of them, aren't you? I should have known you were too good to be true," she said, hoisting the bag and beginning her backswing.

"Miss Price, put the bag down," he said, gently putting a hand on hers. "If you mean am I with Paolo, the answer is no. I'm on the board of the Bohemian Club and received a call last night telling me that someone claimed to have Harry Edwards' owl pin, and that the party would be coming today to sell it. I came to find out what was going on, who had the pin, if it was the item stolen from Dee's shop, et cetera."

"But when did you arrive? I didn't see you in the club's offices?" Penelope said.

"I came up the back stairs so as to go unnoticed by the potential thief."

"So then you're not with the mob? Oh, thank the maker," Penelope said, dropping the heavy bag on her own foot. "Ow!"

Paolo began to moan, regaining consciousness.

"Stanley," Hank said to the desk clerk who, along with the lobby guard, had come out to see what the commotion was about. "We're going to need some rope ... a good deal of it."

"Are the police on their way?" Penelope asked.

"Afraid not," Hank said. "The San Francisco police department prefers to stay out of all club business, opting to leave us to our own devices."

Penelope gulped.

Hank chuckled. "It's nothing nefarious, Miss Price—more of a conflict of interests since so many city officials, including members of the police force, are members of the club. But what is that you were saying about the mob?"

"Paolo, he's part of the Italian mob. They were blackmailing Dan and killed him," Zara said, digging her heel into Paolo's chest.

"Wrong again. Shows what you know, ya stupid cow," Paolo said, spitting on the ground in disdain. "The mob's got nothin' to do with this."

Zara twisted the heel on his chest in response.

"Is this too much rope?" Stanley asked, hauling a skein dozens of yards long.

"Actually, I think that's just enough, Stanley," Hank said with a smile.

**\* \* \* \***

After some deliberation, it was decided that Penelope, Zara, Hank, and their captive would return to Pacific Grove in Penelope's car, with plans to retrieve both Zara's and Hank's vehicles at a later time.

"I'm sorry to ask you to drive, Miss Price, but I'd feel more comfortable staying here in back with Paolo, should he try anything," Hank said.

"As if you could do anything, ya pansy boy, hidin' behind your girlfriend's skirts. You make me sick—all of youz. How many times I had ta bite my tongue ta bleeding not ta tell youz all ta go straight ta hell. How many times I had ta get drunk to work up the guts ta get into bed with that flapping hag," he said, glaring at Zara.

"But Paolo, you proposed marriage to her! I heard you!" Penelope said.

"What you heard was what ya wanted ta hear. Actually, I was only recitin' the menu from the Roma deli back in the Bronx. And I only did it cuz I thought she was rich."

"You ladies mind if I gag him?" Hank asked.

"Please do!" they both shouted.

Throughout the multi-hour drive back to Pacific Grove, Paolo squawked and grunted and protested nonstop. No one could make out a word he said, and were all the happier for it.

"Would you care for some pie, Mr. Edwards?" Penelope asked at length.

"I do believe I would. Thank you," he said, as Zara passed him one of the pie tins and a fork.

"I'm afraid we have no plates, but I'm guessing that won't bother a bohemian like you," Penelope said with a shy smile.

Hank chuckled. "No, it won't bother me at all."

"What I can't figure out is why Paolo stole the brooch, that is, if he's not part of the mob. You don't think he had anything to do with Dan's murder, do you?" Penelope said.

Paolo kicked violently and shouted into his gag in response.

"I would say let's ungag him ... then again," Zara said.

"I'm sure these are questions Walter Harrison can see answered," Hank said. "We should be back within the city limits any minute. I suggest taking Paolo directly to the police station, if it's all the same to you ladies."

"The sooner the better," Zara said.

"And good riddance," Penelope added.

* * * *

It wasn't long before they'd arrived at the police station where they all began talking at once, including Paolo, much to the confusion of Constable Jimmy Matlin.

"Slow down, please," he said. "Mr. Edwards, can you tell me what happened? Police matters are much too complicated for women to grasp. Ladies, I suggest you go home and have a good faint, or whatever it is hysterical females do."

"Well of all the nerve!" Penelope protested.

"Does Chief Harrison know we're here? I believe he'd be quite interested in what we hysterical females have to say," Zara said, making a start for the chief's office.

"Chief Harrison doesn't usually work nights. We have orders not to disturb him with petty affairs."

"You're right, of course," Zara said, turning to face the young constable. "Theft, blackmail, and murder are far too petty to bother the chief of police with, even though the pertinent murder trial takes place tomorrow."

"Call the chief," Hank said, sliding the phone toward Jimmy. "Ladies, if you don't mind my saying so, perhaps it *is* a good idea if you two go home."

"Why of all the misogynistic—" Penelope fumed, her cheeks flushing with affront.

"What I began to say is, you have a very important day ahead of you tomorrow and have already put in a long one today. I'd be happy to stay here and explain things to Walter. Besides, I think the person he'll be most eager to converse with is most likely Paolo."

Penelope thought for a moment. "I suppose that makes sense," she said, pouting.

"Perfect sense," Zara said, guiding Penelope toward the door. "Thank you, Hank."

"It's the least I could do. Don't want Miss Price to oversleep and be late for her day in court after all," he said, waving goodbye and smiling.

# Chapter Twenty-Two

Penelope awoke with a scream. Zara came running into Penelope's room, naked and brandishing a Savage pocket automatic pistol. Penelope took one look at her and screamed again.

"Zara, for the sake of all that's holy!"

"What's wrong? Why did you scream?"

"Because we're late for court!"

"You scared me to death! I thought it was something serious."

"Look at the time!"

Zara tried to focus her eyes on the mantle clock. When she saw the time, she too screamed and ran back to her room, her naked bottom bouncing and the pistol waving.

Penelope's trial was already underway when they pulled up to the courthouse twelve minutes later. As they ran through the long corridor, they could overhear the proceedings through the open door.

"But your honor, we have Paolo Rossi's confession … and several witnesses to his apprehension," Chief Walter Harrison pleaded.

"I'm afraid my hands are tied, Walt," said Judge Houston. "The defendant has fled. She's flown the coop, gone on the lam … Frankly, that's not good. In fact, it's very bad."

"A sure admission of guilt, your honor," Bernard Beekham stated. "You may very well need to throw the book at her."

"Counselor, aren't you supposed to be defending Miss Price?"

"We're here! I'm here!" Penelope said, skidding into the courtroom with Zara trailing.

"Thank the lord," Walter Harrison said, wiping his perspiring brow.

A shared sigh resonated throughout the courtroom.

"As I was saying, your honor, let the punishment fit the crime," Bernard Beekham continued, his expression devoid of emotion.

"You're not suggesting the death penalty?" Judge Houston said.

"Yes, your honor."

"For being tardy?"

Bernard Beekham shrugged.

"Miss Price, this court does not take kindly to those who flout the law and show up late to their own trial," the judge said. "What have you to say in your defense?"

"Your honor, it's my fault," Zara said.

"And who might you be, Miss ehr ..."

"Clark, your honor, Miss Clark."

Stella gasped from the third row. "She used her last name ... This is serious!"

"Miss Price was detained due to my negligence. After last night's unexpected turn of events, I took over her case. I'd asked her to go over the sequence of incidents with me one last time this morning, and I was so fixated on getting the information down accurately, I lost track of the time. Forgive me?" she said, swishing slowly toward the judge's bench, her eyes smoldering and dimples in full force. "I was sure you'd want as detailed an account as possible," she said, placing both hands on the judge's bench and fluttering her eyelashes.

"This is outrageous!" Bernard Beekham said, slamming closed his briefcase and standing up.

Zara walked purposefully back to the defendant's table. "Move aside, Bernie," she whispered, bumping his hip with her own to force him out of the way.

Bernard exited in a huff, then quietly turned back and slid into a seat at the back of the courtroom.

"Have you prepared opening remarks, Miss Clark?"

Zara's mind raced in search of an acceptable answer. "I prefer to let the facts speak for themselves, your honor. After all, my client has nothing to hide. If the court please … or is it *pleases* … I always get that mixed up …"

"Either works for me," the judge said, leaning on his elbow and smiling in enchantment as Zara worked her magic.

"Well then if it pleases *you*, your honor, I'd like to call Chief Walter Harrison to handle my client's opening remarks."

"The state objects, your honor!" a skinny man with a runny noise said, rising wobblingly from behind the prosecution's table.

"Leopold, let me make this easy on you," the judge said. "Your objections are overruled—all of them."

"But I've only made the one!"

"Any and all objections to come, they're overruled. Understood?"

"Not really, I—"

"Walter, come on up and tell us what you know," the judge said.

"Carusi, bring in the prisoner," Walter said as he took the stand.

**\* \* \* \***

Within a quarter of an hour, small town justice had prevailed and Dan's case had been concluded. Even more exciting, the Tea & Sympathy Investigative Agency was lauded for their persistence and bravery in ferreting out and apprehending Paolo Rossi, or rather, Paul Ross.

During his nightlong questioning at the patient hands of Walter Harrison, Ross confessed to killing Dan Cooper in the heat of the moment.

Walter explained, "Paul Ross was a down-on-his-luck actor from New York who came to San Francisco where

357

many of his east coast acting peers had found lucrative theatrical work. Paul did not share their success, and it didn't take long before he resorted to employing his masculine, shall we say, *animal magnetism* to pay the bills. While practicing an Italian accent for an audition, he found that he could get whatever he wanted from wealthy women by playing the Italian lothario. This drugstore cowboy role was the only one in which his acting was believable and appreciated. While *in character*, Paolo met Zara, a woman to whom he was exceptionally attracted—can ya blame him?"

The majority of the men in the courtroom chuckled in agreement. Several of the women struck their husbands.

Chief Harrison continued, "Since Zara appeared to be well-off financially, Paolo rode her coattails down to Pacific Grove. He pretended not to speak English as a way of avoiding answering questions about his background and intentions. Women tended to find his lack of English comprehension erotic and liberating, and they were lax in their conversations around him, divulging all manner of private information in his presence, believing he did not understand."

"No wonder Paolo would never talk to me in Italian … He doesn't really know any!" Vincent whispered to Stella. "Huh … and I just thought he was stupid."

"Who says you were wrong?" Stella replied with a smirk, leaning her head on Vincent's arm.

Walter Harrison described to the court how the stolen owl brooch—found in Paolo's breast pocket, to be returned to Penelope shortly—along with Daniel Cooper's blackmailing and death had nothing to do with the New York mob. Rather, another party had been the blackmailer, threatening to turn Daniel into the authorities for bootlegging if he didn't continue to keep the speakeasy running and cut the other party in on the profits. This other party used the blackmail threat as leverage to force Daniel to steal the owl brooch.

A collective gasp rang through the courtroom.

Stella said aloud what all were thinking. "You mean Dan broke in to the antiques shop to steal the brooch?

"No, Stella, of course not," Chief Harrison said.

All who'd gasped exhaled in relief.

Chief Harrison continued, "Paul Ross here overheard this other party trying to coerce Dan, but Dan staunchly refused, regardless of the blackmail and possible consequences. That's how Paul got the idea to steal the brooch himself. Dan was driving by the antiques shop late that night to drop off a couple of extra pots of flowers for the front entrance as a surprise for Miss Price—"

"I'd wondered where those came from!" Penelope whispered to Zara, placing a hand over her heart.

"Dan saw a flashlight shining around the otherwise dark shop, and he entered, calling out to see if anyone was there. That's when Paul Ross clocked him on the head with a statue, later placing it as inflammatory evidence in Miss Price's bag, certain the hefty object would go unnoticed given the preponderance of items usually found in her bag."

Zara, Stella, Vincent, and Hank chuckled.

"Ross then tracked down the principals at the Bohemian Club and arranged to sell the pin to them for an outrageous sum. He intended to flee San Francisco with the money from the sale of the brooch, abscond with Miss Zara's automobile, and drive to Hollywood to try his luck in motion pictures. There was just one last piece of the puzzle to be found—"

"Eexcuse meh … I beeg your pardon," Hubert whispered as he worked his way down the row of courtroom seats toward the aisle.

"—the person who blackmailed Dan regarding the speakeasy, and took the lion's share of its profits. Sit down, Hubert! You're not going anywhere. Your honor, Hubert Allen is the party who was both blackmailing Daniel Cooper and asked him to steal the brooch."

Shock bombinated through the courtroom.

"Told you there was something shady about him," Vincent said to Stella.

"That brooch behlongs to thee Bohemmians, not some out-of-towneer, and ceertainly not a woman, eespeecialleh *that* woman!" Hubert shouted, pointing at Penelope.

Hank, who'd stood up to enable Hubert to shuffle by him in the row, wasted no time in leveling Hubert with a single debilitating punch to the gut.

Penelope gasped and felt woozy with admiration.

"Your honor, I confess to aggravated assault," Hank said, offering his wrists for cuffing.

"This seems to becoming a commonplace occurrence with you lately, Hank," Walter said.

Hank looked at Penelope then quickly to the floor, his cheeks reddening.

"Denied, overruled, not a chance, Hank!" Judge Houston ruled.

"Your honor, on behalf of the state of California, I charge Paul Ross with manslaughter, and Hubert Allen with blackmail and complicity in murder," Chief Harrison said. "And may I add, all charges against Penelope Price are formally dropped!"

The courtroom exploded in cheers.

"Order in the court!" the judge shouted, pounding his gavel.

All conversation hushed.

"Officer, take Mr. Ross and Mr. Allen into custody," the judge said. "Miss Price, you are hereby exonerated and free as a bird."

"Free as a monarch butterfly!" Stella shouted.

The judge smiled. "I stand corrected, Miss Parker. And now if you'll pardon me, folks, I have a grandchild to meet. As you were, everyone," he concluded with a single tap of his gavel.

Zara blew the judge a kiss that he pretended to catch.

"Miss Price, I owe you an apology, a long overdue one, I'm ashamed to say," Walter Harrison said, pulling Penelope aside.

Penelope stood silent, hoping to at last learn what she'd done to get off on the wrong foot with him when first she came to town.

"It's about my treatment of you. If I've seemed, well, cold, you should know it had nothing to do with you," he said, fumbling with his police hat.

"You could've fooled me, Chief Harrison!"

"The fact is, my issue was with your grandaunt."

"Aunt Dee? But what could she have—"

"Please, let me finish. I harbored a great deal of resentment toward Dorothea for far too long. You see, the truth is, she was the love of my life. And I thought I was hers, but she declined my offer of marriage, claiming it would be too dangerous for me—something having to do with the circles she ran in when obtaining antiquities. I reminded her that I was the chief of police and could take care of myself. But she said she could never forgive herself if anything ever happened to me because of her ... and so she refused me."

Penelope searched his face for several seconds then whispered, "Your laughing eyes. Of course! Why didn't I see it before?"

"Miss Price?" the chief said, worried she may be falling into another *Tell-Tale* fit of some kind.

She unbuttoned the top of her blouse.

"Miss Price!" he cried, looking around to make sure no one was watching.

She unclasped her grandaunt's silver locket from around her neck and handed it to him. "It's you, isn't it? You and Aunt Dee."

He covered his mouth and nodded, afraid to speak lest decades of heartbreak gush out. He ran a rough thumb over the tintype and looked at it for several seconds. "My sweet DeDe," he whispered adoringly. He blinked away his tears and cleared his throat, holding out the locket for Penelope to take.

"I found it in her personal effects. Would you like to keep it?" she asked gently.

He shook his head and took her hand, placing the necklace in her palm. "That won't be necessary. The thing is, Miss Price, when you came to town, I took all my pent-up anger regarding DeDe and directed it toward you—simple as that. I'm more remorseful than I can say. Do you think you can find it in your heart to forgive an old sap like me?"

She paused for a moment, then hugged him. "Of course, Chief Harrison."

"Walter, please."

"Walter, I so want us to be friends. And I'm sincerely sorry for your heartache. I hope someday you find a way to fill the void left by Aunt Dee."

"I think I already have," he said, gazing tenderly at Zara who was laughing in conversation with Stella and Vincent.

"Chief Harrison?" the police lieutenant called.

Walter warmly patted Penelope on the shoulder and excused himself to handle the arraignment of his prisoners.

Elsie Davies ran to Penelope's side, pencil and pad in hand. "Tell us, Miss Price, what is going through your head at this very moment? Our Butterfly Bugle readers are dying to know."

"You really want to know what I'm thinking?" Penelope asked.

"Oh yes, absolutely—your deepest, darkest thoughts," Elsie said, nearly salivating at the prospect of a juicy story. "Attention, everyone, Penelope Price has something to say!" she shouted. "Go ahead, Miss Price. We're all listening."

Penelope wrung her hands for a moment then straightened her shoulders. "I was merely going to comment, Miss Davies, that in my opinion you are as much to blame for Dan Cooper's death as Paolo and Hubert Allen. If you hadn't bullied Dan and pressured him into feeling he needed to make a certain amount of money in order to keep his wife and family happy, he would still be with us today. I dare say if given a choice, his family would far prefer having Dan rather than the latest fashions or most luxurious furnishings."

Elsie gasped and the courtroom fell momentarily silent.

"I believe that should answer your question, Miss Davies. Good day."

"Brava, Miss Price!" Vincent cheered as Penelope trod down the aisle toward the rear exit.

"Attagirl, Penelope!" Stella cried.

"Well done, Miss Price. Well done," Florence Morgan said. "I'll be at your shop at nine o'clock sharp tomorrow morning. I have a number of events to plan with you."

Penelope nodded to the grand dame.

"Miss Penelope Price, you're my heroine," Hank said, taking Penelope's hand as she passed and kissing it slowly, his eyes locked on hers.

She gasped in enthrallment and began to feel instantly dizzy.

"Steady on, old girl," Zara whispered, taking Penelope's arm to ensure she didn't faint. "There's something irresistibly mysterious about that man," Zara said, nodding back toward Hank as they left the courtroom.

Penelope glanced back and saw him smiling as he chatted with Florence Morgan, looking effortlessly dashing in his sartorial splendor. She squeezed Zara's arm in hers and said, "Now that's a mystery I'd be willing to spend a long time solving … perhaps even a lifetime."

## THE END

*As lovers of macarons will attest, few delicacies are as heavenly as ethereal, crispy meringues. With the addition of sweet cream, fresh strawberries and chocolate (optional), this recipe is simultaneously light, simple, and momentous.*

INGREDIENTS

- 2 cups sliced strawberries
- Juice of half an orange
- 2 cups heavy whipping cream
- 4 large egg whites
- 1 cup semisweet or dark chocolate chips; may use additional as garnish
- 1 teaspoon vanilla extract
- 1 cup sugar
- 2 Tablespoons confectioner's sugar
- 1/4 teaspoon salt
- 1/4 teaspoon cream of tartar
- Parchment paper

DIRECTIONS

1. Set the oven to 250°F.
2. Lay a sheet of parchment paper on a baking pan and, using a pencil, draw 2 eight-inch circles on the parchment, as far apart as possible, to prevent them melding in the oven.

3. Place the egg whites in a deep bowl and sprinkle with the salt and cream of tartar.

4. Mix vigorously until the whites turn into fluffy foam. Keep mixing as you sweeten with the cup of sugar, a little at a time.

5. Whip until frothy peaks arise. Slip your spatula in deep, and spread the puffy clouds onto the circles laying in wait. Now slide it all into the yawning mouth of the sweltering oven for one blissful hour, until the meringue tops are hot and crisp.

6. Meanwhile, slice the strawberries 1/4 inch thick and squeeze a half orange over them, tossing them lightly to ensure an even coating of the juice.

7. OPTIONAL - When the meringue disks have finished baking, top each of them with 1/4 cup of the chocolate morsels, turn off the heat, and return the meringue pan back to the oven to let the chocolate melt for 5 minutes. Thereafter, use a spreader to smear the disks with chocolate.

8. Pour the whipping cream into a cool bowl and whip until stiff peaks form.

9. Fold in vanilla and pinches of powdered sugar. Set aside.

10. Place one of the meringues on a serving plate and spoon one half of the whipped cream onto it.

11. Please half the sliced berries in the cloud of cream, adding more cream on top if you needed to ensure the next layer sticks to this base.

12. Top with the other meringue and repeat adding chocolate (optional), cream & berries.

13. FINAL OPTION - If you're crazy for chocolate, melt the remaining morsels and decoratively drizzle over this mountain of deliciousness

14. Serve immediately, or chill and serve the same day

# Author

Joy's vices are afternoon tea and Cirque du Soleil.

She is a former tearoom owner, proud member of the Tea Travellers Societea and founder of Siren School.

In her off hours, she enjoys Fantasy Fitness & Mythic Adventures activities.

If you are an afternoon tea enthusiast, you may enjoy her tearoom guidebook, *The Tea Traveller's Constant Companion*, available in a variety of formats.

# Acknowledgements

Heaps of thanks to beta readers Bonnie, Sanndi and Susan for showing me the error of my ways.

Ongoing gratitude to Carola for her indomitable spirit, for playing proofreader, and for joining me on scores of tea adventures.

Love to Molly and my adopted family, the Ps.

Upcoming titles in the Tea Cozy Mysteries series

*"How do I take my tea?*
*Why, I take it quite seriously, of course!"*
~P. Price

CPSIA information can be obtained
at www.ICGtesting.com
Printed in the USA
FSHW021947210120
66352FS